Riches of the Heart

June Tate

HEADLINE

First published in 1998
by HEADLINE BOOK PUBLISHING

First published in paperback in 1998
by HEADLINE BOOK PUBLISHING

10 9 8 7 6

ISBN 0 7472 5909 7

Typeset by
Letterpart Limited, Reigate, Surrey

Printed and bound in Great Britain by
Clays Ltd, St Ives plc

HEADLINE BOOK PUBLISHING
A division of Hodder Headline PLC
338 Euston Road
London NW1 3BH

To my two wonderful daughters: Beverley, who has the soul of a writer, and Maxine, whose spirit of adventure is awesome; and to my dear husband Alan for his patience and understanding.

Acknowledgements

To my friends, Florence Evens, Carey Cleaver, Pauline Bentley and Jan Henley, who between them taught me so much. To Anita, who always found a solution when I was faced with a problem. And to my lovely agent, Judith Murdoch, who had faith in my abilities as a writer.

Chapter One

Southampton, 1920

The door opened slowly – as she knew it would.

'Lily, where are you, my little darling?'

The words were slurred, and rancid fumes of stale alcohol wafted across the small bedroom, no bigger than a box.

Through the grimy windows the moon shed its diffused light. Lily watched his silhouette as he stumbled towards the bed. She pressed herself against the wall behind the door, holding her breath. Fear made her body tremble.

He searched for her on the bed, cursing when he found it empty. 'Where are you hiding this time? Come on out, you little bitch.' His cruel laughter echoed.

Clutching her clothes and shoes to her chest, Lily fled through the open doorway, the roar of anger from behind filling her with terror. She raced down the stairs and stumbled into the little living room, where her mother, Mavis Johnson, a pale scrawny creature with dull eyes, sat doing a pile of mending by the fire.

Lily appealed to her. 'You're supposed to look after me!' Her voice broke with anguish. 'What sort of a woman are you? Why do you let him do this to me? My own father!'

The thin lips narrowed. 'It keeps him out of my bed, that's why.' Fear was suddenly reflected in her eyes, as her husband appeared at the top of the stairs.

Looking up at the swaying figure, his beer belly hanging over his trousers, face bloated from too much alcohol, Lily knew there was no one to defend her. Any spirit her mother might have had had been beaten out of her years ago.

1

Her courage fired by desperation, Lily faced her father as he descended the stairs. 'I'll kill you before I let you touch me again.'

Jack Johnson, puce with anger and alcohol, grabbed her arm. 'You'll do as I say.' He pushed her towards the stairs. 'Get back to your room.'

She hung on grimly to the bannister, knowing what would happen to her if she did as she was bid.

He raised his hand to her and she lunged at him with all her might. Unsteady with the drink, he went sprawling. Seizing this chance, she made for the front door, her fingers shaking so much she could barely grip the knob. At last the door opened and she ran out into the night, tripping over the pavement in her haste and landing, winded, in the gutter.

Jack swayed in the doorway. 'You little slut,' he spat. 'Clear off. I don't want you in this house again.'

Flushed with relief at her escape, Lily shook her fist at him. 'That suits me fine!' she yelled.

The upstairs window of their neighbour's house opened and Mrs Ryan peered out, a chamber pot clutched in her hand. 'What the bloody 'ell's going on?' She looked at the crumpled heap and asked, 'Is that you, Lily, love?'

Getting swiftly to her feet, the girl darted off without replying. She found shelter in the doorway of the corner shop and, with trembling fingers, dressed herself. Her skirt, with its worn material, and the threadbare jumper were not warm enough to keep out the chill of the hour. She put on one shoe, but a frantic search failed to find its mate. Crouching on her haunches, Lily began to shake, the trauma of the night belatedly taking its toll of the young, defenceless girl. What was she to do now? What if her father came looking for her? Terror made her feel queasy. The best thing to do was to get away.

Rising to her feet, Lily limped along the road with an uneven gait, but this soon became so uncomfortable that she cast the remaining shoe aside. Crossing her arms over her chest, she hugged herself for added warmth.

Turning the corner, she collided with a lascar dressed neatly in his seaman's uniform of dark-blue trousers and matching jacket. As he clasped her by the arms, her legs seemed to turn to jelly and her heart pounded. In the low light from the street-lamp, she saw his white teeth strangely bright against his dark skin. His hair was plastered down with Macassar oil.

'Hello, missy. You want jiggy-jig?'

Overcome with rage she pushed him away. 'You filthy pig! You're just like my father.'

He stepped forward, catching her again by the arm.

'Take your hands off me!' she cried. Swiftly bringing up her knee, she caught him in the groin. He cursed in a foreign tongue as he doubled over with pain.

Free from his clutches, Lily ran down the road, laughing hysterically. Her laughter, born of fear, soon died in her throat and eventually, gasping for breath, she stopped and hung on to a street-lamp for support. There was a pain in her side from running. She held it whilst she recovered. 'No more bloody jiggy-jig for me,' she vowed. 'Not ever.' When at last she could breathe freely she wondered, What am I to do now? Where shall I go? I won't go back. I *can't* go back . . . I hate them. Both of them!

The street in this rundown area of the docklands was silent and empty except for a solitary cat walking across the road, its tail held high, its green eyes shining. Lily watched the animal's elegant passage, wishing she could change places with it.

The night chill seeped through her bones and made her shiver. Best to keep on the move, she thought. I must find somewhere to sleep.

There was an empty feeling in the pit of her stomach as hunger gnawed away at her. There had only been bread and scrape for supper these past few nights, her father having spent the last of the money in the pub.

The enormity of Lily's situation began to dawn on her. There wouldn't even be bread and scrape now. She had no home, no money. But at least there wouldn't be any more beatings and no further invasion of her body, which filled her more with shame than anger. It made her feel dirty. No man would ever make her feel that way again. She'd get by, somehow. Nothing would induce her to return home. I'm never, never going back, she vowed. And yet, even as she swore to survive, she was filled with apprehension. The docks were a dangerous place for anyone, but more so for a fifteen-year-old girl, all alone and in the dead of night. She shivered as the sudden shrill whistle of a goods train made her jump.

Queens Park looked ominous in the dark. During the day the area was a buzz of activity, but now it was eerie. Huge cranes loomed, dark, menacing silhouettes against the sky-line. There were no deep throaty roars from the funnels of an ocean liner, no crowds, only an occasional drunken figure, staggering back, hopeful of finding the dock gates and a warm bunk aboard their vessels, docked silently in one of the berths. A sound of voices raised in anger, a policeman's whistle, carried in the air. Shrubs and trees loomed out at Lily, casting strange shapes and shadows. Branches swayed in the night breeze. Lily tiptoed along the path, glancing all around her, terrified of seeing anyone, and of being seen.

She was making her way towards a wooden bench when she saw, by a shaft of moonlight that suddenly appeared from behind a cloud, the shape of a sleeping figure. She paused beside it. A hand shot out and grabbed at her skirt. Lily screamed. The figure sat up. The smell of filth and decay from the woman made Lily retch. It was Mad Maria, a well-known character around the docks. The old hag pushed her face towards Lily.

'What ya want?'

'I'm looking for a place to sleep,' was the defiant answer.

'This is my pitch. Now bugger off!'

Lily moved quickly away from her as soon as Maria let go, only to almost stumble over a man, snoring, curled up fast asleep beneath a tree. He was wearing a steward's jacket, stained with vomit. Beside him she saw something glitter in the moonlight. Bending down she picked up a sixpence and put it in her pocket.

Two men began to fight outside the closed doors of a pub and she was scared they would come into the park and find her. Across the way, she saw that dimmed lights were still on

4

in the reception area of The South Western Hotel.

Crossing the road, she crept up to the door and pressed her nose against the pane of glass. Inside she could see the night porter asleep in a comfortable armchair. A large potted palm spread above his head like a canopy. His cap was low over his nose, covering his eyes. Lily watched the steady rise and fall of his chest as he slept, envious of his comfort.

There was a wide porchway over the entrance, affording some relief from the night air. She leaned against the stone wall and began to shake. Her teeth were chattering with nerves.

Lily dragged the coconut matting with the name of the hotel emblazoned on it over to the wall in the corner and, using it as a mattress, lay down, curled up in a ball. But she was too frightened to sleep. She could be murdered, kidnapped, taken away on a ship – sold into slavery. Her imagination ran riot. From her foetal position, her eyes watched every movement.

She must have dozed off, but noises in the background disturbed her. A heavy mist had drifted in and the sound of a fog horn made its mournful cry. Cats fought over food they'd scavenged. Five drunken crewmen loomed out of the mist and staggered past after a late-night party, heading for their ship's berth. Lily cowered in the corner, praying they wouldn't see her. Mercifully, they passed by. Still and alert, she listened to the sound of footsteps in the distance, heading in her direction. They sounded just like her father's. She sat up, ready to take flight, her breath caught in her throat and perspiration beading her forehead. The footsteps paused in front of the hotel. Lily froze. A match illuminated the face of a stranger. She felt faint with relief as the man walked on, puffing contentedly on his cigarette. Eventually her eyelids closed without her permission and she fell into a fitful sleep.

Next morning, she wakened confused as to her whereabouts. It soon became abundantly clear when the porter appeared, enraged that his precious mat had been used as a bed.

Kicking out at the curled-up bundle, he was surprised to

hear the cry of pain came from a young female. As blue eyes the colour of cornflowers looked up at him accusingly, he was momentarily thrown. 'What the 'ell's your game, my girl?'

Getting stiffly to her feet, Lily grinned at him in relief that she'd survived her first night. 'I've always wanted to stay in a posh hotel.'

'Less of your cheek, missy. You'll lose me my job if my boss sees you. 'Ere . . . why ain't you at 'ome?'

''Cos I've left.'

'Well, you can't stay 'ere, so be on your way. If I catch you in my porch again I'll call the police. Understand?'

She nodded.

He turned away muttering to himself and went back inside.

Looking at the sixpence she had picked up the previous night, Lily decided that when the workman's cafe along the road opened, she'd buy a cup of tea and a slice of bread. But to do so, she'd have to look a bit more respectable. Brushing the loose matting from her skirt, she ran her fingers through her dark wavy hair, shaking it in an effort to look decent. She walked along Western Esplanade to the drinking fountain, quenching her thirst before washing her face and hands then bathing her dirty feet, trusting no one in the cafe would notice she was shoeless. She hoped it wouldn't be too long before she could get off the street, with its damp March air, into somewhere warmer.

Sitting on one of the cannons beside the fountain, she waited. How am I going to manage? she asked herself. All she had between her and starvation was sixpence. She couldn't get a job. Who would employ her, looking such a mess? She stuck her legs out and stared at her bare feet. The first thing she had to do was get a pair of shoes. No. The first thing she had to do was have a hot cup of tea and something to eat. She felt sick with hunger.

Bitterness welled up inside her as she thought of her mother. How she despised Mavis for letting her daughter be degraded without putting a stop to the brutality. Yet deep down she felt pity for the woman, married to such a

6

monster. Her skin went cold as she thought of her father and of the buckle of his belt biting into her skin. She could still feel the pain, and his filthy, stubby hands touching her. 'I won't think about him,' she said, pushing the ugly images to the back of her mind. 'I won't think about either of them ever.' From now on she had no parents. If anyone asked, she'd say she was an orphan. She grinned impishly, deciding to change her name. She'd keep Lily because she liked it, but she'd have to give some thought to a new surname. Something posh. Yes – something with a bit of class.

Putting her hand in the pocket of her skirt, she clasped hold of the small coin. Thank God it was still there. Looking out past the Royal Pier at Southampton Water, she wished she could sail away to another land like the big liners. Start another life. Well, she had started another life, and today was her sixteenth birthday.

Hidden behind a tree, Lily watched anxiously for the opening of the cafe. Patting her hair, she slipped quickly across the road, opened the door and stood in front of the counter before the owner could see her bare feet.

When he looked round in surprise, she grinned at him. 'Morning,' she said.

'Where the 'ell did you spring from?'

'I was just passing and thought I'd have a cup of tea and a slice of bread. I didn't have time for breakfast this morning, before I left home.'

He eyed the shabby youngster suspiciously. 'Oh yeah? Well, I'm going to be real busy soon, so you be on your way.'

Lily's heart sank, but she was determined not to leave until she'd had some breakfast. Placing her sixpence upon the counter, she glared at the man. 'What's up then?' she said, all hoity-toity. 'My money's as good as anyone else's, ain't it? I'm not asking you for any favours, am I? Now come on, mate, I'm desperate for a cuppa – and I've heard yours is the best around here.'

Bert, the owner, looked at the sixpence, then at her. She was a nice-looking kid, her face shiny clean as were her hands, and he thought she deserved something for her cheek. 'All right, madam. Cuppa and a slice coming up.'

Lily settled at a table near the door. Best thing, she thought, just in case she had to make a hasty retreat. She pulled her legs under the chair to hide the fact that she wasn't wearing shoes.

The tea tasted wonderful, not like the gnat's pee they usually had at home, where Mavis was forced to eke out their meagre supply. This was strong and hot. She munched on her bread slowly, although she had wanted to devour it, she was so ravenous. How long could she make it last, she wondered.

When the door opened, Lily automatically drew her feet further beneath the seat. Looking up, she was surprised at the figure walking past her. This was no workman. He was of medium height, powerfully built, with black sleek hair and wearing a suit of the finest material. He gave her an interested glance and then went to speak to the owner.

They exchanged a few words and the stranger nodded towards Lily. 'Who's the girl?'

Bert shrugged. 'Don't know. She come in off the street.' With a smile he said, 'Spunky kid – demanded I serve her.'

They spoke for a while, then the stranger began to walk towards the door. 'I'll get that to you soon, OK?'

'Fine,' Bert nodded.

The man stopped beside Lily. 'Good morning. You're out early.'

She looked at him beneath long silky eyelashes. 'Yes. Best time of the day, I always think.'

Studying him in greater detail, she guessed he must be in his early thirties. His fine head of black hair receded at both temples. His olive skin was smooth, his dark eyebrows thick above dark-brown eyes. His nose was slightly hooked. He was heavy in stature, but carried himself with a definite air. There was something menacing about him, yet at the same time there was a certain magnetism. When he smiled, as he did now, he looked almost handsome.

'Nice young girl like you should be home, tucked up in a warm bed, not wandering around the streets.'

'I'm not wandering,' was her sharp denial.

Looking at his watch, the man frowned. 'I have to go, but if you want a job, come and see me. I've got a nice little room with a comfortable bed just waiting for you. Good food too.' He put his hand out to stroke her hair. She pulled away. Looking at her shabby attire he added, 'And nice clothes.'

Lily was beginning to feel uneasy. 'You don't know me, so why would you put yourself out to give me a job? What's in it for you?'

He was amused. 'Let's just say I like the look of you. You're a bright girl, nice-looking – and I could help you.'

'No thanks,' she answered spiritedly. 'I can take care of myself.'

He grinned. 'Can you now? I run the Club Valletta, in Bernard Street. Come and see me. Ask for Vittorio.' Opening the door, he left.

Lily was relieved at his exit, but puzzled as well. No one offers a girl such things for nothing, she thought. And anyway, who was he? As she was mulling over the conversation, Bert came across to her.

'Listen to me, sunshine. You keep away from The Maltese.'

'Who?'

'Vittorio Teglia. Everyone calls him The Maltese.'

'Why?'

'Because his family come from Malta, an island in the Mediterranean. He's a dangerous man to know. I'm giving you some fatherly advice, ducks. Don't you have anything to do with him.'

A shiver went down Lily's spine.

The cafe began to get busy, and she slipped out through the door. The park no longer seemed a dangerous place in the daylight. She made her way to an empty bench, well away from the one used by Maria, and watched the street come alive.

The noisy rattle of trams began to shake the air. The road became full of dockers on their bicycles, packed together like a flock of birds, first swaying one way then the other, following the curve of the road. She marvelled that no one fell off. Fruit-sellers were busy setting up stalls for the day. Newsboys called out the latest headlines: 'Lloyd George sends the Black and Tans to Ireland!' A middle-aged woman pushed her flower-laden cart on her way to the National Provincial Bank, where she'd had a daily pitch for years. Lily recognised her and waved.

A throaty roar from a liner echoed as the RMS *Olympic* tested its engines ready to sail to New York. Its four red and black funnels belched out thick dark smoke.

Still suffering from hunger pangs, Lily made her way to Kingsland market, cocking an ear to the banter which passed between the stall-holders getting ready for the day. One woman, setting out some cabbages, clutched two against her breast. 'Nice pair you've got there, gel,' called the man on the next stall.

'Now then, you cheeky monkey. One more word from you, I'll squeeze your tomatoes.'

'Best offer I've had this week,' he replied with a laugh.

'Going to see the new Douglas Fairbanks picture this week, Nell?' called another. 'It's on at the Gaiety.'

'Yeah, not half. He could swash my buckle any time.'

A watery sun made its appearance, and in her own way Lily felt happy wandering around. Thoughts of the night to come were pushed to the back of her mind. She watched carefully as the traders sorted the bad fruit from the good, noting the wooden boxes containing the discarded pieces. She smiled to herself as she watched them serve their customers from the fruit at the back of the display, giving short measure with dexterity.

Waiting until the market was busy and the traders occupied with customers, she filched some rotten apples and a couple of bananas, stuffing them into her pockets. Nonchalantly, she moved away to eat her fill, then went back to replenish her store – leaving before she was discovered.

Next she made her way towards Canal Walk, commonly known as The Ditches. It was a narrow pedestrian-only street that sloped down slightly each side with a ditch running down the middle for the excess rain to drain away.

There were one-roomed shops on either side: pubs, eating-houses, and butchers' shops with their goods displayed – legs of lamb hanging from hooks, and dead poultry with skinny necks. There was a pawnbroker, a bespoke tailor and a jeweller, but it was Mrs Cohen's second-hand clothing shop that was Lily's chosen destination.

The ragged canopy was pulled down and dresses, coats, and men's suits hung from the rusted iron struts. Sweaters and hats in boxes were on display – but it was the pile of shoes that held Lily's interest.

She carefully sorted through them, trying on one pair after another, discarding those that were unsuitable. She couldn't find a pair her size and settled for another, just one size too big. She looked furtively around. Mrs Cohen was inside the shop; the street was busy. She was just about to walk away, when a voice said, 'Oh, no you don't.'

Her heart beating with fright, she turned. Behind her stood a policeman.

'I've been watching you, young lady.' He looked sternly at her.

With trembling lip, Lily asked, 'Why?'

'You were just going to walk away with those shoes.'

Bravely she faced him. 'How dare you accuse me of stealing! I was only trying them on.'

'Now don't tell lies, young lady. I've been lied to by the best and I know a thief when I see one.'

'Look – look!' she said angrily, sticking out a foot. 'They don't even fit. Why would I want a pair of shoes that don't fit?'

'You were just about to leave, wearing them.'

'I beg your pardon.' Lily bristled. 'Here I am still in front of the shop. I haven't gone anywhere. Now if I was down there,' she pointed further down the street, 'that would be a different kettle of fish.'

At that point, Mrs Cohen came bustling out of her shop. 'What's going on?'

Lily knew Mrs Cohen by sight. She always dressed in good clothes, if a tad shabby, but she was known for the hats she wore. Today it was a splendid effort in brown straw with a

11

wide brim and an exotic feather draped around the crown.

Clasping Lily by the shoulder, the policeman said, 'I just caught this girl about to walk away from here wearing a pair of your shoes.'

Lily stared at the woman, wondering what would happen to her now. Would she go to gaol? Had she escaped one prison, only to be shut away in another? Inside she was quaking but as she waited her expression gave away nothing of her inner turmoil.

'It's all right, officer. I told her to have a good sort through.'

Lily thought she was going to faint with relief.

'Well, if you're sure,' blustered the policeman.

Mrs Cohen nodded and beckoned to Lily to enter her shop.

As she stood in the inner sanctum, Lily's legs trembled. She was speechless. Why had this woman saved her from being arrested – and having done so, what would she do to her now?

Rachel Cohen stared at the girl. She knew who she was. Hadn't she seen her many a time outside the pub waiting to get money from her drunken father? And she'd witnessed the brutal way he'd hit her before sending her on her way – empty-handed.

With a grim expression she asked Lily, 'Well? And what have you to say for yourself?'

'He was right, missus. I *was* about to walk off.'

'At least you're honest about it,' said Mrs Cohen with some surprise. 'Why do you want a pair of shoes?'

Lily flushed with embarrassment. 'Because I don't have any. I did have a pair, but I lost them.'

'How on earth can you lose a pair of shoes?'

'My dad threw me out of the house and I dropped one. It was too uncomfortable with just one, so I dumped it.'

The woman looked thoughtful. 'And where are you staying now?'

'With my aunt in Union Street,' she lied.

'Got a job, have you?'

Lily shook her head.

Mrs Cohen pursed her lips. 'Want one, do you?'

Eyes wide in surprise, Lily said quickly, 'Yes, I do.'

'I need help here. The shop could do with cleaning and there's a lot of clothes to be sorted. My son is away buying and I have to keep an eye on the shop, else someone will pinch my stuff.'

A guilty flush rose in Lily's cheeks. 'I'll work hard for you, honest.'

'Then we'd better find you a pair of shoes that fit.'

'Oh thank you, Mrs Cohen. You are so kind.' Her gratitude bubbled forth.

'I'm not giving you them, girl. You'll pay me so much a week out of your wages.'

Suitably rebuked Lily said, 'Yes, yes, of course.'

'One thing you will learn in life, my dear, is that no one does anything for nothing. You just remember that. There's always a price to pay.'

Inside the shop, Lily looked around in astonishment. Clothes hung everywhere. One rack was full of ladies' evening dresses. She'd never seen anything so beautiful. The fragile materials were covered in sequins and coloured bugle beads. Such elegance, she thought admiringly. Day dresses, costumes and men's suits hung nearby. Wonderful creations tumbled out of hat boxes. But it was towards the large tubs full of unsorted clothes that she was led.

'I want you to go through this lot with a fine-tooth comb. Sort the good stuff, and any that is worn and torn you throw over there, into the empty box. All right?'

'Yes, I understand, missus. Don't you worry, I'll be very thorough.'

'If you aren't, then you won't work for me. I don't pay good hard cash for nothing.'

Sorting through the clothes in the dark enclave of the shop, Lily was content. She was off the street and felt safe and secure, for the time being anyway. She was meticulous in her search. After all, if she was earning, she could eat. I wonder when she'll pay me, she pondered.

At lunch-time, Mrs Cohen made a cup of tea and called to Lily: 'Come here, girl.' She handed Lily a mug of the hot steaming liquid and a bagel filled with salt beef. Lily had never enjoyed anything so much.

They sat together on a couple of old straight-backed chairs. Rachel Cohen arched her back, placing her hand against it. 'Getting stiff in my old age,' she muttered. 'If my son Manny worked a bit harder, it would help.'

'How old's your son?' Lily asked.

Rachel pulled a face. 'Thirty and not married. I try to find him nice Jewish girls, but either he doesn't like them or they don't want him. What's a poor widow woman to do? I want grandchildren.' She bit angrily into her bagel. 'And you, Lily, what do you want out of life?'

Sitting back against the chair, Lily stretched out her feet to admire her shoes. 'I don't want ever to be poor again.' She looked dreamily into space. 'I want a nice man to marry me, I want to live in a nice house – I want to be respectable.'

Looking over her horn-rimmed spectacles, the Jewess smiled. 'Well, we all have dreams, girl. I hope you get yours one day.'

'I will, Mrs Cohen. I don't know how, but I will.'

The determination on the girl's face moved Rachel. What chance has she got? she wondered. Not much. She was a pretty girl, with her lovely eyes. But living round here didn't offer a great deal, and she doubted that Lily would ever fulfil her aspirations.

When the shop closed Lily asked, 'When do I get paid?'

'At the end of the week.'

Her heart sank. She was working, but she still didn't have money, only the twopence left after buying her breakfast. She had some mouldy fruit left over, but that was all.

The smell from the fish and chip shop was too much. 'Two penn'orth of chips and some scraps please,' she asked. The scraps – the pieces of batter that came off the fish as it cooked – were crispy and succulent. It would help to quell her hunger.

The cool wind had dropped and it was a balmy spring evening as Lily strolled along the Esplanade, eating her chips. Not a bad birthday, she mused. I got myself a job *and* a pair of shoes. Now all she needed was a roof over her head.

She couldn't go back to the hotel. The night porter was sure to keep an eye out for her and she certainly wasn't going to sleep in the park. Looking across at the Royal Pier, she thought that was as good a place as any. There was no shelter, but it was quiet, away from the pubs.

It was too early to stake her claim to Southampton's Royal Pier, however, so Lily strolled around the old walls and up the steps towards St Michael's Square. She wandered past Tudor House and made her way to St Michael's Church. The evening sun shone on the stained-glass window and the tall spire towered against the skyline. The heavy door was slightly open and she ventured inside.

She was immediately aware of a sense of peace and quiet. A pungent scent of incense hung in the air. Standing at the top of the aisle, she looked in wonderment at the tall ceilings, the graceful arches and, in the distance, the large gold-coloured cross standing on the altar.

Sitting in a pew, she felt a strange calm as she surveyed the surroundings. It was the first time she'd ever entered a church and she found it an awesome experience. This was the house of God. She knew that from the scriptures of her schooldays. God was never spoken of in the confines of her own home.

Would He want her here? she wondered. After all, hadn't she committed a wicked sin with her father? Perhaps she should go – but she wanted so badly to stay. If only someone could tell her what she should do.

As if in answer to her thoughts, a quiet voice beside her said, 'Good evening. I've not seen you here before.'

A middle-aged man dressed in a long black cassock stood beside her. His hair was greying at the temples and he had kind eyes. At Lily's look of anxiety he said, 'I'm John Page, the vicar.'

'Is it all right for me to sit here?' Lily asked uncertainly.

'Of course, my dear. All are welcome in God's house.'

Frowning, she said, 'Even those who have sinned?'

'Especially those who have sinned. If you're worried about it, why don't you pray and ask Him?'

'I don't know how.'

With a gentle smile he said, 'Just talk to Him. That's all a prayer really is. A conversation between you and God.'

Lily wasn't convinced. 'But someone might hear what I say.'

'Then think your conversation in your head. Then it will be for God alone. I'll leave you to it.'

She watched him walk towards the altar. He bowed, crossed himself and disappeared through a doorway at the side. She was alone.

Kneeling on the worn hassock, she put her hands together. 'The vicar said it was all right to talk to You. I'm sorry that I have sinned, but You know it wasn't my doing. I couldn't help it.' She paused as the thoughts tumbled through her brain. 'I'd like to ask You something. If You're really God, why didn't you stop my father?' There was no sound to be heard. I suppose God only talks to saints, she thought and, with a wry grin, muttered, 'Well, that definitely lets *me* out . . . I've got a job,' she continued, 'but I don't get paid till the end of the week. Please take care of me. I'm a good girl really. Thank You. Amen.'

That night, Lily slept outside the Royal Pier. She wasn't molested or disturbed, but during the night it rained heavily. When she awoke, she was soaked to the skin.

Wringing out the water from her skirt, she looked up at the sky, shivering with cold and shook her fist. 'I said take care of me, not bloody drown me!'

Chapter Two

Lily kept her head down as she walked along The Ditches. She knew she looked a fright. Her shoes squelched with each step and tears of indignation pricked her eyes. Muttering angrily she said, 'Bloody funny kind of God you are. What's Mrs Cohen going to say when she sees me?'

Her concern was justified, for when she arrived at the shop, her new employer was appalled. Looking askance at Lily, Mrs Cohen raged, 'And what do you mean, coming to work like that? You look like the wreck of the *Hesperus*.'

'I can't help it,' Lily cried. 'At least I came, and I'm early.' She began to shiver.

Rachel hustled her inside the shop. Throwing a towel across to her she said, 'Get out of them wet things and towel yourself down afore you catch pneumonia.' She started sorting through some clothes. Seeing Lily hesitate, she snapped, 'For heaven's sake, girl, go on. I won't look. After all, you ain't got no different from me, 'cept yours is in better condition.' She cackled at her own joke. 'Here.' She threw a skirt and jumper at Lily, and a pair of knickers. 'It's not for free, you'll . . .'

'Have to pay for them out of my wages,' quipped Lily. 'I know. I won't *have* any bloody wages at this rate!'

Mrs Cohen hid a smile. 'You don't have to pay me all at once. So much a week will do.'

Lily let out a sigh. 'What about my shoes?' She held them out for inspection, almost ready to weep. She'd been so proud of them.

'Give us them here and I'll pack them with newspaper. They should be dry by tonight. You won't need them working inside.'

Warm and cosy at last, Lily drank the cup of tea thrust at her by her employer. As she went to thank her, Mrs Cohen said sharply, 'Can't have you going sick. If you can't work, you can't pay what you owe me.'

Shaking her head, Lily said, 'My, but you're a hard woman.' But in her heart, she knew it wasn't true.

That evening, when she put on her shoes, they still felt damp, but at least they no longer squelched.

'Where you sleeping tonight, then?' Rachel asked suddenly.

'With my aunt,' Lily lied.

'Like you did last night, I suppose?'

Lily met Rachel's gaze unflinchingly. 'That's right.'

'Your aunt's place . . . got a roof, has it?'

Puzzled, Lily said, 'Yes, of course it has. What are you getting at?'

'It rained last night, girl. If you were at your aunt's, why did you come here this morning soaked to the skin?'

'It poured with rain when I left home.'

Mrs Cohen shook her head. 'No, it didn't. It stopped around six this morning. I know 'cos I was up. You've been sleeping rough, haven't you?'

Lowering her gaze, Lily felt her cheeks flush with embarrassment. 'Yes,' she admitted in a whisper.

Her employer tutted loudly. 'Stupid girl. Don't you know how dangerous it is out there? The place is full of foreigners, criminals, drunks and pimps.'

Lily's eyes blazed. 'Don't you think I know that? Christ! Do you think I would have done it if I'd had a choice?'

'It's your drunken bastard of a father's fault, all this. What was he thinking of, kicking you out?' She saw the tightening of the girl's jaw. 'Well, that's your business, but I'll not see you on the street. You can sleep in the back of the shop.'

Overcome by such kindness, Lily could only stare at her benefactor.

'Of course, I'll have to charge you a bit for rent.'

Lily was indignant. 'What do you mean, rent? There's no bedroom, so what are you charging me for?'

'The roof over your head, girl. The one what's going to

18

keep you dry, not like last night. I told you, you don't get nothing for nothing in this world.'

Remembering her discomfort of the night before, Lily was silent.

'Here,' said Rachel. 'There's twopence out of your wages. Go and get a pie for your supper. I don't want you starving to death on me.'

'I'm surprised I've got any wages left.'

'Go on, get off with you afore I changes me mind.'

Lily skipped off down the road singing. 'Thank You, God,' she cried. 'You aren't so bad after all.'

Lily was happy. In the three weeks since she'd worked for Rachel Cohen, she'd made many friends with the local traders. The man in the fruit shop was so captivated with her, he was always giving her 'free samples' as he called it, and one day the fishmonger asked her to go out with him. She refused him gently, so he wouldn't be offended.

Each day, once she'd finished cleaning the interior of the shop, she'd go outside and assist her employer. The clothes on display were of a decent quality and business was brisk. Lily had a natural rapport with people and she made an excellent saleswoman. Mrs Cohen was pleased.

In quieter moments, Lily would gaze in the window of the pawnbroker's opposite, looking at the jewellery on display, unclaimed by the owners. It would be nice to be able to afford such luxuries. She'd watch people file into 'Uncle's' as it was known, pawning their precious belongings – for instance, their only suit – which they would then retrieve a few days later. It was a hard life for many, but she was lucky.

One day, as she was gazing at the jewellery, Abraham the pawnbroker came to the door. 'Vat you looking at, Lily?'

'All these wonderful rings and brooches. Are they real diamonds?'

'Some are. You vant to try some on?' He ushered her into the shop.

She was fascinated by the stock inside. There were musical instruments, old furniture, paintings, military uniforms, medals and old coins. 'It's like Aladdin's cave, Mr Abraham.'

'Vell, you know how it is. Some people need the money more than the stuff.' Abraham looked over his glasses at her. 'I'm here to do the needy a service, my dear.' But she knew that he made a good living out of other people's misery. 'Here, try on this diamond ring.'

Lily held out her hand, eyes bright. 'One day I'll have one of these,' she told him.

'And how are you gonna earn such money? Not vorking for old Mrs Cohen.'

Lily thought it funny that he of all people should refer to Rachel as old. He was balding, his face was wrinkled and his beard was long and wispy.

'One day I'll marry a rich man.'

Abraham laughed. 'I hope you do, my dear. But remember this. Money ain't everything. You have the love of a good man, you have so much more. You have riches of the heart.'

Handing back the ring, she said, 'I'd best go or Rachel will get mad at me.'

He caught hold of her arm with his scrawny hand. 'You come and see me any time, Lily.'

At night, alone in the shop, Lily would try on the exquisitely decorated evening gowns. Tying beaded ribbon around her forehead, she would pick up a long cigarette-holder and prance around, pretending she was attending some grand function. Or she'd dress up in one of the hats and sing one of Marie Lloyd's songs.

Sometimes, Rachel would let Lily wear one of the hats as she served. Her good looks and dark wavy hair were a perfect foil for the creations, and the sale of them escalated.

One Saturday morning, a tall, good-looking young man, his hair the shade of autumn leaves, stopped outside to examine a smart dark-brown gent's suit.

'That would suit you, sir, with your colouring,' Lily piped up, walking over to him.

'Would it now.' As he smiled, his hazel eyes twinkled.

He was neatly dressed. His suit was clean but old, yet his shoes gleamed with polish and around his neck he wore a red neckerchief. In a soft Irish brogue he asked, 'And how much would you be wanting for the suit then?'

'Two and six. Cheap at half the price,' Lily grinned. 'You'll be able to cut quite a dash wearing that. Better with a shirt and tie, of course. Make you look a real gent!'

Chuckling, he asked, 'Are you saying I don't look a gent now?'

Blushing she retorted, 'Did I say that? Well, did I?'

'You did not. What's your name?'

'Lily.'

'Just Lily? Don't you have a surname?'

'Lily Pickford.' She'd decided she'd call herself after Mary Pickford, the film star. 'I'm an orphan,' she added.

'Sure and that's sad,' he said, his voice full of sympathy.

'No, I do all right. Now, do you want to buy the suit before someone else realises they're missing a bargain?'

Laughing he said, 'How can I resist?' His gaze made her heart race. He bought the suit, plus a shirt and a tie, chosen by Lily. Handing over the change, she said, 'Thanks.'

'Now, Lily Pickford, if I dress meself up as a gent, would you come out for a walk and a spot of tea with me tomorrow afternoon?'

Immediately thinking of her own shabby clothes she said, 'No, thanks. I don't go out with strangers.'

'I'll just have to get to know you then. My name's Tom McCann and I'll be back.' With a cheeky wink he walked away, clutching his purchases under his arm.

Lily watched the stranger as he disappeared down the street. His shoulders were broad, his figure upright, like a soldier's. There was a gleam in her eyes as she remembered his smile, his soft voice.

Rachel Cohen had been standing in the doorway listening to the conversation. 'Why did you turn him down, a good-looking man like that?'

'How could I accept, Mrs Cohen? I don't have any decent clothes to go courting.'

'You could always borrow a dress and coat from the shop.'

'You'd let me do that?'

The older woman said, 'Why not? I can't get my Manny married off, but perhaps I can help you. Mind you, spill anything on it and you'll have to pay for it.' In unison they said, 'So much a week out of your wages.'

Lily loved working in The Ditches. It was a lively place, and all manner of life could be observed here. It was particularly festive on Saturday nights, when meat, fruit and vegetables were sold off cheaply. Business for all was brisk. But she found the most fascinating aspect of The Ditches was watching the local prostitutes at work, parading up and down outside the pubs.

She would watch them approach a punter and hear their spiel. 'Hello, darlin', you're looking lonely. Out for a bit of fun, are you? You come with me and I'll show you a good time.'

With a shiver, she would remember her own experience, as she watched them lead the men away to some shabby room nearby. She didn't condemn the women – everyone had to survive. She just didn't understand how they could do it. Not by choice.

She said as much to Amy, one of the prostitutes who bought her clothes from the shop. As Amy slipped a dress over her shoulders, she said, 'There's nothing to it, girl. Blimey! So many of the poor buggers are so eager to shove their pricks somewhere, it's all over in five minutes.'

Lily coloured, but couldn't help laughing.

'Look, love,' said Amy as her tousled dark hair emerged from the neck of the dress, 'it's just a job like anything else. What's wrong with fucking for a living?'

'But it's dangerous.' Lily frowned. 'What happens if you get someone violent?'

'I squeeze his balls till he screams.' Smoothing the dress down over her hips, Amy asked, 'What do you think?'

'Looks lovely on you . . .' But Lily couldn't leave the topic alone. 'Don't you ever get someone you can't handle?'

'Sometimes. It's a chance we all take. One girl got her face cut last week by some crazy bastard. Some of the girls have a pimp to look after them, but I'm not passing my hard-earned cash over to some man to piss up the wall. Of course, I could have worked for The Maltese, in luxury, but that's still

22

pimping. I want all of what I earn for myself.'

Lily felt a chill run down her spine at the mention of Vittorio. 'This Maltese . . . I was told he was a dangerous individual.'

Amy's countenance became serious. 'You heard right. He's into all the rackets – gambling, prostitution, loan-sharking. Not a man to be messed with.'

Lily shuddered.

Late one Sunday morning, Lily carefully locked the shop door behind her, aware of the responsibility she held. Mrs Cohen had warned her: 'You forget to lock up once and you're out on your ear.'

She made her way to the Royal Pier, glad of the coat she'd borrowed as the wind was cool. She paid her penny entrance and walked along looking down through the wooden slats at the water swirling below.

She loved the pier, with its penny arcades. The machine with 'What the Butler Saw' was a favourite of hers. In decent weather, people would sit in gaily clad deckchairs, watching the paddle-steamers sail off to Southsea, Brighton and the Isle of Wight. Some went to Cherbourg on a day's excursion for twelve and six. One day, Lily thought, I'll save up the money and go myself.

Here, on the Pier, she would sit and watch happy families together and long to be a member of one. She'd dream of bringing her own children here one day. Or of getting on to an ocean liner and sailing to New York. Of marrying a millionaire . . . Of walking into The South Western Hotel, well dressed, with the night porter who had chased her from the entrance bowing and scraping. Treating her with respect. Such were her dreams whilst walking on the pier – alone.

Standing by the rail looking out over the Solent, her thoughts were interrupted by a voice behind her. 'Good afternoon, Miss Lily Pickford.'

Turning quickly, she gazed into the smiling eyes of Tom McCann. He was wearing his new suit, shirt and tie. On his head was a smart trilby, which he raised in greeting.

'Well, Mr McCann, you look the bee's knees and no

mistake.' Lily was relieved to be wearing something decent herself and silently thanked Rachel for her generosity.

'I know you don't go out with strangers,' said Tom, the corners of his mouth quirking with amusement, 'but then we're not strangers, are we? We've met before, so how about me taking you along to the restaurant for something to eat?'

Her blue eyes shone with pleasure. 'That would be lovely. How could I say no to such a gentleman?'

Over a meal of cod and chips, he told her about his home and family in Ireland. 'We came over here when I was small, but me ma couldn't stand it. When I was fifteen she went back to Ireland. I stayed and learnt me trade. I'm one of the best caulkers in the docks,' he said proudly.

'Tell me about Ireland,' asked Lily, hungry for tales of life outside her own environs.

'I live in Newcastle, nestling at the foot of the Mountains of Mourne.'

'There's a song about them,' said Lily. 'I know it.' In a sweet voice she began to sing softly: 'Oh Mary, this London's a beautiful sight . . .'

He sat hypnotised by her beauty, her innocence, as she sang the words. 'That was lovely, as are the mountains. Where did you learn the words?'

She spoke before thinking. 'There was an Irish family next door to us, Eileen and Paddy Ryan. She taught me a lot of Irish songs. She had a fine voice.'

'I know a Paddy Ryan – I think his wife's name is Eileen, an' all. I wonder if it's the same one?'

Lily's heart sank. If he knew the Ryans he would find out the truth about her family, and maybe learn her guilty secret. She'd die rather than let anyone know her father had had sex with her.

'My Ryans went back to Ireland,' she said hurriedly. 'Tell me about the mountains, Tom.'

'They stretch for miles. In sunlight, they're a thing of beauty, but on dark days they're menacing and dangerous. Get caught on them in an Irish mist and you're in trouble.'

'Did that ever happen to you?'

'Sure it did, but only once, when I was seven. I went up

near the top of one, when a mist came from nowhere. I couldn't see a hand in front of me face.'

With a look of horror, Lily asked, 'What did you do?'

'Me? Nothing. I stayed put. Curled into a rock and waited for the mist to go. I was out all night.'

'Weren't you scared?'

'Bloody right I was, but me ma always told me to stay put if I got caught ever.'

Lily remembered her first night on the street, waking up and seeing the mist. She knew that kind of fear.

He told her of the McCanns. 'Me daddy has a smallholding and me brothers work it with him. They sell the produce in Newcastle.'

'There's a Newcastle here in England.'

'Yes, you're right, but mine has a wonderful beach and the sea stretches for miles. But wherever you go, you can't get away from the mountains. One of them is called "The Divil's Bite" – or "Bit" as we called it.'

'What a strange name.'

'Well, you see, it's said that when St Patrick chased the Divil out of Ireland, the Divil was so mad, He bit a piece out of one of the peaks.'

Lily chuckled with delight at the tale. Looking across at the man sitting opposite, she saw the strong cut of his jaw, the fire in his eyes and knew his heart was still there, among the mountains.

'And what of your family, Lily?'

Her blood ran cold. 'My parents died when I was little. I lived with my aunt.' The words came out so easily, she surprised herself.

'You must miss them.'

Do I hell, she thought. 'Not any more,' she replied truthfully. 'It was a long time ago.'

They walked back along the Pier. 'Thanks, Tom,' she said. 'It was a lovely meal, and I really enjoyed hearing about Ireland. It sounds a magical place.'

'It is. There are many more stories I can tell you about it . . . if you'll come out with me again.'

Lily felt her heart swell with happiness as she looked up

into his smiling eyes. 'I'd like that.'

'I'll come by the shop and we'll arrange something. I have to go now. I've to meet some friends.' He squeezed her hand. 'Goodbye, lovely Lily.'

She walked back to The Ditches, humming happily about the Mountains of Mourne that sweep down to the sea.

As she settled for the night on her home-made bed, covered with a blanket and an old coat, she went over every moment of her meeting with Tom. It was the first time she'd ever been taken out by a man. She'd so enjoyed being fussed over.

He'd been very generous, too, telling her she could order whatever she wanted from the menu. She'd been a bit nervous about that, not wanting him to know this was a new experience for her, and was quite proud of the way she carried it off. 'I'd enjoy being a lady,' she said. She hugged her knees as she sat up in bed. He really was the most handsome chap. He hadn't tried anything either, just held her arm across the road, like a gentleman. If he took her out again, she wondered how she'd feel if he gathered her into his arms and kissed her. She'd only ever been kissed by one man. She shuddered. It couldn't be like that . . . could it?

Vittorio Teglia walked along Bernard Street and turned into The Lower Ditches, making a few calls on some of his customers. Some of the shop-keepers here frequented his club. They liked to gamble and finish the evening in a private room with one of his girls. Vittorio greeted them all, shopped with them, but was discreet in his conversation. Most of his clients were family men, who spent a lot of money on his premises. His buying their goods made them feel they were getting back some of their lost earnings. But he knew the odds were always on his side.

His eyes narrowed as he recognised the youthful figure setting out a display of second-hand clothes outside Mrs Cohen's shop. The woman's son Manny – a nasty, greasy individual – sometimes came to his club. The girls didn't like him, and neither did Vittorio.

He slowed his pace and watched the trim figure bustling

about, listening to the saucy banter flying between the girl and the other traders. She certainly had character, this one. He remembered the wide blue eyes that had stared hard at him when he'd offered her a job.

'Good morning. We meet again.'

When she saw who had spoken to her, the smile faded momentarily from Lily's face, then she grinned cheekily at The Maltese. 'Told you I could take care of myself, didn't I?'

He nodded slowly. She was better dressed this time, and was wearing shoes. He admired her small waist and rounded hips, and his eyes lingered on the shape of her full breasts. He didn't like scrawny women. Dark waves framed her pretty face beneath a neat hat and around her neck she wore a feather boa.

'Going somewhere, all dressed up like that?' he asked with amusement.

'You know I'm not. It's good for the customers.' Looking at his expensive suit and silk shirt she said, 'Don't suppose I can sell you anything – not from here.'

He laughed loudly, his brown eyes twinkling. Everyone else around was terrified of him, but this girl showed no fear, no respect. It was unusual, and he was enjoying himself.

'What's your name?'

'Lily.'

'Well, Lily, you look as if you're doing all right. But you could do much better.'

There was a watchful expression in her eyes as she replied, 'Oh, really?'

'You could work for me.'

'You setting up a second-hand stall, too?'

Oh, she was brazen, was this young lady. He'd enjoy smacking her plump bottom, Vittorio thought. 'You know what I mean,' he said smoothly. 'You could work in my club.'

Anger flashed in her eyes. 'No, I bloody couldn't. I'm no whore!'

Her temper amused him; he was tired of compliant women. This girl was a fighter. There had been something about her that had caught his interest that day in the cafe. Something different – a certain spirit. He wanted to know

27

her better. To have her in his bed – fighting with him. What a tiger she would be. Hard to control . . . He felt a stirring in his loins at the thought.

'I didn't think you were,' he pointed out. 'There are other jobs to be done.'

But in her eyes, Lily had been insulted and she was bristling with indignation. 'I think you'd best be on your way. I've work to do – honest work!'

Vittorio chuckled to himself. 'I'll be seeing you again, Lily.' He walked away, his shoulders shaking with suppressed amusement. There was no hurry. She was very young, time was on his side. But one day she would be his. He had made up his mind.

Lily knew he was laughing at her. 'What a nerve,' she muttered as she went back inside the shop for more wares to display. But her fingers trembled as she picked up a dress. She had recognised the expression in his eyes. She'd seen it in the eyes of her drunken father.

'What's up, girl?'

'That bloody Vittorio – offered me a job in his club. Cheeky sod.'

'You talking about The Maltese?' Rachel looked worried.

'Yes. Who does he think he is?'

Rachel caught hold of her arm. 'Listen to me, Lily. And listen good. You keep away from him or one day they'll fish you out of the docks.'

Lily paled. 'What do you mean?'

'That's where some that have upset him have ended up.'

'Then why isn't he behind bars?'

Shaking her head Rachel said, 'No proof. He's a clever man, but dangerous. You watch your step. If he's taken a fancy to you, he'll be back.'

Later that evening, Tom McCann entered the public bar of The Sailor's Return. The smell of tobacco and stale beer assailed his nostrils. Walking up to the bar, he greeted Declan, the landlord with: 'Pint of the usual, you Irish peasant.'

Declan grinned. 'Ye young varmint. I wouldn't take that from anyone else.'

Tom studied the contents of the glass placed before him, holding it up to the light. 'Just making sure you haven't given me the dregs of the barrel,' he teased.

'You should be thanking your lucky stars you don't live in America, my friend. For you wouldn't get a drop.'

Laughing at the big man behind the counter, Tom said, 'They wouldn't dare bring Prohibition here, mate. There'd be a bloody riot in the streets. Mostly from the toffs waving empty champagne bottles.'

'Too bloody right,' agreed Declan.

'The news of the Troubles in Ireland isn't good,' said Tom seriously. 'I don't know what Lloyd George is playing at.'

Declan nodded gloomily.

'Still,' said Tom, taking a swig of beer, 'life's not all bad. I had lunch the other day with a beautiful young lady.'

'Did you now? Like the others, is she? I know your type – blonde and flighty.'

Shaking his head, Tom said, 'No. This one is quite different. I don't know, there's just something very special about her.'

Declan clapped his hands in delight. 'Never thought I'd live to see the day when wild Tom McCann, the charmer of the docks, was smitten. The next one's on me.'

Taking his complimentary pint over to a table, Tom sat down. He always chose a seat where he could see who was coming in the door. That way there were no unpleasant surprises.

The Public Bar was L-shaped, with bench-seats around the walls and tables and chairs in the rest of the area. The partitioned end was grandly called the snug. At the opposite end, the regulars would gather to play shove-ha'penny and dominoes.

Looking around, Tom studied the usual seedy collection of customers standing, supping their beer. Two foreign seamen were being entertained by a couple of local prostitutes, fleecing the men for drinks as they fussed around them. They'll have empty pockets before long, mused Tom.

Declan was keeping a wary eye on everyone. Because he

was Irish, his pub was a great meeting place for his country-men living in exile. He was a big burly chap, well able to deal with any trouble that might and often did occur. He had no hesitation in using the shillelagh he kept hidden beneath the bar.

With the constant flow of shipping in and out of the port, the pub had become a marketplace for stolen goods. Many a bale of silk, a case of spirits or a side of beef passed through but the police didn't bother Declan often, knowing he kept the drunks under control. However, every now and then, they would raid all the pubs, trying to clamp down on such illegal dealings. Things would be quiet for a time, but soon trading would start again.

Tom looked up at the door opened and his mate, Knocker Jones, the rag and bone man, walked in.

'Hello, me old mucker. Ready for another?'

Tom handed him his glass. 'I'll have a half in there, thanks.'

Knocker called out his order and waited at the bar. Tall and skinny, with beady eyes, he wore an old suit, a cloth cap and a silk muffler. His narrow features resembled those of a ferret, and his gaze darted everywhere. He watched the two seamen for a while then, after carrying the beer to the table, said, 'Won't be a minute,' and headed over to them.

Tom watched with amusement as his friend bargained with one of the drunken men before buying a handsome watch he was wearing. The prostitute sitting with him gave Knocker a lot of verbal abuse as he walked away, but he just laughed at her.

Sitting down, he confided, 'I've just ruined her night – she'd already copped her eyes on this.' He put the watch on his wrist and studied his bargain. 'I'll get a pretty penny for this tomorrow.'

'Don't you ever stop grafting?'

Knocker looked at Tom. 'You know me better than that, me old flower.' Picking up his glass he took a long drink, then wiped the froth off his mouth. 'God, I needed that. So how are you, me old mate?'

'Never better.'

'You sound dead chirpy. Got a new woman, is that it?'

Tom laughed. 'I don't know what you mean.'

'I know that gleam in your eye. Bit of all right, is she?'

'I did meet a young lady the other day, as it happens.'

'Oh, young lady, is it? That sounds a bit serious. Take some advice from an old friend. You be careful or you'll find yourself in church one Saturday then surrounded by kids before you know what's happened.'

The bar door opened and Amy entered. Seeing Tom, she walked over to him and sat down.

'Hello darlin',' she said to him. 'How about buying an old friend a gin?'

'Business bad, Amy?'

'No, I just thought I'd have the night off. Unless you want me to take care of you?'

'You know I never pay for it. Why should I?'

Amy laughed. 'The trouble with you, Tom McCann, is you're too bloody good-looking. All the women would drop their drawers willingly if you so much as gave a hint.'

'You never have, Amy.'

'You've never asked me to. Anyway, I never give it away, you know that.'

Nudging Tom, Knocker said, 'It's much cheaper in the long run, paying a tom than getting married. *Much* cheaper. The cost of the licence is only the beginning.' Finishing his drink he said, 'I've got to go. See you soon.'

'Well, are you going to buy me a drink or what?' prompted Amy.

Tom willingly complied. He liked Amy. There was no side to her and he admired her spirit. She reminded him in some ways of Lily.

He wondered about Lily. It was sad that she was alone in the world so young. It made him feel protective towards her, somehow. There was an air of innocence about her, despite her sparky attitude and ready quips. A vulnerability. Yet she seemed well able to take care of herself. He found himself thinking that he'd like to be the one to do that.

Chapter Three

'So you're my mother's assistant.'

Lily took an instant dislike to Manny Cohen when he arrived the following morning as she was sorting the stock to be displayed outside.

He was short and fat, and his skin oozed with sweat as he lifted a heavy box of clothes across the floor. He reeked of stale perspiration and there were food stains down the crumpled jacket of his suit. His hooded eyes rested slyly on Lily in a way that made her flesh crawl.

Leering at her he said, 'I won't have to be away so often, then we can be friends.' He caught hold of her as she went to pass by him, his hand brushing her breast.

'Listen to me, you greasy little bastard. I work for Rachel, but that doesn't mean I have to be friends with her son. You lay another finger on me and you'll be very sorry.'

Outside, Lily silently fumed. Everything had been going so well for her. Now she felt uneasy. Knowing that Rachel doted on her son, Lily felt it could make things very difficult for her if he was going to be around.

'I see you've met my Manny,' said Rachel. 'He's going to sort out the stuff he brought today. Will you give him a hand, Lily?'

'I was just going to hang these dresses up,' she protested.

'I'll do that.'

Lily was left with no alternative but to go back into the shop. There, alone with Manny, she tried to be businesslike. 'Here's an empty box for any clothes we have to discard,' she said.

He stood watching her, making her uncomfortable by his presence.

Putting her hands on her hips she demanded, 'Are you going to stand there all day, or are you going to help? There's a lot to be done.'

He looked sulkily at her. 'Don't you talk to me like that. I'm the boss' son, remember?'

'I don't give a toss who you are. Rachel said I was to give you a hand, but it seems to me I'm doing it all myself. Go on outside and help your mother. I can manage.'

He walked towards her. 'No, thanks. It's windy outside. I'd rather be in here with you.'

Picking up an old umbrella, she clasped it tightly 'Keep away from me or I'll clout you one.'

Her angry stance made him wary of her and he backed off and started working. But Lily remained vigilant.

A short while later, Rachel poked her head around the corner. She was grinning. 'Lily? Your boyfriend's here to see you.'

Lily felt her cheeks colour as she went outside.

Tom was standing there in his working clothes. 'Hello, Lily.' His eyes twinkled at her obvious embarrassment. 'Sorry to disturb you, but how about coming to the pictures with me tonight?'

'That would be lovely, Tom. Thank you.'

'I'll pick you up here at six o'clock, all right?' He was staring past her. 'Who's that?' he asked.

Turning around, Lily saw Manny in the doorway watching them, his pudgy hands wiping the sweat from his brow. 'Oh, that's Mrs Cohen's son.'

Tom's expression had darkened from the smiling countenance that had greeted her. 'Does he give you any trouble?'

'I've only met him this morning.' She thought it unwise to elaborate. 'Why?'

'I don't like the look of him – and I'm a good judge of people. If he does anything to upset you, just tell me . . . OK?'

She saw the fire in his eyes and the set of his jaw as he glared at Manny.

'Don't you worry about him,' she said. 'I can take care of myself.'

'You don't have to, Lily. I can do that for you.' He smiled suddenly. 'Anyone gives you a moment's bother, you tell me.'

Anxious to avoid trouble she said, 'Go on back to work, Tom. I'll see you later.'

When he'd gone Manny said, 'Big chap, your boyfriend.'

She glared at him. 'You'd better remember that.'

Later, in the dark of the cinema, Lily felt a tremor of excitement as Tom put his arm around her. He'd bought her some chocolates in the foyer, and they ate them whilst they watched the black and white images on the screen. They laughed together at the antics of Charlie Chaplin until their sides ached.

When at last they left the cinema, Tom took out his pocket-watch. 'We've got time for a couple of drinks before the pubs shut and I take you home. Come on, we'll go to The Lord Roberts.'

Filled with consternation, Lily agreed. What was she to do? She wasn't old enough to go into a pub. Tom obviously thought she was at least eighteen. He might be put off if he knew her real age, sixteen. And she didn't know what drink to ask for. Then she remembered that her mother, on the rare occasions that Mavis drank, had liked port and lemon.

As they went inside the bar door, Lily looked furtively around in case her father was there. She didn't think this was a regular pub of his, but she knew that any pub would do when he felt like a drink. Thankfully, she was safe.

'What would you like, Lily?'

'A port and lemon please,' she said without hesitation.

She sat down at a table and waited, looking at her surroundings with interest. From the banter exchanged, she gathered some of the customers were locals, the others were a mixed bunch of seamen, ships' stewards, talking about their last voyage, and one or two of the local prostitutes accompanied by their clients. Amy, sitting with a group of people, waved.

Lily found the atmosphere exciting.

'There we are,' said Tom, placing the drinks on the table. 'Did you enjoy the film?'

'Oh yes, thank you, Tom. And the chocolates – they were lovely.'

He pushed a strand of hair away from her forehead. 'So are you, Lily.'

The touch of his fingers on her skin sent a quiver through her body. 'What's this – the Irish blarney coming out then?' she quipped, covering her embarrassment.

'Not at all.' He laughed. 'You must know you're a good-looking woman. Any man would be proud to have you on his arm.'

Amy walked over to their table. To Lily she said, 'Hello, darlin'. You watch this Irish devil. He'll charm the birds out of the trees if you don't keep an eye on him.'

As she made her way towards the bar, Lily asked, 'You know Amy, then?'

He looked knowingly at her. 'Yes, I've known her for years – but only as a friend. I'm not one of her clients.'

Lily blustered, 'I didn't think you were.'

'But you wondered, for just a moment, didn't you?'

'No, of course I didn't.' Looking at him she said, 'Well, I did. Just for a second.'

Putting back his head, he roared with laughter. 'Lily, oh Lily. I don't think you could tell a lie if you wanted to.'

Tom McCann, you really don't know me at all, she thought. Since I left home, I've been *living* a lie.

Putting his arm around her he said, 'I've never paid for sex in me life.'

Deeply embarrassed, Lily protested, 'That's really none of my business.'

'But I hope that everything about me is going to be your business.'

Her heart started pounding erratically as she nervously asked, 'What do you mean?'

'I want you to be my girl, Lily.'

She couldn't believe the words. 'What do you mean, your girl?'

'You are the strangest creature. I want you to only go out

with me. Let me look after you, protect you from trouble – like that creep at the shop.'

'Oh, Tom.' She was overcome. Here at last was someone who cared about her. Wanted to look after her. No one had ever done that, not since she'd been born. All she could ever remember was being poor and being brutalised.

He was waiting for an answer.

'I'd like that, Tom. I really would.'

Holding her hand to his lips, he kissed it.

She looked into his eyes. She could trust someone with eyes like that. There was such a gentle expression in them, not one of lust, of hunger for her body. This man was different. He had a strength about him, a pride – and he wanted her to be his girl. She didn't ever remember feeling so happy.

Walking back along The Ditches Tom asked, 'Where do you live?'

'In the back of the shop.'

He looked puzzled. 'Is there a room there?'

'Not a proper room, but Rachel let me make one corner of it mine.'

'This won't do at all.'

'Why, what's wrong?' Lily couldn't understand him. To her, the corner of the shop was her own personal haven. It was safe and warm, if a bit musty.

'I can't have my girl living like that. I'll look for a room for you.'

'But Tom, I can't afford to rent a room.'

'No, darlin', but I can. I told you, I'm going to take care of you.' He gathered her into his arms, and kissed her forehead, her eyes and then, softly, her lips.

Lily, eyes closed, thought she was in heaven. This was not like her father. This was gentle – this was love. This was wonderful. She returned his kisses, holding him tight.

That night, in her bed, she thanked God. 'You *have* taken care of me. Thank You. He's a fine man, this Tom McCann. But I'm a bit worried about Rachel's son – You know, Manny. I don't like him. I know we're supposed to turn the other cheek and all that, but if You don't mind, in his case, I can't. Amen.'

Amy popped into the shop the following day. 'Hey, you lucky tyke.'

'What do you mean?' asked Lily.

'You and Tom. He's about the best-looking man around. I can't tell you the women that have thrown their cap at him.'

'Oh, really. Does that include you?'

'Given half the chance. But don't you worry, love. Tom and me, we're just good mates. Good luck to you, darlin'. He makes good money, and he can take care of himself.'

'What do you mean?' asked Lily, suddenly fearful.

'Oh, he's got an Irish temper on him when he's roused, but for all that, he's a good bloke. Ta ra.'

Rachel Cohen had been listening and had seen the uncertain look on Lily's face. 'I've never met an Irishman yet who didn't have a temper. But as long as he's good to you, don't worry about it. A woman needs a man with a bit of fire in his belly, not some *schlemiel*.'

'He asked me to be his girl last night,' Lily confided.

A look of pleasure crossed Rachel's face. 'I'm happy to hear it, my dear. It's about time you had someone to take care of you. Not thinking of leaving me, are you?'

'No, of course not.' With a mischievous look Lily added, 'Besides, I still owe you money out of my wages . . . And I'm happy here with you.' Looking around she asked, 'Where's Manny today?'

'He's gone up to London, to Golders Green, but he'll be back in the morning.'

Breathing a sigh of relief, Lily said, 'Well, best get on then.'

Later that night, Rachel sat by the fire in her comfortable house, wearing her old dressing gown, eating her gefilte fish and drinking her gin. Her thoughts turned to Lily.

She compared the happy girl she had left this night at her shop to the poor scruffy barefoot waif trying to pinch a pair of shoes. What a sad sight she had looked that day. God knows what she'd suffered at the hands of her drunken father – though Rachel had a good idea.

The confrontation between Lily and Manny had not gone unnoticed, and Rachel let out a sigh. He was her son and although she loved him, she was aware of the boy's bad points. Boy? What am I thinking, she chastised herself. He's a man – thirty yet. She knew he'd been to the Club Valletta, and she knew what for. He didn't gamble, he liked money too much . . . as did his father. He chased women though, just like his father, Hymie. He was a lazy good-for-nothing, but in this he was alone. His father had worked hard for his money, which he saved, scraping every penny together, being miserly about the housekeeping. Rachel grinned sardonically. Poor Hymie, saving so hard for so long only to die suddenly and leave it all to her. She raised her glass. '*L'chayim!* Good health!'

Nobody knew just how much Rachel was worth – certainly not her son. It gave her satisfaction to wear shabby clothes when she was working, but few would have recognised her when she made the odd trip to London, dressed in expensive finery.

Frowning, she thought again of Manny. She needed to find him a wife. Someone who could keep him under control. Someone tight-lipped and tight-arsed. She would speak to the Rabbi again.

Perhaps with Tom McCann, young Lily could at last fulfil her aspirations to marriage and respectability. God knows she deserved it. The girl had crept into her heart, yet she knew that one day she would leave. And how she would miss her. Why couldn't I have had a daughter instead of a feckless son? she sighed, and took another sip of gin.

Lily was up early the following morning, and was already setting out the display when she saw Rachel and Manny walking towards her. Her heart sank. She was going to have that slimy individual around again.

'Morning, Rachel.' She ignored Manny, who just looked at her with a sly grin.

Lily was kept busy on the shop front for most of the morning, but just before noon Rachel said, 'I've just got to go to my solicitor's for an hour. Manny will help keep an eye on the shop. I won't be long.'

Lily cast a baleful eye in his direction as his mother left them. 'You make sure you keep your distance,' she threatened him.

'You should treat me nice, Lily. When Mama dies, all this will be mine.' He looked around the shop. 'This is a good little business. I'll have plenty of cash.'

'If you were covered from head to foot in fivers I wouldn't touch you with a barge-pole!'

'You know you don't mean that,' he said and made a grab at her, catching her by the wrist and pulling her towards him.

Lily was outraged. With all her might she pushed him hard in the chest, sending him flying. He fell awkwardly among the many boxes, knocking the velvet yarmulkah off the back of his head. A feathered hat with a large brim descended and settled on his head as he sat there, dazed from her sudden onslaught.

He looked so ridiculous that she doubled up with laughter. 'Blimey! You could go on the stage at the music halls dressed like that.'

Manny was furious. How dare this chit of a girl ridicule him! Getting to his feet, he grabbed at her once again, gripping her left breast in a cruel hold.

Feeling the sudden pain, Lily clenched her fist and punched him in the face.

With a howl, he let go.

Picking up the old umbrella she'd used before, Lily pointed the steel tip at his throat. 'You touch me again, you filthy bastard, and I'll stab you. Why don't you clean yourself up and find a nice Jewish girl and get married. Make your mother happy. That'll keep you out of trouble.'

Rubbing his jaw, he glared at her. 'You think you're so bloody clever, wheedling your way in here, creeping around Mama. I know your sort – after all you can get from a poor old woman.'

'Poor old woman? Ha! Your mother could make ten of you. Look at you – you're disgusting. Your suit is filthy and

40

you stink. Don't you ever wash? You think any woman would want you? You turn my stomach.' She walked outside the shop to calm down. Muttering, 'I'll swing for that bastard one day if he's around here too often.'

Abraham appeared in the doorway of his shop and, seeing Lily stomping up and down, asked, 'Vat's the matter? You look upset, my dear.'

'Bloody Manny Cohen's what's wrong. I can't bear to be in the same room as him. Trying to paw me all the time!'

Scratching his whiskers, he agreed. 'Vat a disgrace. That poor woman deserves better. My life! If he vas mine, he'd be vorking to earn his keep. Not taking his mama's money. He's a *meshuggener*!'

Manny appeared at the door.

Abraham pointed a scrawny finger at him. 'You leave this girl alone or I'll tell your mama the disgrace you are. Your father if he vas alive would be disgusted with you.'

'Get back to your pawn tickets, old man, and mind your own business.'

'Nobody's talked to me like that since I came here from Poland, thirty years ago. You got no respect for your elders.' Abraham's angry voice brought other shop-owners to the street.

Harry, who owned the fruit and veg stall, strolled over. Shaking a fist at Manny he said, 'You watch your mouth, talking to the old boy like that. You want to take someone on, you try me.'

Manny stepped back, his face pale. An old man was one thing but Harry was another. 'It's nobody else's business. Get back to your shop.'

Harry grabbed him by his coat front. 'Don't give me any of your lip, you little runt.' He pushed him away. 'You all right, Abraham?'

'Sure. That little rat ain't vorth vorrying about.'

Lily had been watching the altercation with enjoyment. She saw the worried look in Manny's eyes, and knew now that he was a coward as well as a slob. 'Thanks, Harry,' she said, 'but it's all right.'

'Any more trouble from him,' he pointed in Manny's

direction, 'you let me know, Lily.'

When the small gathering had dispersed, Manny said, 'I'll pay you back, you little *shiksa* bitch, you see if I don't.'

Seeing Mrs Cohen approaching, Lily didn't answer.

Rachel was immediately aware of the tense atmosphere in the shop. She saw the boxes tipped over and the bruise appearing on her son's face. She was furious. 'Get those boxes put straight,' she told him.

'I was just off for a pint,' he whined.

'Stuff your bloody pint. You do as you're told. It's time you earned some of the money I give you.' She went outside where Lily was folding some clothes. 'Everything all right girl?'

Seeing the worried look in her eyes, Lily nodded. 'Fine, Rachel. Just fine.'

Walking back into the shop, Rachel grabbed the collar of Manny's jacket. 'Been up to your old tricks have you, you little *putz*?'

He looked worried. 'What do you mean?'

'You know what I mean. My life – you're just like your father! You carry your bloody brains in your trouser pockets. Can't keep your hands off a bit of skirt.'

'I never touched her.'

Rachel put her face up against her son's. 'Don't you bloody lie to me. What's this bruise on your face, then? Give you one, did she?' She slapped him hard across the other cheek. 'Now I've done the same.'

Manny looked at her in shocked surprise.

'That girl has had enough to put up with in her young life without you to deal with.' She let go of him.

Manny looked at his mother, his mouth tight with jealousy. 'You think more of her than you do of me.'

'What did I ever do to deserve a son like you? Tomorrow you go to your uncle in Golders Green. This time you work in his tailor's shop. You don't buy for me no more – now you earn your keep.'

'Mama, you can't do that! I'm your son!'

'When you marry a good Jewish girl and settle down, then

42

you're my son. Now, you are nothing to me. You get nothing from me. You earn your own money to spend on prostitutes. Go home. Pack your bags and bugger off.' She crossed her arms. 'I put up with your father for long enough. I don't put up with you. Enough already. *Go!*'

As Manny pushed past Lily, he said quietly, 'You'll pay for this.'

Lily knew that day she had made an enemy.

Chapter Four

The sound of the piano being played in The Sailor's Return could be heard the length of the street. 'My old man said follow the van, and don't dilly dally on the way.' The words of the song were being sung lustily by most of the patrons. In the corner, banging out the melody on an old tinny piano, was Sandy, so named for the colour of his hair.

In his mid-forties, Sandy was paunchy from living too well, his complexion bloated from too much liquor. But his hair, worn long in the neck, curled softly and shone, the overhead lights picking out the chestnut tones. A brightly patterned silk scarf was tucked in the neck of his shirt, over which he wore a maroon-coloured smoking jacket that had seen better days. Nevertheless, it gave Sandy a jaunty, decadent air.

Coming to the end of his number, he stopped playing and angrily tossed his head when a male voice demanded he carry on.

'Shut your face, you old fart. I'm going to have a peaceful drink.'

'Ooooh!' the locals chorused, used to his tantrums.

'Half a bitter please, Declan.' Then turning towards Tom, standing next to him at the bar, he said, 'Honest to God. They don't give a girl a break, that lot.'

With a grin Tom said, 'Don't complain. If they didn't want you to play, then you'd have something to bitch about.'

Sandy looked coyly at him. 'Oh, I do like a strong and masterful man.'

'Where did you get that scarf you're wearing?'

Fingering it lovingly, the pianist said, 'I was given it last

45

week by a Dutch sailor. Now there was a masterful beast.'

'I swear you get worse,' chided Tom, his eyes crinkling with amusement.

'Well dearie, you know what Mae West says: "When I'm good, I'm very very good, but when I'm bad . . . I'm better".' He downed his beer. 'Best get back to the rabble. Any requests?'

' "I'll Take You Home Again Kathleen". It was me mother's favourite.'

'All right, my lovely. I'll play it just for you.'

Taking his drink with him, Tom wandered over to an empty table and sat down. Listening to the familiar strains of the song, he pictured his mother. He missed her, he realised. She was a simple woman who would have made any sacrifice for her family with love and without complaint, but she had been unable to settle in England away from her precious mountains. She and the rest of the family had returned to Ireland. His mother had been in tears when he decided to stay behind.

He hadn't done badly he thought. He'd got himself a trade and the respect of his peers, after many a battle. As a young man, he'd had to learn to stand on his own against all adversaries, and there had been many. Life was a constant struggle for survival in the docks.

He knew now how to handle himself, asking no quarter and giving none. He had survived. Now he thought it was time to settle down. To be honest, he'd only begun to think this way since he met Lily. Before that he was happy as a single man, but somehow she had made him take stock of his life.

He so enjoyed her company. She made him laugh with her ready wit, and she was appreciative of everything he did for her. She was warm, affectionate, and caring. There was a quirkiness about her that he found appealing. He thought of her dark bouncy hair, her blue eyes, the feel of her in his arms. He longed to make love to her, to hear her cries of delight when he caressed her. She was definitely the woman he wanted to be the mother of his children.

He frowned when he pictured the look on Manny Cohen's

face as he watched them that day. He didn't trust the sod. If Manny touched his Lily, he would be sorry. If any man touched his Lily, they'd rue the day.

On their way home from the cinema the following evening, Tom and Lily had their first disagreement.

'But I don't *want* you to pay for a room for me. If I can't afford my own, then I'll stay at Mrs Cohen's shop.'

Tom ran his hands through his hair in frustration. 'I don't understand. Why won't you let me do this for you?'

'It's like being a kept woman – it's not respectable.'

'Oh, for goodness sake! I'm not renting a love nest, somewhere we can run to for sex.'

'Tom!' Lily glared at him, shock in her eyes.

'What's the matter, Lily? There's nothing to be ashamed of. Sex is a wonderful thing between two people in love. How do you think we got born? Our parents had to do it.'

Lily's face was white. All she could think of was her father's heaving body on top of hers. The pain – the disgrace. There was so very much to be ashamed of. She couldn't speak.

'Lily.' Tom's voice softened. He stopped walking, pulling her into a shop doorway. 'Come here.' He held her in his arms, feeling her resistance. 'Relax, darlin'. I'm not going to hurt you, I'd never do that. Now listen to me. If we were married, we'd share the same bed, and I'd take you in my arms and love you. Would that be such a terrible thing?'

She snuggled up against him. His arms held her in a close embrace. 'No, that wouldn't be terrible.'

Putting a finger under her chin, he tilted her head, looking into her eyes. Why were they so full of fear? 'Are you frightened of me, Lily?' She shook her head. 'Then what is it?'

How could she tell him? He thought of her as pure. Untouched. If he made love to her, he would know and she'd have to tell him her guilty secret. It would disgust him. He wouldn't want her after that.

'Let's not rush into anything, Tom. We can wait a while, get to know one another better.'

47

'Don't you like me, Lily?'

'I do, Tom. A lot. I can't imagine my life without you now.'

'Then why do we have to wait? I've fallen in love with you. I never thought the day would come when I'd say that – well, not for some time. But you, Lily, you've crept into me heart. Let's get married. I can afford to rent a two-up and two-down. We'll have a nice little house, then you won't be a kept woman – you'll be Mrs Tom McCann.'

Lily's heart was heavy. Here was everything she had ever wanted. A good man to love her, the chance of a husband earning decent money, a home, respectability. All her aspirations. Her chance at a good life, and she couldn't take it.

She didn't want to lose this wonderful Irishman. What could she do? Who could she ask? Certainly not Tom.

'It's too soon, Tom,' she said evasively. 'You're rushing me. I'm too used to being on my own, I need time to think about it.' She could see the anger in his eyes. His pride had been hurt. Here he was offering her everything and she'd turned him down.

'I do love you, Tom.' She felt a warm glow as she uttered the words. She did love him, but it wasn't as simple as that. 'We have our whole lives in front of us. Let's not rush things.'

'The trouble with you, Lily Pickford, is you're too bloody independent!'

The following day, Lily saw Amy standing outside the pub. She left the shop and walked up to her.

'Hello, ducks. Decided to go on the game, have yer?'

'No, of course not!'

'It was a joke, Lily. A joke. What's on your mind, girl?'

Suddenly feeling shy, Lily said quietly, 'I need to ask you something personal. In private.'

Seeing the worried expression on the young girl's face, Amy realised that, to Lily, this was a serious matter.

'All right. How about I come to the shop later tonight when old mother Cohen has gone home?'

'Would you really, Amy? Thanks, that would be great. What time?'

'About seven, before I go to work.'

Filled with relief, Lily said, 'I'll watch out for you.'

All day she worried as to how she was going to approach Amy. She didn't want to divulge too much about her past, but there were things she must know, and Amy was the only person she could ask.

As good as her word, Amy turned up at seven o'clock and Lily let her in, carefully locking the shop door behind them. In the dim glow from the one light, the two women sat on the shabby straight-backed chairs.

'All right, darlin', I'm all yours. Ask away.'

'Well you see, it's like this,' began Lily. 'If a girl gets married and she isn't a virgin but her husband thinks she is, will he know when he makes love to her?' There. She'd said it.

Amy scratched her forehead. 'How much do you know about your own body, love? I mean your private parts?'

Lily shrugged. 'Not much.'

'Christ! I feel like your mother.'

Lily listened carefully as Amy gave her a completely frank and graphic account of the sex act, as only a prostitute could. 'What's the problem, love?' Amy asked. 'Look, I'm your friend. Anything you tell me I swear to God, I won't repeat it to a living soul.'

Lily studied Amy. The earnest expression and concern in her eyes were genuine, and she trusted her. 'Tom wants to marry me. But I'm not a virgin.'

'How's he going to know? When he first makes love to you, just give a little cry of pain. He won't know any different. Listen, darlin', by then he'll be so bloody worked up, he won't even think about it.'

Lily gave a sigh of relief. 'Thanks, Amy. You're a real brick.'

Realising that Lily was not a girl to give her body to anyone, Amy drew her own conclusions. She took a cigarette out of her bag and lit it. 'I was raped once.' She didn't look at Lily. 'I wasn't much older than you are now. It was an uncle of mine. Took me out for the day. I was really excited. Then he took me to his home . . . Rotten bastard.' She paused.

'Oh Amy, I'm so sorry.'

With a wicked grin Amy said, 'No, don't be. I paid the perverted sod back a few years later.'

'How?'

'I met a couple of sailors when I first went on the game, and we became friends, although they still paid for sex. But they beat him up for me one night.'

With wide eyes Lily asked, 'Did he know why?'

'Oh yes, he knew why – I was there when they did it. I stood and watched.'

I know just how you feel, thought Lily. She wouldn't bat an eye if she saw her father treated the same way. It would be a kind of justice.

'You thinking of marrying the wild Irishman, then?'

With flushed cheeks Lily said, 'Well, I'm thinking about it, but I want to wait a while.'

'You'll have to get your parents' permission.'

Lily felt the blood drain from her face. 'What do you mean?'

'Well, you're under age, aren't you?'

'What?'

'You have to be twenty-one.'

With a forced smile Lily said, 'Well, that's all right then. Besides, I'm an orphan, so it doesn't really count. But as I'm old enough it doesn't matter.'

Amy looked knowingly at her. 'Well, you're a bright kid. I'm sure you know what you're doing. Listen, darlin', if there's anything I can ever do for you, you just ask, OK?' She caught hold of Lily's hands. 'Listen to me, this is a hard old world. If we can't help each other, then it's even worse.' She stood up. 'Now I must go and earn some money.'

'Have you ever been in love, Amy?'

The smile left Amy's face as she answered, 'No, dearie. Many men have wanted to lay me down, but I haven't met one yet that has wanted to pick me up.' She walked towards the door. 'Never mind, I do all right. See you tomorrow.'

Alone in the shop, Lily pondered on this new problem. She was under-age for marriage. Tom wouldn't wait for years without some explanation and she certainly wouldn't go near her father to ask for his consent. Most likely he wouldn't give it anyway. If she lied about her age and got married, would it be legal? She sighed. If she told Tom the truth about her age, would he understand, or would he perhaps be angry with her? And would he still want her? Maybe he'd think her too young for him. She thought she'd go mad with all these uncertainties running around inside her head. Why did life have to be so complicated, just when she had it within her reach to be happy?

Vittorio sat in his leather chair behind a dark mahogany desk, puffing on his Havana cigar. He tapped the edge of the desk with his fingertips. His lips were drawn in a tight line, and his eyes were burning with anger. Picking up some bags of change, he made his way downstairs to the club.

It wasn't yet opening time and the staff were making final preparations for a busy night ahead. Tables were laid with expensive linen and cutlery, the gambling rooms were ready for those who would certainly chance their luck. Upstairs the girls waited, chatting together.

Vittorio walked towards the bar, lifted the flap and went over to the barman, who was polishing glasses. Handing him the bags, Vittorio said, 'Here's the rest of the float. You'd better check it.'

The barman tipped out the florins and half-crowns and counted them carefully under Vittorio's watchful eye, placing the coins in tidy piles.

'It's all here, sir.'

'Then put it in the till.'

The metal drawer was opened and the money transferred. As the last small pile was carefully placed inside, Vittorio slammed the drawer shut, trapping the man's fingers. He let out an agonised yell of pain.

Vittorio pushed even harder. 'You've been dipping into my

money, Johnny, and now you've been caught with your fingers really in the till.'

'No, guv. I haven't, honest!'

'Honest! You don't know what the word means. Not only are you a thief, but you're a fool as well, thinking you can put one over on me.'

Johnny was bent almost double with the pain. 'Please let go,' he pleaded.

Vittorio did so suddenly and the barman withdrew his crushed fingers. 'They're broken!' He stared at his boss in disbelief. 'You broke my bloody fingers.'

The eyes that stared back at him were cold. 'It should be your bloody neck.'

'I've got to get to the hospital.'

'When I've finished with you, you'll need a mortuary.'

Johnny's eyes were filled with terror. 'Please, Mr Teglia. I'm very sorry. I won't ever do it again.'

'Correct. You won't have the chance.' He beckoned one of his henchmen over. 'Johnny no longer works for me. He's been dipping into my money. Deal with him.'

George Coleman, the ex-boxer, tut-tutted. 'What a silly thing to do. I always knew you were a bit fly, but I didn't think you was stupid.' In a steel-like grip, George took hold of the man and led him towards the back entrance. 'Can you swim, son?' The door banged shut behind them.

It was ten o'clock and the club was packed, the dining room filled to capacity. Vittorio looked around at his clients. There were several of the town's dignitaries enjoying the excellent food, prepared by a chef with the highest references. The front of the house was there to create an air of respectability, but behind locked doors it was a different matter.

He gave a sardonic smile. These people sickened him. They were puffed up with their own importance, yet here they were, enjoying good food, many here to gamble, some to have sex with one of his girls, knowing discretion was guaranteed.

It gave The Maltese power. His customers, anxious to have their particular perversions satisfied, were in a position to help him if any difficult situations cropped up with the law. One telephone call was all it took to smooth things out. Not many knew that the Chief Constable liked young boys, for instance. Thus Vittorio was able to run his business undisturbed for most of the time. When a raid was planned, he was informed. He knew where to pay, and who to pay . . . He was invincible.

George Coleman approached. 'The barman's been sorted, guv.'

'Good. When will they learn that I'm not a man to be messed with?'

Grinning, George said, 'I chucked him in the dock. Stupid bugger couldn't swim, either.'

'So what happened to him?'

'I threw him a life-belt and walked away.'

'Well, if he wants to survive, he'll learn to swim to it or sink. Either way he won't mess with me again.'

'Any orders for tonight, guv?'

Vittorio frowned. 'Yes. That young boy – you know, the one whose father owns the Pier – don't give him too much credit. He's a bad gambler and an even worse payer. If he wants a woman, he pays cash, understand?'

'Sure. He'll be no trouble – I'll see to him personally.'

Walking away, Vittorio inspected the restaurant. He was a perfectionist and his staff were aware of this. The clients expected the best and they paid through the nose for it. The Club Valletta had a fine reputation and God help any of the staff who were not on their toes.

Satisfied at last that all was as it should be, Vittorio returned to his office, still annoyed at the audacity of the barman. No one crossed him and got away with it. He was a hard man but a fair one, he liked to think. OK, so he sailed very close to the wind as far as the law was concerned, but he supplied a good service. The Club offered an excellent, if expensive, night's entertainment, the service was impeccable and the gambling honest. The Maltese was no fool. If the punters suspected they were being cheated, they wouldn't come.

He thought suddenly of Lily. When first he saw her in the

cafe, it had been his intention to bring her here as a prostitute, but after meeting her again, he knew he didn't want that. He didn't want any other man to enjoy the pleasures of her body. Vittorio gave a slow smile. She wouldn't have it anyway – she'd made that *quite* clear. The girl was bright, articulate and highly amusing. He would enjoy getting to know her better. But there was no rush. She would eventually be a part of his life, of that he was sure. He could feel it in his bones.

Chapter Five

Lily was unhappy. For the past three months Tom had been badgering her about getting married, and she could see that his patience was wearing thin.

Tonight they had been to the Palace Theatre, one of Lily's favourite places. She so enjoyed the variety programmes, but she especially loved to watch the singers – Marie Lloyd in particular. She herself would love to go on the stage and perform. She imagined herself strutting about, getting the audience singing with her and hearing their applause at the end. It would be wonderful, she thought. She was saying as much to Tom as he walked her home.

But Tom was silent. She noticed that during the evening he hadn't joined in with the singing either. She sighed, knowing what was to come. It was the same old argument.

'You'd rather be doing anything than be me wife, it seems to me.'

'Oh Tom, don't start.' She clung to his arm. 'We're happy, aren't we?'

His stormy expression as he looked at her told her he wasn't. 'I don't understand you, Lily Pickford. There are scores of women who would only be too happy to be asked to share me life.'

I'm not going to have him ruin a lovely evening, Lily thought. Besides, she was fed up with the constant pressure. 'Then I suggest you ask one of them!'

She saw the fire in his eyes. 'Maybe I should.'

They walked back to The Ditches in silence.

Lily never invited him inside the shop. He felt so strongly against her living there that she didn't want him to see her humble corner. She herself was quite pleased with her little abode. She had acquired a clean mattress and bought some bed linen off Rachel Cohen – paid for out of her wages, naturally! She'd placed two screens around the corner of her bedroom to make it private, and with a washbasin and a mirror, she was quite self-sufficient. What more did she need at this time?

'I'm going away, Lily.'

The sudden statement sent a chill through her. 'Going away – where?'

'I'm going to Ireland, to see me mother. She hasn't been well.'

Lily was immediately sympathetic. 'Oh Tom, I'm sorry. I hope it isn't anything serious?'

'She's had pneumonia, but apparently is getting better.'

'You didn't tell me.'

'I didn't know how serious it was meself, until I got a letter this morning.'

'You *are* coming back?'

He hesitated. 'That all depends.'

She felt her stomach tighten. 'What do you mean?'

'Do I have anything to come back for, that's what I want to know.'

Oh God, please don't let me lose him, she prayed fervently. 'You have me, Tom.'

'Do I, Lily? I don't think I do.'

She grabbed at his coat and held on. 'Don't say things like that, Tom. I love you.'

'I'm not even sure of that any more. If you really loved me you would want to be me wife. You would have named the day. We could be planning our wedding, but you keep giving me excuse after excuse.' His expression was cold. 'What else can I think?'

She was beside herself. Yes, she kept putting him off, for she wasn't able to marry him unless she lied about her age, but she couldn't let him go like this. She loved him too much.

Holding his face tenderly in her hands, she kissed him. 'I love you more than life itself. I want to be with you, for ever.'

There was a flicker of hope in his eyes. 'You mean that, Lily?'

'I mean it, Tom. Honest I do. When you come back from Ireland, we'll sort out a date for the wedding.'

He clasped her to him, raining kisses on her lips, her eyes, her hair. 'Oh Lily, darlin', I was beginning to give up all hope. I want you so much. I want to hold you in me arms, make love to you, wake up beside you in the morning and know you'll be there when I get home at night.'

Lily held him tightly, overwhelmed by his words. 'I want those things too.'

He tilted her chin upwards, and kissed her tenderly. 'When I come back, we'll look for a house to rent. We'll choose some nice second-hand stuff. One day you'll have a place to call your own. I'll work hard, you'll see. It will be wonderful, being Mrs Tom McCann. You'll never regret it.'

They held on to each other, exchanging kisses filled with passion. 'We'll make wonderful babies,' he said softly.

Lily felt her cheeks redden. 'Tom!' she chided.

His laughter echoed down the street. 'My, but you're a shy one, for all your cheek.' He kissed her forehead. 'I'll be gentle with you, darlin'. I'll teach you how to enjoy being loved as a wife should. I know you're a virgin, but there's nothing to be frightened of. Love and sex go together.'

As he held her close Lily thought, No, Tom. Sex isn't always about love at all.

'I'll be away a week, unless me mother's really sick. If I'm going to be longer, I'll write to you.'

Her eyes lit up. 'Will you? I've never had a letter in my life.'

'In that case I'll write anyway. Tell you how much I love you . . . and miss you.'

It was late when Tom reluctantly left her and she let herself into the shop, locked the door and sat on her bed, alone. 'Well, I've really gone and done it now,' she said aloud. Then she had a frightening thought. What if she had to produce a birth certificate? Not only would Tom discover her real age, but her name would be different. There would be so much explaining to do – and what would have to be revealed then? Her eyes closed in despair. She had committed herself to Tom, but was frightened of the consequences.

The next day, weighed down with her problems, she was uncharacteristically short-tempered with the customers, telling one woman who was unable to make up her mind over a dress, 'Take it or leave it, missus! If you don't want it, someone else will.'

When the woman walked off in a huff, Rachel pulled Lily roughly into the shop. 'You just lost me a sale. I can't afford to lose money, now pull yourself together. What's up with you?'

Lily apologised. 'I'm sorry. Tom has gone away, back to Ireland to see his sick mother.'

'Humpf! That's no reason to get snotty with the paying customers. He's coming back, isn't he?'

Lily nodded.

'Then I suggest you go out there and work harder. You had better make up the loss by the end of the day, girl, or you'll get a tongue-lashing from me.'

With a sardonic look Lily said, 'I thought I'd just had one.'

That evening, Lily walked down to the Esplanade, thinking the sea air might blow away her troubled thoughts. En route she saw her friend Amy.

'Blimey! You look as if the end of the world is near. If you were to wear a placard saying so, no one would doubt it.'

'I'm in a lot of trouble, Amy.'

'You're not up the spout, are you?'

'No,' said Lily. 'It's worse than that.'

'Oh my God,' said Amy, looking worried. 'Here, let's sit on this bench and you can tell me about it.'

'Tom's gone to Ireland and I told him when he comes back, we'll make a date to get married.'

'Christ Almighty! Is that all? I should have such a worry.'

'But you see,' continued Lily, a deep frown creasing her forehead, 'I'm not old enough. I can lie about my age, but they'll need a birth certificate.'

'That's right, love. Even with your parents' consent. Oh I

forgot, you ain't got none, have you?'

Looking at Amy, Lily drew in a deep breath. 'Well, I have, but I don't want to see either of them ever again.'

Laying a hand on her friend's arm Amy said, 'You don't have to explain to me, love. Now I can see you do have a problem. Maybe I can help after all.'

With a look of disbelief, Lily asked, 'How?'

Leaning closer, Amy lowered her voice. 'Well, dearie, in my game you meet all sorts, and one of my punters is into a bit of forgery now and again. He owes me a favour – I'll see what I can do. Just give me a few days.'

Hugging Amy, Lily said, 'Oh, thanks! I was going out of my head with worry.'

'Well, just keep your fingers crossed. Come on, let's go and have a drink. Cheer us both up.'

The following morning, Lily was singing as she worked. Rachel, watching her, shook her head. 'So yesterday you were hell in shoes, today a canary. What's the story?'

With a smile that could light up The Ditches Lily said, 'I'm going to marry Tom.'

'*Mazel tov!*' Putting her arms around Lily, Rachel hugged her and said, 'That's wonderful news. So why yesterday's long face?'

With a shrug she said, 'There was a little problem, but now it's solved.'

'So my dear, at last you'll get all your dreams. A man, marriage, a home and respectability. I'm so happy for you.' Rachel clapped her hands together in delight. 'At lunchtime, take a jug to the pub, and fetch home some beer. We'll celebrate. Am I invited to the wedding?'

'Of course you are.'

Looking suddenly crestfallen Rachel asked, 'Does this mean you'll be leaving me?'

'Why should it? I can still work for you. I don't see what difference getting married will make.'

'Have you discussed this with Tom?'

'No, why should I?'

With a knowing look Rachel said, 'You don't know men,

my dear. It strikes me that Tom McCann might have different ideas.'

'What do you mean?'

'That Irishman has a lot of pride. He's got a good job, he may want you to be at home, waiting on him.'

With a derisive snort Lily said, 'I'm going to be his wife, not his bloody slave.'

Rachel's laugh was hearty. 'Ay yi! I can see this marriage is going to be very volatile. Still,' she nudged Lily in the ribs, 'making up will be a lot of fun, I'm sure.'

'Really, Mrs Cohen! Such thoughts from a middle-aged lady.' But Lily's eyes twinkled as she chided her.

Tom McCann sat beside his mother's bed, holding her frail hand in his. He'd been dreadfully shocked when he'd first seen her, for she had aged so much since he had last visited. Now she was propped up against her pillows, asking him about his life.

'Are you happy, son?'

'I am, Ma. I've got a good job and I've a lovely girl who's going to be me wife. When I go back, we're going to arrange the wedding.'

Squeezing his hand, his mother smiled softly. 'Ah, that's grand to be sure. Every man needs a good woman to take care of him. And mind you care well for your wife, Thomas. Will you be bringing her home to Ireland one day?'

'I certainly will. I've told her all about the family, Newcastle, and the mountains.'

'Ah, the mountains.' Kathleen McCann looked out of her window and gazed at them, now bathed in late-autumn sunshine. 'Every day I look at them and say good morning. I hope to be well enough to take at least one more walk among them.'

Tom was filled with sadness. The doctor had told him his mother was unlikely to recover.

'One day you, Lily and me will walk them together,' he promised.

Holding his hand tighter she said, 'I don't think so, son. I'm near the end of me days, and I'm happy to go to me

Maker. Just you bring up your family with love and honour – that's all I ask of you. I'm glad you came home and we were able to be together for a while.'

That night, Kathleen McCann slipped quietly away in her sleep.

After the funeral, Tom took a walk along the beach. He breathed in deeply and the smell of seaweed and salt air filled his nostrils. He watched the waves break upon the sand, looked back at the mountains and shed tears for his mother. One day he and Lily would come back here to live, he thought, maybe bring their own children. It would be with them he'd walk among the mountains, for the spirit of his mother would always be there.

The postman popped his head around the door of the shop. 'Letter for Miss Lily Pickford.'

Lily rushed towards him. 'That's me,' she said excitedly. 'I'm Lily Pickford.' She opened it quickly, and the smile faded from her lips as she read.

'Something wrong, girl?' asked Rachel, seeing her stricken expression.

'Tom's mother's died. He's staying on for the funeral and the wake. What's a wake?'

'They hold a party to celebrate the life of the person who's just died.'

'A party?' Lily looked shocked.

'Yes, and what's wrong with that? All her old friends will be there, remembering the happy times. It's not a time for sadness, it's a celebration.'

'Sounds very strange to me.'

'So when will he be home?'

Quickly scanning the letter, Lily said, 'About a week's time. He'll write and let me know.' She blushed as she read the last few words. Rachel diplomatically left her alone.

'I love and miss you, darling Lily. I can't wait to hold you in my arms. Soon, very soon, we'll be together again. Never again will we be apart. Love always, Tom.'

★ ★ ★

Lily was lying in her bed dreaming of Tom and the Mountains of Mourne when something disturbed her slumbers. Rubbing her eyes, she sat up. She noticed one of the screens had been removed. As her eyes became accustomed to the low light from the street-lamps, she saw a figure sitting on one of the straight-backed chairs that had been drawn up at the foot of her bed. Sitting on it, watching her, was Manny Cohen.

Lily gave a cry of fright. Fear gripped her heart. She looked at him in silence for a moment, trying to gather her wits. 'What the bleedin' 'ell are you doing here at this time of night?' She drew the blanket up around her.

Beneath his hooded eyes, Manny's lips curled into a cruel grin. His words were slurred. 'I thought I'd pay you a visit, Lily. I'm sure you get lonely here at night.'

'You're drunk!' she said in disgust.

'Yes, I am. But I had a most interesting drinking companion tonight.'

Something in his manner made her wary. 'What do you mean?'

He crossed one knee over the other and leaned against the back of the chair. 'This man told me the saddest story. It seems that his daughter ran away from home.'

Lily was filled with apprehension as he continued.

'Apparently his wife has left him and he's lonely. He wants to find his daughter. You see, he wants someone to love – to play games with.'

She felt sick inside as she realised that Manny, of all people, had uncovered her past. 'Why are you telling me all this?' she whispered.

'Come, Lily. You can't pretend with me. I know all about you now. You certainly won't want anyone else to hear the truth about you and your father. I reckon you owe me a favour to keep it quiet.'

What was she to do? A million thoughts crowded into her mind. She knew what Manny wanted, had always wanted. Well, she wasn't going to let this fat slob touch her. Those days finished when she left home. She looked wildly around for her umbrella.

Manny leered at her. 'There's nothing you can do. Your weapon has been hidden away. Why don't you just lie back and enjoy it?'

Lily remembered what Amy had told her about awkward customers. If she was clever, she could handle this. Manny was well into his cups, he would be unsteady on his feet. She smiled invitingly at him.

'It seems I don't have any choice, so let's both enjoy it.'

He looked first surprised, then a little wary. He didn't trust Lily. 'What do you mean?'

'Let me get up and get dressed first.'

'I don't want you dressed. I want you naked.'

'Of course you do, Manny, but think of the fun you'll have *un*dressing me.'

He wriggled in his chair at the idea, and she saw the expression of raw lust in his eyes. She looked quickly for the bag that held her savings. She wasn't leaving without them.

'What do you say, Manny? Shall we play games, just you and me? My father taught me lots of naughty things we can do.'

He was almost salivating with excitement.

'I'll get dressed very slowly, so you can watch.'

Speechless, he nodded in agreement.

Lily got carefully to her feet and began to put on her stockings, doing up the garters with deliberation, smoothing her legs as she did so.

Manny's eyes were glued to her every move.

She stepped into a skirt, then slipped a jumper over her head, pulling it down over her breasts. Then she put on a coat.

He looked at her suspiciously.

'All the more to take off, darling,' she promised, gritting her teeth as she did so.

Walking towards him, she stroked his face and ruffled his hair. 'You have far too many clothes on, Manny. Let me take them off, then you can do the same to me.'

Like a lamb, he did as he was told. He stood up, swaying against the chair. 'Kiss me, Lily.'

Her stomach turned at the idea. 'Be patient,' she whispered in his ear. She took off his jacket and dropped it to the floor, undid the buttons of his shirt and removed his tie, fighting with the strong urge within her to strangle him with it. She slid the shirt off his back. 'My, what lovely skin you have,' she said, smoothing his shoulders. Then at last she undid his flies.

Manny's face was flushed with anticipation. Lily turned her head away from his sour breath as he breathed heavily.

Sliding the trousers down round his ankles, she then took down his underpants. Seeing his swollen member, she thought she would be sick. 'Such a fuss over such a little thing.'

For a moment there was a look of awareness in his eyes, but Lily dispelled this. 'I was joking, Manny. You're a fine man. Would you like me to touch you?'

He nodded.

Lily could hear Amy's voice in her head. 'I squeeze their balls until they scream.'

Holding Manny's scrotum gently, she heard him moan with ecstasy – then she squeezed as hard as she could.

As Manny's screams of pain filled her ears, she gripped harder. He begged her to let go, but she ignored him and squeezed even tighter. When she was ready, she released her hold.

Manny writhed on the floor, sobbing.

She looked at him, her heart full of hate. This rotten piece of humanity had ruined her future happiness. Her feeling of disgust for the games she had just played and her hatred for the man on the ground made her devoid of emotion. Ignoring him, she buttoned her coat and picked up a couple of her dresses. Taking the shop keys out of his jacket pocket, she put on her shoes, picked up her handbag and, turning to Manny, spat at him, 'One word out of you about me and my father, and I'll kill you.'

Walking to the front of the shop, she opened the door and left. Carefully locking up behind her, she gazed at the building with tears in her eyes. She'd been so happy here, but she couldn't come between Rachel and her son. After all, blood was thicker than water. The woman had been so good to her, she couldn't do anything that would make her unhappy.

As for her own performance – God! She'd behaved no better than a whore. To her surprise, it hadn't been that difficult. She'd been revolted, but it wasn't as bad as she'd envisaged. He deserved the pain she'd inflicted on him. The scumbag. Her eyes bright with anger, she smirked. It would be some time before he'd want a woman, and that fact gave Lily deep satisfaction.

At least this time she had a little money. She could rent a cheap room, maybe get a job. Sticking one foot out, she gave a rueful grin. And she had a pair of shoes. But now she must start again. Her heart was heavy and her shoulders slumped. She could never marry Tom now. Manny knew about her past, and he would be bound to seek his revenge. If he thought she was going to marry Tom, he would make a point of telling him about her father.

That night, in a shabby room she'd rented deep in the heart of the Docklands Lily wept for Tom. Now that she was settled with a roof over her head, her defences were totally annihilated and she felt raw with pain. She pictured Tom's face the last time they were together. She sobbed when she thought of his return, when he would discover she was no longer there. How hurt he would be. She wept for the loss of her future, of their happiness together. But she couldn't take the risk of his finding out her secret. It disgusted her. How would he feel? Equally disgusted, she was sure. He would never be able to hold her, make love to her, without the knowledge that her father had enjoyed the same pleasures. It would destroy them both.

Chapter Six

As Tom hurried to the shop in The Ditches he caught sight of Rachel, who was in the middle of hanging up a dress. 'Good mornin', Mrs Cohen,' he said, a broad smile on his lips. 'Can I speak to Lily?'

She looked at him, a haunted look in her eyes. 'I'm sorry, lad. She ain't here.'

Puzzled, he asked, 'Where is she then, gone on an errand?'

'No, Tom. I don't know where she's gone. She left about five days ago.'

His eyes widened in surprise. 'What do you mean, left?'

'I arrived one morning and the shop was still locked. When I opened the door, she'd gone.'

He couldn't believe what he was being told. 'Did she take her stuff with her? Did she leave a note? Didn't she say anything?' The questions poured forth. 'I mean, she can't have just disappeared.'

With a worried expression, Rachel said, 'She took a couple of dresses, her coat and her handbag. The keys were returned to me later in the day by some young kid who said a girl had given them to him to deliver.'

Seeing the shocked expression on his face she said, 'Come inside, son, I'll make you a cup of tea. The kettle has just boiled.'

Stunned by the news, Tom followed her and sat down on the chair she put out for him. He leaned forward, elbows on his knees and hands to his head. 'But I don't understand it. We were going to be married.'

'I know. I know. She told me about it.' She handed him a

mug of steaming liquid. Her heart went out to him, and she cursed her son.

'What made her do such a thing? Do you know?'

'No,' she lied.

'I've got to find her, Mrs Cohen. Find out what's happened. She can't have gone far. Did she have much money on her?'

Rachel shook her head. 'She'd been saving, but she couldn't have had too much.'

'But why would she suddenly go off like that? She was so happy here.' He ran his fingers through his hair in agitation. 'God knows I've tried to get her to move to a room, but no. And now to run off . . . It doesn't make sense. Perhaps I should go to the police.'

Her nerves taut with tension, Rachel said, 'You must do what you think is best, my dear.'

He looked at her shrewdly. 'Are you telling me everything you know?'

Immediately defensive, she asked, 'What's that supposed to mean?'

'Where's that son of yours?'

'He's in London, working with my brother. Been there for months.'

Tom sipped the tea. 'I never trusted him. I saw the way he ogled Lily.' His eyes narrowed. 'If I thought your precious Manny had anything to do with this . . .'

'How could he? He hasn't been around for weeks.'

'I'm going to find her, however long it takes.' Tom's jaw tightened. 'I'll never stop looking. But now I'm going to report her missing.' He stood up and, turning slowly, asked, 'Why didn't you do that?'

'Had she not returned my keys, I would have done. But I figured she had a good reason to do such a thing, that it wasn't my place to interfere.'

Tom was angry. 'Well, you should have done! Now we've lost five days.' He stormed out of the shop. 'I'll be back. If she returns, you get in touch with me, leave a message at The Sailor's Return.'

After he'd gone, Rachel Cohen sat down, her body trembling. She'd dreaded the return of Tom McCann ever since she had found the shop locked and her son in a drunken sleep, holding his private parts, trousers round his ankles.

She'd quickly locked the door behind her, calling frantically for Lily. Her cries had wakened her son, who sat up and rubbed his eyes, blanching at the pain between his legs, moaning as he tried to move.

'Where is she?' Rachel yelled at him.

Holding his throbbing head Manny said, 'Don't shout, Mama. For Christ's sake, don't shout.'

She went berserk then. 'Look at you, you dirty filthy bugger.' She kicked out at him, catching him in the ribs. Ignoring his cry of pain, she screamed at him: 'Stand up, get dressed, then you had better tell me the truth of what happened here, or I'll call the police.'

When he tried to concoct some stupid story, she dragged him to his feet. 'The truth, I said. You lie to me, and I'll knock your teeth in.'

Never had Manny seen his mother in such a temper. 'I came to keep Lily company, let myself in with my key.'

Rachel's eyes glittered. 'And then? *The truth*, I said.'

'She said she wanted to play games with me.'

Rachel caught hold of his ear and twisted.

'All right! I wanted her. She said it was OK, then she undressed me and gripped my balls until I screamed.'

His mother let go, uttering her disgust. 'She should have cut them off. Did she say where she was going?'

'How the hell should I know? I was on the floor in agony.'

'Did you hurt her?'

He was furious. 'Just a minute! I'm the one who's hurt here. But if I ever meet her again, I'll pay her back.'

'You just pray her boyfriend doesn't find you first.'

Fear was reflected in his eyes. 'What do you mean?'

'He's due home from Ireland any day and he'll come here looking for her. What do you think will happen when I have to tell him she's done a flit? He'll want to know why.'

He grabbed at her arm. 'You won't tell him, Mama? He'll kill me.'

She looked at her son with loathing. 'It's what you deserve.

You make me sick. I won't tell him, but it's the last thing I do for you.'

He gave a sigh of relief, then, frowning, asked: 'What do you mean, the last thing you do for me?'

'I've been good to you, spoilt you, looked after you since your papa died. All you've done is cause trouble, drink yourself silly and sleep with prostitutes. Ach!' She spat on the ground. 'That's what I think of you. All I ever wanted was for you to earn an honest living. Get married. Stand beneath the *chuppah* with a nice Jewish girl. But no. You're a *meshuggener*! From today I have no son. You leave here and you don't come back, not ever. From today, I'm a poor childless woman – alone in the world.'

The blood drained from his face. 'You can't do this to me.'

'It's done.' She held up her hands as if in surrender. 'I don't care where you go, what happens to you. Because of you, Lily's gone. For that I don't forgive you – not ever.'

Manny glared at her. 'You crazy old woman. You cared more for that slut than you ever did me.'

Rachel looked coldly at him. 'She has more honesty, pride and *chutzpa* in her little finger than you'll ever have.' She threw his jacket at him. 'Get dressed, you look pathetic. I'll send the rest of your clothes to your uncle. Now, get out of my sight. You disgrace my family. That I should know you, makes me want to puke. That I gave birth to you makes me ashamed.'

As she recalled the ugly scene, tears pricked her eyes. To think it was a son of hers who'd tried to have sex with Lily and frightened her away. Lily, whom she had grown to love as a daughter. What would become of the poor girl? How would she, Rachel, cope without her? Her life would be empty now without the cheeky, cheery presence which had lit up her every working day. The girl had brightened her life, made up for some of her disappointments. Yes, she would feel the loss deeply. Perhaps she could find her, get her back. After all, Lily had no one to fear now. Manny had been banished from her life. Yes, Rachel decided. She would have a quiet word with Amy. The prostitute got around – heard all the gossip of the Docklands.

But Amy couldn't help her.

'Blimey, Rachel, what happened to make her scoot off like that? She was so happy the last time I saw her. Tom was due back from Ireland.'

'He's back,' said Rachel, 'and he's going mad with worry. He's out looking for her at the moment.'

'Well, I'll keep my ear to the ground,' Amy promised, 'and I'll let you know if I hear anything.'

Rachel's face was filled with anguish and guilt. 'If you see her, Amy, tell her it's safe to come back.'

Amy gave her a strange look. 'What do you mean, safe? Just a minute – you ain't being honest with me. What happened here? What did you do to that girl?'

Wringing her hands Rachel said, 'I didn't do anything. It was Manny. He let himself in at night.'

'Oh my God!'

'He swears he didn't touch her – in fact, she hurt him. I'm sure she's all right.'

'All right! How can you say that? God knows where she is, what sort of state she's in. How's she going to make a living? How's she going to live? Tell me that.'

Covering her eyes with her hand, Rachel cried, 'I love that girl. I don't want no harm to come to her. I've sent Manny away. I don't have a son no more.'

Compassion for the woman took the place of anger, and Amy held Rachel in her arms. 'There, there, don't you fret. I'll see what I can do. I'll go round all the pubs and ask if anyone has seen her.'

'Thanks, Amy. I'll do anything to make it up to her.'

'Course you will, and I'll tell her that if I see her.'

'Yes yes,' pleaded Rachel. 'You tell her that no more harm will come to her. She can live here rent free – anything she wants – only bring her back please, Amy.'

Pity for the older woman's suffering filled Amy's heart. 'I'll do my best,' she said.

Left alone, Rachel wondered if she would ever see Lily again.

★ ★ ★

Lily was getting desperate. It was two weeks since she'd run away from Manny Cohen and her money was almost gone. So far, she'd been unable to find work. She'd paid the rent but didn't have enough for next week. Although the new room was shabby, she'd cleaned it as best she could, it had a lock on the door and she felt relatively safe. No way was she going back to the dangers of living rough on the street.

The only thing she possessed of any value was a gold cross and chain that Tom had given her. She would rather starve than sell it. Amy would help if she could get to her, but Lily dared not go to the places that Amy frequented, in case she bumped into Tom.

She'd spent part of the day walking up and down the High Street, looking at the shops, but now it was night-time and she was hungry. Outside the fish and chip shop, she saw a man eating. The aroma wafted across her nostrils and she felt faint with hunger. She hadn't eaten that day.

The man looked up and saw her leaning against the wall, watching him. Walking over to her he said, 'Hello, love,' looking at her pretty face with appreciation. 'Want one?' He held out the newspaper.

'Thanks,' she said gratefully.

Seeing the longing in her eyes as she looked at his food he said, 'You wait here. I'll go and buy you some, then we can go for a drink somewhere, if you like?'

She looked uncertain.

'No funny business, honest,' he urged.

The thought of food weakened her resolve. 'All right then.'

Soon he was back with another fish supper and they walked away together, eating and talking. 'Jim's my name,' the stranger said. 'Just docked today. My home's in Liverpool, so I thought I'd have a bit of supper and a few pints.'

'You work on the boats then?'

'Lady! *Ship*, if you please. You row a boat.'

'Sorry,' Lily apologised. 'I didn't know.'

'No, that's all right. It's just one of those things that are important to merchant seamen. How about a drink, then? To wash down the food.'

Lily reluctantly agreed. At least she would be warm, she

told herself. Sitting in the pub, she looked around and was thankful that the bar was full of strangers.

'What's your name?' Jim asked as he sat beside her.

'Lily.'

'Suits you, you're as pretty as a flower.'

She smiled at his flattery. 'What do you do on your ship, then?'

'I'm a bedroom steward.'

'What does that mean?'

'I have several cabins to look after and the passengers that use them during the voyage. You know, change the linen, get them food or drink if they want it. See their clothes are put out, pressed and cleaned if necessary. Clean the cabin, keep them happy and hope they leave a big tip!' He grinned. 'It's a busy life.'

Lily was fascinated. 'How wonderful to be able to travel to other parts of the world. What's America like?'

'We only go to New York – that's hardly America. It's a big noisy city, full of people.'

The next hour passed pleasantly, with Jim regaling Lily with tales of his passengers and their strange habits and demands. He told her he was married. 'I miss my wife and kids. It's a lonely life being at sea if you don't live local. I don't get home that often, you see, and I lack female company.' He looked at her thoughtfully. 'I could come back to your room tonight, Lily. I'm not on duty until the morning.'

Lily looked stricken.

'Look, love, from the way you tucked into that grub tonight, you're down on your uppers. You need money and I'm lonely. I'll pay you well.'

'You think I'm on the game!'

'No, I don't, or you would have come up to me earlier tonight.' His tone was reasonable. 'I can tell you're a nice girl, and we can do each other a bit of good.' He looked at her earnestly. 'I really do miss my wife, Lily. I'm lonely. I want to hold a woman in my arms. I've had a good trip, and I'll see you all right for money.'

The thought of taking a man to her bed terrified Lily. The

only sex she'd ever had was with her father. Yet what was she to do? She had no savings left. She looked into the smiling eyes of her companion. Did she have any choice in the matter?

'How much?' The words came out of her mouth before she had time to think.

'Two quid.'

Lily's breath was taken away by his generosity. If she took him home, she could pay next week's rent and feed herself. Despair overcame her. She was really desperate and if she said no, then she was in real trouble, with nowhere to turn. He looked a nice man, sounded kind. There was no choice.

'All right, Jim. But you pay me first.' She remembered Amy's rule of always getting paid in advance.

He smiled at her and, taking the money out of his wallet, handed it over.

As they walked back to her room, Lily drew the collar of her coat up around her face. She couldn't bear the thought of anyone being able to recognise her and be a witness to her degradation.

Early next morning, she lay back against the pillow and listened to Jim's snoring, closing her eyes to blot out the tears that slowly trickled down her cheeks. She had come to this!

He had been kind and gentle, but as he made love to her her heart was breaking. What price her respectability now? She got out of bed and slowly dressed. Walking over to the window, she watched the dawn break, crossed her arms over her chest to keep out the chill of the morning, and tried to listen to the sounds of the docks as they came alive. The ship's hooter, shrill on the morning air. The sound of coal trucks shunting into each other. The rattle of the first tram. Doors slamming as workers left home. But her thoughts precluded all things. What was to become of her? Was this to be her life? Was this the only way she could survive? If this was it, did she want to face the days ahead?

Tom. She longed for him with every fibre of her being. What had happened, she wondered, when he returned from

Ireland and found she had disappeared? How hurt and confused he must have been. Angry, even. Would he hate her now? It made no difference; he was lost to her for ever. She could never tell him the truth. Never tell him about Manny. If she did, he would find him, then Manny would divulge her guilty secret. There was now no way they could ever be together. She was filled with despair.

Jim stirred. Looking around, he saw Lily by the window. 'Good morning,' he said.

She didn't want to answer, to turn and face him. If she did, she would be facing her own shame. She heard him dressing, then walking over to her, he caught hold of her by the shoulders and turned her round.

'Don't feel guilty, Lily. You kept me company, and I'm grateful.'

She tried to smile. 'I know. And I'm grateful too.'

He kissed her forehead. 'I've got to get back. It was a quick turnaround this trip, we sail this evening. Maybe when I come back next time, we can do this again?'

Taking a deep breath she said, 'Why not?'

Tom stood at the bar of The Sailor's Return, looking morose and unhappy.

'No news then?' asked Declan.

Shaking his head he snapped, 'The police are bloody useless. I've searched and searched, but I can't find her. Amy's been looking too – but there's no trace of her. I don't know what else to do.'

'Maybe she doesn't want to be found.'

Tom glowered at Declan. 'What the hell do you mean by that?'

'Don't take this wrong, but you don't know the reason for her running off. All I'm saying is that something may have happened that she doesn't want to explain . . . For all you know, she may have left Southampton.'

Tom shook his head. 'Rachel Cohen said she didn't think she had much money. God, I hope she hasn't left this place or I'll never find her.'

'That's something you may have to face, my friend.'

With a grim expression Tom said, 'I hope you're wrong. I love that girl. I had such plans. We were to get married and one day I was taking her back to Ireland. She wanted these things too. None of it makes sense.'

Declan looked puzzled. 'It only makes sense if something happened to change her mind.'

'She did need a bit of a push to name the day,' said Tom thoughtfully.

'What happened to persuade her?'

'I told her I might not come back from Ireland, because I thought she didn't love me.'

'And?' prompted Declan.

'Well, then it all changed. She said she didn't want to lose me. It all ended all right, but then I went to Ireland with the promise we'd make plans on my return. It's all so crazy.'

Declan shook his head. 'It certainly is, but then I've never understood the female mind and I've been married for six years. Why don't you go home and try to get some sleep? You look all in.'

Tom emptied his glass. 'No, give me another pint. If I'm on me own, I'll go mad.'

Amy was getting worried. She'd spent the last few weeks visiting every pub in the dock area talking to the other prostitutes, describing Lily, but no one had seen her.

She'd been tempted once or twice to tell Tom about Manny, but if Lily hadn't turned up, what difference would it make? Besides, she didn't know for sure what had happened that night. It must have been something pretty traumatic to make the young girl turn tail and run. Maybe something she wouldn't want Tom to know. Anyway, the poor bugger was in a bad enough state as it was – Rachel Cohen too, for that matter.

'Bloody Manny!' Amy cursed as she left yet another pub. If I could get my hands on that little sod, I'd do for him myself.

She worried as to how Lily would manage. She hoped she could get a job of some kind. Well, at least the kid had guts. She was a survivor. If only she'd get in touch with me, Amy thought. I told her I'd always help her if she got into any trouble.

Lily stood in the shadows opposite the Club Valletta and watched the comings and goings. She was getting really desperate. She remembered Amy saying she could work in comfort for The Maltese. She didn't want to be a whore, but he had said there were other jobs and she wondered what he could have meant. Then she remembered the expression in his eyes. If she went there and asked for a job, they'd make her a whore. Who was she kidding? And after her night with Jim, was she any better?

The club seemed very busy. It was fascinating watching the different types enter the doorway. Lily was surprised that so many of the members seemed to be well-dressed. This was no cheap brothel.

There was a man on the door. He didn't wear a uniform, but he was well-dressed, too. He was big and broad, built like a wrestler or a boxer. She noticed how the members treated him with a nervous respect. No doubt he was there to keep trouble and unwelcome clients at bay. Two seamen tried to enter, but they were soon sent on their way. Obviously not up to standard, thought Lily.

She drew deeper into the shadows as she saw Vittorio come out of the club. Beside him stood a tall girl, dressed in the latest fashion, her cloche hat matching her expensive-looking coat. She was very striking to look at, and her cultured voice carried on the air. Lily wondered who she was and what she was doing there. A car drew up and The Maltese kissed the woman on the cheek before helping her inside. He waved as it drove away, and stood on the steps, talking to the man on the door. He turned slowly and peered across the road through the darkness in her direction, almost as if he felt he was being watched. Lily felt the chill of fear down her spine. She slowly backed off around the corner, quietly. Then, turning, she hurried away.

Chapter Seven

'Come along home with me, Tom, and have a cup of tea.'
Bill Harris looked at his work-mate with a worried frown.
This lad needed taking out of himself, he thought. Ever
since his girl had run off, he'd lost his sparkle.

With a nod Tom said, 'Thanks, that's real kind of you.' He
shivered. 'It's getting so parky these days, a hot cup of tea is
just what I need.'

When they arrived at his house, Bill opened the door and
called, 'Mary!'

A tall girl peered around the scullery door. She had a head
of riotous black hair and green eyes like a cat. 'Hello, Dad.'

'This is my mate Tom. Make us a cuppa, there's a good
girl.' Turning to Tom he nodded towards the scullery. 'My
daughter – works as a maid at the doctor's house.'

Tom thanked Mary as she put two mugs in front of them
and smiled to himself as he saw the nervous tremble of her
fingers. 'I don't bite, you know.'

She was embarrassed. Looking at him shyly she said, 'I
don't suppose you do.' Then she left them alone in the room
that served as both kitchen and living room.

Bill lit his pipe and, tamping down the tobacco, quietly
puffed on it to set it going. Sitting back in his chair he asked,
'So how are you these days?'

Tom shrugged. 'All right, I suppose. I guess I have to just
get on with life, but it isn't easy.'

'Women are strange creatures, but there'll come a day
when you'll be able to put it all behind you. Life is for living,
lad. You're a bloody long time dead.'

As he sat beside the range in the warm cosy room, quietly

drinking his tea, Tom felt at peace for the first time since Lily had disappeared. He supposed he had to accept that she really didn't want to be found. He still couldn't understand it. He had experienced all kinds of emotions – shock, worry, despair and a sort of grieving for her. Now he was angry. His pride had been hurt and he wondered just how she could do such a thing to him. Offering marriage was a holy commitment, one for life. She'd thrown it back in his face. She couldn't have loved him – how could she? It had all been lies. Yes, it was time to put it behind him.

Downing the dregs of his mug, he got to his feet. 'Best be off. Thanks for the tea.' He called, 'Thanks, Mary.'

She came into the room and said, 'You're welcome.'

He walked towards the door and stopped. Turning around, he asked, 'I don't suppose you'd like to come to the pictures with me on Friday?'

She looked surprised, then glanced over towards her father, who nodded his approval. 'Thank you, I'd like that.'

'I'll pick you up about six then,' he said with a smile that made his eyes crinkle.

'Fine. I'll see you then.'

When he'd gone, Mary said to her father. 'That was a bit unexpected.'

Bill let out a sigh. 'Poor chap. He was going to be married, but his girl ran off.'

She looked thoughtful. 'Oh dear. Why on earth did she do such a thing?'

'I don't know, neither does he, but he was very cut up about it. Still, if he's asked you out, he must be feeling better. He's a nice bloke, Mary. Be gentle with him, he's still a bit fragile.'

'He looked man enough to me to take care of himself.' She walked back into the scullery. Whilst she washed up the dirty mugs, she wondered who would be mad enough to run away from marrying such a good-looking man.

It was late November and the weather was cold and miserable. In the streets of Southampton, there had been a two-day fall of snow, which was now beginning to turn to slush.

Lily shivered as she stood on the corner of the street, her feet frozen in the thin shoes that needed repair and let in the wet. She'd been forced to go on the game to keep body and soul together. She was a reluctant whore, only taking a punter when she needed the rent and to buy food. She hated what she'd become, and cursed Manny Cohen every time a strange man's hands moved over her body, touching her.

She tried to be careful in her choice of client, because here in the dock area there were many undesirable and dangerous people. But she'd learned the hard way that the decent-looking men were sometimes the worst. Sometimes she smiled wryly when Amy's words came true – when her time with a punter was thankfully over quickly.

She saw Jim from time to time. It was a welcome respite for her. Despite the fact that he paid her for sex, he took her out for a meal, brought her gifts from America, treated her with respect and never questioned her about herself.

But tonight she felt ill. The rent was paid, but she hadn't been able to face the street and all its horrors for days. She was weak with hunger, shrammed to the bone, and tonight had been forced to leave the safety of her room and try her luck.

Fred Bates was strolling along the street, happy to be out of prison at last and looking forward to his first pint in several long weeks. Having been released earlier that day, he had been home to dump his small parcel of possessions and was now ready to slake his thirst. He had stopped to light a cigarette, when a girl stepped out of the darkness and spoke to him.

'Hello, dearie. You look lonely. Could you do with some company?'

In the low light from the street-lamp, he looked at her with interest. She'd pulled the collar of her coat up around her face to keep out the cold; all he could see was a pair of wide, deep-blue eyes, fringed with long silky eyelashes. The voice lacked the harsh tones that most of the toms possessed, through years of degradation. He was curious.

'If I knew who I was talking to, I might be interested.' He

leaned forward and opened up the collar, and was surprised at the youthful appearance of the girl. Despite the dark hollows beneath her eyes, she was a pretty little thing.

'How old are you?' he asked.

She gave him a cheeky grin, tucked her arm in his and said, 'Old enough.'

He caught hold of her hand, which was like ice. She staggered against him, and he clutched at her, to stop her falling. She was shivering.

'You shouldn't be out on the streets like this. Come on. I'll take you into the pub and give you a pie and a drop of whisky, or I can see I'll have a body on my hands.'

He ushered her into The Dog and Duck, sat her down and went to the bar.

'Hello, Fred,' the barman greeted him. 'Just got out?'

'Yeah, this morning. And I'm never bloody going back.'

The man laughed. 'That's what you said last time.'

'Yeah, but this time I mean it. Give us a pint of bitter and a Scotch. Got any hot meat pies?'

'Yes. I'll get the wife to fetch one for you.'

Lily sat huddled in a corner, blowing her breath into her hands, trying to warm them and observing the stranger at the bar. He must be in his thirties, she guessed. His build was wiry and his thin face was kind. He glanced back at her with a worried frown and gave her an encouraging grin. She smiled wanly back at him.

He walked over to her, handed her a glass and said, 'Sip this, love. Slowly, mind. Don't want you choking on me.'

The fiery liquid slid down her throat, burning as it made its slow passage, warming her. Then she tucked into the pie, brought over by the landlady. It tasted so good, she relished every mouthful.

Fred didn't speak but watched her with fascination. What was she doing on the street? This was no usual tom. There was a vulnerability about her, almost an air of innocence, which he found very strange when she was out there selling her body. 'Feel better?' he asked as she swallowed the last crumb.

'Mm,' she answered with a sigh of satisfaction. 'That was

82

very kind of you. Thanks. Now where do you want to go?'

'What do you mean?'

'Well, you bought me a drink, gave me something to eat. Do we go back to your place or mine?'

Her words shocked him – but why should they? After all, she'd propositioned him. There was no secret about what she was offering for money.

'How long have you been on the game, love?'

Lily lowered her gaze for a moment then, lifting her head defiantly, answered, 'That's none of your business.'

Fred smiled inwardly. So there was fire there. A spirit that was not yet extinguished. For no particular reason it pleased him.

'You're quite right, it isn't. Sorry if I offended you.'

Perked up by the whisky and the pie, Lily grinned. 'No, I'm not offended. What's your name?'

'Fred.'

She held out her hand. 'Hello, Fred. I'm Lily.'

Amused, he took her hand, shaking it solemnly.

'What's your game then, Fred?'

He scratched his chin. 'Well, to be honest, I've just come out of prison.'

Lily's smile vanished and a wary look was in her eye, a worried note in her voice as she asked, 'What for? What did you do?'

'I haven't killed anyone, girl. I'm a dip – a pickpocket.'

She relaxed against the seat. 'Oh, is that all.'

Chuckling he said, 'I wished the magistrate what sent me down thought like you do.'

'How long did you get?'

'Three months – this time.'

'Why do you do it, then?'

'I've been doing it all my life, Lily. My father was one of the best dips on the South Coast. When I was a kid, we used to go to the markets or busy streets. I'd cry, pretending to be lost, then when people gathered round, my father used to pick their pockets.' The way he told it, with a mischievous grin, it didn't seem a crime at all.

'What are you going to do now?' Lily asked.

Sipping his pint he said, 'I'm going to try and keep out of trouble. Go straight.'

'It must be awful being in prison.' Lily looked troubled.

Fred nodded. 'Yeah, it is. There are some pretty mental people in the nick. It's a dodgy place to be . . . that's why I'm never going back.'

'Will it be easy to find a job? I mean, you'll have a record.'

'True, but my friend Knocker Jones, the rag and bone man, wants me to give him a hand.' He lit a cigarette. With a sudden note of pride in his voice, he told her, 'I've got my own little house – a two-up and two-down. It belonged to my dad, the only good thing he got from crime. So you see, sometimes it does pay. Want another drink?'

Lily relaxed. The drink and food had made her feel better. Fred was a good companion who made her laugh.

He, however, was still curious about this young girl. 'Do you live alone, Lily?'

'Yes, I've got a little room not far from here. Bit grotty, but it's home.'

She'd undone her coat now she felt warmer and Fred could see her curvaceous figure. This girl should be at home with a husband to care for her, not out on the streets in the docks. God knows what could happen to her, or already had. Something must have sent her out there. He knew enough about toms to know that most of them had a sad story.

'What are your plans for the future, then?' he asked.

The change in Lily was astonishing. Gone was the smile, the friendliness.

'Future! What future?' The expression on her face was one of bitterness. Two Scotches on an empty stomach had loosened her tongue. 'Do you think I want to go on like this day after day, year after year? I *have* no future.'

Fred looked around to see if anyone had heard her outburst. The bar was fuller now than when they had entered, but the people drinking were immersed in their own world. Here, in these parts, folk just survived. They had enough problems without being involved in other people's.

But Lily's words had upset Fred. This lovely girl needed someone to care for her, that was evident. He couldn't bear to think of the consequences if she was left alone. He knew how tough life could be on the streets without a penny to your name. It made you do all kinds of crazy things. Maybe for once in his life he could help someone down on their luck. He felt he had to try.

'You come home with me, love – I'll take care of you. I'm going to be working, I'm going to be legal and all that. No more prison. You needn't go back on the game. How about if you look after me and the house, cook my meals, and in return I'll look after you?'

'What's in it for you, Fred?'

He looked at her quizzically. 'I'm not saying I wouldn't want to share my bed with you, Lily, but only if you want me to. I've never forced myself on a woman yet.' He paused, then asked, 'What do you say – give it a try?'

Lily was feeling so desolate that she thought, Why not? It couldn't be worse than what she was forced to do now. She looked across at Fred. He seemed decent enough, and if she didn't like the situation she could always leave.

'All right.' She perked up a bit. 'My rent's paid until the end of the week, so I'll give it a try until then. If it doesn't work out, I'll leave and you can pay my next week's rent.'

He chuckled. 'You strike a hard bargain, I'll give you that. OK, it's a deal.'

'Half a mo. What happens if I don't want to sleep with you?'

'Nothing. I've got a spare room. You'll be a kind of housekeeper.' There was a twinkle in his eye as he added, 'But if you change your mind, I won't say no.'

Men never do, thought Lily. Why did they have to be born with all that tackle between their legs? It was ugly and was the cause of a lot of trouble. Some said a lot of pleasure, but up to now she hadn't found it so.

The barman winked at Fred as the couple left. Fred pointed a warning finger at him, daring him to utter a word.

Lily followed Fred into his house. The front door opened straight into the living room. She was surprised that it was so clean and tidy. In the polished black-leaded range a fire was burning. She immediately went over to it, turning her back to the flames, loving the warmth creeping through her clothes.

When Fred lit the gas-lamp, she looked around at what was to be her new home. There was an old leather settee, covered in a bright rug. The linoleum on the floor, though cracked, was clean. In the centre of the room stood a table, covered in a maroon chenille cloth. Two armchairs were drawn up on either side of the range. The room was welcoming and cosy.

'This is the scullery.' Fred led her through the door. Then, opening the back briefly, closing it when Lily shivered, he told her: 'There's the lavatory and a clothes line where I hang me washing. In the bin is the coal for the range. If you come upstairs, I'll show you the rest.'

Lily followed him, thinking, Now we come to the real business.

He opened one bedroom door, inside which was a double bed, a wardrobe and chest of drawers. 'That's my room.' He walked over to the other door and pushed it open. It contained a single bed, with a small cupboard beside it. 'This is your room, Lily.'

She looked at him in surprise.

With a sardonic grin he said, 'Didn't believe me, did you? I'll leave it up to you which you choose to use.'

'Thank you,' said Lily sincerely. 'Tomorrow I'll have to get my things from my room.'

He put his hand in his pocket and handed her a key. 'This is the spare. It's yours for as long as you like.'

She looked at the key in her hand, then at Fred. She was still uncertain. It all seemed too good to be true and she wondered what was going to happen next.

Fred meanwhile walked downstairs and put the brown kettle on the hob. 'Take your coat off, my girl, and make yourself at home. I'll brew us a cuppa before we go to bed.'

Later, Lily and Fred sat either side of the range, not speaking, listening to the crackle of the burning wood and the soft whistle of the kettle on the hob, both lost in their own thoughts. Fred was wondering which room she would choose, and Lily was wondering what would happen when she went into the spare room.

'You go on up,' Fred said at last. 'You look worn out. I'll see you in the morning.'

Lily went into the smaller room, closed the door, got undressed and waited. She heard Fred's footsteps on the stairs and held her breath, but he walked on and she heard him close the door to his room.

That night, Lily slept more soundly than she had for several weeks.

The following morning, she ventured downstairs somewhat nervously.

Fred was already up and dressed. He smiled at her. 'Good morning. Sit down, Lily. I'm just frying some eggs and bacon. I'll get you a cup of tea in a moment.'

'Shouldn't I be doing that?' she asked. 'If I'm supposed to be your housekeeper, I should be waiting on you.'

'Later, love. I've got to go out and do some shopping first. Did you sleep well?'

Nodding she said, 'Yes, thanks. Like a log.'

They sat at the table together, Fred urging her to eat up. 'You need to get some flesh on your bones, girl. Get rid of them dark circles under your eyes.'

They sat companionably eating. She was quiet, a bit shy with the situation.

'I've got to go out and see my mate Knocker. Will you go and fetch your gear, then?' There was a note of uncertainty in his voice as he asked the question. And a look of relief when Lily answered.

'Yes, I thought I'd pop over early, before anyone realises I'm not there and nicks my stuff.'

'Right then, love. I'll see you later.' He gave her a quick smile as he opened the door and left.

Lily sat drinking her tea, looking around her. Somehow she felt at home in these strange surroundings. She thought it odd that she should be living in a house with a man other than Tom. This had been their dream – a place like this. Where was he now? Pull yourself together, she thought. You could be on the street. This is a thousand times better than that and Fred hasn't once bothered you or attempted to touch you in any way. It seemed she'd found a gentleman, and she knew to her cost that there weren't many around.

Days passed into weeks, and Lily didn't return to her room. She and Fred got on well together, shared the same sense of humour. She enjoyed cooking for him and he was always appreciative of her efforts. It was an easy alliance.

That Christmas was the happiest Lily could ever remember. Fred had been busy working steadily for Knocker Jones. He'd given Lily money to buy food for them both, and some extra, to do some Christmas shopping. She'd bought a small tree, put some soil in the pot and placed it in the corner of the room, lovingly decorating it with a few bright baubles she'd found in the market. Then she had sat admiring it, filled with childish delight at its festive look.

It had been more than a month now since she had first entered the house, and Fred, good as his word, never approached her in any way. She cleaned and cooked for him, happily. They lived almost like an old married couple, walking around the market together at the weekend, going to the local for a drink, eating together. But they still slept apart. Now it was Christmas Eve.

Lily heard his key in the door, and realised how much she had grown to look forward to the sound. 'Hello, love,' Fred said as he walked in.

Then he espied the tree. 'Oh, Lily!' He stood back and admired it. Turning to her he said, 'It looks lovely.' Looking below it, he saw a small parcel, and smiled. He took a parcel of his own out of his pocket, walked over to the tree and put it beside the other.

Lily jumped to her feet, ran across the room and picked up the parcel, shaking it to see if it would rattle. She was like a child and Fred, though happy to see such joy in her face, was struck by her youthful innocence. It made all his thoughts of holding her, making love to her, almost obscene.

'What would you like to do tonight?' he asked.

'Could we walk up the High Street, look at all the shops with their decorations?'

'If that's what you want. Then we'll go to the pie and mash shop and get some supper, so you won't have to cook.'

She couldn't believe her luck. Fred was so good to her, so thoughtful and caring. She was suddenly saddened. Tom used to be the same. She wondered where he would be spending his Christmas, and with whom.

Seeing the sadness in her eyes, Fred wondered who it was that filled her thoughts. It was like a knife going through him when he thought she might have loved someone. The fact that she'd had other men when she was on the game didn't bother him one bit. But he was falling in love with this lovely young girl and he didn't want anyone else sharing her heart.

The evening was crisp and cold. The sky was almost clear and the moon shone. Church-bells were ringing and Lily had an overwhelming desire to go to church. She knew there was a midnight mass, although she didn't know what a mass was. Turning to Fred she asked, 'Do you ever go to church?'

He looked at her with some surprise. He never knew what this girl was going to say next. 'I used to go to St Michael's,' he admitted. 'And guess what? I even thought of joining the choir when I was a kid.'

It was Lily's turn to be surprised. 'Can you sing then?' She didn't remember him doing so round the house.

He chuckled wickedly. 'Tone deaf, love. But they used to give the choirboys tea and buns.'

'Oh, you!' she chided.

'Would you like to go?' he asked gently.

'Could we go at midnight?'

When Lily had first visited St Michael's Church, she'd found it a profound experience, but that was nothing to what she felt as she entered the door that Christmas Eve.

The lights were bright, illuminating the lofty roof and the wonderful arches. The altar and pulpit were decorated with holly and flowers, and the scene of the nativity, its figures carved from clay, was laid out in its simplicity, for all to admire.

Fred handed Lily a prayer book, opening it up for her to follow the service. They looked at each other with conspiratorial smiles as the choir made its way up the aisle. As the service went on, Lily was transported to another world. She joined in the carols, singing enthusiastically in a sweet pure voice, which surprised Fred, standing beside her.

This girl who shared his home was an unknown quantity, he realised. He watched her face, aglow, enjoying the pomp and ceremony of the festive occasion, and he saw her breathe in the incense ecstatically as if it had magical powers.

They stayed in their seats, observing whilst people took the sacrament. Lily was filled with peace and wonderment. At the end of the service, they slowly filed out of the church. The vicar was standing at the door. A look of puzzled recollection crossed his face as Lily stopped beside him.

'Hello, Vicar. That was a beautiful service. Thank you.'

He saw the happiness shining in her eyes and said, 'Thank you, my dear. God bless you.'

'Oh, He does,' she said. And walked away, holding Fred's arm.

That night, as he settled down to sleep, mulling over the events of the night, Fred heard his door open. Lily climbed into the bed and snuggled down beside him. Kissing him on the cheek, she whispered, 'Happy Christmas, Fred.'

Chapter Eight

Tom McCann spent Christmas Day with the Harris family. Bill's wife, Jessy, was like a small bee, flitting in and out of the room, bearing food, keeping up a constant happy chatter.

Mary looked across the table at Tom and grinned as he politely refused yet another helping of Christmas pudding.

'So help me, Jessy, I have no room for another morsel!'

'Well, if you're sure.'

'Whist your hush, woman,' said Bill. 'Just sit down and relax. You make me tired with your rushing about.'

They all sat around the range, luxuriating in the warmth, subdued by too much food.

A while later, Mary rose from her seat and began to clear the table. As Jessy went to help her, Tom got up. 'You sit still with your husband, I'll help Mary.'

When they were alone in the scullery, Tom drew Mary to him and kissed her lingeringly upon the lips.

As he released her, she chided him softly. 'Behave yourself, Tom. They may come in and see us.'

'Don't be silly, girl, of course they won't. They were young themselves, you know, and after all, it isn't as if we've just met.'

As she washed the dishes, passing them to Tom to be dried, Mary thought about the previous months. She and Tom had been going out together regularly, but he'd not made his intentions clear, and she wondered if he would ever get round to popping the question. There was no doubt in her mind that Tom McCann was the man for her.

Mary had plans. She didn't want to stay in the dock area for the rest of her life. She wanted to move away and live in a small house. One with a garden for her children to play in, near a nice school, with nice refined children, not ruffians. She conveniently forgot, of course, about her own schooldays.

Working as she did for the doctor and his wife, Mary had acquired the taste for better things: good manners, decent clothes, gracious living. She wanted some of that for herself, and Tom was the man to give it to her. He was a skilled man, earning good money in the docks, and he was handsome. She was the envy of her friends.

He never spoke of the girl who had jilted him, and once when she'd brought the subject up, he'd quelled her questions so adamantly, she'd never dared mention it again. But often, she wondered about her. Who was she? What was she like? Where was she now? And . . . would she ever return?

Humming softly to herself, Lily made her way to the market, an empty basket on her arm. It was good to be alive and she was content. Since she'd crept into Fred's bed on Christmas Eve, their relationship had blossomed. Fred was delighted in their intimacy and couldn't do enough for her. Lily knew he was in love with her, and she felt a pang of guilt that she couldn't return such feelings. She was very fond of him and at ease in her newfound way of life, but there was only one man who had claimed her heart. However, as time passed, she'd grown philosophical about it. If this was second-best, it wasn't at all bad.

She missed Rachel and Amy, but that was all behind her now. The dark rings under her eyes had long since faded. Fred was earning, and they didn't go short. True, they didn't live the high life, but they had enough for their needs, an occasional drink at the local, and they had each other.

Fred sometimes fretted about the difference in their ages, telling her she was living with an old man, but she laughed him out of such moments. A younger man would be off at the pub most nights, leaving her all alone, she told him. Fred was content in her company, although she did urge him to go and meet his mates, which he did on occasion.

Lily enjoyed the market, exchanging banter with the

market-traders. She especially liked shopping when the light had faded and the stalls were lit by paraffin lamps. It gave the place a jaunty, festive air.

She'd made her purchases and was walking away when she spied Vittorio Teglia coming towards her. She stopped abruptly. Until now, she'd not encountered anyone from her days in The Ditches, having kept away from the old haunts, and it threw her completely.

'Hello, Lily. Where on earth have you been these past months?'

'I've been around.'

'Then how is it no one has seen you? I went to enquire at Mrs Cohen's, but she was very evasive.' His dark-brown eyes seemed to bore right through her. 'Why did you suddenly disappear like that?' He caught hold of her arm as if to stay her flight.

Feeling his hand upon her, Lily experienced tingles of both fear and excitement. What was it about this man that affected her so? She knew The Maltese was a bad person; perhaps that was part of the fascination.

Holding her head high, she tossed her hair back and met his steady gaze. 'Disappear? I didn't *disappear*. I just had a better offer.'

He raised an eyebrow and looked at her apparel. Though clean and neat, her coat had definitely seen better days. He gazed into her eyes. 'It wasn't as good as *my* offer. Why do you waste your talents on those who can't give you what you deserve?'

Lily's eyes flashed with anger, her nostrils flared. 'How dare you stand there and say such things! All you want me to do is whore for you in your club!'

He smiled with amusement and said, in a voice both soft and seductive, 'Not true. You have no idea what plans I have for you, Lily. But I can give you my word, you would not be a whore.'

Suddenly, she was curious. 'What do you want of me, then?'

His eyes were twinkling. 'I see I've got your interest at last.' He chuckled. 'I will tell you only when you come to me.

You won't be dressed as you are now, that I can promise you. It would give me the greatest pleasure to take care of you. You, Lily, will want for nothing.'

'I don't want for anything now, ta very much.'

'You enjoy being poor?'

She was highly indignant. 'I'm not poor!' She held out her basket of vegetables. 'Look. Poor people can't afford all this.' She picked up a wrapped parcel. 'This is rabbit.'

He gave a cursory glance at the basket. 'And you are going home now, wherever home might be, to cook it, I suppose?'

'Yes, of course I am.'

He caught hold of her hand, his tapering fingers smoothing her skin, sending shock waves through her body at his touch. 'You, my dearest Lily, should have someone to cook for you. Living with me, you would enjoy a life of luxury such as you've never dreamed.' He lifted her fingers to his lips. 'One day, Lily, you will come to me and share my life. It is your destiny. All I have to do is wait.'

Watching him walk away, Lily was totally unsettled by the encounter. The most peculiar thing was that, ever since she'd first met Vittorio, she'd had the strangest notion that their future *was* somehow entwined. It was an eerie feeling. Today, he had put as much into words. She suddenly shivered.

'Things are getting real tight, Knocker. I'm going to have to do something else to earn a few bob.'

Knocker Jones nodded in agreement. Looking at Fred he said, 'I know. Things are tough at the moment. I'm finding it hard meself.'

The two men sat drinking mugs of tea in the room Knocker grandly referred to as his office. It was in fact a corner of a shed, filled to capacity with old tat he'd picked up with his rag and bone cart. He had a small goods yard where he stored everything, and housed Charlie his cart-horse in a tumbledown stable.

Loosening his grubby white silk scarf from around his neck, Knocker said, 'There is a whisper of something coming through the docks. Bit dodgy of course, but I've got

94

me finger in the pie, so to speak. Might be a few quid in it for you, Fred.'

Frowning, the other man answered, 'Well, beggars can't be choosers. Count me in. I've got commitments these days, I need the money.'

A sly smile crossed Knocker's face. 'Yes, I heard you've got a woman. Keeping her under wraps, ain't ya?'

'Not at all,' Fred protested. But in fact, he'd been afraid to introduce Lily to his friends. Afraid she might meet a younger chap and leave him. Now, he felt more secure about their relationship, and occasionally Lily's name crept into his conversations.

'Why don't you bring her to The Sailor's Return tonight?' Knocker went on. 'We can have a drink together and I might be able to fill you in a bit more. I've got to meet a mate of mine who knows more than I do about it. Besides, I'm curious to meet the woman daft enough to take you on.'

Lily was nervous about meeting friends of Fred. Until now, the pair of them had kept pretty much to themselves, and she'd only popped to the little local with him, not to his usual pub where he met all his mates. After all, they were living in sin. What reaction would that bring from his friends?

But from the moment Lily walked into the bar of The Sailor's Return, she was made most welcome. Declan, the landlord, had teased her about Fred. 'You should have met me first, love. He doesn't deserve a lovely girl like you!'

Knocker Jones was enchanted with her ready wit, and Sandy the pianist was delighted to discover that she had a good voice as she sang along with the others. It developed into quite a party.

'How about giving us a song on your own, Lily?' entreated Sandy.

Flushed with embarrassment, she said, 'Oh, I couldn't.'

Fred, delighted that she'd made such a hit with his friends, encouraged her. Putting an arm around her shoulders he said, 'Go on, love. I remember hearing you sing them carols in church last Christmas. You have a lovely voice.'

Sandy, who had taken a break from his playing to have a drink, said softly, 'Come on, Lily. You're a natural if ever I saw one. What songs do you know?'

Before she could protest, she was led to the piano, and began to sing all the Marie Lloyd songs she knew. Gathering confidence as she sang, she really began to enjoy herself, remembering how at the Palace Theatre she'd wished so often she could be on the stage, singing with an audience. Looking around at the happy faces of the customers, singing along with her, she was thrilled at how easy it had been.

Knocker Jones leaned over to Fred. 'Where did you find such a charmer?'

'We met quite by chance one evening.' He glanced over towards Lily, eyes shining with love. 'She's the best thing that's ever happened to me.'

'Wouldn't like to swop her with my old duck, would ya?'

'Not bloody likely!' He sat and listened to Lily singing, 'If you were the only girl in the world', but she changed the word 'girl' to 'boy', and looked over at Fred as she sang. He sat smiling contentedly, aware of the glances of envy from many.

Sandy insisted Lily take a break. 'We'll sit over here, dear,' he said fussily. 'Fred and Knocker are deep in conversation. Let's leave them to it.' He went to the bar and came back with two halves of beer. 'Declan says it's on the house.'

She raised her glass to the landlord in thanks.

'Have you done any singing in public before?' Sandy asked now.

Lily burst out laughing. 'You joking or what?'

'No, I'm serious. You have a good voice . . . and you have the personality that goes with it.'

'I used to love watching Marie Lloyd,' she admitted. 'And when I did, I always thought how much I'd like to perform too.'

With a speculative look, Sandy said, 'You know, you could make a bit of money at it, if you wanted to.'

Lily's eyes widened. 'What do you mean?'

'There's lots of pubs in the area that have singers in over the weekend. They either pay them, or let them make a collection among the customers. There's a few quid to be made.'

'I couldn't do that.'

'Why not?' He raised his eyebrows in question. 'I could help you, all girls together.' He looked a little abashed. 'I used to work the halls myself, when I was younger.'

Lily's eyes lit up. 'You did?'

Sandy nodded. 'I was a pianist with a few good singers in my time. I could show you how to move, how to present your songs, tell you what clothes to wear. You'd enjoy dressing up in all your slap and a posh frock, wouldn't you?'

With a chuckle Lily said, 'I don't have any clothes like that, you daft hap'orth.'

'No, but I do – and we're about the same size.'

Lily looked at him in surprise.

'Well, a girl likes to have a few frocks to wear on special occasions.'

'Oh Sandy, you are a card.' She started laughing. 'I've never met anyone quite like you.'

He smiled archly. 'There's a lot of us old queens about, dearie. What do you think? Are you interested?'

She shook her head. 'No, thanks. It's lovely of you to offer, but I've got Fred to look after.'

'How on earth did you end up living with *him*?' Seeing the look of anger in her eyes, he quickly added, 'I didn't mean any offence, love. Fred's one of the best, but look at you. Young, good-looking, great personality. So much to offer.'

'Look, Sandy.' Lily was deadly serious now. 'Fred has been good to me. I owe him a lot. As long as I live I would never let him down.'

He patted her arm. 'He's a lucky bloke. If you ever need to earn a few bob, remember what I said, though. All right?'

'Thanks.' She hugged him. 'You'll be my manager, will you?'

'Stranger things have happened at sea. Now – how about another tune?'

'Why not? Do you know "I'm forever blowing bubbles"?'

Across the room, Knocker looked at his watch and frowned. 'He's late. Never mind, fancy another pint?'

Fred nodded. 'Wouldn't mind.' He watched Lily and thought how lucky he was. The customers were all enjoying singing along with his girl. He'd seen the looks of interest in the other men's eyes. Many of them, he was sure, desired her. But it was in his arms she lay at night. His hands that caressed her. His words that comforted her, when she had a bad dream. Yes, he was the luckiest person in the world.

'Know any Irish songs?' called Declan.

'I do.' Turning to Sandy, she said, 'How about "When Irish eyes are smiling".' This was happily received, but when she sang 'Danny Boy' the poignancy in her voice hushed the room.

There was a spontaneous burst of applause as the final notes died away. Lily looked around, her cheeks flushed with embarrassment. Never had she been such a centre of attention, and she loved every moment.

'You make me feel quite homesick,' said Declan, bringing over another two glasses of beer. 'Do you know the one about the Mountains of Mourne?'

Lily hesitated, the memory of singing it to Tom in the cafe on the Royal Pier suddenly stark in her mind.

'Never mind,' said Declan, his voice full of disappointment. 'It's just that it's one of my favourites.'

Sandy, catching the look of consternation on her face, waited.

Lily looked at him. He just raised his eyebrows. She nodded, and he began to play the opening bars of 'The Mountains of Mourne'. Lily's sweet voice filled the silent bar with aching poignancy.

As Lily sang the final words of the first verse to a hushed audience, emotion flooded through her. She looked across at Fred's happy face, but it was Tom she saw there.

Sandy, aware that something was going on in that beautiful head, watched her carefully as she started the second verse, not knowing if she was going to be able to complete the song. He was the only one who realised that something had deeply moved her. He was still observing her when the door opened, and it was he who witnessed the blood drain from her face, saw her clutch at the piano for support.

'Tom!' called Knocker jovially. 'Over here!'

Chapter Nine

When Tom pushed open the bar door and heard the sweet voice of Lily, he stood still, his face white with shock. As she looked at him he heard her voice falter. He vaguely heard someone call to him, but he couldn't move. He blinked, sure that the vision standing by the piano was a figment of his imagination. But she was still there.

Again he heard his name and looked over towards the table where Knocker Jones was beckoning him. He walked in that direction, his legs shaking, his breath caught in his throat.

'You all right?' asked Knocker jovially.

'Fine. I'm fine.' He fought to collect his thoughts. 'Sorry I'm late,' he mumbled.

'This is Fred Bates,' said Knocker. 'Pity you didn't come earlier. We've been having a great time, mainly due to Fred's lovely lady.' Looking across the room he called, 'Hey Lily! . . . Over here!'

Tom turned round.

Lily looked at the pianist, her eyes wide and frightened like those of a small animal caught in bright lights.

'What is it, dearie? Can I help?' Sandy asked quietly.

She took a deep breath and straightened up. 'No, Sandy – but thanks. This is something no one can help me with.' She moved forward, towards her friends – and Tom.

She saw the tightening of his jaw, then the anger reflected in his eyes, and felt as if someone had gripped her heart with a steel glove.

Knocker held out his hand to her. 'Come and join us, Lily. This is me old mucker, Tom McCann. Tom, this is Fred's lovely lady. He's a lucky fellow, don't you think?'

'Yes, indeed,' said Tom. '*Very* lucky. How do you do, Lily?' His fingers gripped hers so tightly she nearly cried out.

Fred made room for her beside him and put his arm around her shoulders. 'Lily's been singing for everyone,' he said proudly. 'You missed a real treat.'

Tom smiled, but his eyes remained cold. 'I'm sure I did. Perhaps I can catch your next performance.' His gaze seemed to imprison her with its intensity.

'I don't perform,' she said. 'We just had a singsong, that's all.'

Declan called over, 'She knows lots of Irish songs. She was singing of the Mourne Mountains when you came in. Did you hear her? We could have had a real celebration if only you'd been here earlier. This lad's just got himself engaged,' he declared.

Lily looked stricken. She wanted to run away. Away from this tortuous situation, from the anger in Tom's eyes. She suddenly shuddered and Fred looked at her, filled with concern. 'Are you all right, love?'

'I have a bit of a headache. Do you mind if I go home?'

'I don't like you going on your own this time of night, but I've got a bit of business with the lads.'

Sandy, who had been listening closely to the conversation said, 'I'm off now, Fred. I'd be happy to escort Lily home if that's all right with her?'

She looked towards him with an expression of relief. 'If you wouldn't mind.'

'No trouble at all. Shall we go?' He caught hold of her arm, firmly, and led her outside.

Once out of the door, Lily slumped against the wall. 'Give us a cigarette, Sandy.' She took it with trembling fingers.

He held the match for her but had to take her hand to steady it. 'Come on. What you need is a strong cup of tea with plenty of sugar. That's what they give people suffering from shock.'

When they got to the house, she handed him the key and he opened the door. Lily walked straight to one of the chairs by the fire and slumped into it. Burying her head in her hands, she started to sob.

Apart from handing her a handkerchief, Sandy ignored her. He filled the kettle and put it on the hob after raking out the slack in the fire and replenishing the coal. He searched around for the tea, sugar, milk and mugs, then sat down opposite Lily. He lit a cigarette and waited.

Eventually the wracking sobs subsided and Lily blew loudly into the handkerchief, wiped her eyes and let out a deep breath. She looked across at Sandy through red eyes and swollen lids.

'Better now?'

She shook her head. 'I feel like shit.'

The kettle started to whistle and he made the tea and waited for it to mash before pouring it out. He handed a mug to Lily. 'Drink up, girl. Tea cures all ills.'

'If only that were true.'

They sat in silence, broken only by the gentle hiss of the steam from the kettle.

Looking up, Lily said, 'Aren't you going to ask me what this is all about?'

'No, my dear. If you want to tell me, that's different. But I don't poke my nose in where it's not wanted.'

She leaned over and patted his hand, then sat back in the chair, wiped her nose one last time and confessed: 'Tom McCann is the only man I have ever loved.'

'I thought it was something like that. I saw your face when he walked into the bar.'

'We were to be married.'

Sandy looked at her in surprise, but didn't question her further.

She closed her eyes for a moment, then said softly, 'But I ran away.'

'I'm sure you had a very good reason for doing something quite so dramatic.'

'I did, Sandy. I really did. You may understand, but I doubt that Tom will. Ever.'

'You think you'll see him again?'

'Yes, I do. He hates me now.' She pursed her lips. 'He won't let it pass. He can't.'

'Does Fred know about him?'

She gave him a wan smile. 'No. Fred knows little about me, and he's never asked. He's a wonderful man – I can't hurt him.' Finishing her tea she said, 'I think I'll go to bed, if you don't mind. I don't want Fred to see me like this. But thanks for bringing me home.'

Sandy rose to his feet. 'I hope it all works out for you, dearie. Life can be hell . . . If you ever need a pianist, or a friend, you know where to find me.' He squeezed her hand and let himself out of the door.

Lily was in bed when Fred returned home. He crept up the stairs and climbed carefully in beside her. 'Are you awake, Lily?' he whispered. She didn't answer. Putting his arm across her body, he settled down for the night.

As she listened to Fred's steady breathing, Lily wished she too could sleep, but all the time she kept seeing that look of cold hatred in Tom's eyes. She could still feel the grip of his hand on hers. Her heart ached for him. It wasn't until he stood before her in the flesh that she realised just how much she still wanted him. Until now, she had managed to delude herself that life was grand. But now, after tonight, she knew it was all a sham.

The following morning, as she cooked breakfast, Fred glanced at her with a worried expression. 'Are you all right, love? You look a bit pasty. Still got a headache?'

'No, I'm just a bit tired, that's all. Too much excitement last night.'

He gathered her to him in his arms and kissed her softly. 'You were wonderful. I was so proud of you. I love you, Lily. You know that, don't you?'

'Yes.' She kissed him back. 'I know you do. Although I don't know why.'

'Love is not an emotion with reason, Lily. It's from the heart, not the mind. We don't have any choice in the matter.'

How true, she thought, as she saw Fred off to work. How very true.

An hour later, when she was washing up the breakfast dishes, she heard a knock on the door. With racing heart and trembling legs, she walked forward and opened it.

There, standing before her was Tom, his body taut and his eyes cold.

'Come in,' she said. 'I've been expecting you.'

He stood in front of the table, back rigid. 'Well, what have you got to say?'

There was so much she wanted to say to him. *Hold me. Kiss me. Love me. Take me with you* . . . But she knew she could never say such things to him, ever again.

'Oh, for goodness sake, sit down!' she exploded. 'Standing there like a soldier, you make me feel I'm on trial. I'll put the kettle on.'

Her sudden attack surprised him.

'You're not on trial. But I think you owe me an explanation, Lily Pickford.'

'And I'll give you one if you sit down.'

He grabbed hold of her arms. 'Sit down! Is that all you can say? You appear out of nowhere after being missing for months, then you tell me to sit down. I ought to shake the living daylights out of you.'

The nearness of him, the feel of his hands on her, robbed her of movement. She looked into his eyes and felt weak with emotion. This was her beloved Tom.

'I could kill you.'

Here was the Irish temper she'd heard about, and it was awesome. Yet she had no fear of him. She shook herself free. 'And you'd have every right, but let's just calm down a minute. I can't talk to you when you're like this. Please . . .' She indicated a chair by the fire, into which he reluctantly lowered himself.

She busied herself getting the tea, fighting for time to gather her thoughts, to choose her words. This was probably the most important moment of her life. She was committed to Fred; she couldn't tell Tom about Manny and her past. She had no choice, she had to get rid of him – for ever.

Handing him a mug of tea, she sat opposite. Taking a deep breath, she said, 'I'm sorry I ran off like that, but when it came down to it, I didn't want to get married.'

Anger and indignation oozed from him. He glared at her. 'Is that it? You tell me you love me, want to spend the rest of your life with me, are ready to name the day, then you can't go through with it? That's a load of crap.'

Oh it is. It is. I want to run away with you now, leave everyone, be only with you. But she looked at him coolly. 'You put too much pressure on me, Tom. Telling me you wouldn't come back from Ireland. You forced me into a corner I couldn't get out of. I wasn't ready for marriage. I had no choice except to run.'

'Have you any idea the worry you caused?' His anger was bubbling like a cauldron. 'I searched the streets every single night for weeks. I was almost out of my mind with worry. Demented. Amy looked for you everywhere she could think of. Rachel was going mad with worry. But you didn't care about any of us. Least of all me.'

I did care, her heart cried. She was overcome with guilt. Poor Rachel – and Amy, her friend. If only Amy had found her, how different things might have been. She always had an answer for everything. She'd have known what to do.

At her silence, he gave her a baleful glare. 'You didn't love me. You never loved me.'

'I did, Tom,' she said softly. About this she refused to lie.

'How could you have loved me and run away like you did? It was all lies. Well, Lily, you certainly had me fooled.' He looked around the room, his gaze resting on the washing drying on the fireguard – her underwear, next to Fred's. 'You soon found someone else, I see. Soon lost your shyness for – *sex.*'

She could feel her own anger beginning to rise. 'And so did you. Congratulations on your recent engagement.'

'At least I found a woman I could trust.'

How hurt he was. How hard it was for her not to reach out and ease his pain. 'I'm sorry about your mother,' she said softly.

His anger abated for a moment. 'Thank you. I told her about you, about our plans for the future.' But the bitterness in him rose once again. 'Thank God she died before she too was disappointed.'

'I'm sorry. But things have changed. I'm with Fred now, he's a good man.'

'*I* am a good man! But obviously you didn't think so. Well, I wish you joy with your lover.' He spat out the words. 'Now I can get on with my life.' He got up suddenly. 'There seems little point in my being here any longer. We have no more to say to each other. It's all water under the bridge now.' He walked towards the door then paused as he opened it. His tone softened for a second. The anger in his eyes was no more. 'At least you're still alive. At one time I wondered if you were . . . That was the worst part, Lily.' He stepped outside, closing the door behind him.

She quickly crossed to the window, only to see him walk away. She put out her hand to touch him, but her fingers met only the cold of the window pane.

She slowly wandered back to her chair. Desolate.

As Tom walked down the street, his emotions were in turmoil. Lily, his beloved Lily was alive and well. Looking as beautiful as he remembered, her eyes still of the same deep-blue hue, with those long lashes . . . but she was living with another man, damn her!

One moment he wanted to strangle her with his bare hands for the torment she'd put him through, the next he longed to take her in his arms. But another man had this privilege now, holding her in bed at night, making love to her as Tom had yearned to do. The images were driving him mad.

Why did she leave him? She said it was because she didn't want to marry, but he didn't believe it, not for one moment. Could she have possibly left him for Fred? Surely not. Fred was a nice enough chap, but so much older than Lily. He suddenly pictured the look in her eyes when she had said she did love him. That he believed.

When he turned the corner, he stopped and lit a cigarette. He couldn't think straight. What was he to do? What *could* he do? Last night when Fred had put his arm around her shoulders, he'd wanted to knock the man's teeth down his throat. Jealousy had coursed through him and today to be inside the house they both shared, with the bed upstairs they slept in together, filled him with a blind rage. And if that was not enough, he himself was to be married to another woman. God! What a mess.

He looked at his pocket-watch. He was an hour late for work, and that would mean his foreman would have a go at him. Well, he'd better be careful what he said, because for two pins, Tom would throw him in the dock, he was in such a foul mood.

Standing at the end of the gangway, Burt Haines looked again at his watch. McCann was an hour late. His eyes gleamed. When the Irishman arrived, he'd really be able to have a go at him. Put him in his place.

There was no finer man at his job throughout the docks than Tom McCann, but his sharp tongue and hot Irish temper didn't always make him friends. One of the many enemies he'd made was Haines, the foreman.

By nature, Burt was a surly man. At home, his wife nagged him continuously. He was totally cowed by the woman, but made up for it at work. Once he walked through the dock gates, he became a man. He ruled his workers as his wife ruled him. Relentlessly.

The one person he couldn't ride was Tom. He was unable to match the Irishman's sharp tongue. McCann always got the better of him – and he hated him for it.

He saw Tom walking towards him in the distance and thought, Cocky bugger. Walks like he owns the place. He waited.

As Tom got to the bottom of the gangway, about to board the ship, Haines caught hold of his arm. 'What time do you call this?'

Tom checked his own watch. 'It's eight o'clock. Your watch is right. Nothing wrong with your eyes.'

Burt's face was puce. 'Don't you give me any of your lip, my lad.'

Looking down at the other's hand on his sleeve, Tom said, 'I'm late, but I had my reasons. Now let go of me, Haines, or I'll put you in the bloody drink.'

Haines sensed the menace in Tom's voice and had no doubt he would carry out his threat. He quickly let go. 'Well, make sure this doesn't happen again,' he blustered.

'Or what?' Tom glared at the foreman, daring him to say another word. Wanting him to, so he could vent his anger on someone.

'Get on with your work. We're already behind.'

As he watched Tom stride up the gangway, he muttered. 'I'll have you one day, you Irish bastard, see if I don't.'

Lily sat in the chair by the table, wondering about the woman who was to become Mrs Tom McCann. Even if she herself had been free, Tom had already made plans for his future. A future in which she played no part. Knowing she'd have to go through the rest of her life without him was bad enough, but to picture someone else taking her marriage vows beside Tom was more than she could bear. Yet she had no right to feel this way, had she? She was living with another man.

Was it possible that Tom felt as badly as she did? His expression had softened when he spoke those last few words to her before leaving. Could he still love her? But, even if he did, what was the use? The night she'd left Rachel's shop had shaped their future destiny. And she could blame no one but herself for the results of her actions. Except perhaps Manny Cohen. How she hated that man. But he'd done the worst he could to her, and she'd survived. It wasn't in his power to hurt her further.

Fred was getting desperate. He felt in his pocket, and there was very little there. The deal with Knocker had gone cold and the rag and bone trade was slack. What was he to do? He walked around the High Street shops. There should be a few rich pickings here, he thought, as he flexed his fingers and went to work.

A little later, his mood had improved considerably. The old fingers were still dextrous. He'd systematically worked the High Street shops, then made his way to Edwin Jones, in East Street. The lower floor was doing a good trade. He picked out a likely-looking target who was inspecting a gent's suit. Fred sauntered up to the man, stumbled and bumped into him, apologising profusely as he pocketed his wallet.

But to his surprise, the man grabbed hold of his wrist and held on tightly, calling for the manager.

Fred tried desperately to get away, but the customer had told the assistant who'd been serving him to catch hold of Fred as well, declaring, 'This man is a pickpocket!'

A small crowd gathered, while Fred loudly protested his innocence. When the manager arrived on the scene, Fred was dragged off to his office.

'This man is Fred Bates, a well-known pickpocket,' the target said. 'I recognised him in the store. Then when he bumped me, I knew why. Look in his pocket and you'll find my wallet there.'

Despite Fred's protestations, the manager searched him, and was surprised to find several wallets about his person. He looked at the customer with some consternation.

'That wallet is mine,' said the man who had grabbed Fred. 'Inside it you'll find my warrant card. I'm Police Constable Castle – and you're nicked, Bates.'

Lily rushed to the police station when she got word of Fred's arrest. She sat opposite him in the interview room, while a policeman kept watch by the door.

'Fred, how could you? You promised to go straight.'

His face was ashen. 'I know, love. I'm so sorry, but I was running out of money. The rag trade was bad and I had to take care of you.'

She looked angrily at him. 'You stupid idiot. Why didn't you tell me things were bad? What good are you to me if you're in prison?'

'I didn't want to lose you, Lily.'

She looked at the distraught man sitting opposite, and her heart was filled with pity. 'You're never going to lose me, Fred. I promise.'

He rubbed his forehead. 'How will you manage? You've got a roof over your head, but there isn't any money.'

Catching hold of his hands she said, 'Don't you worry about that.'

'But I do worry, Lily. I don't want you to have to go back on the game.'

She brushed his words aside. 'I won't. Sandy said he could get me work singing round the pubs if ever I wanted. I'll go and see him.'

'Now listen, Lily. I want you to promise me you won't visit me in the nick. I couldn't bear it, seeing you and not being free.'

She patted his hand. 'All right, Fred. But just you take care of yourself. I'll still be here when you get out.'

The look of uncertainty in his eyes hurt her deeply. She owed this man so much. 'Where else would I want to be, Fred, but with you?'

The look of relief on his face was her reward. 'I love you so much, Lily.'

'I know. And I love you, Fred.' It wasn't a lie. In her own way she did love this man. Not in the way she loved Tom, but in her heart was a warm affection for Fred Bates. She would never leave him. How could she?

In court the next day, the magistrate sent Fred down for six months.

Chapter Ten

When Lily walked back into the house, it seemed empty, lifeless. She had been stunned to hear the sentence. Fred had looked at her with a tragic expression on his features. She'd smiled bravely across the courtroom at him, but was devastated when she saw him led away.

Looking in the larder, she saw she had enough food for a couple of days. Meagre offerings perhaps, but she remembered when such things would have meant a feast. There was no time to waste. If she was to survive, she would have to see Sandy. She would take herself off to The Sailor's Return tonight.

Declan was the first to see her as she entered the bar, somewhat uncertainly. 'Lily, me girl. How are you? Come on over here.'

Sandy was sitting talking to a young man at one of the small tables. He looked up when he heard Declan greet her, made his excuses to his companion and came over right away. 'Hello, Lily.' Something about her demeanour caused him concern. 'What's the matter?'

She gave a wry smile. 'I always seem to meet you when I've got a crisis.'

'Then perhaps we had better sit down. Let me get you a drink. What'll it be?'

'Half a bitter will be fine, thanks.'

He carried the drinks over and sat beside her in a quiet corner.

'Fred's in gaol.'

'Oh dear.' He frowned. 'Been dipping again, has he?'

She nodded. 'I'm afraid so. I have a roof over my head, but no money, so I need a job. You said if I wanted to sing around the pubs, you'd help me.'

'I did and I will. But if you're going to make a success of this, you need a bit of training. You come round to my place tomorrow and we'll rehearse. I'll set you up with the right gear, and we'll go from there.'

'How long will it take, Sandy? I'm broke.'

He fished in his pocket and produced two one-pound notes. 'Here, this will keep you going for a bit.'

She put up her hand and shook her head. 'I can't take that.'

Tossing his hair back with a flourish, he said, 'Now, dearie, don't play the prima donna . . . that's *my* role. You can pay me back later.'

With a thankful smile, she took the money.

'Poor old Fred.'

Sandy's sympathy brought tears to her eyes. 'When they took him away, he looked awful.'

'Well, being in the nick is no picnic.' Sandy put his hand on her arm. 'Don't you worry now, pet. I'll teach you everything I know. With me as your manager, you'll be fine.' He winked. 'And I won't expect to sleep with you. Your honour will be intact.'

The wicked twinkle in his eye made Lily chortle, despite her problems.

'Look, I'll write down my address,' he said, 'and you come round tomorrow afternoon. Best not say the morning in case I get lucky tonight.' He looked across to where his boyfriend was waiting. 'It looks quite promising. What do you reckon? . . . Good-looking, isn't he? Think I stand a chance?'

'I don't know.' Shaking her head, Lily said, 'I refuse to get drawn into your love-life. I'll see you tomorrow. And thanks.'

The following afternoon, Lily made her way to Bond Street, checked the number on the scrap of paper, then knocked on the door. Sandy opened it, a broad grin on his face. 'Come in, dearie. I'm all ready.'

He was wearing a loose, brightly coloured silk shirt over

his trousers, his cravat around his neck – and carpet slippers.

'All you need is a feather boa, and you'll do,' said Lily, amused at his appearance.

'Cheeky.'

He took her coat, and sat her down at the table in the middle of the room. Lily looked about her. The settee had bright cushions on it, the floral curtains were frilled and the rag rug was a riot of colour. 'Are you sure you're not colour blind?' she teased.

'Listen, darling, this bloody world is dark enough. This is my answer to it. Now, I've got a lot of sheet music here. We'll go through it and see which numbers you know, then we'll work out a programme.'

They pored over the music together; the songs Lily already knew were put to one side, while Sandy hummed the others to her. Those she liked they kept, and the rest were put away for the time being. Lily began to enjoy herself.

'Right.' Sandy clapped his hands. 'We have to mix the tempo. Some jolly old singalongs, others that you can sell to them as a solo.'

'What do you mean, sell to them?'

'Put them over. You know, all soulful-like. Tear at their heartstrings. Like "Danny Boy". When you sang that in the pub, you could hear a pin drop. Then a nice jaunty number. "A Little of What You Fancy Does You Good", would be about right. You can be good and cheeky with that, you know, a nod and a wink here and there. Then perhaps a bit of raunch.'

Her eyes twinkled. 'What's a bit of raunch when it's about?'

He frowned and scratched the back of his head. 'Let me see, how can I make you understand? I know.' Getting up from the table, he ran to the stairs. 'Won't be a minute.'

She gave a puzzled frown. What was the old devil up to now?

To her amazement, Sandy eventually appeared in a long evening gown, high-heeled shoes and a feather boa.

'Tra la!' He stood hand on hip, head tilted, a provocative expression on his face and started to sing: 'After you've gone, there's no use crying. After you've gone, there's no denying . . .' He really put his heart and soul into the number. He was amazing.

When he had finished, Lily applauded enthusiastically. 'That was terrific! I think *you* should be the one singing.'

'I'd be locked up. But you see what I mean?'

Lily looked perplexed. 'I do, but I couldn't do that.'

'Listen, dearie, dressed in the right clothes you can do anything. Clothes give you a character. It's like as kids we used to dress up to play games. It helps. Come upstairs and I'll show you.'

When he opened the wardrobe door, Lily was astounded. There were several evening gowns and dresses, hats and shoes. 'Are these all yours?'

'Lovely, aren't they, darling? Aren't you just a teeny weeny bit jealous?'

Seeing the mischievous grin on his face, she shook her head. 'You old queen, as a matter of fact I am.'

Taking out a red gown decorated with sequins he said, 'This ought to fit you. Try it on.'

'What, now?'

'Of course now. I'll wait downstairs. Here.' He handed her a small black hat with an osprey feather across the front. 'Put this on as well, and these.' He passed her a pair of long black gloves.

'Blimey, Sandy. I'll look like a bloody toff in this lot.'

'You will, my dear. You certainly will.'

Lily was thoroughly enjoying herself now. It reminded her of the days at Rachel Cohen's shop when she used to dress up, all by herself. When she was ready, she walked carefully down the stairs and struck a pose, leaning against the door, puffing on an imaginary cigarette. 'How will I do?'

Sandy, who had changed back into his trousers and shirt, smiled in satisfaction. 'You look wonderful. I don't think you know quite what a beauty you really are. You should always be dressed in beautiful clothes, you carry them so well.'

'Don't give me that old flannel.' She was embarrassed by what she knew to be a genuine compliment.

'Right. Then let's get started.'

116

For the next three hours, Lily worked really hard. Sandy, she realised, knew his business and she listened and learned. At the end of the session, they were both exhausted and collapsed into a couple of chairs.

'I need a pick-me-up,' he wailed. He went into the scullery and returned with a couple of glasses and a bottle of Guinness. 'Here, drink this. It's full of iron – do you good. What am I saying? It will do us both good. Frankly, I'm knackered.'

After they'd taken a rest, Sandy said, 'Look, love. If we work every day, we'll start at The Sailor's Return at the weekend. You were a hit the other time you sang with me. Think of it as practice. Then we'll start moving around.'

Lily was suddenly overcome with nerves. 'Do you really think I can do it?'

Placing his hand over hers he said, 'Lily, my dear, I told you that first night. You're a natural. You have a gift. All you need is a little polish to be like a professional, and I can give you that. Now off you go. Come back at the same time tomorrow.'

Whilst Lily was practising her routines, ready for the new start to her life, Mary Harris was planning the campaign to start hers, as Mrs Tom McCann.

Things were not going at all well. She couldn't put her finger on the reason, but suddenly Tom didn't seem quite so enthusiastic about naming the day. He kept making excuses as to why the time wasn't right.

'I need to save a little more money, Mary. I don't want us to go into debt as soon as we get married. I want a small nest egg at the back of me.'

'I have a little saved,' she insisted. 'What with us both working, and you earning good money, I don't see what the problem is.'

He became irritated. 'Now listen to me, you'd better get used to the idea that I'm the one who makes the decisions – now . . . and certainly when we get married!'

She moved across the room and stood behind his chair, putting her arms around his neck, snuggling her cheek into his. 'Of course you are, darling,' she wheedled. And was put out when he pushed her away.

'What's got into you, Tom?'

'Nothing's got into me,' he snapped. 'What are you on about?'

Mary gave a childish pout. 'These past few days, you've been acting very strange. You've been almost distant. You've hardly kissed me.'

'Don't be so bloody ridiculous!'

Mary's green eyes deepened in anger. 'There's no need to swear. It's common.'

Getting up from the chair, he said, 'For God's sake leave me alone, woman. You're turning into a right nag – and I won't put up with it.' He grabbed for his coat, lifted it off the hook behind the door and walked out, slamming the door behind him.

Storming off down the road, Tom felt a stab of guilt. Mary was right, of course. Ever since he'd seen Lily, he'd been cool with his fiancée. He couldn't get Lily out of his mind; Mary had become an irritation. She wanted to get married and soon. All of a sudden he wasn't so sure. There was and always would be only one woman for him, and she'd turned him down . . . twice. First by running away and now by living with another man. That still stuck in his craw, but in his heart Tom knew that if she changed her mind tomorrow, he would take Lily back.

When Declan told him that night over a pint that Fred had been sent down for six months, Tom's first thoughts were of Lily. How would she manage? He left his drink on the counter and walked out of the bar without a word. Declan looked on in amazement.

Knocking on Lily's door, Tom found his heart was pounding. The very thought of seeing her again sent the adrenalin surging through him.

'What do you want?' demanded Lily when she saw him standing there. 'Come to insult me all over again?'

But this time, there was no anger in his eyes, only concern. 'No, Lily, I promise. Can I come in for a moment?'

Reluctantly, she stepped aside. She'd been shocked to see him at the door and didn't think she could bear to have him in the house, so near to her. She had to be on her mettle. 'Well?'

'Look, tonight Declan told me about Fred. I'm really sorry and I wondered how you would be able to cope without his money coming in. Can I help in any way?'

Her heart was bursting with happiness. Tom wanted to help her. He must still love her. But she remained distant. 'No, thanks. I'm going round the pubs with Sandy, singing. He thinks I should do all right.'

The wonderful spark in her eyes . . . It was still there. He caught hold of her arm. 'Is it really too late for us, Lily?'

Lily wanted to die. All she wanted was Tom, but again she'd have to turn him down. 'I told you before. It's over.'

There was a sudden flame in his eyes. In a low, husky voice he asked, 'Is it, Lily? I don't believe it is.'

Before she knew what was happening, he pulled her to him, held her firmly in his arms and kissed her. His lips traced the shape of her mouth, exploring it gently, making her legs tremble. At first she fought against him, but as his mouth moved over hers, opening her reluctant lips, exploring her mouth with the tip of his tongue, she couldn't help herself. She kissed him back with all the love that she felt for him and had to deny.

'Oh Lily, Lily,' he murmured against her cheek, before again searching for her mouth. His hands slipped beneath her jumper, caressing her back, sending tingles down her spine. He kissed her eyes, her neck. 'I want you, Lily,' he whispered against her throat. 'Let me make love to you. I need you. God! I've been crazy all these months thinking you were dead. Then to find you. I want to make love to you – now. Don't deny me. Please.'

How could she deny him? The fire of passion was building inside her; she wanted him too. Taking his hand, she led him upstairs.

'Not in his bed,' said Tom sharply.

'No,' she said, 'in here.' They went into the spare room. Lily closed the curtain and turned to face him.

He drew her slowly towards him and slipped the jumper she was wearing over her head. Her exposed breasts filled him with an even greater desire. He cupped them gently in his hands and kissed them.

Lily moaned with delight.

Tom slid the skirt from her rounded hips and removed her undergarments. Picking her up, he laid her on the bed. 'You are so beautiful, Lily. I can't tell you the number of times I've dreamed of this moment.'

'Tom. Oh Tom,' she groaned as he explored her body with his sensitive fingers, probing, stroking until she thought she'd go crazy.

He slipped his own clothes off and lay beside her.

She felt the hardness of his manhood pressing into her side, sending shivers of expectancy through her. She caressed his broad shoulders, kissing his chest, nibbling his ear. Ran her fingers through his auburn hair, calling his name as he brought her to the point of ecstasy.

As he gently entered her, she cried out with joy.

That night, for the first time, Lily slept with a man for love.

The next morning, they awoke early and made love again.

'What are we going to do, Lily?'

'About what?' she whispered, her head buried in his chest.

'About Fred.'

She froze in his arms. 'What about Fred?'

He felt the sudden tension in her body. 'You can't stay with him, not after last night.'

'Last night was wonderful, Tom. But it doesn't change anything.'

He sat up and looked at her as if he couldn't believe her words. 'It changes everything.'

Shaking her head she said, 'Look, Fred took me in when I had nothing and nowhere to go. He looked after me. Now he's in prison. I promised him I'd be here waiting for him when he came out. And I will be.'

His hazel eyes blazed. 'So what in Christ's name was last night all about?'

She stroked his face, and he grabbed hold of her fingers. '*Well?*' he demanded.

'Last night was about love, lust, total satisfaction of two people who wanted each other and couldn't deny each other's needs. Don't spoil it, Tom.'

He swung his legs off the bed and started to dress. 'I don't understand you! I thought you wanted me . . . for ever. Not just one night.' He looked at her, anger pouring forth. 'It seems you've made a fool of me again.'

She got out of bed and put on a wrap. 'No, Tom. I wanted you. I still love you, will always love you, but I can't just let Fred down. Not now, when he needs me most.'

He pulled her to him roughly, his gaze burning into her. '*I* need you. Think about that.' His kiss was not one of tenderness, it was brutal, and when he let her go, Lily held her fingers to her bruised lips.

At the bedroom door, he turned. 'You think you can take me into your bed, let me touch you, kiss you, love you – then turn me away? Well, you picked the wrong man. This is not over yet, by a long chalk!'

That weekend, Lily made her debut as a professional singer at The Sailor's Return. She was sensational. The bar was packed. Apart from the locals, there were many crew members in there off one of the liners that had docked that day. The men had had a good trip and were more than generous when Sandy made his collection. The local prostitutes with their clients were also appreciative. The music had put their punters in a good mood, and money was flowing over the counter.

Declan poured out a free port and lemon for Lily. 'You can work here on a regular basis,' he said with a grin.

'You'll have to talk with my manager about that,' she said, with a look of delight in Sandy's direction.

He hugged her. 'I told you you were a natural, didn't I? We'll do well, you'll see.'

She smiled when she saw Sandy hurry over to the bar and get into deep conversation with Declan later on that evening. She knew they were talking business. Arranging when she would be able to perform. She was elated.

Sandy was proved correct. As the weeks passed, Lily performed in various pubs around the dock area, and did well, but on Saturday nights, she was booked permanently at Declan's.

Just as she was preparing to start her programme the following Saturday, who should walk into the bar of The Sailor's Return but Amy and Tom.

As soon as the girls saw each other, they flung their arms around one another with cries of joy.

'I couldn't believe it when Tom told me you were all right.' Amy stood back from Lily. 'Look at you – you look marvellous! If only Rachel could see you now.'

Lily's eyes clouded over. 'How is Rachel?'

Amy shook her head. 'She was really cut up about you running off. Blamed her Manny, but didn't dare tell Tom. He'd have killed him. She kicked Manny out, you know.'

'Oh no!' Lily looked shaken. 'I only ran away so as not to come between mother and son. I had better go and see her.'

With a worried expression, Amy said, 'I wish you would, Lily. She hasn't been the same since you left. The spark seems to have gone from her somehow. She wanted you back, you know. Made me hunt for you.'

'I'm so sorry, Amy. I put you all through so much.'

'Tom was the one who suffered the most. At one time I feared for his sanity. Are you back together?'

Lily shook her head. 'You'll have to come round to the house and I'll tell you all about it.'

Sandy intervened at this point. 'Are you working tonight, madam?'

'Whoops! I'd better go, Amy. I'll talk to you later.'

When it was time for Lily to sing 'After You've Gone', she looked over at Tom for the first time. His eyes were on her as she started the number. His expression didn't change throughout, but his mouth got tighter, and his jawline firmer. Lily knew that she hadn't shaken loose from him. In her heart she was glad, but she fretted about Fred. He was relying on her.

When she'd finished her routine, Amy beckoned her over. 'You're terrific!' she exclaimed with admiration as Lily sat beside them. 'Isn't she, Tom?'

'Oh yes,' he replied, 'Lily is quite a performer. She knows just how to get the heart of an audience and leave them wanting more.'

Lily gave him a sharp look.

When Amy went to the bar for some drinks, Tom caught hold of Lily's wrist. 'When are you going to come to your senses?' he demanded.

'Don't start, Tom.'

'Start! I haven't even begun. You can't throw away our future. We belong together. You know we do.'

'Not any more. When will you accept the fact?' She got up and left him sitting alone.

The following day, Lily made her way to The Ditches. It was like walking down Memory Lane. Various shopkeepers called out to her as she passed, and she waved back, returning a cheery remark. Ahead of her was Mrs Cohen's shop. It was open, but Rachel was nowhere to be seen.

Lily paused outside. This was where she'd been most happy after leaving home. She looked at the dresses and suits, still hanging from the rusty struts of the blind. The boxes with the hats . . . and the shoes. How well she remembered the shoes. She touched them with the tips of her fingers, a smile on her lips. Then she walked into the shop.

Chapter Eleven

Peering into the dark recesses of the shop, Lily called, 'Rachel! Anybody home?'

A figure shuffled towards her. 'What is it? Can't you wait a minute?'

'Hello, Rachel.'

The Jewess suddenly stopped, looked over her horn-rimmed glasses and in a faltering voice, asked, 'Lily? Is that really you?'

Tears welled up in Lily's eyes and her words choked in her throat. She walked over to Rachel and taking her in her arms whispered, 'Yes, it's really me.'

The two women clung together without speaking, tears streaming down their cheeks. 'Oh Rachel, I'm so sorry I ran off like that.'

'My dearest Lily. I thought I'd never see you again. Let me look at you. Come to the light, I can't see nothing here.'

Rachel Cohen held Lily at arm's length, her eyes shining with tears, a happy smile on her lips. 'How well you look, my dear. So how is life with you?'

Lily was shattered when she got a close look at Rachel. The older woman's skin was sallow. She'd lost weight and looked ill.

'Never mind me. How are you, my dear friend?'

Rachel shrugged. 'What's to tell? I'm still in business.' She clutched hold of Lily's hands. 'I sent Manny away. It was his fault you ran off like that. I'll never forgive myself.'

Leading Rachel to a chair, Lily sat close beside her, still holding her hand. 'I'm sorry you felt you had to do that. I ran off because I didn't want to come between mother and son.'

Rachel smoothed her cheek. 'So thoughtful a girl. But tell me, Lily, I have to know. Did he touch you that night?' She looked haggard with worry.

'No,' Lily assured her. 'He didn't get the chance. Anyway, he was very drunk.'

With a sly smile on her face Rachel said, 'But *you* touched *him*. He was still in pain the next morning. I told him you should have cut his balls off.'

Both women collapsed with laughter. Rachel held her side. 'Ay yi, I have the stitch. I ain't laughed so much since you left. Oh Lily, it's good to see you.'

'Where is Manny now?'

'In London – Golders Green, where he's having to really work for his living.' She grinned wickedly. 'Do him good. I should have done it years ago. I don't see him – I have no more a son.'

Lily was filled with sadness at such an outcome. 'I'm so sorry. I feel it was all my fault.'

'Look, my girl, it was no one's fault but his. He's no good. Never has been. Ach, he's no great loss. Now, have you seen Tom?'

The laughter stilled as she said, 'Oh yes, I've seen him.'

'And? You still together?'

Shaking her head, Lily said, 'No. I'm with another man and Tom's engaged to some woman.'

'*Oy vey!* Such a waste. Never have I seen two people more suited. Can't you do nothing?'

Lily shook her head. 'I'm afraid it's too late for that.'

'You listen to me, girl. Don't you let your happiness slip away without a fight. He'll want you back.'

With a sigh Lily said, 'He does, but I've promised I'll stand by Fred. He was good to me, Rachel. He gave me a roof, kindness, love. I can't dump him.'

'Pity. Such a pity. Will you come and visit with me again?'

With a fond smile Lily said, 'I certainly will.' Then with a wide grin, she added, 'I still owe you a quid out of my wages.'

Laughing, Rachel said, 'The debt is cancelled.'

'What? Rachel Cohen letting someone get away with a

debt? My, I never thought I'd live to see the day.'

'Don't you go spreading the word. Anyway, who would believe it?'

Looking at Rachel intently, Lily asked, 'And you, are you well? You look a bit pale to me.'

'My life! I don't see you in months and you start fussing. Me . . . I'm just fine. Getting old is all. So you – are you working?'

With a gleeful look on her face, Lily said, 'I'm a singer round the pubs. I really like it and I'm making money.'

'*Mazel tov!* Some night I'll come and see you for myself.' Hugging Lily to her, Rachel said, 'Now don't forget me, eh? Your old Yiddisher momma.'

Gazing fondly at the older woman, Lily said, 'I could never do that. The happiest time of my whole life was here with you.'

'Me too,' said Rachel.

'Why don't you come to The Sailor's Return?' Lily suggested. 'I sing there every Saturday night. We'll have a party.'

Rachel beamed with happiness. 'Yes, I'll come. It'll be a change.' Shaking her head she said, 'Lily, Lily. It does my eyes good to see you.'

The following Saturday night Lily was delighted when the bar door of The Sailor's Return opened and Rachel walked in. She rushed over to her. 'My dear, how smart you look.'

The Jewess was wearing a green coat and matching felt cloche hat, with a splendid pair of fox furs around her shoulders. She tossed her head somewhat arrogantly and said, 'I've got some decent *schmatte* for special occasions and this is one, ain't it?'

Lily hugged her and laughed. 'Indeed it is. Come and meet my friends.' She introduced Rachel to Declan, who shook her hand, then to Sandy, who bowed gracefully.

Rachel raised her eyebrows in Lily's direction. 'Such fine men you know.' She gave a sly smile and said to Sandy, 'But in your case . . .'

Sandy burst out laughing. 'Now don't get naughty, darling. Come and sit down. What'll you have to drink?'

It was a great evening. Lily sang her heart out and Rachel, topped up with gin, danced a strange kind of Irish gig with Declan.

Amy arrived in the midst of the celebrations and after a few drinks, she and Sandy demonstrated their own hilarious version of the Tango, the new dance which was all the rage. The rest of the customers were soon carried away with the festive spirit that filled the bar, and sang at the top of their voices, as Sandy played all the popular songs of the day.

Lily was so happy, here with her dearest friends around her, and was thrilled to see Rachel having such good fun. When it was closing time, they all declared it had been a night to remember.

Fred Bates stood waiting patiently for the warder to release him from prison. With the heavy door finally unlocked, the warder stood back.

'Don't worry, Bates. We'll keep your cell warm. By the time we've changed the bedding, you'll be back.'

'Piss off! You rotten screws are all the same.' Fred stepped through the opening and wrapped his muffler around his scrawny neck, clutching his meagre belongings in a brown paper parcel, tied up with string. 'This is the last time you'll see me.'

'They all say that, Bates. But most of them come back.'

Fred heard the door clang behind him. The sound always made him feel sick to his stomach. This time he meant what he said. He'd spent too many years banged up and it was getting harder to survive inside. His cough was no better either. It kept him and his cell-mates awake at night, which had caused even further trouble.

His thoughts were all of Lily and how badly he'd let her down. She'd written to him, telling how well she was doing. He'd worried that she would be forced back on the streets; he would never have been able to forgive himself if this had been so. He felt such a failure. Looking at the paper parcel he thought it just about summed up his life. But it seemed from Lily's letters she was doing fine, and she had sent him the money for the train fare home. He couldn't wait to see her.

Taking in a deep breath of air, he wondered wryly how it could smell so sweet from this side of the prison walls, when in the exercise yard it smelt quite different.

He took a packet of Woodbines from his pocket and lit one, inhaling deeply. It made him cough violently for a moment, but nevertheless the nicotine tasted good. All he needed now was a pint of beer. As soon as he got back to Southampton he would have one, before going home.

The lunch-time trade was busy. Declan looked at his watch, thankful he'd be able to call last orders soon. Tom was standing at the counter talking to him when the bar door opened. 'He's just made it,' remarked Declan.

Tom looked round and frowned when he recognised Fred Bates. But he was shocked as Fred walked over to them. His build was naturally slim, but now he looked like a bag of bones, and his prison pallor didn't help.

'Hello, Fred. You look as if you could do with a pint,' he said.

Before Fred could answer he had a fit of coughing. Tom, filled with concern said, 'Here, best sit down. I'll bring you a pint over.'

Wiping the beads of sweat from his forehead, Fred thanked him. 'I need this before I go home. Lily will be waiting.'

The words were painful for Tom to hear. Looking at Fred, he knew that any plans for him and Lily to be together were now doomed. It was obvious that Fred was ill. Lily would certainly never leave him now.

'You well, Tom? Got yourself married yet? The last time we met you'd just become engaged.'

Shaking his head Tom said, 'No, not yet. There's plenty of time. Drink up, we must celebrate your first day of freedom.'

'No thanks, best not. I'm anxious to get home. I haven't seen Lily since I was sent down. I wouldn't let her visit me, you see, and I can't wait to be with her. I'm sure you understand.'

Taking a deep breath, Tom tried to hide his despair. Oh yes, he could understand only too well how Fred felt. 'Take care then.' He watched Bates leave the bar, knowing that he was going to the woman he loved. He would be holding her, making love to her . . . His thoughts were tormenting him, driving him insane. Getting up from his seat, he called to Declan, 'I'm off back to work.'

Lily looked up as the front door opened to see Fred standing there, an expression of uncertainty on his face. 'Hello, Lily.'

She was shocked at how pale he was, the circles under his eyes, the new grey strands in his hair. He looked so ill. My God! She thought. He's come home an old man. She saw his trembling fingers holding his paper parcel and her heart was filled with compassion.

'Well, don't just stand there, you daft bugger. Come and give me a kiss. I've waited long enough.'

Breathing a sigh of relief Fred stepped inside the room, shutting the door behind him. Putting the parcel on the table, he caught hold of Lily tightly, like a child needing comfort from its mother. He could smell the carbolic soap she'd washed with. To him it was as great an aphrodisiac as any expensive French perfume. He felt her warm flesh, her bosom like a soft pillow as he nestled his head against her. He was filled with a physical longing for her so strong, the pain was almost unbearable.

Feeling his arousal, Lily lifted his head and kissed him passionately. Softly she said, 'I'm glad they haven't knocked all the stuffing out of you.'

He started to tremble as he caressed her bosom. 'Talking about stuffing, Lily – let's go to bed.'

'I was going to fill you a bath in front of the fire. I had it all planned.'

With a lopsided grin, he said, 'Don't be bloody silly, girl. I've been without a woman for six months. Do you think I've got time for a bath?'

Kissing him on the forehead she whispered, 'Come on upstairs then. I'll give you the time of your life.'

As he preceded her up the stairs, he said, 'I stopped off for a pint before I came home. Tom McCann bought it for me. He looked well.'

Lily's heart lurched within her. The last time she'd climbed these stairs with a man, it had been Tom. She was filled with guilt. To have been unfaithful to Fred in his own house was unforgivable. Never again would she be tempted. Now her main task was to get Fred well.

The following weekend in The Sailor's Return, Tom waited for a quiet word with Lily. 'How's Fred?'

She shook her head, her face etched with worry. 'He's not good. If he doesn't improve, I'll get the doctor in.'

Tom's gaze searched hers. 'Does this mean there is no chance of us ever having a future together, Lily?'

'How many times do I have to tell you, Tom, before you believe me? Fred is my life.'

He stared at her, his face full of sadness. 'I wish with all my heart it could be different, Lily. I'll always love you, you know that?'

'I know,' she said with a sigh, 'but the gods have decided differently. Get on with your life, Tom. Forget me.'

Tom's heart was heavy as he watched her walk away. She was all he wanted in the world. But he understood that now she must look after Fred. She wouldn't be his Lily if she left the man who so obviously needed her care. With a deep sigh, he finished his drink and left.

The following day, Tom and Mary made a date for their wedding.

On Friday evening, when Lily was performing at The Lord Roberts, Vittorio came into the bar accompanied by the big man Lily had seen outside the Club Valletta.

For a moment the buzz of the patrons died down, such was the reputation of the man, but as he sat quietly with his glass of whisky, the place returned to normal.

The Maltese looked with interest at Lily standing by the piano whilst she went through her whole programme. He applauded her performance enthusiastically, then beckoned her over.

Sandy muttered, 'Watch your step with him, girl.'

He looked very surprised when she grinned at him and said, 'Don't you worry, we're old friends.'

Sitting beside Vittorio, Lily said, 'Good evening. I haven't seen you in here before. Slumming, are you?'

His slow smile was mesmeric. His eyes seemed to see into her very soul as he looked at her. Catching hold of her hand, he said softly, 'I don't usually come to places such as this, my dear, but you've been making quite a name as a performer. I thought I should see for myself if you are as good as I'm told.'

'And?' she asked cheekily, raising her eyebrows.

His fingers were caressing her hand and she was beginning to feel unnerved by his touch. She made to pull her hand away, but he tightened his grip. 'You are very much better.'

Lily was delighted. 'Thank you.'

He looked around at the peeling paintwork of the bar with distaste. 'But what on earth are you doing in a place like this?'

'What's wrong with it?' she asked indignantly. 'It's full, and with honest people too.'

His gaze searched her face, looking at every feature. Lily was uncomfortable under such close scrutiny. 'You are even more beautiful now,' he declared. 'You've matured since the first day we met.'

Her eyes sparked with pleasure. 'And you, Vittorio, what about you? You don't look any different. Making an honest living these days, or are you still in the same dodgy business?'

He burst out laughing. 'Oh, Lily. You are an extraordinary girl. No one speaks to me the way you do.'

'Frightened of ending up in the drink, I expect.'

She saw his expression change. His smile didn't falter but the sudden cold look from the piercing eyes made her quake inside and she knew that everything she'd been told about Vittorio was true.

'You are sometimes very foolish, Lily,' he said smoothly, 'but I put that down to your inexperience. Come and have dinner with me one night. I might have an interesting proposition for you.'

Tilting her head on one side, she asked, 'What sort of proposition?'

'I see you are a little intrigued. You will like it, I promise.'

Lily glanced over towards the piano where Sandy was playing soft music, keeping an eye on her. She looked back at Vittorio. 'I'm sorry, but I'm not free to accept such invitations.'

The smile left his lips. 'Don't tell me you're married?'

Shaking her head, Lily said, 'No. But I'm spoken for.'

The sudden anger in Vittorio's voice made her start. 'What is wrong with you? I can give you everything a girl could desire and you waste yourself on some useless man.'

She was angry. 'Fred isn't useless. He's a lovely person and at the moment he's not well, so don't you talk about him like that.'

He calmed down. 'I see I've upset you. I'm sorry, that was not my intention. I'm sure this character you're involved with is an upright figure of the local community.'

'Yes, he is.'

The same small smile played in the corners of Vittorio's mouth. 'But can he give you what I can?'

'And what would that be?'

He appraised her figure. 'You have a great body, a beautiful face and a dream of a voice, but in this setting, it loses so much. You could sing in my club, with my band. I could make you a success. You would be somebody. I could lift you out of these sordid surroundings. Clothe you in the most expensive gowns. You would have money, jewels, position . . . and me.'

Lily's eyes widened. This was far more than she'd bargained for. 'What do you mean . . . and you?'

He brushed his finger gently down her cheek. 'You would be my mistress.'

'Your mistress?'

He chuckled. 'Is the idea so repugnant to you?'

'What does repugnant mean?'

'Don't you like the idea? Is it distasteful to you?'

Looking at his smooth skin, his powerful figure in his well-cut suit, the spotlessly clean shirt, tapering fingers with clean nails and his fascinating smile, she couldn't honestly say yes, so she didn't answer.

There was a look of satisfaction on his face as he said, 'I see it isn't. That gives me great pleasure. If only you'd let me help you, Lily. You have talent. You need someone to take care of you.' He smiled. 'I would very much like to be the man to do that.'

'Well honestly, Vittorio, you've really taken me by surprise. I don't know quite what to say.'

He chuckled. 'For the first time, Lily, I do believe you are at a loss for words. Think about it. I know one day you'll come to me, but I just hope it's sooner rather than later.' He kissed the back of her hand. 'Until that day, my dear.' He excused himself and left the bar.

Lily was stunned. Yet she was aware that she had been the centre of attention; the customers were still gazing at her with speculative looks.

Sandy came rushing over. 'What the hell was that all about?'

'I've just been propositioned.'

'By The Maltese? What did he want?'

With a grin she said, 'He wants me to be his mistress.'

Sandy's eyes nearly popped out of his head. 'Oh my God! I need a drink and so do you, I shouldn't wonder.'

They sat together with a glass of brandy each. 'Medicinal purposes only,' said Sandy as he took a sip.

'Well, what do you think?' Lily asked him.

He looked at her in astonishment. 'You are joking, I hope?'

'Why? Don't you want to see me dripping in diamonds?' Her eyes were twinkling with delight. 'You saw the power he has. He walked in here and there was silence. Power, Sandy. And he's rich.'

The pianist couldn't believe what he was hearing. 'You surely aren't considering his offer?'

'No. Of course not, you silly old fart. But don't you think it's worth putting to the back of my mind for a rainy day?'

'Stop messing about, Lily.' Sandy was becoming agitated. 'You know the man's reputation. He's dangerous.'

'Yes, he is,' she agreed. 'But frankly, he's also quite fascinating. I actually like him!'

'Then you're probably the only person that does.'

'Rubbish. He's got a mother somewhere. She must love him.'

Shaking his head Sandy retorted, 'That man wasn't born. He's the Devil's issue.'

'You think I'm being tempted by the Devil? How exciting.'

'Don't joke about it, Lily. Please, do me a favour. Forget about Vittorio Teglia.'

But Lily knew she couldn't. There was still only one man she really wanted, but there was something about Vittorio. Always had been. Somehow he was to be a part of her life. She knew that, and so did he.

Chapter Twelve

Today was Mary Harris's wedding day, and she was beside herself with excitement. Today she would become Mrs Thomas McCann. There was a time when she had thought this day would never come, but all of a sudden Tom had had a change of heart and wanted to rush the wedding through. She wondered what had changed his mind, but pushed any doubts to the back of her thoughts.

Tom had rented a two-up and two-down in the adjacent road to her parents. She'd pleaded with him to look further afield, but he'd become stubborn. 'I don't want to walk bloody miles to work, woman, just so you can say you live in a better neighbourhood than your friends.'

It would be a start at least. Later, when they'd saved and had a child, then she would insist on a move and a good school. She could wait. She insisted, however, she have her way with the furnishings, telling Tom that after all she was used to nice things at the doctor's house and had good taste. He gave in for the sake of peace and quiet.

Now she stood before the long mirror in her bedroom and looked at her reflection. Her wedding dress was of the palest ivory satin, scalloped around the hem of the skirt. On her head, covering her riotous raven black hair, held in place with tortoiseshell combs, was a short veil, with artificial flowers in a crown to keep it in place. She was to carry a small posy of cream and peach-coloured roses.

She was pleased at the pretty picture she made, but couldn't stem a feeling of trepidation about becoming a wife. She'd let Tom kiss and fondle her during their courtship because she thought she'd lose him if she didn't, but she hadn't enjoyed these moments of intimacy very much. She was ignorant about her marital duties, for Jessy had not taken her aside to explain them, and she wondered what would happen tonight . . . But as she smoothed her dress and twirled around she resolved to put aside these worrying thoughts and enjoy the day ahead.

As Tom dressed for his wedding, he was already regretting the haste with which it was taking place, but he'd been so devastated when Lily confirmed there was no future for them, he'd rushed headlong into it. Now it was too late. Anyway, he thought dispiritedly, it was time to get on with his life. Today would be a new beginning.

After the wedding ceremony, the bride walked nervously from the registrar's office clutching her posy of roses in one hand, her new husband's arm with the other.

They were immediately surrounded by family and friends offering their congratulations. Mary smiled shyly at Tom as they were showered with confetti.

Tom, dressed in a new navy suit, looked at her with an encouraging grin. 'Well, Mrs McCann, you look beautiful. In fact, I'd go so far as to say we make a very handsome couple.'

'Oh, go on,' Mary scolded, but was thrilled with the compliment.

As the small procession of guests followed them through the narrow dingy streets towards her mother's home in College Street, Mary tried to adjust to the fact that after the wedding breakfast, she would leave as a married woman, with a home of her own and a man to look after.

Her worries about her wedding night resurfaced briefly, and the thought of sharing a bed with a man loomed large in her mind as they entered her parents' house.

'God, I could kill a pint,' one of Tom's cronies said as he walked into the parlour. Looking around he exclaimed, 'My! This looks good.' Mary's mother Jessy had done her proud. The table was laden with sandwiches and sausage rolls, the sideboard covered with bottles of beer and milk stout.

Jessy had already discarded her hat and was putting on her

wraparound apron. 'Dig in, lads,' she called, on her way to the scullery.

The younger women gathered around the bride. 'You are lucky, Mary,' one of them twittered. 'That Tom McCann is such a fine catch . . . and so good-looking. I wouldn't kick him out of bed, I can tell you.'

Mary eventually made her way to the kitchen in search of her mother. To her relief, she found her alone.

'The food is lovely, Ma. Everyone's tucking in as if there's going to be a siege tomorrow.'

'Well, you know what men are, love. I expect the beer's moving too. Me, all I want is a nice cup of tea.' She bustled around filling the kettle and setting out the cups and saucers.

'Can I ask you something?' Mary was hesitant.

Jessy, catching the note in her daughter's voice, wiped her hands on her apron and with a concerned look on her face asked, 'What is it, child?'

Mary couldn't meet her mother's gaze. She felt a flush of embarrassment creep over her. 'About tonight. I don't know what to do.'

Jessy became flustered and began to fuss with a plate of sandwiches. 'There's more to marriage than bed. It's only a small part of it, more important to men than us women. You just have to put up with it.' She looked sternly at her daughter. 'You be a proper wife, mind. Your man has a good job, you're a lot better off than many round here. And remember this, Mary. A man who gets all his comfort in his own home won't go searching elsewhere for it.' With a shamed look she confided, 'I usually think about the shopping I've got to get when your father's performing. It makes the time pass quicker.' Picking up a plate of sandwiches, she walked briskly from the room.

'So here's my bride.'

Mary, startled, looked up.

Tom, his tie awry, walked towards her and, putting his arms around her, kissed her expertly on the mouth, at the same time placing his hand on her left breast, caressing it gently.

Mary pushed him away. 'Tom! Behave yourself!'

He pulled her roughly towards him. 'You've never objected before.'

'Yes, but that was in the dark when we were alone.'

He glared at her. 'You're my wife now, so don't come it. As from this morning, I have the right. And don't forget it.'

She watched his retreating figure with a sinking heart. She had tried to keep him at arm's length most of the time, and it hadn't always been easy. Tom was a passionate man, and tonight he would claim his right as a husband.

Her mouth suddenly went dry; she felt sick with nerves. Seeing a bottle of sherry on the side, with trembling fingers she filled a glass then drank the liquid down in one gulp before going into the other room.

It was dark when the last of the wedding guests took their leave. Mary lingered over her goodbyes to her parents, anxious to stay within the security of familiar surroundings as long as possible.

'Come along, Mrs McCann. Time we went home.' Tom took a firm grip on her arm and led her towards the door.

She looked apprehensively over her shoulder towards her mother. 'Good night, Ma, Pa. Thank you for a lovely do. See you tomorrow, perhaps.'

Putting the key into the lock of number 27, Chandos Street, Tom opened the door and lit the gas-lamp in the kitchen. It was warm inside, the embers still glowing from the fire he'd lit earlier in the day.

'Shall I put the kettle on?' asked Mary.

'No, darlin',' he answered, slurring his words. 'I'll just go to the privy then I reckon it's time for bed.' His gaze lingered on the soft curves of her breasts and he felt a stirring in his loins. 'Hurry up and get undressed,' he said huskily.

As she washed her face under the cold water of the scullery tap, Mary heard Tom curse as he stumbled over something in the dark. Taking a deep breath, she went upstairs to the bedroom.

Closing the curtains, she slipped out of her dress, hanging it carefully in the wardrobe. She pulled her nightdress over her head and climbed into bed, pulling the covers up to her neck. She closed her eyes tightly, as if to shut out the inevitable. Kissing and cuddling was one thing, but what was expected of her now?

She heard her husband's footsteps on the stairs, the handle turn as he entered the room. As he moved about, she closed her eyes even tighter to shut out the vision of him getting undressed. She felt him turn back the bedcovers, and tensed. The bed sagged as he climbed in beside her. She could scarcely breathe, she was so frightened.

'Come here, Mary,' Tom whispered softly as he drew her towards him. She could smell the beer on his breath, feel the stubble on his chin as he kissed her. His mouth covered hers, forcing her lips apart. She recoiled as his tongue slipped gently into her mouth. But he held her head firmly. For her there was no escape.

Tom could feel the rigidity of Mary's body. She was paralysed with fear. 'Relax, darlin', I'm only going to love you, not murder you. Relax.' He just held her, but as soon as he moved she was stiff in his arms. He stroked her gently, kissed her softly, encouraged her to let go, talking to her continuously, coaxing her, trying to reassure her. He softly caressed her bare breast, but as he suckled gently on the pink pinnacle, he heard a gasp of distaste from her lips.

Still fondling her, he tried to allay her fears. 'This is quite a natural thing between two people in love. This is how babies are made, after all.' He stroked her stomach, her legs, the inside of her thighs; he tried every way he knew to help her, to stir within her the fire of passion, to reach that inner core of her emotion, but to no avail. He knew he hurt her, when at last he entered her. But he'd tried to give her satisfaction. She just wasn't responsive. His passion spent, he lay beside her, his arms about her, murmuring words of love.

He lay wondering if Mary was suffering with wedding nerves. Perhaps it was just her innocence? Or could his new wife be frigid?

Mary lay stiff in his arms, listening to his steady breathing.

How could he sleep after the dirty, filthy things he'd done to her?

She felt violated.

She lay still, tears trickling down her cheeks. She could hear Tom's deep breathing as he slept beside her. She turned away from him and curled herself into a tight ball. *I want my mother*, she wept silently, then angrily brushed the tears away. If this was married life, she hated it.

'You have to put up with it,' Jessy had said. Well, if there was one thing she was sure of . . . she wouldn't.

The following morning, Mary woke early, looking around at the unfamiliar surroundings, wishing she was at home in her own bed, alone. She gazed at the motionless figure of Tom and wondered how he could sleep. She felt sore and her muscles ached. Was this what they called love?

Mary slipped out of bed quietly so as not to disturb Tom and quickly dressed. As she folded her nightdress, she was horrified to see it marked with bloodstains. It wasn't her time yet. She ran downstairs to the privy. There was just a smidgen of blood on the paper. She wondered if perhaps the excitement of the wedding had brought her period on early, but somehow she didn't think so. Last night in bed, Tom had hurt her. Maybe that was the cause.

Returning to the scullery, she washed her hands and face, put on her pinafore over her black skirt and set about clearing the ashes from the range, before re-lighting it, and then looked in the mirror over the mantelpiece, tilting her head from one side to the other. Quite what she expected, she didn't know. But she was surprised that she looked just the same.

Hearing footsteps above, she put the large brown kettle on the hob and went into the scullery to fetch a frying pan out of the cupboard. As she stood up, she felt Tom's arms around her waist. She froze at his touch.

'For heaven's sake, Mary, will you stop this? Every time I touch you, you are like a board. You didn't do this when we were courting. You let me caress you then. For goodness sake, I'm not going to hurt you, woman.'

She spun round. 'You hurt me last night.'

'I'm sorry, darlin'. It was because you were a virgin. Last night was your first time, you'll soon get used to it. Tonight will be better, you'll see.'

Putting her hand to her throat, she retorted, 'You're not doing it again to me.'

Tom looked at her in dismay. 'What are you talking about?'

'I don't want you to touch me like that, it's not decent.'

The sudden anger that was reflected in his eyes frightened her.

'Now you listen to me. Marriage is more than a kiss and a cuddle. I tried my best to help you last night but you wouldn't relax. I won't have this nonsense, Mary. You are my wife. And by God, you'll be a real wife to me, with or without my help. It's up to you. Now get my breakfast.'

Tom was seething as he sat at the table. How ironic, he thought. Tom McCann, the successful lover of countless women, marries a wife who is frigid. Was this some kind of retribution? He remembered the passion shared with Lily, and his heart was heavy.

As she let the doctor out of the front door, Lily was trembling. He had been thorough in his examination of Fred. Putting his stethoscope away, he looked across the bed at Lily and nodded towards the door. 'Let's go downstairs, my dear.' Once they were alone, he took hold of her hand. 'I'm sorry, but your man has TB. It's only a matter of time.'

She let the doctor out of the house and lowered herself into a chair. Fred was dying. Tears filled her eyes. Dear Fred, who had been so good to her. She couldn't bear the thought of his leaving her for ever. Not this way.

'Lily!'

Looking up at the sound of his voice, she swiftly wiped away her tears. 'Coming.'

As she walked into the room, Fred looked at her intently. Poor Lily. He knew he was on his last legs and now so did she. This last spell in prison had done for him. The prison doctor had gruffly told him the bad news, but he'd hoped that once at home, he might improve. What could he do for Lily now? At least with her singing she was making enough money to keep her when he wasn't around, but who would watch out for her safety? He would have a word with Knocker. 'Could I have a cup of weak tea, love?' was all he said.

She kissed his cheek. 'Of course. Do you want me to stay in tonight? I can easily tell Sandy you're not well.'

He shook his head. 'No, you go, dear, I'll be fine. But if you see Knocker Jones, ask him to come round and see me, will you?'

She nodded her assent.

As she left, Fred had a sudden spell of coughing which wracked his whole body. When it was over, his handkerchief had the telltale bloodstains all over it. He felt saddened that he would not be around for much longer. The time here with Lily had been the happiest in his life and he thanked God for it. At least his last days would be spent with her and in comfort. It would have been far worse in prison. She looked after him so well. She was a good girl and he loved her dearly.

There was a subdued air in The Sailor's Return that night as Lily passed on the message and told Sandy, Declan and Knocker the doctor's verdict.

'Poor bugger,' said Knocker. 'I had no idea. Tom said he looked unwell when he saw him, but I put it down to his spell inside.'

'Is there anything we can do?' asked Declan.

Lily tearfully shook her head. 'He says he wants me to make him a bed in the kitchen; he hates being alone upstairs. If you want to come and see him, he'd be pleased.'

'I'll bring a couple of bottles of the black stuff,' said Declan. 'That will help him a bit. And I'll give you a hand to move the bed.'

Left alone with Sandy, Lily looked at him in despair. 'What will I do without him?'

'You will have to get on with your life, my darling. Everyone faces the loss of a loved one at some time or another. The pain is great for a while, but in time you learn to live with it. You've got to.'

'I can't sing tonight, Sandy.'

'Of course you can't. You go home to Fred.' He put his arm around her shoulders. 'If things get too unbearable, you know where I live.'

'Thanks. You're a good friend.'

The following day, with a forced air of gaiety, Lily moved Fred's bed downstairs with Declan's help. They rearranged the room to make Fred as comfortable as possible. Declan produced a bottle of Guinness and proceeded in his own way to cheer the invalid though, truth to tell, Declan was very shocked when he saw how Fred had deteriorated. It was only a matter of weeks since the man had been let out of prison.

Knocker Jones called, bringing some grapes and a paper for Fred to catch up on the news. He settled himself beside his friend. 'You wanted to see me, me old mucker.'

'I did.' Lily was upstairs, so Fred lowered his voice. 'I don't have much longer for this world, Knocker. Lily is earning, thank God, but I need to know someone is keeping an eye out for her. Will you do this for me? I'll go to my Maker a happier man if I know you're looking out for her.'

'Course I will. You don't have to worry about her, Fred.' He smiled broadly. 'That girl has more friends than you and me put together. We'll all keep an eye out for her, never you fear.'

When Tom was told of Fred's impending demise, he was saddened. He'd quite liked the man and had he not been the lover of Lily, they might have got to know one another better. But he was frustrated beyond measure. Soon Lily would be free, and now he was a married man.

And he wasn't happy. Not only was Mary a very reluctant partner in bed, but she was obsessed with moving up in the world, forever pushing him to better himself. It had led to many rows during their short marriage. They'd had a particularly bitter one that morning.

'I don't understand you, Tom,' she'd expostulated. 'You're a fine worker, and you hate your foreman. Haven't you ever thought of going after the man's job?'

He looked at her as if she'd gone mad. 'I don't want his job. I'm happy doing my own.'

'You have no ambition,' she blazed at him. 'If you want to get on in the world, you must have ambition.'

'It seems to me,' he said sarcastically, 'that you have enough for both of us!'

She glared at him, her mouth narrowing with anger. 'What if we have children? I would want them to go to a decent school, live in a better home than this.' She looked scornfully around her.

This was too much. Tom's temper exploded. 'How dare you! It is better furnished than your parents' place, so it is, and yet still you complain. And as for children – how do you think you'll ever get pregnant? You have to spread your legs first.'

Mary's face was white. 'Trust you to bring everything down to sex. You're sex mad.'

'Chance would be a fine thing. We've been married for two months now. Either you buck your ideas up about being a wife, or I'll go and find a woman who's willing!' This threat silenced Mary at last.

'Talk to your mother, or someone,' he advised. 'I'll not be patient for ever.' He stormed out of the house.

Sandy was on his way to Lily's house. During these past three months since Fred's illness had been diagnosed Lily had put on a brave face and performed as usual, though her heart wasn't in it. He knew she needed the money to take care of herself and Fred. But for the past week Fred had been so poorly, she'd stayed at home during the evening.

Seeing the front door ajar, Sandy hesitated, but then he realised he could hear the sound of someone sobbing. Putting out his hand, he slowly pushed the door open.

In the kitchen he could see the still form of Fred Bates in his chair by the fire, his arm hanging limply from his shoulder. On the floor beside him was Lily, her arms around her man.

Sandy stood silent for a moment, loath to encroach upon her grief, yet knowing he had to do something. Stepping softly towards her, he called her name, then gently put his hand on her shoulder.

She looked up at him, her face swollen with crying, her eyes red raw. The pain etched on her face reminded him of a wounded animal, trapped in a snare.

'He's gone. My poor Fred's gone.' She clutched at the body and shook him as if trying to instil life into the inert form. 'Don't leave me, Fred,' she begged. 'Please don't leave me.'

Sandy eased her away from the dead man, firmly but gently. She sobbed in his arms. 'He didn't deserve to die like this. He was worth better.' She clung to Sandy. 'What am I going to do without him?'

He led her to a chair. 'I'll make you a cup of tea, then I'll send someone to the funeral directors.' He watched her closely, her distraught state giving him grave concern.

He sent for the doctor, who gave Lily smelling salts and a mild sedative, then arranged for the body to be removed. Sandy would never forget the anguish on Lily's face as Fred was taken away.

He sat beside her, and comforted her. 'I'll stay here with you if you like, dearie.'

'Oh please do, Sandy. I couldn't bear to be alone.'

'No, of course not. I'll stay with you as long as you need me. Do you want to remain here or go to my place?'

'I'll stay here, I think, because if I walk out now, I doubt if I could ever come back.'

The funeral was a sad affair. There was a heavy frost that morning and the trees, bereft of their leaves, stood like silent sentinels guarding the graves as the simple casket was lowered into the ground. The few mourners stood around watching, their breath hanging on the crisp air.

Lily, clinging to Sandy's arm on one side and Declan's on the other, stood beside the grave. There was a quiet dignity about her as she threw a handful of earth into the deep cavern.

'Ashes to ashes. Dust to dust,' intoned the vicar.

Later, alone at the grave, Lily looked down at the coffin. 'You were a good man, Fred, and I loved you,' she whispered. Then, turning away, she walked towards the cemetery gates.

To her surprise, Tom was waiting for her nearby. He stepped forward and took her arm. They walked together. 'I'm sorry for your loss, Lily. I know how much he meant to you.'

The smile barely touched the corners of her mouth. 'Thank you. He was a good man, you know.'

'He must have been, darlin', for you to have stayed with him. I'm just sorry he was taken so soon. If there's anything I can ever do, you've only to ask.'

'Thank you. How are you, Tom? How's your wife?' There was no bitterness in her voice. Her interest was genuine.

'She's fine.'

'I really hope you're happy, Tom.'

How could he burden her with his troubles on such a day? 'Yes, Lily, I am. Mary is pregnant.'

Her voice faltered for just a second. 'That's wonderful news. Congratulations.' They'd reached the gates and Sandy stepped forward.

'Ready to go home, dearie?'

'I need a very stiff drink, Sandy. Medicinal purposes, you know.'

'Oh, like that, is it? Then come with me. I have half a bottle in a drawer.'

Later, two figures holding on to each other for support arrived unsteadily at Lily's house. She fumbled with the key. As the door opened, they both fell in, a tangled mess of limbs as they rolled on the floor, helpless with laughter. As Lily eventually managed to pick herself up, she looked at Sandy still sprawled out. With great difficulty and a lot of giggling, she hoisted him onto the sofa. Throwing a blanket over him, she said, 'You'd better sleep there, you old fart.'

'Such unkind words,' slurred Sandy. 'If I spend the night on your sofa, your reputation will be in ribbons, dearie.'

They both laughed hysterically at the idea. Lily looked towards the stairs and shook her head. There was no way she'd be able to climb those. She'd sleep in Fred's chair by the unlit fire.

She had known that the only way to cope with this terrible day was to get roaring drunk. Wrapping herself in Fred's blanket, she curled up, breathing in the scent of him as she did so. It brought her a strange kind of comfort.

'Good night, Fred,' she whispered. 'God bless you.'

Chapter Thirteen

Lily pushed open the door of The Sailor's Return and looked around, thankful that it was quiet. It was now two weeks since Fred's funeral and she couldn't stay a minute longer on her own in the empty house. It was too full of painful memories.

Walking up to the bar, she asked for a small glass of beer. Declan poured one for her and passing it over the counter said, 'It's on the house, Lily. You all right?'

She looked at him, her face drawn. 'Frankly, I feel buggered.'

'It's to be expected, girl. Anything I can do?'

Shaking her head she said, 'No, thanks. I just have to work my way through it.' She wandered slowly over to a table in the corner and sat down.

Sandy closed the lid of the piano. His heart went out to Lily when he saw her disconsolate air. He'd become very fond of his protégée, and was concerned for her. Walking over to the table, he sat beside her and looked at her drawn face and red-rimmed eyes. 'Hello, you old tart,' he said fondly. 'I wondered when you'd surface. I've missed you.' It had been a week now since he'd returned to his own house, at Lily's insistence.

She smiled at him. 'You're probably the only one who has.'

'Rubbish! You'd be surprised at the number of friends you have, dearie.'

With a deep sigh she said, 'I miss him so much, Sandy. He was so kind. I know he got into trouble again, but he only did it for me. He tried so hard to take care of me.' She sniffed loudly.

Putting an arm around her shoulders he said, 'I know. But he wouldn't want you to fret so for him. You must pick yourself up, my dear. Go on with your life. The best thing is work.'

'I don't think I can.'

'You must. Look, the one thing that helped Fred in his last days was the fact that he'd left you with a roof over your head and that you were capable of earning a living – could keep yourself. You can't let him down, he had such faith in you. Besides, if you're busy, you don't have time to think. Anyway, girl, you've got to make a living. You won't last long on thin air.'

Lily knew this to be true. She was now down to her last pound note. Taking a deep breath she said, 'You're right, of course. Give me a couple of days.'

'Saturday night, here, where you're among friends. What better place to start?'

Various customers approached her, shyly, offering their condolences on her loss, and she knew that Sandy was right. It was time to start again.

Just a few weeks before Christmas, the bar was festooned with paper chains and holly. The patrons were in a festive mood, singing along to the carols, led by Lily. She'd picked herself up and started work again, but when she went home at night, the empty house was almost more than she could bear.

Amy was sitting at the bar with one of her punters, when a big Dutch seaman began to pester her. The man with her was getting annoyed and it was obvious that there was going to be trouble.

'You come with me,' the Dutchman insisted. 'I like you. I pay you more than him.'

'Bugger off!' Amy told him. 'I'm with a friend.'

He leered at her. 'He's not a man.' He thumped his own chest. 'I am a man. I have big dick. Women like big dick.'

'Go and shove it somewhere else,' retorted Amy.

The big man made to grab at her arm, as Declan leapt over the counter, shillelagh clasped in his hand. 'Get off her, you bastard! I'm not having any trouble in here.' He dragged the seaman away and hustled him towards the door.

Looking over his shoulder, the foreigner glared at Amy. In a harsh voice full of menace he said, 'I'll have you one day, you bitch.'

The bar had been hushed throughout the disagreement, but now that the danger had been removed, the hubbub began again and Lily started to sing 'Daisy, Daisy, Give Me Your Answer Do'. Looking over at Amy, she was concerned when she saw how pale she looked.

Later, Amy told her the foreign seaman was known among the girls as Dutchy. 'No one will go with him, Lily. He's a sick bastard. He cut one of the girls one night. He puts the fear of God in me.' Her fingers trembled when she lifted her glass to her mouth.

Thinking there might be more trouble, Amy's punter had made his excuses and left. Lily didn't want her friend walking home alone and offered to walk with her. 'Look, why don't you come back with me tonight?' she suggested. 'I could do with the company.'

With a look of relief, Amy readily agreed.

They stepped outside to find the streets swathed in thick fog. 'Blimey, where did this come from?' asked Amy.

'One of the deep-sea divers told me earlier that it was forecast. Here, hold my arm.'

As they made their way around the narrow streets, past back alleys, they listened to the haunting cry of the foghorn, giving an eerie feel to the night. A cat suddenly screeched in a side alley, making them jump.

'I hate the fog,' complained Amy. 'Give me a nice moon any night. I like to be able to see where I'm going.'

Rounding a corner, they both collided with a sailor and the two women cried out in fright. The man mumbled his apologies. As he walked off Amy and Lily started to giggle. 'Couple of stupid schoolgirls afraid of the dark,' joked Lily. But she felt nervous and tense and longed to be home.

Turning into Orchard Lane, she began to relax. 'Nearly there,' she said, but her words were cut short as Dutchy loomed out of the fog.

'Hello, girls.' His deep, guttural voice startled them; his huge frame blocked their path.

'What do you want?' asked Lily.

Taking out a cigarette and using his coat as a shelter, Dutchy lit it then offered the packet to Amy. She shook her head.

Lily could tell that he enjoyed their terror. She could see their fear excited him. She waited, her limbs trembling.

Ignoring Lily he said to Amy, 'You come with me. No need to stay out in the cold and damp. We'll go to a little hotel and have some fun.'

Amy shook her head violently. 'No, thanks. I'm going home.'

Grabbing her arm Dutchy said, 'Don't lie to me, bitch. My money's as good as anybody else's.' He tried to drag her away, but Lily started frantically to beat him off.

'You leave her alone, you bastard. She ain't going nowhere!'

With one swift movement, Dutchy swiped Lily with his arm, knocking her sideways. She hit her head against the wall and was momentarily stunned by the blow, unable to move.

Amy was screaming and struggling. She was no match for the big man, yet like an eel she struggled hard enough to make him lose his grip. As she escaped his clutches, she ran to Lily and clung to her, calling loudly for help as she did so.

Cursing, Dutchy reached for Amy once again. 'Come here, you little tramp or I'll cut you. No one will want you then.' He pulled out a knife from his belt and held it towards her.

Amy's face went white. She stood shaking, her voice stilled.

Lily, still dazed, was only dimly aware of what was happening. She shook her head, trying to clear her thoughts. Then she pushed her friend behind her and bravely faced the Dutchman, trying not to show her fear. 'She's not lying,' she told him. 'She's going home. Finished for the night.'

An evil grin spread across Dutchy's features. He played with the knife. The women's gaze was glued to the blade.

Waiting – terrified at what he was going to do next.

He put the point of the knife against Lily's throat. She didn't move or speak.

'Get out of my way, whore. I want the other one. Now move.'

Lily could feel her legs trembling. The point of the knife pricked into her flesh and she felt a trickle of blood. Christ! she thought, I'm going to die.

Suddenly from behind Dutchy, a figure emerged out of the fog and hauled the seaman away, sending him sprawling.

Lily almost collapsed with relief and clutched at Amy as she watched the two men struggling on the ground. As they got to their feet and exchanged blows, the knife came scudding across the pavement and Lily picked it up, holding it, ready to fend off any attacker.

The stranger kneed Dutchy in the groin. As he doubled over with pain, his assailant brought up his knee under the seaman's chin. Dutchy cried out and slowly crumpled to a heap on the ground. As a finale, their rescuer kicked him viciously several times with his metal-tipped boots.

'You all right, mate?' asked Lily, running over to him. And when he looked up: 'You!' she cried in surprise.

Tom McCann picked up his cap and brushed the dirt from his clothes. He grinned at Lily. 'Who were you expecting, the Archangel Gabriel?'

Amy looked down at the still figure. 'You haven't done for him, have you?'

Shaking his head Tom said, 'No, he's just knocked out, but you'd better scarper before he wakes up. Come on, I'll walk you home.'

'Amy's coming to my place, just up the road.'

'I know where it is, Lily. I've been there before, if you remember.'

Lily didn't want to remember. Fred's death was still too raw; she couldn't cope with her guilt. 'How did you happen to come along this way?' she asked.

'I popped in to see Declan,' explained Tom. 'He told me of the bit of trouble in the pub and that you two had left together, so I thought I'd better see if you got home safely.'

'Thanks, Tom,' said Amy, still shaken by the experience. 'I don't know what would have happened if you hadn't shown up.'

There was bitterness in Tom's voice as he said, 'Best not dwell on what might have been in this life. It can destroy you.'

They arrived at the door. Lily put her key in the lock, ushered Amy inside and turning to Tom said, 'Thanks. I don't know what else to say.'

'You could invite me in,' he said without hesitation, looking at her with an intensity that seared her soul.

Shaking her head, Lily said, 'No, Tom, I don't think so. But again, thanks. Take care going home. Your wife will be worried about you out in this.' She walked into the house and closed the door.

She took a half-bottle of gin out of the cupboard and poured two stiff measures. Handing one to her friend she said, 'Here. This will calm your nerves.'

Amy, hands still shaking from the ordeal, took the glass. 'Christ, Lily, I thought we'd had it tonight.'

Nodding, Lily said, 'So did I.' She put her hand to her throat and touched the dried blood on her neck.

Seeing her gesture, Amy said, 'Oh my God! He cut you. Let me see.' After inspecting Lily's neck she went into the scullery and came back with a damp cloth and washed the blood away. 'You were lucky, my girl. It's only a scratch. Thank goodness Tom came along.' Without looking at Lily, she added, 'He still loves you, you know.'

'Bloody lot of good that is. He's married and his wife's pregnant!'

'Oh Lily, why does life have to be so complicated?' Amy sat back in the chair and lit a cigarette. 'I tell you, if I could meet a decent man with a bit of money, I'd take him. Get off the streets.'

Lily immediately thought of Vittorio. She had a chance with a rich man. Why did she keep turning him down? she wondered. She could live in the lap of luxury. Have nice clothes, be spoilt. And she wouldn't have to come home to an empty house every night.

If Tom was free it would be different. But the loneliness was crucifying her and she didn't know how much longer she could stand it.

Christmas had come and gone. Lily had spent Christmas Day at The Sailor's Return, with Sandy, Declan and his wife. The pub had closed after the lunch-time session, which had been a pretty boozy affair. Lily remembered the Christmas turkey and Christmas pudding, but not too much after that. This way she shut out the memories of the previous year's festival and Fred. This year she couldn't face going to midnight mass.

She was barely making enough money to survive. January and February were notoriously bad months. People who had any money were suffering after the Christmas spending. The ships were in dry dock for their winter overhaul, so the pubs were quieter. Money was tight.

Lily was depressed, wondering where her life was going. Amy was her only consolation. That day, she arrived bearing bad news.

'Rachel is in hospital.'

'What happened?' asked Lily.

'She's got pneumonia.'

Lily was shaken. 'Where is she?'

'At the South Hants Hospital. I only heard today. Old man Abraham told me.'

'I'm going to see her,' said Lily.

'Let me know how she is,' said Amy, 'and tell her I'll be in tomorrow.'

Sitting in the tram on the way to the South Hants Hospital at visiting time, Lily's thoughts were full of her days in The Ditches. Of the time Rachel discovered she'd been sleeping rough and took her in. Of the warmth and unspoken love she'd received from the elderly Jewess.

As she walked through the stark hospital corridors, which smelled of ether, Lily was filled with foreboding. 'Please God let her be all right,' she prayed beneath her breath.

The ward sister showed her to the bed. 'Don't stay too long, dear. She gets tired quickly.'

Quietly pulling up a chair, Lily sat beside the bed and looked at the sleeping figure. Tears welled in her eyes when she studied the pale hollowed face of Rachel Cohen.

Catching hold of the older woman's hand, she whispered, 'Hello, Rachel. It's me, Lily.'

For a moment there was no response, then the eyelids fluttered open. 'Lily, is that you?'

Patting her friend's hand she answered, 'Do you think they could keep me away?' She leaned forward and kissed her cheek. 'I don't know, I can't leave you alone for five minutes.'

The patient smiled. 'I am so much trouble.'

Lily smoothed her forehead. 'What can I do for you, darling?'

'Just sit with me, my dear. Let me look at your pretty face. Hold your hand.'

She did so, for the rest of the afternoon.

Rachel dozed off and on, but every time she opened her eyes and saw Lily, she would clasp her hand tighter and smile. Once she softly said, 'I loved you like my own daughter.'

'And you were a better mother to me than my own. You are my Yiddisher momma and I love you very much.'

When Rachel was sleeping peacefully, Lily went to the Matron. 'Can you tell me, is Mrs Cohen going to get better?'

The Matron smiled but asked, 'Are you a relative?'

'I'm her adopted daughter.'

'Sit down, my dear. Your mother had influenza and she wasn't taking proper care of herself, thus it developed into pneumonia. But she's a tough old woman. With rest and proper care, she'll get back to normal.'

'I see. She's not going to die, is she?'

Lily looked so stricken the Matron put a hand on her arm. 'I wouldn't think so for one moment.'

Sitting once again by the bed, Lily looked around the ward. It was clean but there was little comfort, with the rows of iron bedsteads and a strong smell of disinfectant. Tomorrow, she'd bring some flowers and perhaps a bright cover for the bed. Try and make it look a bit more homely.

For the next three weeks, Lily visited Rachel every day and

was relieved that, indeed, her condition did improve.

Today, she was sitting up against the pillows looking quite chirpy when Lily arrived.

'Hello, Lily dear. Am I not a miracle? The Rabbi says that God doesn't want me yet.'

'He's been to see you?'

'Of course.'

'And what about Manny? He's not been. At least, I've not seen him.' Lily hadn't questioned Rachel about her son until today.

The old spark was back. 'Why should he? He doesn't know. I have no son, so how can he be told? When I'm dead will be soon enough. Then . . .' She shrugged. 'Why should I care? Come and give a hug to a foolish old Jewish woman.'

She sat chewing on the grapes Lily had brought with her. Putting another in her mouth Rachel gave a mischievous smile. 'Good for the bowels.'

They both giggled.

'Soon I can leave here,' she announced suddenly.

'You can't live on your own. You need someone to care for you.'

Patting Lily's hand Rachel said, 'Don't have a panic. I'm going to stay in a nice recovery home until I'm really well. If they are any good, maybe I'll stay there.'

'Where?' asked Lily with some concern.

'There's one in The Avenue. It's Jewish, so the food will be kosher. It's full of posh people so, who knows, maybe I'll open a stall.'

'Rachel!' Lily was appalled.

With a wicked cackle she said, 'Don't be silly, my dear. I'm joking. What do you think I'm going to do? Arrive with suitcases full of second-hand clothes? Maybe I'll meet a nice Jewish man there. I reckon I've got a few miles left in me yet.'

Lily gave a sigh of relief. But then with a frown she asked, 'What about the shop in The Ditches? It's been closed for weeks.'

'It's all right, I've got a few bob put by. This time of year, business ain't so good. Think of the money I'm saving on lighting and heating.'

'What heating?' Lily demanded.

'I've got a small electric fire.'

'You never used it when I worked for you.'

Rachel gave a sly grin. 'Why would you want it? Haven't you got young blood racing round your veins?'

'I don't know about racing. There were times I was sure it was frozen solid.'

'Rubbish.' Rachel's eyes twinkled with amusement. 'How do you think I saved my few bob – by keeping you warm? Besides, you moved quicker when you were cold.'

'You wicked old woman.'

Rachel clasped her chest dramatically. 'That's no way to speak to a sick woman. What a girl. I could be dying here in my hospital bed.'

Lily's laughter echoed around the ward, bringing a shush and a frown from the Matron.

Nodding in her direction, Rachel whispered sagely, 'She don't know that laughter is as good a cure as an enema.'

Lily knew then that her beloved friend was getting better.

Putting her hand over Lily's, Rachel asked, 'And you, my dear? How are things with you?'

'Not so good.' Lily admitted reluctantly. 'Money is scarce.' She paused. 'There is a way round it if I want to take it.'

Rachel's eyes narrowed. 'Why do I get the feeling I'm not going to like what you're going to say?'

'I'm thinking of working for The Maltese. Singing in his club.'

'You don't have the clothes for it,' snapped Rachel.

'He'll buy them for me. He's going to pay me a good wage, so I'll be making money. He's the only one doing any business at the moment.'

Rachel's gaze held Lily's. 'And what price do you have to pay for the privilege?'

Lily felt the flush of embarrassment in her cheeks.

'Well?'

'I will be his mistress.' Her face felt warm but the blood in her veins ran cold as she looked at her friend, waiting for her reaction.

Rachel's voice remained calm. 'And why are you doing

this, Lily? Tell me, because I really want to understand. Don't bullshit me. I want the truth.'

The flush of Lily's cheeks had faded. Her face was white and pinched. 'I can't go on alone, struggling. I need someone to take care of me for a change. It's not the clothes and jewellery he promised me, or the good life, although that would be a nice change. I need someone to lean on. To comfort me. To care about me. Can you understand?'

With a shrug Rachel said, 'You think an old Jewish woman doesn't want the same things? Sure, I understand. But with Vittorio Teglia? *Oy vey!* That I don't want . . . Anyway, I should be so lucky he'd look my way.' She gazed with affection at Lily. 'Yes, this man is rich and attractive, but he's only one step ahead of the law.'

'So he's a businessman. He runs a brothel.' Lily leapt to his defence.

'I know that!' Rachel's eyes flashed with anger. 'You say that as if I don't know already. My Hymie spent enough money there on prostitutes.'

Lily gasped with shock. 'I didn't know.'

'When I found out, I made him sleep in another room. You think I wanted him in my bed, maybe give me some disease?' She frowned. 'You want to be part of this world, Lily?'

Shaking her head, Lily tried to explain. 'Vittorio can be charming, kind. We laugh a lot together. I really like him. No one is all bad, Rachel.'

'Have you really thought it through? Isn't there an alternative?'

Lily laughed bitterly. 'Oh yes. I could go back on the game! I tried it once, but I hated it.'

Rachel was shattered. Taking Lily into her arms, she said, 'Oh, my dear. I'm so sorry, I didn't know. Was it when you ran away?'

Lily nodded.

'Oh my God. I take the blame for that. It was all because of Manny.'

Lily eased away from Rachel's hold. 'That wasn't anyone's fault. I made the decision to go and I had to eat.'

161

'Let me help you financially,' pleaded Rachel.

Lily shook her head.

'What about your house?' asked Rachel. 'You got a house, why don't you take in lodgers? Then you wouldn't be lonely.'

'No, it isn't the same. There would be people there, and I'd make some money, but I need more than that. I want to feel a man's arms about me. Someone to hold me when I'm sad. To care how I feel. No, my dear. I'm seriously thinking of accepting Vittorio's offer. I just need a little more time to make up my mind, that's all.' She kissed Rachel's cheek. 'I'll come and see you next week in the home of recovery.'

'Take care, my child,' whispered Rachel as she watched Lily walk down the ward towards the exit.

It seemed like fate that the one person Lily should meet on her way home was Vittorio. With her eyes downcast, she didn't see him approach until he said, 'Hello, Lily. What's so interesting about the pavement that you study it so carefully?'

She looked up into his smiling eyes, but the despondency she was still feeling tempered her response. 'Hello.'

He frowned. 'Something's troubling you. Can I help?'

She shook her head.

Taking hold of her arm, he said, 'Come along. This won't do at all. You're coming with me.'

'Where are we going?' she protested. 'You can't just drag me off.'

'You'll see,' he said as he hailed a taxi. 'Dolphin Hotel please, driver.'

He didn't make conversation on the journey, just held her hand, which to Lily was strangely comforting. When they arrived at their destination, he led her into the dining room and ordered tea and cakes for two.

Once the waiter had served them he asked softly, 'Now you must tell me what's the matter. I don't think I have ever seen you like this. Where is the fire in you that usually burns so brightly?'

She gave a wry smile. 'I suppose I forgot to light it today.'

As she poured the tea he said, 'You need someone to take

care of you, Lily, my dear. You're too young and lovely to be alone. You need a man in your life.'

She gave him a sardonic look.

'No, I don't mean like that. Well, not entirely. Life is for sharing. We all need someone to share our joys, our sorrows and to laugh with. People are not meant to live alone.'

'You do.'

His slow smile crinkled his mouth. 'Yes, but that is my choice.' His eyes twinkled. 'Mind you, I could be persuaded to change that . . . if you were to take up my offer.'

She looked at him, trying to fathom the man. Despite his kindness and his teasing manner, there was still that hint of danger in his background. It was both worrying and fascinating.

'But let's not go into that now,' he said. 'Let's just enjoy each other's company. Then I'll take you home.'

Later, Lily sat alone thinking about her afternoon with Vittorio. He'd been a wonderful companion. He had chivvied her out of her sombre mood and soon they were in hearty discussion about a number of different subjects. It had been stimulating and interesting. Yet again she had seen another side of this strange man.

When he'd left her at the door of her house, he kissed her cheek and said, 'Come and see me soon, Lily.'

He didn't try to pressurise her like Tom did. His was more like gentle persuasion. It was very tempting.

Chapter Fourteen

'What do you mean, you're not going to be singing round the pubs any more?' Sandy, sitting in Lily's living room, looked perplexed.

'Business is bad, you know that. And I'm fed up with my life! I've decided I need a change.' There was a look of defiance in her eyes.

'And how are you going to work such a miracle, I'd like to know?'

Taking a deep breath she said, 'I'm going to see Vittorio.'

Sandy choked on the tea he was drinking. 'You're *what?*'

'I'm going to take Vittorio up on his offer.'

'Are you mad?' Sandy was dumbfounded. He leaned forward and clasped her wrists. 'Tell me you're joking – having me on.'

Shaking her head Lily said, 'No, I'm deadly serious. I can't go on like this. We're scraping a living and I'm sick of being alone. I've tried to find work but no one will give me a job. If Tom was free it would be different, but without him, what does the future hold for me? Nothing. So why not take up his offer? What have I got to lose?'

Sandy stood up from his chair and threw his cigarette end into the embers of the fire. He turned to face her, his voice reverberating with anger. 'For God's sake, Lily, I can't believe you've taken leave of your senses like this! Do you know what you're letting yourself in for?'

'What do you mean?'

'Vittorio runs a brothel, for God's sake!'

'So? I'm not going to be a prostitute. I'm going to be his mistress.'

'You think that makes you any better than a whore?'

His cruel words, though true, infuriated her. 'Yes, it bloody well does. I'll be his woman. It's no worse than living with Fred.'

'You can talk of Fred in the same breath as that bastard? You should be ashamed!' Seeing the stricken expression on her face, Sandy resumed his seat. In a calmer voice he said, 'Well, before you do, perhaps you should know a few things about the Club Valletta.' He leaned back in the chair. 'It looks very respectable from the outside. The front part is a bar and dining room, all very legal, but behind closed doors there's gambling and prostitution.'

'So, what makes it so different from many other places?'

'Vittorio! He provides many perverted services. Did you know the Chief Constable likes young boys, for instance?'

Lily's eyes widened with surprise.

'Oh yes. I've known a few that have been used there. Kids that are starving – and are pretty. You have to be good-looking, of course.'

Lily leapt to Vittorio's defence. 'For goodness sake, Sandy – we all know these boys are on the streets. At least at the club they'll be taken care of.'

'What are you saying?' asked Sandy angrily. 'That they'll be raped in comfort?'

'Don't be ridiculous. They go there willingly – it isn't rape. In the docks some of them are attacked by these perverts and not paid at all. At least in the club they'll get their money and can at least feed themselves!'

Sandy refused to be drawn further into an argument. 'The Maltese is into all sorts of rackets. Not only gambling, but loan-sharking, and receiving stolen goods off the liners. He's pretty thick with a few Chief Stewards.' He frowned. 'He'll never go short of good meat and booze.'

Lily glared at him. 'So he's a good businessman,' she shrugged. 'Look, I've seen lots of dodgy stuff come in and out of The Sailor's Return. What's the difference?'

'The difference is The Maltese. He's a nasty piece of work. You go to him, you'll never be free again. He likes to control: what's his is his. Once inside his net, you can struggle as much as you like, but you belong to him. He'll own you. That's scary.'

'I can take care of myself.'

'Lily, oh Lily,' he said sadly. 'You'll be completely out of your depth. To control a few drunks in a bar is one thing. No one controls The Maltese. *No one.*' He got up. 'If you go to him, what will you do with this house?'

'Keep it. It will give me somewhere to come when I want some peace and quiet.'

Sandy looked at her with an earnest expression. 'Please don't do this.' He kissed her on the forehead, then quietly left.

Alone, Lily mulled over the things that Sandy had told her. She had no doubt they were true. But as Vittorio's mistress, they need not be a part of her life. She could carry on singing, which she loved to do. At least she would be in full employment, and despite what Sandy had said, she could save her money and eventually leave, if she wanted to.

She gazed around the comfortable home. Despite being a shabby abode, it did have such a warm and cosy feel to it. But what good was that when there was no one with whom to share it? The only man she wanted was Tom, but he was married and soon to be a father. Vittorio had offered to take care of her. She sighed. How nice that must be, to have someone to lean on, to share your troubles, take away the worries. Vittorio was such a strong person. With him she would never have to struggle again. It wasn't the promise of new clothes and the good life that drew her to him. It was the thought of the future, being alone, which terrified her.

She looked into the mirror over the fireplace. She was still young, just eighteen, but without a steady job she wouldn't survive, and she'd rather be dead than go back on the streets – suffer the same degradation as before. No, she couldn't face that again. She yearned to be cared for and Vittorio had offered to do so. There seemed to be no alternative. And at least she wouldn't be lonely.

George Coleman, standing outside the club entrance, was very surprised to see Lily walking towards him that evening.

He knew who she was, of course, from the time he'd accompanied his boss to the crummy pub where the girl was singing. He could see the attraction she held for Mr Vittorio. She walked with a cocky kind of air about her. Head held high – as if she owned the world. He'd thought she put over a song very well and had a good voice and, of course, she was a very pretty girl.

She stopped beside him. 'Hello,' she said with a sweet smile. 'I want to see Vittorio, please. Will you tell him I'm here? Lily Pickford is the name.'

He hid a smile. Cheeky madam. 'You'd better come inside.' He led the way.

Lily looked at her surroundings with some surprise. This might be a brothel, she thought, but the place had class. There was a small entrance hall lit by a crystal chandelier, a good carpet on the floor and flowers, tastefully arranged. She followed George through into the large dining room and seated herself on a plush chair.

The well-stocked bar was in one corner of the room. There were many tables made up to sit various numbers, set out with pristine linen tablecloths with matching napkins and expensive cutlery. In the centre of each table was a small but beautifully arranged posy of flowers. At the far end of the room was a small stage. This she looked at with particular interest.

If this was to be where she performed, it certainly was very different from the shabby bars in the different pubs she was used to. Surrounded by such opulence she suddenly felt the clothes she was wearing were cheap, and she began to feel uncertain about the wisdom of coming here. She was ready to take flight when George walked back into the room.

'Mr Vittorio will see you now, Miss Lily.'

She liked that – Miss Lily. 'Thank you,' she said, and followed the man up the richly carpeted stairs to the first floor.

Vittorio was seated behind a dark carved mahogany desk, which was covered with business papers, and a telephone. In front of the desk was a high-backed chair.

As she entered the room, he said, 'Thank you, George.

That will be all.' He placed his hands together, his fingertips beneath his chin and looked at her with a piercing gaze from his deep-brown eyes and smiled. 'Well, well. This is a pleasant surprise, Lily. What can I do for you?'

Looking around, she said cheekily, 'So this is the lion's den, is it?'

He chuckled. 'Is that how you see me? A lion in its den?'

'To be honest, Vittorio, I'm not at all sure how I see you!'

'I like the idea of being a man of mystery.' His voice was deep and mellifluous. 'Have you perhaps come to find out for yourself – at last?' His eyebrows arched in question.

'Maybe.'

'Then perhaps you'd better sit down.' He indicated the chair opposite him.

She sat and looked at The Maltese. There was no doubt about it, he fascinated her. But what it was about him that did so was a mystery to her. She thought if he was dressed differently, he'd be a bit like Rudolph Valentino. She grinned across at him, her smile lighting up her eyes. 'You made me a proposition that night in The Lord Roberts and again the other day. I've come to find out a bit more about it!'

He lowered his hands and, taking a gold case out of his pocket, offered her a cigarette. She took it and felt her fingers tremble when he got up from his chair and walked around the desk to light it for her. He then leaned against the desk and looked at her.

'What do you want to know, Lily?'

'You said I could sing in your club, with your band.'

'I did and you can.'

'You also said I would be well paid.'

He nodded, 'That's right.'

'How much?'

He mentioned a figure that sent Lily's senses reeling. She tried not to show her pleasure. 'You promised me good clothes and jewellery too.'

'Indeed I did. I am a generous man, my dear, as you will learn if you accept my offer.'

His close proximity was unnerving, and Lily was beginning to feel flustered.

'I also said you would be my mistress.'

'I know you did. I hadn't forgotten.' She returned his gaze, unflinchingly.

He chuckled softly, 'I think we will have a great time together.'

She felt a sudden chill seep through her, wondering what sort of a lover he would be. 'I won't be a whore!'

His head went back as he burst into laughter. He leaned forward and cupped her chin in his hand. 'Darling Lily. You won't be a whore. You will be my woman. That is something quite different.'

With a trace of anxiety in her voice, she asked, 'Is it, Vittorio? Is it really?'

He smoothed her cheek. 'I can assure you it will be. I told you we were destined for one another. I know it and I'm sure you do too, deep inside you.'

She frowned, and seeing her expression of consternation, he asked, 'What is it, my dear? What's troubling you?'

'Why me, Vittorio? You could have your pick of women. I don't understand.'

His smile was benign, his voice soft. 'It's not so difficult, Lily. You have such charm. You also have talent, which I hate to see go to waste. I can help to make you a star in your field.'

'But you could do all this without my being your mistress.'

He gave a throaty chuckle. 'That is quite true. But from the moment I first saw you, you have interested me. You are bright and beautiful. There is so much I can teach you, but I don't want just to be your teacher.'

She looked at him uncertainly. 'No?'

Shaking his head, he said, 'No. I want much more. I want to teach you how to be a woman.'

She looked suddenly indignant. 'I am already a woman.'

'Of course you are, and a lovely one. You are very desirable. I don't want another man discovering these delights. I want you to be mine.'

There was a note of possession in his voice which she didn't like. 'You can't own me, Vittorio. I'm not a piece of meat you can buy at some market stall.'

His laughter echoed. 'Of course not. Oh Lily, you are such a delight. I'm so pleased to see the fire back in your soul.' He caught hold of her hand. 'We will have so much fun together.'

She looked into deep-brown eyes that were bright with amusement. She wasn't foolish enough not to realise that most of the rumours she'd heard about him were probably true, yet as she looked at him, she felt no fear. Trepidation certainly, anxiety about the unknown, but not fear. She did like Vittorio, but she knew if she accepted his proposition, she would have to tread warily. She grinned mischievously. 'But I haven't yet seen the room you promised me time and time again.'

'Then we'd better put that right. Follow me.'

They ascended the stairs to the third floor. Again the decor was luxurious, the deep red of the carpet contrasting with the white walls hung with expensive paintings. Small mats draped the wall. She looked at him with a puzzled expression. 'Shouldn't they be on the floor?'

His dark eyes shone with amusement. 'They're prayer mats.'

'You'd have to be a bloody contortionist to kneel on them, wouldn't you?'

He chuckled as he led her to a door and opened it, stepping back for her to enter.

With her heart pounding, Lily entered Vittorio's bedroom. Its grandeur caught her breath. The bed was huge. The bedstead was made of brass. On it were black silk sheets and an extravagant black cover, embroidered with Chinese concubines. The centre light was a large candelabra, with matching lights on each table placed either side of the bed. There was a huge wardrobe and a tallboy, on top of which, placed carefully and fastidiously, were silver-backed hair brushes and small cut-glass bowls with silver lids.

Vittorio sat in one of two matching buttoned-backed velvet chairs and, with an amused expression, watched Lily inspect the room. Picking up the brushes she turned to him and impishly said, 'You do well for yourself, don't you!'

'I like nice things, Lily. So will you.'

She walked to the wardrobe. 'Can I look inside?'

He nodded.

It was packed with hand-made suits, next to a selection of shirts and ties. 'There'll be no room for my stuff,' Lily complained. 'That's if you're going to buy me new clothes, like you promised.'

'You will need a cupboard of your own, of course.'

'Of course,' repeated Lily. Then with childish glee she said, 'Because I'll have a lot of clothes, won't I, Vittorio?'

'Yes, you will.'

Her expression changed. 'I won't be dressed like a whore. I want good-class stuff.'

'Naturally.' He looked at her with twinkling eyes. 'I would certainly expect my woman to be as well dressed as me.'

'You would?' She was pleasantly surprised.

'Of course.'

She saw a closed door and asked, 'What's in there?'

'Open it and see for yourself.'

She did so. Inside was a bathroom and toilet. Her eyes lit up in delight. Hot water. No tin bath . . . no going outside to the lavatory. How wonderful. She closed the door quietly and turned to face Vittorio.

'Very nice,' she said.

'We need to get a few things clear,' he said. 'Sit down, Lily.'

She sat on the edge of the bed, wondering what he was going to say.

'I've agreed to all your demands, but now you must listen to mine.'

She felt suddenly apprehensive.

'You will have all that I've promised you, but in return, you will not only share my bed, you will entertain my business guests.'

Her eyes opened wide with fear. 'In what way?'

A soft smile lifted the corners of his mouth. 'I don't mean sexually. You will help entertain my clients. Chat to them. Make them feel comfortable. Flatter them. I'll train you so you'll know how to do so, although you have a natural rapport with people anyway. You'll do well, I know.'

She breathed a sigh of relief. 'What happens if after a time I decide I don't like the arrangement?'

His expression changed. His eyes glittered. 'I would not be pleased about that, Lily. Beside, why wouldn't you be happy here with me?' He studied her thoughtfully. 'Why did you suddenly decide to take up my offer?' The sudden look of vulnerability on her face touched him deeply. This girl, with her womanly attributes, looked so much a child at this moment, he wanted to take her in his arms and reassure her that all would be well.

She looked at him and said, 'I just want to be taken care of.'

It was a simple request. The ring of truth in her words made him feel immediately protective towards her. 'It will be my pleasure, Lily. I and I alone will be responsible for you, if you stay.'

She knew that this was the moment of decision. Sandy had been right: if she stayed, she was Vittorio's. There would be no turning back. Looking around the room, thinking of all the things he'd promised her and gazing at the man who fascinated her so, she took a deep breath and asked, 'Then when do we go shopping?'

'Tomorrow,' he said with a smile of satisfaction.

'Right. But tonight I sleep alone.'

There was a devilish glint in his eye as he took her to another small bedroom and ushered her in. 'Tonight this is yours. But tomorrow, you sleep with me.' He closed the door behind him.

Lily lay on the bed, fully dressed, her limbs trembling. She'd made the decision, for better or worse and tried to justify it to herself. 'I'll never be hungry again,' she whispered. 'I'll be working, earning money . . . excellent money. I'll have decent clothes. I'll never have to feel poor. I'll be taken care of.' Then there was Vittorio. He was the unknown quantity in all this. Without him, none of the other things was possible. And if this was whoring, at least it was with one man, someone she knew, not a stranger. Someone who was clean and presentable and who would care about her if she kept him happy. It had to be better than a quick fuck in some dark alley or shabby room. Was it such a bad deal? No, she didn't think so, compared with the awful alternative.

Worn out by these developments, she undressed and climbed into bed. She could scarcely ask God to take care of her – that really would be pushing her luck. She settled down for the night, filled with trepidation about the morrow.

Lily awakened with a start. Standing before her was a young girl wearing a neat black dress. In her hands she held a breakfast tray. Before Lily could speak she said, 'Morning, miss. Mr Teglia said I was to wake you.'

Sitting up in bed, Lily asked, 'Who are you?'

'I'm Beatrice, the maid, miss.' Placing the tray by the bed, she went to the door and opened it, returning with some towels. 'These are for you, miss.' Walking over to the window, she drew back the curtains and peered out. 'Not a bad day. May rain later, though. Sky's a bit dark over yonder.' Turning towards Lily she said, 'Mr Teglia said to be ready in two hours' time.' She placed a small clock on the table. 'You're going shopping.' With an anxious look she added, 'He don't like to be kept waiting, miss.'

'Right. I'll remember that. Thank you, Beatrice.'

When the girl had left, Lily stared longingly at the food, savouring the aroma before tucking in to the eggs and bacon, buttering the toast and drinking the coffee, luxuriating in its rich flavour. She stretched contentedly, like a cat. Later she lay in a hot bath, smothering herself with scented soap. If this was typical of her new life as Vittorio's mistress, she was really going to enjoy herself.

Exactly two hours later, there was a tap on her door. With trembling legs she walked across the room and opened it. Standing on the threshold was The Maltese. Lily felt unsure of herself. But she'd got into this situation and now she'd have to see it through. Putting aside her concern, she smiled cheerfully at Vittorio. 'Good morning.'

He, as usual, was dressed immaculately. He smiled back at her and, holding out his hand said, 'Good morning, Lily. Are you ready for our expedition to the shops?'

'Yes, I'm ready, but I'm warning you, Vittorio,' she said

with a cheeky grin, 'I've very expensive tastes.'

He looked amused. 'You really are an extraordinary creature. Fortunately, I've more than enough for your needs. Come along, I can see we are both going to have a stimulating time.'

Walking downstairs on Vittorio's arm, Lily was aware that she was the centre of attention of many prying eyes. Doors were opened just a fraction, staff looked at her with interest, if unobtrusively. She looked straight ahead. Back stiff, head held high. After all, she was Vittorio's mistress. Well, technically not until tonight, to be strictly accurate. But as far as anyone else was concerned . . . she already was.

Outside a taxi was waiting. As Vittorio helped her into the car, Lily felt very much the lady. She sat back against the seat, watching the passing scene.

The day exceeded all Lily's expectations. Vittorio dismissed the taxi outside a small but exclusive gown shop. Gazing at the expensive models displayed in the window, Lily felt a surge of excitement. Was she really going to be wearing such wonderful clothes?

As they entered the shop, she looked around the swish interior. It had wall to wall carpets which her feet seemed to sink into as she walked.

'Sit there, Lily,' Vittorio commanded, pointing to a tall velvet chair. As she settled herself into it, Lily fingered her coat, knowing it was shabby in comparison to the exclusive clothing hanging on the rails. But she held her head with pride. From now on, things were going to change.

In an authoritative voice, Vittorio asked for the manageress. When she bustled towards them, he pointed to Lily and said, 'I want this young lady taken care of. We want day dresses, costumes and several evening gowns. Money is no object here, you understand.'

Lily's eyes widened at the attention bestowed on her. So this was what it was like to be rich. She smiled across at her benefactor in delight as the manageress measured her and sent several assistants scurrying off in all directions.

Vittorio sat in a chair, puffing a Havana cigar and watching as Lily emerged from the changing cubicle in one creation after another, deciding whether he liked it or not. Those he didn't were quickly discarded.

Inside the cubicle, helping Lily into yet another dress, the manageress said softly, 'Your husband is a very generous man.'

Looking at the woman with feigned innocence Lily said, 'He's not my husband.' And hid a smile at the shock registered on the other woman's face. 'Wives don't get all this – only mistresses.' She thought the manageress was going to pass out with embarrassment. It added considerably to her enjoyment.

Vittorio went along the rack of evening gowns and chose four. 'Try these on, Lily.'

She looked longingly at one in pale lemon that had taken her fancy. 'Can't I try that one too?'

'No. I don't like it.'

The tone of his voice forbade argument.

As Lily slipped a gown of beaded gossamer over her head, she thought of the gowns she used to try on alone at night in the back of Rachel Cohen's shop, and wished with all her heart she could still be there. True, the gowns had seen better days and some of them had smelt musty from storage, but when she wore them, there was no price to be paid. What was it Rachel had told her? In life, no one does anything for nothing. What charge would Vittorio make against his generosity, she wondered. Would it be more than she was prepared for?

Vittorio picked out an exquisite claret-coloured coat, trimmed with black fur, and one of the chosen dresses, made of soft brown velvet trimmed in beige satin, and told Lily to wear them. Then he ordered the rest of the purchases to be sent to the club that afternoon. As they were about to leave the shop, the manageress came hurrying out with the clothes Lily had originally worn that day.

'What shall I do with these, sir?' she asked.

'Burn them!' snapped Vittorio as he opened the shop door.

Lily felt her cheeks redden with shame.

From there, they went to a shoe shop, where Vittorio

chose several pairs for her. On to a hat shop, the packages to be delivered. And then, to Lily's acute embarrassment and that of the assistant who served them, they visited the lingerie department of the largest store in town. Lily chose several sets of underwear in soft pastel colours. When she'd finished, Vittorio chose even more, in black.

Lily felt the anger rising inside her. How dare he humiliate her so. 'I'm hungry,' she said abruptly. 'Good food was one of the things you promised me, so when do we eat?'

'Something upsetting you?' he asked caustically.

'Why all black underwear?'

'I find black sexually stimulating. The other colours don't do anything for me. The black lingerie was to please me, not you.' He looked at her, the corners of his mouth twitching with amusement. 'After all, I must get some personal pleasure from today, surely?'

She glared at him. 'You're not going to order my food too, are you?'

'Don't be ridiculous!' His eyes twinkled. 'Come on. You're not the only one who's hungry.'

Walking into The Tivoli restaurant was another strange experience, but wearing new clothes gave Lily the necessary confidence. Many heads turned to look at her and her companion. The waiter led them to a table and, holding out a chair for her, helped Lily to be seated. When he laid a napkin across her lap, she smiled sweetly at him as if this was an everyday occurrence.

She began to relax until Vittorio handed her the menu. Her fingers trembled as she held it. It was large and impressive, not like the simple one she'd been given when first she'd had a meal with Tom.

'Would you like me to order for you?'

She shook her head. 'No, thank you. I can manage perfectly well.' If this was to be her new way of life, she thought, she had to start as she meant to go on. She deliberately ordered the most expensive dishes.

As she gazed at her surroundings, Lily knew she looked elegant in her new clothes. For once she felt as good as all the well-heeled clients sitting at the other tables. She experienced the first stirrings of the power that money could buy, and she enjoyed it. She couldn't help but compare this moment to the time she had stood outside the fish and chip shop the night she first met Jim. The night she was near to starvation.

She watched carefully to see which cutlery her companion used, having been somewhat startled at the array beside her plate. Finishing her lobster soup, she waited for the steak to arrive. It looked and smelt wonderful. Oh, if only they could bottle this aroma, she thought, I'd wear it behind my ears. She remembered to eat slowly, not wanting to let Vittorio know that for the past weeks she'd been living on bread and scrape and potato soup.

'Have you enjoyed your day, Lily?'

The quiet humiliation she had suffered still angered her. *You'll pay for the black lingerie*, she thought. 'You mean it's over?' she said innocently. 'No more shopping?'

He looked surprised. 'I thought we'd covered everything.'

Slowly she ran her fingers through her hair. 'I seem to remember you mentioned jewellery, when you were trying to tempt me. I don't want a diamond tiara, just a bauble or two to celebrate our new relationship.'

He shook his head. 'You're in the wrong business, Lily. You strike a harder bargain than any businessman I know.'

Nevertheless, there was a look of respect in his eyes. If I want to keep that respect, she thought, I must never let him think he's got the better of me.

As she sat opposite him, she mused that he might be the blackest villain around the dock area, but he was a fine-looking man, with his olive skin, powerful build and jet-black hair. Dressed in a tailored suit and silk shirt, he blended well with the upper crust. His air of power was like a force field around him as the waiters hovered nearby, ready to fulfil his every wish.

Lily was consumed with curiosity about him. Who was he really, this man with whom she had made such a bargain?

'Let me order the dessert,' The Maltese suggested. 'They have a speciality here that I'm sure you'll enjoy.' He called the waiter over and quietly spoke in his ear.

Lily was intrigued.

When the man returned he was pushing a trolley, on top of which, to Lily's surprise, was a dish with a flame beneath it. 'Crêpes suzettes, sir,' he said and proceeded with the intricacies of the dish. When he flambéed the crêpes, Lily gave a cry and sat back in her chair.

Vittorio watched with amusement.

The waiter placed two pancakes on her plate and spooned the liquor over them. 'Bon appétit, mademoiselle.'

She tasted the dessert carefully, her expression one of pleasure as she ate it.

'Is it nice, Lily? Do you like it?'

'Mm, I do. It's delicious! Could we have it again one day?'

With a smile, The Maltese said, 'Of course, if that is your wish.'

'Oh it is,' she said. 'At least twice a week.'

Whilst they ate their dessert, Lily said, 'Tell me about yourself, Vittorio.'

He looked surprised. 'Why do you want to know?'

Shrugging, she said, 'Why not? I know nothing about you, only what people have told me. And no one can be *that* big a bastard.'

His gaze held hers. 'Don't be too sure, Lily. Most of it is probably true.'

'Tell me how you started, how you became so rich.'

His expression didn't alter. 'All you need to know, my dear, is that I am. You will be well looked after, as long as you do as you're told. Would you like some coffee?'

'Yes, and a brandy, please.' She felt as if she was going to need it, if only 'for medicinal purposes', as dear old Sandy used to say. This man gave nothing away. She wondered perhaps if it was because he had so much to hide. She determined she would learn as much about him as she could. Being his mistress ought to give her some advantage, and such information might come in useful some day. She pushed to the back of her mind the thought that such knowledge might lead her into danger, rather than be the means of her survival.

After leaving The Tivoli, Lily was delighted when Vittorio

took her into a jeweller's shop. He bought her an expensive cameo brooch and a diamanté necklace with matching earrings. 'To wear when you perform in the club,' he said.

There was an unexpected softness in his tone when he added, 'I hope you like them, Lily, and the other things we bought today.' She felt a pang of guilt. He did promise her all these things, but he need not have kept his word. She kissed him impulsively on the cheek.

'Thank you, Vittorio. I've had a truly wonderful time.'

He looked both surprised and pleased. He pulled her into his arms and softly covered her mouth with his. It was the briefest of kisses, but it had a profound effect on Lily. Her knees felt like water. She looked at him with surprise. 'Why did you do that?'

'Because I wanted to. Now let's go.'

That night, bathed and wearing a black negligée, Lily lay on the bed waiting for her lover. This, she thought, is where I start to earn my keep. She longed for Tom, to hear his voice, to feel his arms about her, his lips on hers. But it was not to be. She'd made her decision. Her dream of respectability was in ribbons for ever. But at least she was not on the streets.

Smoothing the silk sheets, she looked with childish delight across at the new wardrobe Vittorio had installed for her, containing all her new clothes. The hat boxes on top of the cupboard, full of expensive creations. How generous he had been. She recalled the feel of his mouth on hers. Now he could claim far more. She suddenly felt nervous.

The bathroom door opened and Vittorio, wearing a silk dressing gown, entered the room. Closing the door behind him, he stood and looked at Lily, waiting.

She could almost hear her heart beating, it seemed so loud. She felt tense and apprehensive.

Crossing over to the bed, Vittorio knelt beside her and stroked her cheek. Gently kissed her lips. Lily began to relax. She saw that around his neck he wore a gold chain, from which hung an exquisite ring. She held the ring in her hand. 'What's this?' she whispered.

'This belonged to my mother.' There was great tenderness in his voice. 'It's my most valued possession, Lily. I always wear it.' Slipping the straps of the negligée from her shoulders, he said, 'Take this off.'

She did as she was bid.

His hands, soft and gentle, caressed her full breasts, playing with the pink nipples. His gaze studied her form, lingering on the soft and curly mat of her pubic hair. 'You're even more beautiful than I imagined. You have a body crying out to be loved. I know exactly what you want, Lily my dear, and it will also give me great pleasure to give it to you.' He smoothed her hair. 'You are such a wonderful mixture. Half-woman, half-child.'

Vittorio was an accomplished lover. His deft fingers, slowly exploring Lily's body, touched all the places that sent her senses reeling. She was responding purely from passion that had been aroused by a master. His kisses, at first gentle and searching, became more passionate and demanding. She responded willingly to them. His kisses covered her body, teasing, taunting. She moaned sensually as she arched her back, unable to stem her body's response to him.

'You are truly more than I hoped for, Lily,' he whispered against her lips. His mouth crushed hers. His kisses were filled with fire. With raw lust.

He slowly entered her and she cried out with delight.

When he reached the zenith of his passion, he quickly withdrew, spilling his semen on her. His eyes, piercing and demanding, looked into her eyes. She instinctively knew what he wanted to be told.

'Vittorio, that was wonderful.'

He gathered her into his arms, kissing her neck, her ears, her mouth, until they both lay back against the pillows, exhausted and content.

Who was this man? she wondered. Sandy had warned her against him, but as yet she'd seen nothing in Vittorio to fear. She realised that this was only the start of their relationship. How would it progress? she wondered. Whatever was before her, the choice had been hers, and hers alone.

Chapter Fifteen

The following morning, Lily awoke clasped in Vittorio's arms, still confused about her reaction to his love-making. She was not in love with The Maltese, but he'd stirred within her feelings she didn't know she had. She looked at the sleeping figure beside her. His smooth olive skin shone and his dark hair was tousled. At this moment he didn't look at all like a man who was feared by so many.

Beside her, Vittorio stirred. He smiled lazily at Lily and drew her closer. 'Good morning,' he said, softly nuzzling her ear. 'Did you sleep well?'

'Yes, I did.'

'So did I. Thanks to you.' He ran his hand over her breast as he kissed her gently. Raking her hair with his fingers, he said, 'I like your hair like this. It makes you look like a child.'

Lily lowered her gaze. She'd been looking at his fine frame. The powerful build had not one spare ounce of flesh on it.

Slipping his hand beneath the bedclothes, he stroked her soft flesh. 'You are everything I'd hoped you'd be, Lily.'

She looked puzzled. 'And what is that?' She felt his hand move between her thighs.

'A little tiger.' He gave a throaty chuckle. 'I like it when you're soft and naked in my arms.' His finger slipped inside her. 'And you are a creature of passion. I like that too.'

She felt herself responding to his caresses. He kissed her. 'Lily, you're getting lovely and wet. You are a delight.' He lay on top of her and she felt his erection. They made love, but this time it was gentle and slow, even more satisfying than before.

When it was over, Vittorio sat up. 'Much as I would like to stay in bed with you, I have things to do. Run my bath, Lily, whilst I sort out my clothes.'

When she returned from the bathroom, she saw he'd laid out an outfit for her. She frowned. 'What's this?'

With his back to her he said, 'I'm having some important people to lunch today and I want to be sure you're wearing the appropriate clothes. I particularly like this dress.'

She sat on the bed, suddenly defensive. 'And you don't think I would know, is that it?'

He looked at her with amusement. 'Yes, that's it exactly. How bright you are.'

'Not "bright" enough to dress myself though.'

Walking over to her, he drew her into his arms. 'Don't sulk, Lily. You will be moving in different circles now. Dressing correctly is an important art. Think of this as part of your training.'

When Vittorio emerged from the bathroom wearing a towel around his waist, Lily was on the bed propped up by pillows, brushing her hair. She watched as he dressed with care.

He said, 'I'll send Beatrice up with your breakfast. Lunch will be served at one o'clock. I want you down in the bar to greet my guests at twelve-thirty.'

'What am I supposed to do until then? Stay a prisoner in my room?'

'Of course not,' he said with an indulgent smile. 'You can look around the club, familiarise yourself with the place. But don't leave the building. I don't want you wandering around and arriving back late. You understand?'

She tossed her hair back and with a flippant shake of her head, said, 'Of course . . . I'm very *bright*, you said so yourself.'

She heard his quiet chuckle as he left the room. What a strange man he was. This morning, in bed, they had been as one, and now he'd become businesslike. Dictatorial. She found it irritating. She'd certainly never met anyone like him before.

There was a knock at the door and Beatrice came in,

looking at Lily shyly as she put down the breakfast tray. 'Good morning, miss.'

Lily liked that. It made her feel important. 'Good morning. Now tell me the lay-out of the club, Beatrice.'

The girl looked startled. 'What do you mean, miss?'

'Mr Teglia has given me permission to look around later.' She gave Beatrice a conspiratorial grin. 'I don't want to walk into the wrong places, do I?'

The girl grinned back at her. 'No, miss. On this floor, apart from this room, there are others that Mr Vittorio keeps for his special guests. On the floor below are the girls with their rooms. Best not go into those, miss.'

Lily raised eyebrows in question. 'No?'

'They wouldn't like it. Downstairs in the front you've already seen.'

'And the back?'

Beatrice shook her head. 'Apart from the kitchen, I don't know.'

Lily was intrigued. 'Really? Thank you, that'll be all.'

Once dressed, she seated herself before the dressing table that Vittorio had installed for her and looked into the mirror at her reflection.

The red dress chosen by Vittorio, made of fine wool, looked elegant. The neck was round and neat and the long sleeves had a fine double frill at the cuff which matched the frill around the hem. She brushed her hair, patted it in place, quickly put on some lipstick then, taking a deep breath, left the room. When she reached the floor below, she saw three girls wearing silk dressing gowns standing together in a bedroom doorway, chatting. They looked at her with interest.

'Good morning,' she said as she walked by. Two of them smiled at her and answered, the other, a tall redhead, glared spitefully at her and was silent. But as Lily walked on she heard the girl's remark. 'So that's Vittorio's new whore. Nice and young, just as he likes them.'

Lily flushed with anger. She'd sort out that one as soon as possible. She wasn't going to take any nonsense from any of them. Those days were behind her.

When she got to the dining room, her gaze went immediately to the double doors at the back of the room. She caught hold of the handles, but the doors were locked. George Coleman happened to be walking by at that moment and seeing her he asked, 'Anything I can do, miss?'

'No. I was just looking around.'

He eyed her carefully. 'Perhaps I can give you a tour?'

She gave him a wide smile. 'That would be lovely.'

He showed her the kitchen and introduced her to the chef. He walked her up on the stage for her to get the feel of it, for as he said, 'I believe this is where you'll be performing.'

She stood centre-stage and looked out over the dining room, feeling her stomach tighten. What if the patrons didn't like her?

Sensing her dismay, George said quietly, 'You'll do just fine, Miss Lily. I heard you sing in The Lord Roberts, remember?'

'I hope you're right. What's behind the locked doors?' she asked casually.

'No doubt Mr Vittorio will show you at some time, miss.'

He sat her down at the bar to wait with a cup of coffee and the morning papers. She couldn't concentrate on the daily news, becoming more nervous as the time passed, and was relieved when Vittorio ascended the stairs from his office.

He walked over to her. 'You look lovely, my dear.' There was a sudden burst of laughter and conversation coming from the entrance and Vittorio glanced away. Putting out his hand towards her he said, 'Come and meet my guests.'

There were four men in the party, all from the White Star Line's *Olympic*: big bluff Ned Saunders, the Chief Steward; Teddy Green, the Head Chef; Reg Mathews, a quiet man smoking a pipe who was the Chief Engineer; and sophisticated Richard Carter, the Purser.

The men made their way to the bar, where they were greeted by Vittorio. Turning to Lily, he introduced her to his guests. They all shook her by the hand, Ned holding on to Lily for much longer than was polite. She noted the lascivious look in his eyes as he said, 'I do hope this beautiful young woman is to be seated next to me at lunch?'

Vittorio gave a benevolent smile. 'If that is what you want.'

The men drank heavily whilst they chatted. Vittorio refused several drinks on Lily's behalf, which didn't annoy her in this instance as she wanted to keep her senses about her. Finally they were led to the table by the head waiter.

The conversation was stimulating. These were men of the world and Lily plied them with questions about New York and life at sea. 'You must come on board when we dock next trip,' said Ned. 'I'd enjoy showing you around.'

I bet you would, thought Lily. Before I knew where I was I'd be cornered in your cabin. Looking across the table at Vittorio, she said, 'We could manage that, couldn't we?'

With a slow smile he said, 'I expect so, if you'd like to go.'

'If you're busy, Vittorio, I could take the little lady. You know I'd look after her.'

Lily looked anxiously across the table at The Maltese.

'I'm sure you would, Ned. But Lily is solely in my care.'

She saw the disappointment in the other man's face. She also felt the pressure of his knee against hers beneath the table. She moved her leg away. He moved his too.

After the dessert, coffee was served and the men lit cigars. Lily gave a start as she felt Ned's hand on her knee. She looked across with wide eyes at Vittorio, who was watching her carefully. The rotten swine, she thought. He knows exactly what's going on!

Ned's hand crept higher, pushing the skirt of her dress out of the way. Lily's lips narrowed. 'May I have a cigarette, Vittorio?'

He handed over his gold cigarette case and she took one. Still Vittorio's gaze didn't leave her. Lily drew on the cigarette until the tip was long and red. She flicked off the ash, drew on it again, then swiftly stubbed it out on the back of Ned's hand.

He gave a cry of pain, then sucked on the burnt skin. He turned to Lily, a curse on his lips.

'Yes?' she said.

The others, now aware of what had been happening, chided their friend good-naturedly. Still Vittorio remained silent. Observing.

Turning to Ned, Lily said clearly, 'If ever we sit together again, I expect you to keep your paws on the table. I don't like being mauled.'

Ned looked thunderous, but his friends roared with laughter. Vittorio held up his glass to Lily in salute. She wondered if this had been some kind of test. If so, she'd apparently passed.

Their guests were the last to leave the club, with Vittorio at the door to see them off the premises. As Lily walked past the bar, seated on the high stools were the three girls she'd seen that morning. The redhead looked her up and down with disdain.

'I suppose you think you're better than us with your fancy new clothes.'

Lily looked hard at her. 'Watch your mouth or you'll be sorry.'

'Humph! She thinks she's God Almighty.'

Lily put her hand in the centre of the girl's chest and gave a mighty push. The redhead toppled over backwards onto the floor. She was still sprawled there when Vittorio walked over.

'What's going on?'

'Nothing I can't handle,' was Lily's spirited answer.

'Been opening your mouth again, Iris?' said Vittorio. 'I think you'd better apologise to Lily.'

She scrambled to her feet. 'Sorry, Lily.'

'Miss Lily to you, Iris.' She glared at the girl, defying her to disobey.

Iris, puce with anger, glowered at her. 'Miss Lily,' she repeated.

Lily stalked away, followed by Vittorio.

'Come into the office,' he said. She did so, closing the door behind her. He took her into his arms. 'You did well today. I like the way you handled Ned – and Iris.'

'Nobody treats me like those two and gets away with it!'

'Quite.'

Still furious, she asked, 'Why didn't you do anything about that bastard, Ned? You knew what was going on, I could tell. You just sat there!'

'I had to see if you could handle men like him. I would have stepped in if necessary.'

'I should hope so.'

'You are mine and, as such, you are due respect. In time people like Ned will learn this lesson. Remember that.'

'Does that go for you too, Vittorio?'

The slow smile she was beginning to recognise crossed his lips. 'We'll see. This afternoon before we open I've asked the band to come in and rehearse with you. Sort out your programme with the leader. You will sing here on Saturday night.'

'And you will choose my gown, no doubt.'

His smile didn't fade. 'Any of them will do. I chose them carefully.'

'In other words, I can't go wrong.'

'Precisely.'

She looked at him with curiosity. 'Do you ever do anything that isn't calculated?'

Shaking his head, he said, 'No. That's why I'm successful and rich. Now I have work to do.' He kissed her on the forehead and walked over to his desk. 'The band will be here at five o'clock.'

The leader of the five-piece band looked at her with a thinly disguised expression of disdain. 'Right, miss. What key do you sing in?' he asked in a flat voice.

Puzzled, Lily said, 'How the hell should I know?'

He looked at his colleagues in despair.

Already irritated by his tone, Lily took off at him. 'What's your name?' she snapped.

'Harry.'

'Right, Harry. I know what you're thinking. This bit of skirt is Vittorio's latest piece!'

The man was taken aback by her candour.

'And you think you've got to please the boss and tolerate me, knowing that I have no talent. Well, that's right, you do. But I can sing. Believe me, I can sing. Now you tell me what bloody key, all right?'

He nodded.

Lily started to give a beautiful rendition of 'Danny Boy'. As her pure voice rang out in the empty room, various members of staff crept in to listen. The band soon joined in, playing the melody in the right key. In the leader's eyes grew a look of respect. When Lily had finished, there was a flurry of applause from her small audience, joined by the members of the band. And the leader.

She looked at Harry, the expression in her eyes a definite challenge. 'Well?'

He bowed to her. 'I owe you an apology, miss.'

'Lily. My name's Lily.' She beamed at him. 'I think we'll work well together. Now here's my programme.'

Later, she and Vittorio had dinner together in the club dining room. Looking across at her he asked, 'How did the rehearsal go?'

She smiled inwardly but said, 'Fine. No problems. We got on very well.'

'Excellent. Saturday night is usually very busy, so you'll have a good audience.' Seeing the look of anxiety in her eyes, he leaned across the table and took her hand in his. 'You'll be fine, my dear.'

'I hope so. I'll certainly do my best.'

'Have you enjoyed your first day with me, Lily?'

She nodded. 'Thank you, Vittorio. It's certainly been different – strange, even – although that Ned is a dirty old man. Don't you ever leave me alone with him, will you?'

He laughed loudly. 'From what I saw, he's the one who should be saying that.'

'Is he a friend of yours?' she asked.

'No. Just a business acquaintance.'

Lily was relieved. If it was just business between the men, with luck she wouldn't encounter Ned very often. He made her flesh creep.

Weary after her busy day, Lily looked across the table at the end of the meal. 'Do you mind if I go to my room? I'm really tired.'

'No, you go, my dear. I have some papers to clear before I've finished. I'll see you later.'

She was half-asleep when he came into the room.

Vittorio climbed into bed. 'Are you awake, Lily?'

'Mmm,' she murmured.

He leaned over and kissed her cheek. 'Good night,' he said as he gathered her into his arms. 'Sleep well.'

As she lay there, she was surprised yet pleased that Vittorio just wanted to hold her. In her experience of men, with the exception of Fred, all they had wanted from her was sex. It was nice just to be held in a warm embrace, Vittorio's firm body at her back, his arms gently around her. It was something she'd yearned for, for so long. How strange it should be the feared Maltese, who should be the one to give it to her.

It was Saturday night, the club was full and Lily was feeling nervous. She sat in front of the dressing table brushing her hair, her heart beating like a steam engine.

Vittorio emerged from the bathroom, dressed in evening wear. Walking over to her he said, 'For goodness sake, relax.' He laid his hands on her shoulders and began to massage them. 'Good heavens, you're wound up tighter than a spring. If I didn't think you were good enough for my establishment, you wouldn't be here. Trust me.' He leaned forward and kissed her cheek. 'I'll see you downstairs in the bar.'

When he had gone, Lily took a deep breath and gave herself a talking to. 'You're here of your own free will and you want to go on singing,' she hissed, 'so pull yourself together. Sandy said you were a natural, so go and give them the performance of your life.'

Choosing an emerald-green dress, which was made of satin and trimmed at the neck with black jet beads, she looked into the mirror at her reflection and she was pleased. The beads on her dress sparkled, as did the diamond-paste necklace and earrings that Vittorio had bought for her.

As Lily descended the stairs, she saw that the dining room and the bar were already full. Vittorio, standing at the bar, called her over. He ordered a drink from the barman and handed it to her. With a kindly smile he said, 'Take this, it will calm your nerves. You'll be just fine. Go up there and

191

enjoy yourself.' He kissed her forehead and gently pushed her towards the stage.

Lily walked over to the band. Harry, the leader, winked at her. 'Ready, ducks?'

Taking a deep breath she said, 'As ready as I'll ever be.'

He squeezed her arm. 'You look lovely. Within minutes you'll have this lot eating out of your hand.'

She started her programme with a cheerful 'Margie', which soon caught the attention of her audience. Her rendition of Marie Lloyd's songs was enthusiastically received, especially when she draped a woollen shawl around her head and sang, 'I'm one of the ruins that Cromwell knocked about a bit'. And 'A little of what you fancy does you good' brought forth raucous laughter. But as usual it was the ballads that caught at the heart of her audience, the songs a perfect foil for the cheeky numbers she'd sung earlier. At the end of her performance, the applause rang out. 'Encore!' shouted several voices. She thanked them; then, turning to Harry, she nodded for him to play in the first notes of her encore, 'After you're gone, there's no use crying . . .' She smiled to herself as she thought of dear Sandy and his bit of raunch, as he called this song. She remembered exactly how he taught her to put the number over and the applause was noisy and enthusiastic.

This time her heart was beating fast with relief. She looked over at Vittorio, who was smiling and applauding along with the rest. He beckoned her over. Putting an arm around her shoulders, he hugged her. 'Didn't I tell you? You were wasted in those shabby pubs. This is where you belong, amongst those who can appreciate your talent.'

She looked at him, her eyes bright, and defended her friends. 'They too appreciated me. They just didn't have as much money, that's the only difference.'

His eyes sparked at her show of defiance. 'True, Lily. But none of them could help you. Here in this room are men of position who can be of use to your future . . . and mine. *That's* the difference and it's an important one. You have a lot yet to learn. However, this is not the time for a lecture.'

He handed her a glass of champagne. 'Here's to your success.'

She took a sip and wrinkled her nose as the bubbles burst in the glass. She thought of Tom and wished he could have been here tonight. But of course, then he would have known she was the mistress of The Maltese. For a moment the reality of her situation really hit home.

Several clients came up and congratulated her on her performance. Lily forgot her concerns and enjoyed her popularity. She chatted happily with the men, flirted outrageously with many – and became a star.

Vittorio looked on, an expression of pride and amusement on his face, but his eyes were ever-watchful.

Two days later, Lily made her way to the home of recovery in The Avenue to visit Rachel. She was shown into a small private room.

Rachel was sitting in a comfortable chair by the window, wearing a dressing gown, reading a newspaper, glasses perched on the end of her nose. She turned as the door opened. Taking off her glasses, she looked at Lily, her glance taking in every detail of the girl's new apparel. 'Hello, darling! Come in. Come in.' Looking at the nurse, she asked, 'A tray of tea for two, please, and some biscuits.'

'Well!' exclaimed Lily, looking around the comfortable room. 'You're doing all right for yourself.'

With a wry smile Rachel said, 'So are you, my dear, if I may say so. Walking in here like the bloody Queen of Sheba. That's some expensive *schmatte* you're wearing. The Maltese always had good taste.'

Lily blushed. 'How do you know so much about him?' she asked.

'I knew the family after they came to live in Southampton; not long after the mother died. Such a pity. The father was a handsome devil, but it was the uncle I took a shine to. Yes, The Maltese has come a long way since those days. I admire him for it, really. But enough of that. Come and sit down,' urged Rachel, pointing to another armchair. 'Tell me your news. I've been thinking about you a lot, wondering how you made out. How is Vittorio treating you?'

Lily was suddenly overcome with shyness about her lover. 'He's been really good to me. He's not the awful man people think.'

Rachel raised her eyebrows. 'Is that so? Then I'm happy for you.'

Shaking her head, Lily said, 'No, you're not. You don't approve, so don't pretend you do.'

Shrugging, the Jewess said, 'What difference does it make what I think? If you are happy, that's the main thing. Are you, though? That's the question. Tell me the truth now.'

'I am, honestly,' Lily assured her friend. 'Vittorio's really a nice man. He's kind, gentle. He's taking care of me.'

With a wicked glint in her eye Rachel asked, 'Is he good in bed?'

Lily looked shocked. 'Really, such a question!'

With a cackle Rachel said, 'Listen, my dear, when you become someone's mistress, it's bloody awful if he's no good between the sheets. You think my husband was the only man I knew?' She looked with amusement at the interest mirrored in Lily's eyes. 'Listen, when Hymie went off with his prostitutes, I had a few lovers. One was a gentile – don't tell the Rabbi.'

Lily began to laugh. 'The longer I know you, the less I know you.'

'Listen, my girl, as a young woman, I was a good-looker.' Rachel's eyes crinkled with amusement. 'This man taught me more about sex than my husband ever could. He was such a virile man. What a body.'

'Rachel!' Lily protested. 'This is not the sort of conversation you should be having with me.'

'I should tell the Rabbi, is that what you're saying? He'd have a fit.'

'You'll be telling me next you like bacon sandwiches.'

'Only if the bacon is crisp,' came back the quick retort. Both of them laughed helplessly.

The tea arrived and as Lily began to pour, Rachel asked, 'Have you sung at the club yet?'

Lily regaled her with her success.

Rachel clapped her hands. 'Great. Well, maybe after all, you made the right decision.'

'When will you be well enough to leave here?' asked Lily.

'A couple of weeks' time. I'll take it easy, but I must go back to the shop. Earn a few shekels to pay for all this.'

'Perhaps I can help you in the shop,' suggested Lily.

Rachel gave a snort. 'I don't think Mr Vittorio would like that, my dear. Amy is going to give me a hand for a while. I'm going to sell the shop eventually. It's not the same no more. Not since you left. I'm fed up with it. But I need to think of doing something else in the future. I can't stay at home all the time. I need something to keep me occupied.'

Lily looked perplexed. 'Can you afford to retire? I have an empty house that Fred left me. You could live there.'

Rachel looked at Lily with affection. 'Such a kind girl you are. No, my dear, thank you, but I've a few bob put away. Enough for my needs, but I don't forget you offered. You think of some kind of business I might be interested in, you let me know, OK?'

As Lily went to kiss her goodbye, Rachel said, 'You come and see me in The Ditches. I'll even put the electric fire on for you.' She clasped hold of Lily's wrist. A frown furrowed her brow. 'You take care, Lily. It's early days with The Maltese. Watch your back. If you get into trouble, you come to me.'

Lily hugged her. 'I will, I promise.'

As Lily made her way home, she knew that Rachel was right. It *was* early days. And with a man like Vittorio, there was always an element of risk. She didn't know enough about his business to judge how near the edge he was. The Club Valletta seemed all right on the surface, but she knew she didn't see half of what went on.

Chapter Sixteen

Swaying on his feet, Tom held the front-door key in his hand and searched for the keyhole. Why did it seem so much smaller tonight? Eventually, after much cursing and fumbling, he managed to open the door.

Inside, the room was dark apart from the low embers of the range. Mary was obviously in bed, for which he was thankful. He sat in the chair beside the fire and breathed a deep sigh. He wanted Lily so much it was like a constant pain nagging inside him. Never a day passed when she was not in his thoughts. His only consolation was the drink. It was the one thing that dulled the pain. The hangover the next morning he treated as a kind of penance. The more he hurt, the more he loved.

Putting his hand inside his flannel vest, he pulled out a scarf that Lily used to wear when they were courting. He held it in both hands and buried his face in it, breathing in the scent of her.

Lily, Lily, where are you? His heart cried out for her.

He looked around the living room at the ornaments above the fireplace, all carefully dusted and placed precisely. They never must be half an inch to the left or the right. He couldn't count the number of times he'd seen Mary push one back into place if he'd put something on the mantelpiece and inadvertently moved a china figure. Filled with a sudden rage, he got up from his chair and swiped the lot onto the floor with his hand. The broken pieces littering the floor gave him a demoniacal pleasure. Tucking the scarf back inside his vest, he went to bed.

Later, in the twilight time between being awake and

asleep, he could smell her, feel her warm flesh beside him. The drink was like a magic elixir, conjuring many wonderful dreams and feelings. He put his arm around the warm body and held her to him. He could smell the scent of her. 'Lily. Lily,' he murmured as he fell asleep.

Mary, hearing the name of another woman on the lips of her husband as he held her, was outraged. This man she'd married who'd got her pregnant with his disgusting habits was now calling for another. Hadn't she suffered enough, without this? She took the arm that was around her waist and angrily cast it aside.

Downstairs the following morning, Mary gave a cry of horror on seeing her precious things in smithereens. 'That drunken bastard. How dare he?' It was just one more thing with which to berate him.

Tom was ill-prepared for the onslaught that greeted him when he arrived in the living room.

'How dare you come home the worse for wear and destroy my belongings! Well, you can damn well replace them.'

He looked coldly at her. 'No chance. I didn't like them. I want no more ornaments up there. They clutter the place. Now get on with me breakfast, woman.' He picked up the strop to sharpen his razor.

Seeing the leather strop in his hand and the baleful look in his eye, Mary smothered her anger and prepared the breakfast, banging the plates on the table, banging the kettle on the top of the range, banging the frying pan onto the stove. Suddenly her wrist was gripped in a steel-like clasp.

Eyes blazing, Tom yelled at her, 'Stop this at once or I'll swear I'll take the back of me hand to you!'

Mary looked both startled and outraged. 'For God's sake, Tom. I'm five months gone. You'd hit a pregnant woman?'

'I've never raised me hand to a woman in me life, but you would drive a saint to the devil and I'm just a man. Enough, do you hear?' He sat down and ate his breakfast in silence. Then, grabbing his coat from behind the door, he put it on, and his cap, and left the house, slamming the door behind him.

The noise made his head hurt. He was in an ill-humour as he made his way to work, thinking of the shrew of a woman who was his wife. It was an unfortunate start to the day, which grew steadily worse as it progressed.

Tom worked like a man demented that morning, trying to get the anger out of his system by sheer hard graft. During the morning break, he soothed his ruffled feathers by taking the rise out of Burt Haines.

With his quickfire repartee, Tom had humiliated the foreman in front of his workforce. The derisive laughter that had followed Burt's departure as he walked away, unable to find the words to hold his own with the Irishman, still rang in his ears. Now anger raged within *him*.

Later that afternoon, Haines had his revenge; he constantly found fault with Tom's work, clever enough not to make his remarks personal, then enjoyed seeing Tom trying to control his temper. He gloried in the unique situation.

Tom knew what was going on; he realised he'd gone too far earlier in the day. Being proud himself, he knew he'd battered the other man's ego with his barbed comments. Fair enough! Let Haines have the chance to get his own back.

However, one final criticism that wasn't warranted was more than he could stomach; it was the last straw. He was aware of tension in the air as his peers watched, waiting to see how far the situation would go.

Throwing down his tools, Tom faced his foreman. 'All right, that's enough! There's nothing wrong with me work. You know it, and I know it.' He stood within inches of the other man, clenching his fists, longing to punch the living daylights out of the foreman. 'You've had your fun at my expense. Now we're quits.' He pushed Burt Haines in the chest, sending him staggering backwards. The workmen around him laid down their tools to witness the scene before them. 'Bugger off and let me get on with me job,' he growled.

Burt might well have been satisfied with this and let Tom continue, but in the distance he'd seen his own boss approaching. Aware that the confrontation had been observed by his superior but not overheard, his heart sank at the prospect of being questioned about the incident and having to explain it away. Once more, he'd look a fool.

'You're fired, McCann! Take your tools and report to the office.' The words had a wonderful ring about them and Burt savoured the moment. He had longed to say them for many years – and now the situation had presented itself.

Tom looked at him in amazement. There was a buzz of surprise from his colleagues. 'Don't be bloody silly, man,' Tom fumed. 'This joke has gone far enough.'

Haines stood tall, chest puffed out with importance. 'I'm not joking, McCann. I'll make sure your money's made up at the office for you. Now, get off this ship.'

'You bastard – you're serious!' Tom's face was pinched white, and his hazel eyes blazed.

Smirking at him, Burt said, 'You're not so funny now, are you? I don't see you laughing. What, no witty repartee?'

Seeing the big boss approaching, Tom had the sense for once to curb his temper. He grabbed hold of the front of Burt's overall. 'I'll have you,' he said menacingly. 'When you walk down a street on dark nights, you'd better have your wits about you, because I give you me word, you gutless little sod, one night I'll be there waiting.' He wiped his index finger across his throat as he spoke.

The foreman looked back at him, fear in his eyes. Tom saw it and leaned closer. 'You've just taken me living away from me and that's unforgivable.' He let go of Burt's overall. Pointing a finger at the man, he said, 'I'll be seeing you very soon.' Picking up his tools, he threw them into his bag and stomped off.

During the time Tom had to wait for his wages to be made up, his anger increased. He tightly clenched one of his fists and rubbed the taut knuckles with his other hand, picturing the triumphant look on Haines' face. The arrogance of that bastard, to fire *him*, Tom McCann, who could work the socks off him any day. Snatching his pay-packet from the fingers of the startled clerk, Tom marched out of the docks, the rage within him fermenting and bubbling like a volcano about to overflow.

Walking down the road, he wondered how he was going to

tell Mary. He wasn't married a year, his wife was pregnant and he was without a job. If he could get his hands round the throat of that bloody foreman right now, he'd do for him. He'd be worth swinging for.

The sound of the piano being played in The Sailor's Return broke through his tumultuous thoughts. Tom looked along the road towards the pub. He needed a stiff drink. God! Didn't he need something to cheer him up before he went home?

As he entered the bar, Knocker Jones greeted him. 'Hello, lad. Come and sit down. What do you want to drink?'

'A large whiskey.'

Whilst he waited for his friend to be served, he began to calm down, his anger replaced by a deep depression. He'd prided himself on the fact that he'd always been a working man, even during hard times. It had never occurred to him that one day he'd be unemployed. It had been a matter of personal pride to him. But now . . .

Knocker placed the glass in front of him. 'What's up, me old flower? I can see that something is seriously wrong.'

Taking a stiff swig of his whiskey, Tom said, 'I've been fired. I'm out of work.'

Knocker sat quietly listening to his account of the morning. 'The bastard!' he exclaimed when he heard what Haines had done.

'God knows what Mary's going to say, with the baby coming and all.' Tom raged on. 'I've never been out of work, not since I started in the docks. That rotten sod has ruined all me plans. I thought I'd be working until the end of me days.' Leaning towards his friend, he said, 'If I see that bastard, I'll do for him, so help me God.'

'What you gonna do now?' asked Knocker with a worried expression.

'God knows! It's no good me going back to Harland & Wolff's. That bloody foreman will have put the mockers on me ever getting back into the docks. And you know how hard it is to find work elsewhere. Look at the poor buggers back from the war. They risked their lives in the trenches at the Somme, and now they're out on the streets selling matches! Some land fit for heroes, this is. But I'll look around, of course.' Picking up his glass and downing the contents, Tom concluded, 'To be honest, I can't think straight, so I'm going to have another bloody drink.'

Knocker thoughtfully rubbed the stubble on his chin. 'I may be able to put a few jobs your way, if you're interested. No questions asked.'

With an earnest look Tom said, 'Thanks. I'll do anything. I've got to earn some money somehow.'

'Right, me old flower. I'll let you know.'

Tom nodded. 'You're on. Let's have another drink.'

Mary was frantic. Here it was, almost eight o'clock, and still Tom had not returned home. She knew that sometimes he stopped off at the pub on his way home, but he was never this late.

She tried to eat her supper, but she'd no appetite. She pottered about, cleaning, dusting, trying to keep her hands busy and her mind occupied, but eventually she gave up and sat fretting beside the fire. What if Tom had met with an accident? How would she manage? Five months gone, she couldn't get work. What if he was dead? Her skin broke into goosebumps. Who would support her and the baby?

It was a further hour before she heard the singing.

'I'll take you home again, Kathleen . . .' The door opened and Tom staggered in, barely able to stay on his feet. He made his way over to his chair with difficulty and collapsed into it, gazing up at Mary with a vague alcoholic grin. 'Hello, love. Is me supper ready?'

Mary's fury, sparked with relief at his homecoming and anger for his drunken state, was formidable. 'Your supper. *Your bloody supper*. Is that all you can say?'

The smile left Tom's face.

'I've been sitting here waiting for you to come home for hours. Christ! I've had you dead and buried I don't know how many times. And look at you. You're a bloody disgrace.'

'Don't start on me, woman,' he growled. 'I've had one of the worst days of me life.'

Even in his drunken state, the anguish he was feeling showed and Mary stopped her railing. 'Why? What's happened?'

Tom looked at her through glassy eyes. 'I've been sacked. Can you believe that? I've been bloody fired.'

Mary looked shocked. 'Has the work run out, then?'

'No. It's that sodding stuffed-shirt foreman. Can't take a joke.' He sat up straight, muttering, 'He took away me livelihood. I'm going to kill the bastard.'

'What on earth happened?'

'I took the piss out of him in front of me mates and he didn't like it. Later the clever bastard thought he'd get his own back. Then he fired me.'

Mary was furious. 'You never learn, do you? You know Burt Haines doesn't like you, but you've still got to be clever. Now what are we going to do? I won't bring my child up in poverty.'

'Who the bloody hell do you think you are? You've never lived in poverty. Your father has always earned. Since you were married, you've had more money to spend than your mates. Don't think I don't know how you shoved that down their throats!'

With flushed cheeks, Mary blustered at him, 'You've ruined all my plans.'

His eyes narrowed. 'I think you only married me because you thought I earned enough to give you what you wanted. I had plans too, but you never ever thought of that, did you?' He saw the look of guilt on her face. 'Everything with you is planned,' he continued. 'You spend your life to a routine. I know what you are doing every hour of every day.'

Mary was highly indignant. 'I don't know what you mean.'

'At eight o'clock on a Monday, you start washing. On Tuesday you go to the butcher's. In the afternoon you do the ironing. We have the same meals on the same day every week. I'm sick of it! I don't want fish on Fridays. I want sausages.'

'Now you're being childish.'

His gaze was cold and calculating. 'You've never ever had a moment of spontaneity in your whole bloody life. Certainly not in bed!'

She looked at him, cheeks flushed with embarrassment.

'It's like making love to a board. No feeling, no nothing. Apart from that, nothing I do is ever good enough for you, Mary. You're never satisfied.'

'But how will we manage? I can't go back to work, not now I'm pregnant.'

Tom's mouth tightened. 'I'll earn money somehow. You've not married an eejit, you know.'

With a spiteful look Mary said, 'I can always go to my father. He'll give me some money.'

Tom's bellow of rage filled the room. 'You'll do no such thing! No man has ever paid my way in life, not since me family left me here to earn a living, and they won't start now.' He glared at her. 'You'll just have to tighten your belt, woman. Learn how to live economically.' He got unsteadily to his feet and with a certain drunken dignity, said, 'You can always go home to your mother if you don't like it here.' Then he made his way upstairs and went to bed.

The following morning Tom, in a morose mood, left the house and made his way to the Board of Trade building in the hopes of finding work. To no avail. They told him the unemployment benefit had gone up from fifteen shillings to eighteen a week, which didn't cheer him at all. That wasn't enough to keep the wolf from the door for long. His confidence was sorely dented as he made his way home.

It was early evening a couple of weeks later and Sandy was sitting quietly having a drink in The Sailor's Return, hoping there would be some business that night, when the door opened and Tom walked in. He ordered a half of beer and sat beside the pianist.

'It's quiet, isn't it?' he remarked.

Sandy nodded gloomily. 'No one's got any money, dear. By the way, I'm sorry to hear about your trouble. It's hard to be out of work these days. Any chance of getting back to your job later?'

Tom shook his head. 'That bloody foreman wouldn't have me back at any price.' He looked around. 'Where's Lily these days? I haven't been in here the past fortnight.'

Now what am I supposed to say? pondered Sandy. He's

bound to hear about her soon – perhaps it's best it comes from me. 'She's singing at the Club Valletta,' he said quietly.

'She's *what*?' Tom looked appalled. 'What the bloody hell is she doing working for The Maltese?'

'Well, dearie, she needs the work. She's got to live.'

'Yes – but *there* . . .' grumbled Tom. 'I hope she knows what she's doing.' He looked sideways at Sandy. 'Singing, you say. I hope that's all she's doing.'

Sandy remained silent. There was no way he was going to tell Tom Lily was Vittorio's mistress. No way. 'How's your wife?' he asked, changing the subject.

'Not a happy woman.' Tom frowned. 'Being out of work makes things difficult with the baby coming and all. But Knocker said he may have something for me. I was hoping he'd be in tonight.'

'Maybe later,' said Sandy. 'Well, I'd best go and tinkle the ivories. Get the old fingers working.' He got up from his seat and left Tom mulling over his news of Lily.

Sipping his beer, Tom McCann's forehead creased with concern as he thought of Lily working at the Club Valletta. Why the hell had she decided to go there, of all places? Still, as Sandy said, she had to make a living. But Tom was worried. Who was keeping an eye on her, making sure she was safe? No one. Well, he'd not rest until he knew for himself that she was all right.

At that moment, Knocker Jones limped into the bar on crutches. 'Thank God you're here, Tom.'

'What on earth has happened to you?'

'I had a few bevvies the other night and tripped up coming out of a boozer. Broke my bloody toe! I can't do my rounds like this, so will you do them for me? I'll make it worth your while.'

'Of course I will. Be glad of the money.'

'That's what I thought. You'll have to take the horse and cart. Have you ever had any experience with horses?' He sounded anxious.

Tom reassured him. 'Yes, me old mate. When I was in Ireland we used to ride at the local farm. Me and horses get along fine.'

Removing his cap, Knocker vigorously scratched his head. 'Thank God for that. Come around to the yard about eight-thirty tomorrow morning. I'll give you your instructions. Now if you go to the bar for me, I'll buy you a pint.'

It was the last week in March and the morning air was crisp. There had been a heavy frost and the lawns in the parks were still white. Tom McCann sat on the high seat of the cart, muffled against the cold in warm jumpers and an old coat. His flat cap was low over his ears. He held the reins of the old chestnut horse in his gloved hand.

'Gee up, you lazy nag. Get a move on!' The horse snorted, his breath hanging like a mist around his nostrils.

'Rag and bone! . . . Any old rag and bone?' Tom called as he traversed the streets of the Polygon area of Southampton.

These past three weeks Tom had enjoyed himself sitting behind Charlie, the old horse. It had given him a sense of purpose, a feeling of pride. Of being a man again. It had been hard for him to be out of work, but now he was content.

It never ceased to amaze him, the bits and pieces that people threw away. The more wealthy the client, the more bizarre their goods. On his cart now were a chamber pot, a brass bedstead, an old military uniform, a large drum and a hat stand, plus a selection of good-class clothes and a rather worn tiger rug. The creature's head looked quite fearsome with its wide eyes and long, sharp teeth.

Tom enjoyed travelling around the tree-lined roads in this better-class area. With his Irish charm, he found he could sweet-talk his way into paying a pittance for the goods removed, and he enjoyed flirting with the parlourmaids, persuading them into giving him cups of tea and a sandwich occasionally, and now and then a stolen kiss. And sometimes he even could talk clients into paying *him* to take their stuff away – a talent that Knocker noted with approval when he accompanied Tom soon afterwards.

'You've missed your vocation in life, me old flower!' he said to his friend.

'What are you talking about?' asked Tom.

'You with the touch of the blarney. You're making more money than I do on me tod.'

Laughing, Tom said, 'Then perhaps you'd better keep me on.'

Scratching himself, Knocker said, 'I've just been thinking the same thing. How would you like to do this on a regular basis?'

'You serious?' Tom asked, in amazement.

'Why not? Besides,' Knocker gave him a dig in the ribs, 'I've still got a few jobs we can do together, after hours. Until you get back in the docks of course,' he asked hastily, knowing that was Tom's dearest wish. 'What do you say?'

Tom grinned broadly. 'Why not? I'll give it a go. To be sure, there's no other jobs going at the moment, and it's better than being out of work.' Holding out his hand he said, 'Put it there.'

That evening, Tom was eager to tell Mary his good news. He was not a stupid man and had seen for himself the potential for making a profit these past weeks. He would once again be bringing regular money into the home.

'I've got a job,' he announced with shining eyes as he entered the front door.

Looking at the happiness in his face, Mary felt a pang of guilt. Tom had been a generous husband when he was earning and since he'd been fired, she'd felt the pinch. It was difficult for her. She enjoyed being superior to her few friends, and having to lose her position of importance was hard.

She was thrilled at the news. 'Oh Tom, that's marvellous! When do you start back?'

He shook his head. 'No, Mary. It isn't in the docks.'

She looked puzzled. 'Where is it then?'

'It's everywhere,' he said with a chuckle.

'What on earth are you on about? Talk sense.'

Sitting opposite her he said, 'From now on, I'm working full-time for Knocker Jones.'

There was a look of horror on Mary's face. 'But he's a rag and bone man!'

The derogatory tone in her voice killed Tom's enthusiasm. He immediately became defensive. 'I've been doing it these past weeks. You haven't complained before.'

'Well, I thought it was just a temporary measure.'

'It's an honest occupation. What's the matter, Mrs McCann? Think it beneath you to be married to a rag and bone man?'

She remained silent, but the expression on her face spoke volumes.

'Not good enough for you, eh?' He gave her a hard glare. 'Well, listen to me, woman. I'll be putting bread on the table and you'll eat it and be thankful.' Turning on his heel, he slammed out of the house.

Stomping along the road, Tom fumed. Was there no pleasing that woman? His Lily wouldn't have looked down on him that way. Not her.

Unconsciously his steps took him to Bernard Street and the Club Valletta. In the darkness, he stood opposite the entrance, just as Lily had done months before. He watched the comings and goings of the clientèle and wondered where she was. He assumed she was still living in Fred's house and wondered what time she finished work.

Taking out his pocket-watch, he looked at the time. It was seven-thirty; she would probably be working. He'd come back later and walk her safely home. He longed to see her again. It was as if a part of him was missing, like being without a limb.

Just as he turned away, a sound of laughter made him look back. There was Lily, dressed in an expensive claret-coloured coat trimmed with black fur, with a matching fur hat, walking out of the club on the arm of The Maltese. They stood and waited for a moment until a car pulled up in front of the entrance, looking at each other as they had an animated conversation. He heard Lily's laughter and the deep throaty chuckle from her companion. He also saw the way Vittorio looked at her. And he didn't like it. Not one bit.

Chapter Seventeen

Tom and Knocker Jones approached the dock-gates, pushing a large hand-cart loaded with second-hand clothes. It was dark, except for the street-lamps. The light was on in the police post by the gate and the docks policeman on duty was standing in front of it. He stepped forward. 'Where do you think you're going, Knocker?'

'Let me do the talking,' Knocker whispered to Tom.

''Ello, Len. I'm off to pick up some odds and sods from some of the crew on the tugs. They're a bit short of cash. You know how it is.'

The man laughed. 'You'd sell your own mother, given half the chance.'

'You making an offer, mate?'

The policeman waved them through. 'Go on then, you cheeky sod.'

Knocker doffed his cap. 'Thanks, old dear. See you later. I won't be long.'

Letting out a sigh of relief, Tom said, 'That was easy, thank God.'

'Nothin' to it,' laughed his friend. 'I'm always in and out. I make a point of it. I bung them a bottle now and again. Keeps them happy.'

There was an eerie atmosphere within the dock-gates. The darkness was scarcely broken by the low glow from the street-lamps. Reflections of ships' lights quivered on the water, moving with the tide. Figures emerged through the darkness, then disappeared as quickly.

Knocker headed towards a large warehouse which loomed out of the night. He parked the cart beneath an iron staircase, pushing it out of sight in the dark recess.

Sitting on the cart, he patted the space beside him. 'Might as well sit down, me old flower. We'll have some time to wait.'

From their vantage point, they watched a small cargo-ship dock. The hawsers were tied by a crew of stevedores. There was a loud rattling of chains as the anchor was weighed, then a gangway was noisily lowered. Voices carried on the air as the crew hurried ashore to catch the pubs before they closed.

There was a sound of footsteps coming closer, and Tom felt Knocker's hand on his arm, drawing him further into the shadows. His heart pounded; every muscle in his body went rigid with tension. He held his breath as a policeman walked past them, unaware of their presence. As the sound of the footsteps faded into the distance, he felt perspiration break out on his forehead.

Within minutes there was a sound of rustling as a figure appeared from the dusk, a few feet away from them, making Tom jump.

A voice with a foreign accent called softly: 'Knocker. You there?'

Getting off the cart, Knocker gestured to Tom. 'Come on.'

The foreigner – a big man dressed in navy trousers, a thick navy jacket and peaked cap, looked suspiciously at Tom. 'Who's that? What's he doing here?'

'It's all right, Dutchy – he's a mate. Now, have you got the stuff?'

Hearing the name, and recognising the guttural voice of the stranger, Tom lowered his head, pulling his cap further over his face. Dutchy! The man he gave a thrashing to when he was threatening Lily and Amy. Christ – just his luck.

The seaman handed over a hessian sack. 'Be careful.'

Knocker passed it on to Tom. ''Ere, put this on the cart.'

Tom left the two men together talking in low urgent tones, grateful to slip back into the anonymity of the shadows.

The rag and bone man returned and rapidly pulled some coats and old jumpers out of a bag. ''Ere, cover those over the sack. We don't want any awkward questions asked. Keep your head down and say nothing.'

They walked casually back to the dock-gates, where the same policeman as before was on duty. Tom watched anxiously as Knocker stopped the cart and, picking up one of the coats, walked over to him.

'Hey, Len. Got a nice bit of stuff 'ere might fit you. You interested?'

'Get off with you before I run you in for trying to bribe an officer of the law!'

'Would I do such a thing?' asked Knocker in an injured tone.

'Too bloody right you would!'

They cleared the dock-gates without further trouble, Tom breathing freely for the first time since they'd entered the area earlier in the evening.

He was concerned about Dutchy. He must warn Amy that he was around. Lily would be safe from the foreigner's wrath while she was working, for he wouldn't be allowed through the doors of the smart Club Valletta. But what if he found out Lily's home address? Perhaps he'd better go round there later and warn her.

'You did well, Tom,' said Knocker, breaking into his thoughts. 'Kept a cool head. Didn't panic.'

'You were pretty cool yourself.'

'Bit of bluff fools a lot of people, me old flower.'

They headed towards The Ditches.

When Knocker drew up opposite Mrs Cohen's second-hand shop, Tom looked at it and remembered how he'd first seen Lily there. He pictured her bright eyes, her cheeky smile, her laughter. The memory was painful.

Knocker tapped on the window of Abraham's pawn-broker's shop. Then looking around furtively, he rang the bell and waited.

Abraham's bespectacled face peered out as he lifted the curtain, then he opened the door and beckoned to Knocker to come inside.

Lifting the sack off the cart, the rag and bone man told Tom to push it around the corner and wait for him.

Tom puffed on a cigarette as he waited, contemplating how he was forced to be involved with such matters, just

211

because his foreman had sacked him. He thought of Lily – of Mary – and what a mess he'd made of his life.

Fifteen minutes later his friend joined him, a broad smile on his lips. He handed Tom a five-pound note. 'Thanks, me old mate. I finally got a good deal after a lot of argy-bargy with that tight-fisted old sod. He's hard as nails, but I like the old bugger.'

Tom folded the white note and put it in his pocket. 'That was easy money. Thanks.'

Scratching his chin, his friend said, 'Yeah, but it isn't always so. I can do with a man who doesn't lose his nerve. You interested if I need you again?'

Tom nodded his agreement. After all, what choice did he have? He had to earn every penny he could.

Stopping off at the nearest pub for a well-deserved pint, Tom waited until closing time then made his way to Lily's house. He knocked on the door, but there was no answer so he leaned against the wall and lit a cigarette. He was too early. Time passed and still he waited until the man next door, returning home from a late shift, asked him what he wanted. Tom told him.

'You'll have a long wait, mate,' the man said. 'Lily doesn't come here much these days.' He winked at Tom. 'Why would she? She's living with The Maltese.'

Tom felt the blood drain from his face. For one awful moment he thought he was going to pass out. The man caught hold of his arm. 'You all right, mate?' he asked anxiously.

Nodding, Tom held up his hand. 'Yes, thanks . . . I'm fine.'

He walked slowly down the street, wiping his forehead with his red neckerchief. How could she do it? He shook his head. Not his Lily. He didn't believe it. He knew she was singing there, but living with The Maltese . . . Surely the man was wrong. Then he suddenly remembered the intimate look that had passed between Lily and her companion that night outside the club. He pictured the elegant clothes she was wearing . . . and he knew.

★ ★ ★

Amy let herself into her shabby room and sat in an easy chair by the fire. The embers were nearly dead, but she leaned forward and raked them, trying to coax a little flame. Something caught at last and she went to lie back in her chair, but out of the corner of her eye, she saw a movement. Turning, she stifled a cry of terror as she saw Dutchy sitting on the old settee. Although Tom had warned her of his return, she had been vigilant and, as she hadn't set eyes on him, she had been lured into a feeling of false security.

He leered at her, his gold tooth gleaming. 'Hello, bitch. Now you don't run away. Now you stay with me. This time I don't pay. You owe me for the beating I took. You pay good.'

Amy was stricken with fear; she couldn't move. Dutchy crossed the room, moving swiftly for such a big man.

'How did you get in?' she cried.

He ignored her question. Putting out a hand he grabbed her by the neck. He put his large hand across her mouth to stifle the scream that rose in her throat.

Terrorised, she tried to struggle. She saw the excitement reflected in his eyes.

Taking a knife out of his belt, he laid the cold blade against her cheek. 'You don't want to die, do you?'

Fearful that he would cut her she shook her head, slowly.

'Good. You make one sound – it'll be your last. Understand?'

She nodded and stared at the Dutchman, mesmerised by the cruel eyes staring right back at her. She saw his tobacco-stained teeth as he grinned with pleasure.

Amy's heart was thudding so hard she felt it was going to burst. She could hardly breathe. As he removed the knife she felt faint with relief. *Please God don't let him hurt me*, she prayed as Dutchy began to remove her clothing. The feel of his fingers on her flesh made her feel sick. He removed her coat but he couldn't undo the buttons on her blouse quickly enough. He sliced the front of the garment open. Amy felt the trickle of blood on her skin.

She began to shake.

She saw him smile as he gazed upon her bare breasts. She flinched as he enclosed one in his enormous hand, squeezing it crudely. His eyes glittered as she gave a cry of pain. He slapped her face.

He pushed her to her knees and opened his trousers. She tried to resist him as he pushed her down on the ground, flat on her back, and wrenched up her clothes, but he was too strong for her. She clawed at him frantically, to get his sweaty hands off her, but when he held the knife to her throat, she lay still.

He laughed as he ripped her undergarments and parted her legs. Thrusting himself inside her, he covered her mouth with his. She felt his hot skin on her face and caught the odour of his bad breath mixed with the taste of stale beer.

She lost consciousness for a moment and was only vaguely aware of the Dutchman getting hastily to his feet before she passed out again. Then sounds began to penetrate the fog around her – a voice; knocking on the front door; and the slamming of a door at the back of the house as her assailant fled.

'Amy!' called Tom. 'Open the door. It's me, Tom McCann.' He tried the handle of the door and to his surprise, it opened. Stepping inside he called, 'Amy! Where are you?'

He waited for an answer but heard instead a sound like an animal in torment. Turning on the light, he saw before him on the floor a figure, huddled in a small ball.

'Christ! What's happened, Amy love?' He rushed over to her, lifting her to a sitting position. It was then he saw that the shredded blouse was soaked with blood and her other clothes were in disarray. She looked at him with a glazed expression in her eyes. 'Amy!' he pleaded. 'Speak to me.' But she just stared at him vacantly.

Gently picking her up, he placed her in a chair. After a quick search of the downstairs, he raced upstairs, did a lightning check that the place was empty, then pulled a blanket off the bed. He ran back down again, nearly tripping in his haste. Solicitously, he tucked the blanket around the injured woman. 'I'm going to telephone for an ambulance,' he told her, and went out into the street.

When he returned, he sat holding her until it arrived.

'What happened?' asked the driver, as he stooped beside Amy.

'I don't know. I found her like this about twenty minutes ago. She hasn't spoken since.'

'We'll get her to the South Hants Hospital – they'll take care of her. Can you come along? They'll need some details – her name and so on.'

Tom nodded. 'Yes, of course.'

He would have to let Lily know. He was terrified that Dutchy had got to Amy and taken his revenge. If so, Tom would have to sort him out for good and all. Poor Amy. She didn't deserve to be treated like that. His one worry was that she might not recover. Yes, he'd inform Lily as soon as he could.

Early the next morning, a quiet tap on the bedroom door woke Lily. Slipping out of bed, she ran across the room and opened the door. Outside stood Beatrice, an anxious look on her face.

'Sorry to wake you, Miss Lily, but there's a man downstairs asking for you. He says it's an emergency. His name's Tom McCann.'

Lily felt her heart constrict. She glanced back at the bed and was relieved to see Vittorio was still fast asleep. Grabbing her black silk dressing gown she put it on as she ran down the stairs in her bare feet. What on earth could have happened to bring Tom here?

He was standing inside the door, cap in hand, looking around the palatial room. When he saw Lily, he walked quickly over to her. 'I'm sorry to disturb you, but Amy is in hospital.'

Eyes wide with shock Lily asked, 'What's wrong with her?'

He twisted his cap nervously in his hands. 'I think that Dutchy got to her. I found her in a terrible state last night. She's in the South Hants Hospital.'

'Thanks, Tom. I'll get dressed and go to her.' She pulled the front of the gown across her breasts and ran her fingers through her tousled hair, suddenly conscious of him seeing her this way.

The actions were not lost on him. 'I see I got you out of bed.' There was anger in his eyes as he went on: 'I didn't know you lived here until a little while ago. At first I wouldn't believe it.' He looked her up and down. 'I know now it's true.'

Hearing the bitterness in his tone, Lily was filled with guilt. 'You'd best go, Tom. Thanks for letting me know.'

He stared at her with such a hurt expression it nearly destroyed her. 'How could you let *him* touch you!' He turned on his heel and left the building.

For a moment, she couldn't move. She was shaken by the news about Dutchy and by seeing Tom inside the club. At last he knew about Vittorio. But first of all, she must think of Amy.

As she returned to the bedroom, Vittorio stirred. 'What's going on?'

Knowing he would certainly hear of her early visitor, she said, 'A friend of mine is in hospital, badly injured. A man came to tell me.' Opening her wardrobe she said in a choked voice, 'I must go and see her.'

'Get George to call you a taxi. Who is this friend?'

'She's called Amy.' She glanced over to Vittorio. 'She was a good pal to me. She needs my help now.'

He nodded. 'Do whatever you have to, Lily.'

She was so relieved at his understanding, she leaned over the bed and kissed him. 'Thank you.'

'Is there anything I can do?' he asked.

Shaking her head she said, 'No. I don't know too much about it at the moment, except that she's badly hurt. I'll let you know more when I've been to the hospital.'

When she walked into the ward, Lily was shocked at Amy's appearance. Her face was swollen and bruised, as was her neck, but the thing that shattered Lily most of all was the vacant expression in Amy's eyes.

The Matron, on learning that Lily was a close friend and from now on would be taking care of the patient, told her, 'She has been brutally raped. She's in shock still. Stay with her, hold her hand. Talk to her. Perhaps you'll get a response. So far she's not spoken to anyone.'

To Lily it was like seeing Rachel all over again. But Rachel had recovered. Looking into Amy's eyes, she was afraid that her friend would never get over this.

Drawing the curtains around the side of the bed she said, 'Hello, my love, it's Lily. Tom told me you were here.' She took one of her friend's cold hands in hers and stroked it gently. 'Now, don't you worry. I'm going to take good care of you.' Sitting on the bed, she put her arm around Amy's shoulders and held her, crooning softly.

Lily kept talking to her. Recounting their days together in The Ditches. Relating little stories about Rachel, and the times they had together. She smoothed her forehead, murmuring words of encouragement. She bathed her face, gave her a drink of water. 'Sorry, darling, there's no gin in it,' she said with a smile.

Amy looked up at her, a spark of recognition at last. In a faltering voice she said, 'Lily. Oh Lily. I'm so pleased to see you.' The tears welled in Amy's eyes and she began to cry.

Lily held her tightly until the wracking sobs subsided. Then, wiping Amy's face, she said, 'You've nothing to worry about now, my love. I'm here, and I'm going to take care of you.'

Amy relaxed in her arms and slept.

The Matron stopped by the bed and with a look of relief said, 'She looks peaceful at last.'

'What happens to her now?' asked Lily.

With a frown the Matron answered, 'She needs to stay under observation for a while yet. There's nothing broken, thank goodness. Except perhaps her spirit. The police have been round, but I told them she was too ill to be questioned.'

'When can she be moved?' asked Lily anxiously.

'It's too early to say yet, my dear. But the fact that she recognised you and spoke – well, that's a good sign. She'll need care and understanding when she leaves.'

Looking at the sleeping face of her dearest friend Lily said, 'She'll get that, I can promise you.'

Lily stayed with Amy all day. She eventually wakened and

took a little sustenance with Lily's encouragement. 'Now come on, Amy love. You won't get better if you don't take something.' She spooned into Amy's mouth a little broth, then waited outside while the doctor attended to the patient.

'What are you doing here?' asked Amy when Lily returned to her bedside.

'Where else would I be?' asked Lily.

'But shouldn't you be at the club?'

Shaking her head Lily said, 'No. Vittorio knows where I am. And I'll be back tomorrow and every day until you're better.'

With a wan smile Amy said, 'God knows when that'll be.'

'Now listen to me, my girl. These things can't be rushed, but in time you'll be back to your old self.'

Amy shook her head. 'I'll never be my old self, Lily. I'll never go back on the street after what Dutchy did to me. I'd be too scared.' Her face paled and her bottom lip trembled. 'I've never been so terrified in all my life.' She began to cry softly.

Whilst she held her friend in her arms, Lily raged inside. So Tom was right – it *was* that Dutch bastard. Well, she'd fix him. She'd see to it that he could never do this to anyone else again.

The nurse finally gave Amy a sedative and settled her down for the night with Lily's promise to return in the morning.

When she paid the taxi-driver outside the club, Lily raced up the stairs to Vittorio's office and, opening the door, barged in.

He looked up in surprise as she strode angrily over to him. 'I'm going to ask you a favour and please don't say no!'

His eyes narrowed at the expression on her face. 'I can't possibly say yes or no until you tell me what you want. Sit down, Lily. You look as if you're going to explode at any minute.'

That was exactly how she felt! Taking a cigarette from his case on the desk, she lit it, drew deeply on it and said, 'Today I saw my friend who had been brutally raped by a foreign seaman off the *Rotterdam*. I want him seen to.'

The Maltese raised his eyebrows in surprise. 'What precisely do you mean, my dear?'

Lily's face was white with anger. 'I want him dealt with in such a way that he'll never return to Southampton – or England, for that matter.'

His eyes glittered as he asked, 'Are you saying you want him removed permanently?'

She met his gaze without flinching. 'He can be wiped off the bloody face of the earth for all I care!'

'Are you asking me to have a man killed?'

'Yes!'

'Do you realise what you're asking of me?'

'Well, it wouldn't be the first time, would it?'

Vittorio gazed at her coolly. 'Just supposing your request was granted and you were told this man no longer breathed,' he said. 'Could you live with yourself afterwards?' He looked at her, trying hard to make her realise the consequence of her demands. 'Conscience is a very strange thing. It can give you sleepless nights and years of remorse.'

'As far as this bastard goes, I have no conscience. He doesn't deserve one.'

A slow smile touched the corners of his mouth as he saw the anger burning in her eyes. 'My, Lily. I've never seen you in this mood. Who exactly is this monster that has moved you to make such a request?'

'He's a big hulk of a man, known as Dutchy. Feared by all the prostitutes. He carries a knife and he's the scum of the earth. If I was a man, I'd do it myself . . .' She gulped, fighting back tears. 'He once held a knife at my throat. The tip of it cut my skin. I thought I was going to die.'

Vittorio's expression hardened. 'When was this? You never told me about it.'

'Before I came here. Amy and me were going home from the pub when he accosted us. Some bloke came along and saved us, otherwise I might be dead because of him.'

'I see.' The smile had disappeared. 'Which ship did you say?'

'The *Rotterdam*. It's a cargo-boat – probably sailed by now. But he'll be back.'

'You look tired, my darling. How was your friend when you left her?'

'Still shocked.' The anger in Lily had seeped away and she looked harrowed. 'I need to take care of her, Vittorio. You do understand, don't you?' she pleaded.

He nodded. 'Of course. She must be very special to deserve such loyalty.'

'And the other matter?' Lily asked.

'He will be dealt with.'

'Thank you. I'm going to bed now. I feel shattered. Shall I wait for you?'

He shook his head. 'No, Lily. Get some sleep. I'll not disturb you tonight. You don't look as if you have an ounce of energy left in you. That wouldn't do for me.'

She walked around the desk and kissed him on his forehead. 'I'll see you in the morning.'

The following day, Lily arrived at the hospital, arms filled with flowers, and carrying a basket of fruit and a new peach-coloured nightdress with matching negligée.

Amy managed a smile when she saw her friend. When Lily unpacked the night attire, she even showed a trace of her old spirit. 'Blimey! If I was fit, dressed in that lot, I could charge a fortune.'

'You're never going back to whoring, Amy,' Lily declared. 'I've had a brilliant idea. When you're well enough, you can live in Fred's house. Look after it for me, like a housekeeper. I'm earning good money – I'll pay you to do it.'

There was a lump in Amy's throat and she could hardly speak. 'You can't afford to do that.'

'Rubbish! I've decided. It's no good having an empty house.' Catching hold of Amy's hand she said, 'You would do the same for me.'

As she spoke she saw in the distance a figure coming towards her. Her voice faltered as she said, 'You have another visitor, Amy.'

Tom McCann had also brought flowers. He leaned over the bed and kissed Amy on the forehead. 'How are you, love?'

'Not so bad. It was you that brought me here, wasn't it?' she said weakly.

Tom nodded. 'I called round to see if you were all right, but sadly I was too late to save you.' He looked across the bed at Lily. 'How are you?'

Putting on a bright smile, she answered, 'Fine, Tom. Thanks for letting me know about Amy. I'm so grateful.'

They both sat with her until lunch-time, when the Matron suggested that Amy needed to rest. Lily looked anxiously at her friend.

'Go home, Lily. Come back tomorrow,' Amy said sleepily. 'I'll be fine. To be honest, I am a bit tired. Thanks for all the goodies.'

Tom and Lily walked out of the hospital together in an uneasy silence. Outside, she turned to walk away, but he caught hold of her hand. 'We need to talk, Lily.'

She nodded. 'Yes, I suppose we do.'

They went into a small cafe where Tom ordered a pot of tea for two. After the waitress served them, he said, 'I need to know the truth. Why didn't you want to marry me? The real reason, please. I can't rest until I know.'

Lily stared into the face of the man who meant everything to her. After all, now she had nothing to lose. He knew about Vittorio. He might as well know the full story.

So she told him about her father, his abuse of her. 'I couldn't marry you, Tom, without you discovering all this. I was only seventeen – I would have needed a birth certificate. We also needed my parents' permission, as I was under-age. It was a hopeless situation.' The anguish she felt was etched on her face. She omitted the part that Manny had played. Compared to the rest of her story, it was insignificant.

'Why didn't you tell me? I don't understand.'

She caught hold of his hand. 'Would you have been able to make love to me, knowing what my father had done?'

'Lily, Lily,' he chided. 'Don't you know that nothing in this world would have made any difference? Why couldn't you have trusted me?'

She gazed into his hazel eyes, studied the firm jaw, the full lips. There was not a feature she didn't know and love. 'I was afraid you'd be disgusted.'

His jaw tightened. 'The only thing that disgusts me is that you are Vittorio Teglia's mistress! I find that hard to stomach. Why? How could you?'

To her surprise, Lily found that she was defending Vittorio. 'He's given me a new start. I sing in his club, he pays me a good wage.'

'And you pleasure his bed.' Tom's lips narrowed in anger.

'As your wife does yours,' Lily retorted.

Tom gave a derisive snort. 'Not if she can help it. She's a cold fish who thinks only of being one-up on the neighbours. To her, sex is dirty. She hates sharing my bed.'

At once Lily could see the unhappiness mirrored in his eyes.

'Oh Tom, I'm so sorry. I thought you had a good marriage. When you told me at Fred's funeral you were to be a father, it was as if a knife had plunged into my heart. But at least I thought you were happy, so it didn't seem so bad. Why didn't you tell me?'

'How could I? It was the wrong time.'

She thought how sad this meeting was. Two people so in love, never to be together. She gave a deep sigh. 'What a mess we've made of our lives. Do you blame me for it?'

He gripped her wrists. 'Yes! Yes, I do. If you hadn't run away, we could be together.' There was still anger in his voice as he coldly added, 'Of course you wouldn't be dressed nearly so expensively. I can't afford the same things as The Maltese.'

'Don't do this, Tom. I am what I am – I make no excuses. We lead different lives. We have no choice. Not any more.'

His tone softened. 'I still love you, Lily. More than ever. I want to be with you, hold you, kiss you . . . love you. I want you in my bed. I can't bear the thought of him touching you.'

She got up from the table. 'Enough! This is dangerous and stupid talk. Vittorio would never let me go, and you're about to become a father.' Putting a hand on his shoulder she softly said, 'We had one night together. That will have to do for the rest of our lives.' She bent and kissed him on the lips. 'Goodbye, Tom.'

He watched her walk away. She was the only woman he had ever wanted. He felt as if his whole world had collapsed.

Chapter Eighteen

It was two weeks before Amy was ready to leave hospital, and Lily once again needed Vittorio's help. He was in the bedroom, changing before the evening business. Lily walked up to him and winding her arms around his neck, looked at him intently. 'I need another favour, Vittorio.'

He raised his eyebrows in surprise. 'Someone else has upset you?'

She shook her head. 'Amy is due to be released from hospital. I would like to bring her here, just for a few days.'

He looked perplexed. 'I'm not so sure that's a good idea. No one enters my premises unless they are clients. Much of what goes on here is confidential – you know that.'

She did know what Vittorio meant. It wouldn't do for Amy to see the Chief Constable making his way to the large room at the end of their corridor, his arms around two teenage boys, as she'd encountered them one evening.

'I know,' coaxed Lily, 'but we must have a room on this floor that I can use for about three days. Amy won't leave it, I promise. I just want to be sure she's all right before she goes home on her own. Please, Vittorio.'

He hesitated. 'I'm beginning to be concerned about your strong attachment to this friend. I wouldn't like it to get in the way of our relationship. You know I wouldn't put up with such a thing, Lily. My considerations come first.'

She ran her fingers through his hair. 'You always come first, you know that. I'm yours, to do with as you wish. Whenever.'

The deep-brown eyes stared into hers. But there was a look of respect in them. 'You are good at bargaining, I'd forgotten. You are a schemer, Lily. A devious schemer.'

'Does that mean yes?'

'Three days only. And she stays in her room. Bring her here before ten-thirty in the morning – and no visitors!' he snapped.

She gave a cry of delight. 'I promise.'

'This is an exception, Lily. Don't ask again.'

Amy looked apprehensive as the taxi pulled up at the door of the club. She smoothed down the new coat that Lily had bought for her. 'Do I look all right?'

'Of course you do. Now just follow me and don't look at anyone.'

She paid the taxi-driver and walked Amy through the dining room and up the stairs to the room next to her own. She opened the door and ushered Amy in. 'There, what do you think?' she asked with more than a little pride.

The room had a feminine air about it. It contained a large double bed, covered with a chintz spread that matched the curtains. There was a bedside table with matching wardrobe. A small bathroom led off the room, which Amy much admired. On the bedside table was an ice-bucket with a half-bottle of champagne in it, two glasses and a plate of dainty sandwiches. 'They're in case you get hungry,' Lily told her. 'Come on, let's open the bubbly now to celebrate. Apart from that, it's a great pick-me-up.'

Amy sat on the bed and looked about her new surroundings. 'Oh my, Lily. I can see how you like living here. You wouldn't think it was a brothel, would you?'

Somehow these words drove home. Lily never ever considered she was living in a brothel. She saw the girls take their punters upstairs, of course, but she'd managed to shut her eyes to the reality. She'd been allowed behind the closed doors of the gambling room where there were roulette tables and card games, but she was never allowed to gamble. Not that she wanted to. She'd seen too many people lose too much money. But now, she'd been made to face up to it. Yes, this was a house of ill-repute, and she was part of it.

Picking up the half-bottle of champagne she forced a

smile. 'Hold the glasses whilst I open this.'

The two women sat on the bed, drinking and nibbling on their sandwiches. 'This is lovely, Lily.'

She dismissed Amy's words with a smile. 'You can only stay here for three days,' she said, 'but by then I'll have the house ready. I'll get some food in.' She looked at Amy with an anxious expression. 'Will you be all right there on your own? I could ask Sandy to stay with you at night. He could sleep in the spare room.'

'If he would just for a while, Lily.' Amy's brow furrowed as she asked, 'Have you heard anything about Dutchy?'

'I don't think you need worry any more about him. He won't be coming back – ever.'

Amy gave a knowing nod. She was sure from Lily's tone that her problem had been solved one way or another, and she didn't want to know the details.

Lily insisted that Amy get undressed and into bed early. She handed her some magazines she'd bought. 'Matron said you have to take it easy. I'll pop in just before I go down to the bar to work, OK?'

'Don't you worry about me. I'm enjoying every moment.'

'Remember,' warned Lily. 'Stay in your room, don't venture outside.'

'Of course not. I promise.'

When Lily knocked on the door later, she found Amy propped up in bed, reading. She gave a gasp when she saw the creation that Lily was wearing. 'Turn round, let me see. Oh, Lily. You look beautiful.'

Lily gave a twirl. 'Vittorio's bought this and three others for me last week,' she said as she danced around the room. There was a knock on the door. Opening it, she was surprised to see The Maltese standing there.

'I thought I'd come and meet our guest.'

'Of course.' She turned and said to Amy, 'Vittorio has called to see you.' She saw the look of apprehension on her friend's face.

Vittorio entered the room and, walking over to Amy, shook her by the hand. His expression didn't change when he observed the bruising on her face, but he smiled inwardly when he saw the peach nightdress and negligée, guessing that Lily had purchased them. He said softly, 'I do hope you are comfortable?'

'Oh yes, Mr Teglia,' she murmured. 'Thank you for allowing me to stay.'

'It's a pity it's for such a short while, but that can't be helped. Anything you need, ask Lily. Beatrice, the maid, will bring you your meals. Order anything you like from the menu.' He walked towards the door. 'Lily – call into the office on the way down, will you?'

She nodded. 'I'll only be a minute.'

After Vittorio had gone, Amy beckoned Lily over to the bed. Quietly she said, 'He's lovely. I had no idea. Everyone is terrified of him, but Lily . . . he's really handsome.'

Her friend gave a cheeky grin. 'He's all right when you know how to handle him.'

Walking down one flight of stairs, Lily made her way into Vittorio's office. 'You wanted to see me?'

He pushed the local paper over to her. 'Read that.'

The article said a badly decomposed, unidentified body had been washed up on the shore. It was the mutilated body of a male. Foul play was suspected.

Lily looked across the desk at Vittorio and smiled. She felt no remorse. Surely her actions were fully justified! In her mind, this man could have been a murderer. But for Tom's intervention both times, Dutchy could have committed murder, and she might easily have been one of his victims. Passing the paper back, she said, 'Thank you.'

'You've made it clear to your friend she must stay in her room?'

Lily nodded. 'She understands. You have no need to worry.'

'You had better be right. This will be the first and last time. No more lame ducks, Lily.'

'Amy isn't a lame duck. I owe her a lot,' she retorted.

'You owe me more and don't you forget it.'

Filled with indignation, Lily asked, 'Didn't you feel a little bit sorry for her when you saw her condition?'

His mouth tightened. 'Of course. I'm not a monster, you

know. I'm not without some feelings.'

She sat on the chair opposite him, and with Rachel's words in mind asked him, 'Have you ever been in love, Vittorio?'

He frowned. 'Why do you ask?'

'I'm curious.'

'No, Lily. It's an emotion I can't afford in my business.'

She persisted with her questions. 'Don't you ever want a family? Children?'

'No.'

'Why not?'

His eyes narrowed. 'I've no need to explain. And you would be wise not to question me about anything. Do I make myself clear?'

She stared at him, trying to fathom the man. He was a mystery that she would like to solve, but it wouldn't be with his help. 'Yes. If you say so.'

'I do. Now run along, I'm busy.'

'You sometimes talk to me as if I'm a child.' She pouted.

'Sometimes you *are* a child. Now go and play.'

She walked towards the door and paused. 'I'm not a child when I'm in your bed, am I, Vittorio?' She didn't wait for an answer.

Vittorio frowned and put down his pen. He leaned back in his chair as he pondered Lily's questions. It wasn't that he was incapable of love. He'd adored his mother and was devastated when she died. As a boy of five, it was difficult to understand. His sense of loss had been tremendous and the pain still lived within him.

Dreamily, he remembered her beautiful hair, the colour of ebony. The Square where the women used to congregate with their laundry around the communal washing area for a gossip, whilst he played at their feet. When she'd died, he couldn't go near the place. He thought of the simple house where he'd spent so many happy hours and was filled with nostalgia.

After the death of his mother, Vittorio's father, uncle and his family had all left Malta and come to England in the hopes of making a fortune. For them it had been a futile venture. Not so for Vittorio himself.

He lit a cigarette and thought about his father for the first time in years. Mr Teglia had been a fine, handsome man who showed affection only to the many women who came into his life. There was none for his son – only contempt.

Vittorio felt the anger rise within him as he remembered his father's words to him: 'Stop this snivelling. Your mother was too soft with you. You must learn to be strong. Be a man!' There were no comforting arms or soft words to ease his tears as he cried for his mother. To a small boy, used to love and affection, those were dark days.

Puffing on his cigarette, The Maltese recalled the dirty sleazy brothel his father used to run. Vittorio hated it. As he grew, he hated it even more – and despised his father. His mouth narrowed at these memories, and the bitterness within him surfaced.

Angrily stubbing out the cigarette in an ash-tray, Vittorio walked over to the window. Bernard Street was not a bad place. Although it was still part of the dock area, it was better than the dirty back streets of his childhood in England. *His* brothel had class – a thing his father didn't have and couldn't understand.

He had his teacher to thank for his good taste. She saw the intelligence beneath the surface of the boy whose exterior showed little emotion. She introduced him to books and art, and encouraged him. After leaving school, inspired by her faith in him, he'd educated himself even further. He would always be grateful to her.

When he was seventeen, his father had been stabbed to death by a seaman. Vittorio felt no loss at his demise. But left to fend for himself, he discovered that he was good at wheeling and dealing and eventually had acquired the Club Valletta. Slowly he had built up its reputation . . . and his own.

He was determined that no one, ever again, would get close enough to hurt him. Then Lily came into his life. He smiled to himself as he always did when he thought of her. She was like a breath of fresh air in the murky and dangerous life that he led, and he was aware that she was slowly breaking down the barrier he'd built around himself. The situation was as disconcerting as the girl herself, and he didn't know where it was leading . . . Picking up his pen, he returned to his paperwork.

It was Amy's last night and the girls were having dinner together in her room. 'Sorry it's so late,' apologised Lily, 'but the bar was busy and I had to sing a couple of extra numbers.'

'I could hear you – and the applause. You went over well.'

Lily gave her a puzzled look. 'How could you, when you are so far away, and the door was closed?'

Amy was uncomfortable; she squirmed beneath Lily's steady gaze. 'Well, to be honest, I opened the door and listened.'

With a horrified gasp Lily asked, 'Did anyone see you?'

'Only some tall geezer with a couple of boys.'

Putting her hand to her mouth Lily said, 'Oh my God! If Vittorio gets to hear about this, I'm in real trouble. He doesn't like strangers to see his punters.'

'He didn't see much of me. I wasn't outside the door. Well, only for a minute.'

'Just where were you when he came up the stairs?'

'I heard him coming and I popped back inside. He just saw my face only for a second. He was drunk anyway. He won't remember.'

'Let's hope you're right. It's just as well you're leaving in the morning.' She ran her fingers through her hair. 'I told you not to leave your room, Amy. Why did you do it?'

'Sorry, love. I just wanted to hear you sing, that's all.'

With a worried frown Lily said, 'Don't tell a soul about this, please.'

'Cross me heart and hope to die. Christ! What's that?'

There was a crashing noise from along the corridor and raised voices, then the sound of running footsteps. They both sat quietly listening. Then there were more footsteps, and voices in a panic.

The bedroom door opened and Vittorio stepped inside, shutting it behind him. 'I want you to lock this door behind me when I go and don't open it until I tell you. Under-stand?' he instructed the women.

Lily nodded. It was the first time she'd seen him ruffled. Once he'd left, she locked the door and waited.

Outside there was a lot of commotion – much to-ing and fro-ing. The girls wondered what on earth was going on. But Lily knew that whatever it was, it was serious . . . and it meant trouble.

Eventually, things quietened down and there was a tap on the door. Vittorio was standing there, a thunderous look on his face. 'Everything is all right now, Lily. But I suggest you get your friend settled for the night. She must leave early in the morning, by eight o'clock. Understand?'

She nodded. 'Are you all right, Vittorio?'

He just raised his eyebrows. 'I'll see you later. It's best if you go straight to our room.'

After saying good night to Amy, Lily went to her own room and undressed. She sat up in bed, brushing her hair, filled with curiosity and concern.

Vittorio looked so angry when he came into the room, she didn't dare question him. He took off his tie and threw it across the bed, then removed his clothes and carefully hung them up, as was his habit. With a deep sigh, he sat on the edge of the bed and lit a cigarette.

'Have you calmed down now?' asked Lily softly.

'That stupid bastard!' he fumed.

'Who do you mean?'

'Our illustrious Chief Constable. Things got a little nasty for him tonight and I had to get him out of a mess. He'll owe me a huge debt and I'll make him pay.'

'What happened?' Lily asked quietly, surprised at Vittorio taking her into his confidence.

'His games became a little rough and the boys took exception. They both turned on him. He won't be at work for a while, the state he's in.'

'Will you get into trouble?'

He smiled his slow smile. 'Me? Oh no. I'm well covered – I made sure of that. But one thing's for sure. He won't be allowed in here again.'

Lily was anxious. 'But won't he make trouble for you?'

Vittorio shook his head. 'Not with the evidence I'm holding against him. He wouldn't like the pictures I have to fall into the wrong hands.' He turned to her. 'I've told you before, Lily, I don't do anything without calculating all the angles first.' He rolled over on his stomach. 'Massage my shoulders, darling. My body is full of tension and I won't sleep.'

She did so, but was filled with foreboding. Despite Vittorio's assurances, she was worried. Any scandal was dangerous, but one involving such an important member of the public . . . What would happen next?

The following morning, Lily took Amy by taxi to her new abode. As they walked into Fred Bates' living room, Amy looked around with delight. Lily had put pretty net curtains up at the windows, the furniture was nearly new, and on a table in the middle of the room stood a small vase of flowers. In the hearth a fire was already laid.

Lily struck a match to the paper and soon the flames caught. Taking her friend to the larder, she showed her the well-stocked cupboard. 'This should set you up for a while. Every Friday, you'll get your money. The milk float comes every day and the fishmonger with his cart on a Friday morning. Now you can lead the life of Riley! No more standing on street corners. The only sex you need have is by choice.'

Shaking her head Amy said, 'I find all this hard to take in.' She looked at her friend with tear-filled eyes. 'It's like a dream, Lily. I'm just so afraid I'll wake up.'

'Don't be such a daft bitch. I've sent word to Sandy, by the way. He's willing to come here and stay at night with you for a bit, but I can tell you for sure now that Dutchy won't be back. All you need to worry about is getting better and enjoying life.'

Amy gave Lily a hug. 'Who'd have thought it. You, that young girl at Mrs Cohen's, and now this.' She stared hard at Lily. 'I hope it's been worth it, love.'

With a shrug the younger girl said, 'I made my choices.

They weren't what I wanted by a long chalk, but on the whole, I'm not complaining. Just one other thing,' she added. 'Should the Old Bill come round asking questions, you stayed with me for three days and saw nothing as you never left your room. You heard nothing out of the ordinary – all right?'

Nodding her head Amy said, 'Whatever you say.'

There was a knock at the door.

'Probably Sandy,' said Lily.

The pianist bustled in, closing the door behind him. Looking at Lily, he said, 'Heard you had a bit of trouble at the club last night.'

'Why do you say that?'

'Because in the early hours of the morning, I had a visit from two young boys looking for sanctuary. They told me all about it.'

Lily's face turned pale. 'What did they say?'

Undoing his silk cravat he said, 'They were hustled out the back door after they beat up the old man they were with. Vittorio's man gave them some money and told them to keep their mouths shut, or else. They were scared shitless!'

'Where are they now?'

'At my place.'

'Then get rid of them,' urged Lily.

With an anxious look Sandy said, 'Don't worry. I've told them to go to London this morning – to get right away. I don't want to be involved, and neither do they.'

Amy had been sitting quietly listening to it all. 'That's all right then.'

With a frown Sandy said, 'Don't be too sure. I've heard rumours. The Chief Constable has been under suspicion for some time. I think this whole thing is going to blow up in everyone's faces.' To Lily he said, 'You be very careful, my girl. You don't want to be dragged into a scandal.'

'I only sing at the club. I don't know anything.'

'Don't be so bloody naive. It's a known fact you're the mistress of The Maltese. You need to be very careful.'

'I'd best be getting back to the club,' she said, filled with concern. 'To warn Vittorio.'

★ ★ ★

As soon as she entered the club, she knew she was too late. It was swarming with police. 'What's going on?' she asked, her voice steady.

A man in plainclothes approached her. 'Detective Inspector Chadwick,' he said, producing his warrant card. 'You'd be Miss Lily Pickford, no doubt.'

She gave a winning smile. 'That's right. What can I do for you?'

'Were you here last night, Miss Pickford?'

'Yes I was. All evening.'

'Where were you?'

'After an early meal, I was in my room getting changed for my performance. Then I sang for the guests. After that I went back to my room and went to bed.'

'Yours and Mr Teglia's room, I think you mean?' There was a sneer in his voice.

'Yes, that's right, officer.' She stood tall, looking at him with a certain arrogance. 'It's not a secret that I live with Mr Teglia.'

'Did you hear anything unusual?'

She looked puzzled. 'Like what?'

'The signs of a fight – a struggle, perhaps.'

Shaking her head, she said, 'No, sir. Nothing.'

Behind him she saw Vittorio coming down the stairs with two police officers. He looked calm enough, but knowing her man as well as she did, she could sense the tension in him.

He walked towards her and put his arm around her shoulders. 'I see you've met Miss Pickford.'

The Detective Inspector nodded.

'Was she able to assure you there had been no trouble?'

'As far as it goes, sir.' He looked at Vittorio with scarcely veiled hostility. 'You've been very clever up to now, Mr Teglia, yet I can't help but feel you're living on borrowed time. I can still see you banged up in a nice cosy cell.'

The slow smile crossed Vittorio's features. 'Not really my style, I don't think. Do you?'

The Detective Inspector gave a sly grin. 'Well, we don't have a brothel in the nick, if that's what you mean.'

'A brothel!' Vittorio looked at him in surprise. 'Are you suggesting these premises are used as a brothel?'

'Do you deny it?'

'I most certainly do. Businessmen come in here for a few drinks, a fine meal and a pretty hostess to sit with them and to dance if the client wishes to do so. That hardly constitutes a brothel, officer.'

'But it's what happens after the dancing, isn't it, Mr Teglia?'

Vittorio looked indignant. 'My hostesses are under strict instruction not to fraternise with the clients after hours. They would lose their jobs if they did. They know that.'

Lily was filled with admiration at Vittorio's composure.

'That's not true, and you know it.'

With a steady gaze Vittorio asked, 'Have you any proof to the contrary?'

The detective ignored him. Looking at the closed doors at the back of the dining room he asked, 'What's in there?'

Lily's heart constricted, thinking of the roulette tables.

'Take the gentleman to see the room, Lily.'

She looked at Vittorio in surprise, but he just smiled. 'Come along, my dear, these men are busy.'

She led the way, her temples throbbing with tension and fear. The double doors opened to her touch, and she walked in. The room now resembled a tasteful salon, with comfortable easy chairs, tables and magazines.

She stood back and let the detective sniff around. Over her shoulder she looked into the smiling eyes of Vittorio. He closed one eyelid in a sly wink. She smiled broadly at him. Crafty sod. This must have all been done in the night. As usual, Vittorio had foreseen every move the police would make. She was filled with admiration.

Looking around, Detective Inspector Chadwick gave a rueful smile. 'Very cosy, I must say.'

'We have a fine dining room with excellent food, Inspector,' said Lily. 'You should consider holding some of your official meetings here.'

'Don't push your luck, love!' he snapped. 'You're in this as deep as everyone else.'

Further searching by the police drew no evidence that would convict Vittorio in any way of breaking the law and the officers reluctantly withdrew.

When at last they were alone, Lily breathed a sigh of relief, and Vittorio looked at her with amusement. 'Official police meetings? Bit cheeky, wasn't it?'

She shrugged. 'Anyway, why were the police here?'

Suddenly he looked angry. 'Apparently, when the Chief Constable's wife saw the state of her husband, she first called the doctor, then the police.'

'That must have put the fear of God in him,' said Lily. 'Mind you, I don't suppose for one minute she has any idea of her husband's little weakness. But that doesn't explain you being raided.'

'I have it on good authority that the powers that be are out to get the Chief. They knew he dined here. After all, it wasn't a secret. He did many a time with other notable city officials, strictly above board luncheons. But you can't keep secrets in the force and they thought they had him at last.'

'By the short and curlies, if you'll pardon the expression,' said Lily with a grin. 'Weren't you the least bit worried?' she asked.

He shook his head. 'Why should I be? Once we cleared the gambling room and cleaned the room upstairs, there was nothing for them to find.'

'Well, my bloody knees are knocking. Give me a drink, please,' she asked the barman. 'And make it a double.'

Vittorio chuckled as he watched her down the fiery liquid. 'We'll have to be careful. Shut the gaming room for a while. Keep the girls off their backs. It'll soon settle down again.'

'What about the old geezer that got done up?'

'He won't dare come back here. You'll see – things will be back to normal soon enough.'

She grimaced. 'I hope you're right. This is no good for my nerves.'

He caught hold of her arm. 'You did remarkably well, Lily. You kept calm, and you were utterly convincing.'

'What else could I do?' But she was now deeply concerned for Vittorio. She'd seen the determined look in the eyes of the detective. He was out to get The Maltese. Of that she was sure.

A few days later, there was an article in the local paper, reporting the early retirement of Chief Constable Bartlett for health reasons. As Sandy put it: 'He's been rumbled, dear – caught with his pants down – and the police wouldn't want it all to become public knowledge.'

During the following three weeks, business in the club slackened off considerably, as was expected. But Vittorio said it would be only a five-minute hitch. And sure enough, things did begin to pick up a little eventually. Aware that the police were keeping his club under observation, The Maltese played it by the book. In the evenings the girls were allowed to sit with the clients and dance, but that was all. Being a shrewd businessman, he made sure they didn't lose out financially. That way the girls were content, and they stayed loyal. For their part, the girls enjoyed themselves. As one said to Lily, 'It's like being on holiday.'

During this time, Vittorio arranged for Lily to be schooled in the intricacies of running a business. To her surprise, she loved the technicalities of it all. Such was her enthusiasm that even the head waiter took time to teach her his skills: the correct way to lay a table; uses for the different types of cutlery; the proper way of serving and how to choose wine. The chef explained his menus to her and the different ways of balancing the different courses. She was bright, and she learned quickly.

Vittorio watched with delight as she soaked in all the details like a sponge. One day she would be even more of an asset to him than she already was.

One Saturday evening, Lily, even more confident with her newfound knowledge, was talking to Vittorio and some of his clients when suddenly over his shoulder she saw a familiar figure enter the club. It was Tom McCann. She stiffened.

'What is it?' asked Vittorio.

'Nothing,' she said quickly. 'Someone walked over my

grave, that's all. I'll leave you with your friends.'

Walking casually over to the bar, greeting one or two clients on the way, she went and stood next to Tom. 'What are you doing here?' she asked abruptly.

He looked at her with an intensity that shook her. 'I wanted to see you again. I can't get you out of my mind. It's driving me crazy knowing you're here, with him.'

It was obvious to Lily that Tom had been drinking. His eyes were reddened, his face flushed and his speech slurred. He was spoiling for a fight. She was terrified that he would cause a scene.

'For God's sake, Tom. Don't cause trouble for me, please. Not here.'

'Why not here? Frightened I might upset your lover?' He spat out the words.

'Please don't do this to me,' she pleaded.

'I must talk to you.'

'We have nothing more to say to one another.'

'I have plenty to say.'

The anger in his expression disturbed her. His mouth was set in a cruel line, and his voice was threatening. She was seeing a different side to the man she loved, and she didn't like it. 'But not now,' she urged.

'Then when? And where? I won't leave until you arrange some place.'

Lily was becoming agitated. 'Right then. Tomorrow afternoon at Fred's house. Amy's living in it now. I'll be there at three o'clock. But only if you leave here – now.'

'If you insist,' he grumbled, and made his way out of the club.

Lily turned slowly and walked upstairs.

Vittorio had been discreetly observing the scene. Now he frowned, and his eyes narrowed. Who was this man – and what was he to Lily? This was no casual customer. He'd seen her agitation and how pale and upset she had been as she left the bar. He got up from his table determined to solve the mystery.

Walking over the bar, Vittorio asked the barman, 'That man who just left, do you know him?'

'No, sir. He's not a regular, but he has been here once before.'

'When?'

'He came early one morning to give Miss Lily a message about a sick friend.'

That night as Vittorio hung up his suit-jacket in the bedroom he shared with Lily, he casually remarked, 'Your friend didn't stay long.' He observed closely the sudden watchful expression on Lily's face as she sat before the dressing-table mirror.

'Who do you mean?'

'The man at the bar you spoke to. He left rather abruptly, didn't he?'

'He was in a hurry to get home to his wife.'

Walking over to Lily, he began to massage her neck and felt her tense beneath his touch. In low, even tones he asked, 'What's his name?'

'Tom McCann.'

'What's he to you, Lily?' He saw the anxious look in her eyes.

'Nothing. He used to be a regular in one of the pubs I used to sing at.'

'Was he ever your lover?'

Lily vehemently denied it. 'No. Never!'

Vittorio stared at her expressionlessly. 'I saw the way he looked at you. If he was a nobody, why were you so upset?'

With her heart pounding in her breast, Lily glared at Vittorio. 'He was drunk – I was afraid he would cause trouble. When he's got a few beers under his belt, he becomes a handful. He's Irish, and you know what they're like.'

He gripped her shoulders tightly. 'What did he want?'

Lily winced with pain and looked at Vittorio in the mirror. Her gaze didn't falter. 'He wanted to know how Amy was.'

'Is that all?'

'What is this, the bloody third degree?' Lily threw off his hold and stood up, turning to face him. 'You've been mixing with too many coppers lately!'

He grabbed her by the arms and drew her roughly to him, his brown eyes shining with anger. 'Now you listen to me. Things are very difficult at the moment and I'm having to be very careful. I don't want something or someone to come along out of the blue and mess it up. I don't want any surprises, Lily. And believe me, neither do you!'

Lily was fearful. What would happen to her – and to Tom – if Vittorio knew they were to meet again? It would have to be the only time, for both their sakes. 'There are no surprises. Honestly.'

He studied her face. He wanted to believe her but deep inside, his sixth sense told him differently. 'You belong to *me*, Lily. I don't want anyone from your past cropping up, ever. I would only have to deal with them and I can assure you it wouldn't be pleasant. Do I make myself clear?'

She felt the blood drain from her face. She had no doubt that Vittorio would carry out his threat, and she must make Tom see the danger he was putting her in. Yet her indomitable spirit surfaced. She would never show her fear.

'For Christ's sake, Vittorio, give it a rest, will you. The man came to ask about Amy. That's all.' Her tone softened. 'I know you've had a tough time lately. But you're seeing danger where it doesn't exist. You look tired. I'll run you a bath, that'll relax you.' She smiled at him, trying to coax him. 'Come along. It's been a hard day.'

He let out a sigh. Perhaps she was right. Maybe he was getting jumpy. But still he felt uneasy. As he lay in the warmth of the soothing water, he wondered what he would do if his suspicions about this Tom were confirmed. For the first time in his life he was jealous. Deep down he was seething with it. He couldn't bear the thought that this stranger might have meant something to Lily. Might have laid with her, made love to her.

He was still trying to come to terms with these strange emotions as he climbed into bed beside her. Taking her into his arms, he kissed her with a vicious passion born of jealousy, trying to impose himself and his will upon her. There was no gentle foreplay. No loving words. No soft caresses. No consideration. He thrust himself into her as if driven by demons, until with a shuddering orgasm he spilled his seed over her.

He lay back against the pillows, his emotions drained.

He was suddenly aware of her silent weeping and was filled with remorse. Taking her gently into his arms, he whispered soothing words of comfort to her as he kissed her wet face. Tasted the salt of her tears.

Chapter Nineteen

Lily lay awake later that night, still clasped in Vittorio's arms, wondering what had brought on this assault of her body. Never had he been like this before. Always he'd been a considerate lover. His attack had frightened and upset her. Yet, when it was over, he'd been as always, gentle. As if trying to make up for his treatment of her. Not that he made any verbal apology. She wondered if it was because he was under so much strain, what with the police causing him grief and business dropping off. It was bound to affect him.

Well, she had her own problems. Would Vittorio stay at the club and continue to run it, or would this be the time for him to move on? If that was so, what would become of her?

Tom, too, was a problem. How could he come here and make trouble for her? Was that the action of someone who loved her? It was selfish. She remembered the look on his face and shuddered. He would have caused a scene here tonight and not cared a toss about her. The very thought of the consequences made every nerve in her body tense.

For God's sake, Tom was a man with responsibilities. She put herself in his wife's place. How would she feel if, heavy with child, she discovered her husband chasing after another woman? She felt a pang of sympathy for Mary. She must be nearing her time now. He wasn't being fair to either of them. Well, after tonight she'd had enough. She would have to put a stop to all this tomorrow when they met.

Lily felt jumpy as she made her way to the house. She took a long detour, glancing over her shoulder several times to ensure she wasn't being followed. She was worried that

Vittorio hadn't been convinced by her story the previous night. Maybe that had something to do with his vicious lovemaking. Now she was angry when she thought about it. Whatever his problems, he wouldn't treat her like that again. She felt used, like a whore.

When the coast seemed clear she headed towards the house, arriving with a sense of relief. She knocked on the door, then opened it and walked in. 'Amy!' she called.

Her friend emerged from the scullery, wiping her hands on a towel. 'Lily! What a lovely surprise.' She sensed that something was amiss. 'What's wrong?'

As she sat down by the fire, Lily gave a deep sigh. 'I had to make sure I wasn't followed. You see, Tom came to the club last night.'

'What?' Amy was shocked.

'I know. I had a fit when I saw him. He was drunk, and demanded that we meet. I had to say yes to get rid of him.'

Amy looked gravely concerned. 'Christ, Lily. If Vittorio finds out . . .'

Lighting a cigarette, Lily nodded. 'I know. I've asked Tom to come here. I hope you don't mind. It was the only safe place I could think of.'

'Of course I don't mind, this *is* your house after all.' But Amy was cross. 'Honest to God, Lily. You will have to put a stop to this. You know The Maltese. Nice as he can be, he won't tolerate it. Then where will you be? Floating in the bloody docks, that's where!'

Lily's expression was full of concern. 'You're right, of course. He questioned me enough last night.' She turned towards her friend. 'I can't go on like this. Tom has got to leave me alone. He can have no place in my life now.'

Amy looked surprised. 'But I thought you loved him?'

'Yes, but I've got to think of my future, and Tom's no part of it. If you'd seen him last night, Amy . . . he was drunk, and vicious with it.' She said firmly, 'He reminded me too much of my father. In fact, I'm coming to the conclusion I'd be better off on my own. Free of all men.'

'How would Vittorio like that?' But before Lily could answer, there was a knock on the door.

'I'll make myself scarce,' said Amy, heading for the stairs.

Lily felt her fingers tremble as she opened the door and stared into the hazel eyes of Tom McCann. Her breath caught in her throat. She stepped back, unable to speak.

He walked purposefully into the room and, throwing his cap onto the chair, immediately took her into his arms. 'Let me look at you, Lily. Let me hold you.' He pulled her to him and held her close.

For one glorious moment Lily gave way to her true feelings and held him tight, feeling the strength of his arms about her. Then she pushed him away.

He looked at her, a hurt expression in his eyes. 'Why did you do that?'

'Because this is madness. Don't you ever stop to think? Why did you come to the club? Are you trying to make trouble for me?'

He caught hold of her and, gazing deeply into her eyes, said, 'Lily, me darlin', I could never hurt you, you know that. I love you more than life itself.'

She was suddenly angry. 'No! I don't believe you. If you really loved me you would be concerned for my safety. Instead you go out and have a few drinks, then full of Dutch courage you come to the club and demand that we meet. If I hadn't agreed, who knows what might have happened.'

His eyes blazed. 'What do you expect? You leave me easily enough. First you live with Fred, then you move in with the biggest villain in the docks. How do you think that makes me feel?'

She stood defiantly in front of the fire. 'I am not interested, Tom You have no right to disrupt my life. You'd do better to look after your wife – after all, she's pregnant with your child. She didn't manage that on her own!' Seeing his petulant expression she added, 'What sort of a man are you, anyway? How can you come hounding me when you have such responsibilities?'

'I worry about you, but you won't listen to me.'

Taking a deep trembling breath, she said, 'Tom. Sit down, please. We have to talk.'

His fingers shook as he took a cigarette from a packet, lit it and sat beside the fire.

Sitting opposite him, Lily started to speak. 'How can I make you understand? I am not your responsibility any more, but your wife and child are. You are married and I'm with Vittorio. That's the end of it.'

His jaw tightened. 'What are you saying?'

'Vittorio won't tolerate me meeting another man.'

He leaned forward and taking her hand, said passionately, 'Then come away with me. We'll go somewhere safe.'

'For goodness sake, don't you ever listen? Mary is about to give birth to your child. You owe it to them both to be with her.'

Putting his hands over his eyes, Tom said, 'I know. I know. I have to be with her. But perhaps later, we can plan to be together. I'll look after Mary and the child, but she doesn't love me. She doesn't need me, only what I can provide.'

'Oh Tom, I'm so sorry. I hoped you'd be happy. When the baby comes, things will be different, you'll see.'

'I'll get a divorce.'

'Don't talk rubbish.' Lily felt her anger rise.

'Are you telling me you don't want me? Is that it?'

Lily's eyes glittered as she said, 'Don't let your male ego get in the way, Tom. It seems to me you're simply angry that I'm with Vittorio. You haven't asked if *I'm* happy. You haven't given a thought to your child, growing up without a father. All you can think about is your own injured pride.'

His face was white with anger. 'You can't possibly be happy with that man. How can you be?'

Lily held his gaze. 'Well, I am. He's a gentleman.'

Tom rose to his feet, his mouth twisted with rage. 'So you'd rather be the whore of a rich man than the wife of a poor one, is that it?'

Lily felt her stomach tighten at his insult. She leapt to her feet and slapped him hard around the face. 'He's more honest than you are. He never made me promises that he couldn't keep. You already have a wife, remember? I suggest you go home to her and try to be a decent husband. Get out!' She pointed a trembling finger at the door. 'Get out – now!'

His face flushed at her dismissal. He put his flat cap on and strode to the door, slamming it behind him.

Lily, her whole body shaking, sat down.

Amy came rushing down the stairs. 'Blimey, that was a bit strong, wasn't it? I couldn't help overhearing. The whole road must have heard the two of you.'

Lily, still raging inwardly, said, 'I don't give a damn. Perhaps now he'll leave me alone to get on with my life in my own way.'

'I'll put the kettle on,' said Amy, not knowing what else to do.

At the Club Valletta, Vittorio was having his own problems. Sitting at the desk in his office, he listened to the words of Detective Inspector Chadwick.

'I thought I'd come myself and break the news, Mr Teglia.'

'And what news is that?'

'We have a new Chief Constable. Quite different from the last one.'

Vittorio's slow smile crossed his lips. 'I do hope so. I read the other one retired through ill-health.'

The policeman looked at him, his jaw tight. 'We both know why he resigned. But this new man doesn't have the same perversions. In fact, he is going to campaign to clean up Southampton – the red-light district, the brothels, the clubs that run above the law.' He paused. 'He's also cleaning out the few bad apples in the police force.'

The Maltese raised his eyebrows. 'You are admitting there are bent coppers?'

'You should know – you pay most of them.'

'Really!' said Vittorio in mocking tones. 'That's tantamount to slander.'

'Only if I was lying. So you won't be getting your information any more. There will be no more privileges for you, sir.' He added in a derisive tone: 'Your time is running out.'

Vittorio held the other man's gaze. 'I run a strictly legitimate business.'

Chadwick allowed a smile to cross his features. 'Probably for the first time in your life. And only because you know we're watching you. But your takings are well down.'

For one moment Vittorio's eyes narrowed.

The detective got to his feet. 'You can't go on much longer. Once this Chief makes his aims known, what business you have . . . will cease.' With a triumphant smile he said, 'I've got you just where I want you.'

Vittorio chuckled. 'We all have our illusions, my dear fellow. You keep yours. They won't last long.'

A look of fury crossed the detective's face. 'Not this time, you bastard. You're on your way out.' He walked to the door. 'I'll keep a cell waiting for you – sir.'

As his office door closed, Vittorio's smile vanished and his expression hardened. He knew that the man was right. Unless he made other plans, he was finished in the club business. Getting up from his chair, he crossed to the door, opened it and called, 'George!'

He motioned to George Coleman to sit down. 'We have a new Chief Constable who's not going to be a friend. I want you to collect all the outstanding gambling debts and the loans. I need to accumulate all my assets. But take care, we're being watched.'

When he was alone, Vittorio sat back in his chair. If the police made it impossible to continue with the club he would have to sell up, move to another town. A legitimate business wouldn't bring in the revenue he was used to and he'd been wealthy for too long to lower his standard of living. He'd worked too hard to do that.

Later that evening, Lily, sensing the concerns of Vittorio, tried to find a solution. 'I know that you weren't too keen on making the club legitimate, but these past weeks haven't been so bad. If you were to get rid of the rest of the girls and decorate their rooms as guest rooms, you could have a thriving business, within the law.'

Her lover's lips twitched with amusement. 'You are determined to turn me into a pillar of the community, aren't you, Lily?' He looked suddenly serious. 'It's not that simple. We are to have a new Chief Constable who's on a crusade. He will certainly want to close me down.'

'But he won't be able to,' she persisted. 'Look – there is always a need for hotels for the passengers arriving and wanting accommodation until their ship sails. There are businessmen, needing beds. Commercial travellers. You could use the old gambling room as a room for business meetings. If you're running a legal place, what can he do?'

'You think the reputation of the place won't put people off?'

Lily gave a wicked grin. 'Quite the opposite. It'll give them a thrill, staying in a place that used to be a brothel. And there's another thing. I remember you saying it's not what you know, but *who* you know. You have the contacts to bring in business. Use them.'

He looked thoughtful. 'You may have something. Besides, there are many ways to skin a cat.'

'What do you mean?'

'It's as I told you, supply and demand. People always want money. Some banks won't take them, but I could set up a business dealing in finance. The percentages would be high, of course.'

'But you do that now.'

'True, but not on a legal basis. A proper company with accounts would be legal.'

'In other words, you'd still be in the same business, except for the prostitutes?'

He leaned back, a satisfied look on his face. 'Exactly. Do you think I'd let some jumped-up Chief Constable get the better of me?'

Lily was filled with trepidation. 'So it would just be a cover?'

'Look, Lily. All kinds of businesses are some kind of scam, people trying to put something over those in authority. It's the way of the world. You just have to be clever about it, that's all.'

The following morning, Vittorio called his girls into his office one by one, explaining that he was having to dispense with their services. He gave them all a small bonus, which made the parting easier for them, with the exception of Iris.

'So you're just going to chuck me out on the street?'

Vittorio looked at her coldly. 'Be careful, Iris. Don't let that big mouth of yours get you into trouble.'

'I'd have thought it would have paid you to keep me on, Mr Teglia,' she sneered at him, her mouth twisted spitefully.

He raised his eyebrows in surprise. 'Oh, and why is that?'

'I know what's been going on here. You wouldn't want me to tell anyone, would you?'

He didn't raise his voice or change his expression. 'I can't believe you are stupid enough to try and blackmail me, Iris. Even you couldn't make such a big mistake.'

Her smile faded. 'It's just that I don't understand why I can't stay.'

'Don't question me, you little bitch. Just be grateful that you lasted so long. If you hadn't been so good with the clients and so handy with a whip, you would have gone a long time ago.' His eyes flashed with anger. 'Now get out, and remember who you are dealing with.'

George, who had been helping his boss, looked at Vittorio. 'Do you think we'll have trouble with her, guv?'

'You follow her and make sure we don't.'

'How far shall I go?'

'Teach her a lesson, then put her on a train to somewhere a long way away. Tell her if she comes back, she'll leave in a box.'

The following day, Vittorio called Lily into his office. 'Sit down, my dear, I want to have a serious talk with you.'

Lily felt her stomach plummet. Things had been so unsettled, she was sure that Vittorio was going to impart bad tidings. Or had he found out about her meeting with Tom?

Sitting back in his chair, he studied her at length.

With a feeling of discomfort, Lily challenged him. 'What is it? What's wrong?'

He chuckled softly. 'Darling Lily. How quickly you are on the defensive. Nothing's wrong, I can assure you.'

She let out a sigh of relief.

'I have a proposition to put to you that I think you'll like.'
She looked apprehensive. 'I will?'

That slow smile touched his lips. 'You know, you've come a long way since the first time we met. You've blossomed into a lovely young woman. Your intelligence has been a revelation, your ability to learn a pleasure to watch. All of which can now be put to great use.'

Lily looked at him with suspicion. 'Get to the point, Vittorio.'

His laughter filled the room. 'That's one of the things I love about you. You don't beat about the bush.' He lit a cigarette and, blowing the smoke out slowly, said, 'I've decided to take your advice.'

Her eyes widened with surprise. 'About what?'

'Becoming legitimate.'

For a moment she was speechless. 'What do you mean?'

'Making the club legal. Using the rooms for paying guests, the gambling room for business meetings. What is more, I'm thinking of putting the club in your name – transferring the licence. It will be your name over the door instead of mine.'

'You're *what?*'

'You see, Lily, if it's to be a success, I must step back from it. Then the police may leave me alone. If they think I'm still around here, then we'll be hounded until we have to close.'

'But I can't run it on my own! I don't have the experience.' Her face was white with shock.

He agreed. 'Of course you don't. I will still run it, but from behind the scenes. You will front it. After all, you've learned a lot. And in some areas, you're capable of overseeing things. As far as the public and the police are concerned, you will be in charge.'

She looked uncertain. 'You think I can carry it off?'

'Yes, I do.'

'What about the staff? Will they mind if they think I'm their boss?'

He shook his head. 'That won't be a problem. I'll speak to the head waiter and the chef. Things will carry on as before. They've always done a good job. Nothing will change on that score.'

She looked thoughtful. 'I do have a few ideas of my own, if we're to start again.'

Vittorio looked surprised. 'Do you? Like what?'

Lily was filled with enthusiasm. 'It would be nice to have a doorman in a uniform. It looks classy. I saw a picture of one in a magazine the other day. After all, this won't be a brothel any more. We have to show the punters some difference. The man on the door is the first impression they get.'

With a thoughtful look, Vittorio said, 'Yes, that's a good idea. I'll find the man.'

'Not one of your bruisers!' exclaimed Lily.

With a chuckle Vittorio said, 'No. But it will be somebody who can cope with trouble if it happens.'

'I've got another idea too,' said Lily tentatively.

'Go on.'

'Well, don't you think it would be rather nice to have a pianist play during the lunch-time period? In the evening we have Harry's band, but during the day, the place has no atmosphere.'

Vittorio's slow smile played at the corners of his mouth. 'My goodness, Lily. You have been doing a lot of thinking lately.'

'I know just the man,' she said eagerly.

'Very well. Get him in. We'll see how it goes.'

Leaning back against the chair, Lily was filled with excitement. She was convinced the club could be made to pay, but she wasn't sure that she could handle it. 'The idea of running this place frightens the shit out of me!' she confided.

'You will have to learn to temper your language, my dear.'

Frowning she asked, 'You're not expecting to make a lady out of me, are you?'

He nodded. 'Yes – a very successful one. You can do it, Lily,' he urged. 'You know you can. Look how you manage the crowd when you sing, and after. No one works the tables like you. Already you have learned so much.'

Pondering on Vittorio's words, Lily knew that he was right. She grinned cheekily. 'You really believe I can?'

'When I've finished showing you the ropes, yes!'

There was a sudden look of anxiety in her eyes. 'What are you going to be doing?'

'I'm opening a new business. I'm going to rent a shop in the High Street and set up a finance company. It will all be legal, don't worry.'

Lily looked sceptical. 'Oh, really?'

Chuckling, he added, 'We will be separate. My business affairs will not have anything to do with you.'

'But what about account books for the club? I don't know anything about keeping books.'

'I will still be doing them. They won't be your concern.'

Lily was both excited and afraid. 'What happens if it's not a success? I might lose your money for you.'

'I can assure you, I won't let you. I'll be keeping a close eye on everything. Go away and think about it. We'll talk again this evening.'

She hesitated. 'Where will you live?'

He looked at her with his dark-brown eyes shining with amusement. 'I will still live here, of course. The only difference is that I won't be downstairs in the club. However, I'll have a small window put in the wall of my office. Then I can keep a watchful eye on the proceedings.'

Getting up from his chair he walked around the desk and, taking her into his arms, he held her to him. Brushing her ear with his lips, he said softly, 'You are still my woman, Lily, and I'm certainly not going to miss my more intimate moments with you.' He covered her lips with his and kissed her until she could hardly catch her breath.

Pushing him away, she gasped for air. 'Vittorio!' she cried. 'For goodness sake! You'll smother me.'

'Later darling. Now go away and think over my idea.'

Later that day, Lily made her way to Sandy's home in Bond Street, praying she would find him there. To her relief, in response to her knocking, he opened the door almost immediately.

Sandy looked at her in surprise. 'Good God, Lily. What the 'ell are you doing here?'

She stepped into the living room and planted herself on

his settee. 'I've got a proposition to put to you.'

He sashayed over to her and sat down. 'Darling, how wonderful. I've not been propositioned all week!'

'Behave yourself, you old queen. I'm being serious,' she protested. 'How would you like a job, playing the piano every lunch-time at the club?'

His eyes widened. 'At the Club Valletta?'

'Of course at the Valletta. Where else?'

'But I don't have decent-enough clothes, darling. I mean, I could hardly wear my frocks now, could I?'

Lily chuckled. 'I don't think Vittorio would approve of that. You'd quickly be out on your ear.' She opened her handbag and took out two five-pound notes. 'I seem to remember this happening before – the other way round! Here, take this.' She thrust the money into his hand. 'Buy yourself a nice velvet smoking jacket, a pair of smart trousers, and a decent shirt.'

He looked at the money and then at her. There was such an expression of affection in his eyes, that Lily felt choked with emotion. 'You will do it, won't you, Sandy?' she pleaded.

He put his arm around her shoulder and gave her a smacking kiss on the cheek. 'I certainly will. I can do with the money as you well know. How can I ever thank you?'

She gave him a playful nudge. 'Listen to me, you old tart. Where would I be if it hadn't been for you? We've always looked out for one another.' She stood up. 'I'll see you on Monday, about eleven-thirty. By the way, you'll be pleased to know, the piano has a wonderful tone.' She kissed him on the cheek and left.

Lily made her way to The Ditches to tell Rachel all the latest news.

The two friends sat together in the back of the shop mulling over the details.

'*Mazel tov!*' cried Rachel as Lily told her of Vittorio's plans. 'That Maltese. What a clever bastard. He knows you can do it where he can't.'

'What do you mean?' asked Lily.

Rachel clasped Lily's hands in hers. 'Don't you see, you silly girl? The police wouldn't let it succeed with him still there. With you, it's different. Sure, you're his mistress, but you're not on their lists.'

Lily's eyes widened. 'Does Vittorio have a criminal record?'

With a snort Rachel said, 'Him? Never in a month of Sundays, even though the police have been after him for as long as I can remember. But, he is a villain all right. Everyone knows that. There was just never the proof. But you . . .' she held out her arms '. . . pure as the driven snow!'

'Hardly that,' said Lily, doubling up with laughter.

Shrugging Rachel said, 'OK, but you know what I mean.' She looked pensive. 'Much better if he wasn't involved at all.'

'Oh, Rachel, of course he has to be involved. He has the money.'

Her friend looked thoughtful. 'Yes – a shame that. But never mind. You do it, my dear. Here is your chance at respectability. Remember that was your dream?'

With a bitter laugh Lily retorted, 'A bloody lot of good it did me.'

'No, darling. Don't you see? If you run a successful business then no one can touch you. You will have earned respectability, maybe by a roundabout route, but so what?'

Lily left the shop and walked towards the Pier, needing to be alone. The June sun was beating down and she sat in one of the deckchairs and watched the swirling water beneath the wooden slats. Then, leaning back, she closed her eyes, letting her mind wander. It seemed a very long time ago since she had walked here and met Tom. She recalled the day he took her for a meal in the cafe. The beginnings of her first love . . . what pain and joy it had brought. Surely love wasn't meant to be like that?

Getting up from the chair, she walked restlessly around the Pier and stood at the rails staring out over the Solent River. Across the water lay the Isle of Wight, and beyond that yet another world. She watched the paddle-steamer making its way to Ryde, fascinated by the sounds of the swish of the water as the massive wheel turned, and remembered a day trip she and Tom had taken to Cherbourg. How strange and different it had seemed to them. The foreign food. The language. It had been such an adventure.

Walking back towards the club, she wondered if one day she would be able to move away from here, away from the filth and the bustle of the docks. She waited as a freight-train passed by into the dockyard, looked at the lime-washed walls of the buildings in Canute Road. This, and the shopping area of the town were the only places she really knew well. She realised that, apart from the occasional jaunt to the Common as a child, she knew nothing else. She suddenly wanted much more. She wanted to be her own person, not reliant on anyone. If she made a success of the club, then maybe one day she could leave. Go on to other things. Other places.

When first she'd gone to Vittorio, all she had wanted was to be cared for. Now she felt secure. Her independence had grown as she had. The world had to be bigger and better than this small part of it. Now she was curious about it. Wanting to know what was out there. One day, she vowed, she would find out.

Later that evening, a well-dressed woman was shown into Vittorio's office. He smiled at her and politely offered her a seat. He gazed with appreciation at her stylish and expensive attire. 'You are looking particularly elegant this evening.'

Rachel Cohen smiled back at him. 'Better than when you see me working in my shop in The Ditches, eh, Vittorio?' She looked around the richly appointed room. 'You do well for yourself! Yes,' she said, 'when I think of the snotty-nosed kid that used to run wild in The Ditches, when first you came from Malta, it's hard to believe he turned out to be the feared Maltese.'

He chuckled with amusement. 'But not feared by you, Rachel.'

'So what's to be scared of, when I've seen your bare

bottom hanging out of your trousers. Your father had such a time with you.'

'You, of course, knew my father well.' His deep-brown eyes hid a look of amusement, but his mouth twitched at the corners.

Rachel smiled to herself. 'Yes, I knew him. Liked the women too much, he did, but it was your uncle I knew better. Such a man. What a physique! I should have met him before my Hymie. But then I would have had to marry out. *Oy veh!* What a scandal that would have caused!'

'Especially as he already had a wife,' added Vittorio with a wry smile.

Rachel shrugged. 'Wife, yes. Such a pity that. My, when your family first arrived in Southampton from Malta, all the female hearts were aflutter. Your papa, he wasn't such a good man. I used to wonder if you were like him.' She saw the sudden anger in his eyes. 'But after you met Lily, I knew you were different.'

'Really? How?'

'She told me you treated her well, so I thought you couldn't be so bad after all.'

Vittorio burst out laughing. 'I'm happy to hear it.'

'But shall I get to the point of my visit?'

He nodded in agreement. 'Indeed. What can I do for you? I assume that this is not a social call.'

She looked at him, her gaze steady. 'It's what I can do for you would be more to the point.'

He was surprised. 'And what might that be?'

'Lily tells me you have offered her a business proposition and I've come to offer you another.'

His interest was aroused. 'Carry on.'

'First I must ask you a question, and don't give me any old bull!'

He raised his eyebrows at her directness. 'And what is that?'

'Are you concerned about Lily's future?'

He took out his cigarette case and lighting a cigarette, drew on it deeply before replying. 'Of course I am.'

Rachel let out a sigh of relief. Leaning back in her chair,

257

she began: 'You have a big problem with the police, and they want to close you down. You think putting the place in Lily's name will get you off the hook.' She shrugged. 'Well, maybe it will and maybe it won't. But if you sell me half of the club and put the other half in her name, then it certainly *will* work. The police couldn't touch you.'

He looked at her, his slow smile touching the corners of his mouth. 'You don't honestly believe I would do such a thing, do you?'

'Why not? You want the police off your back. How long before they realise that it's all a con? But with me as a partner . . .' Seeing his hesitation she continued: 'I want to secure a future for Lily. It's as simple as that. I have the cash, so finance isn't a problem. I'm selling the shop, but I want an interest. With my years of experience, I can help her. And if anything should happen to you, she has no worries.'

His eyes narrowed. There was a look of calculation in his expression. 'You think this place will go as a legitimate concern?'

'Not if you are within a mile of it.'

He thought for a moment then said, 'I believe you have a point. But tell me, why is Lily so important to you, Rachel?'

She answered without hesitation. 'Because I love that child and I won't see anyone else cause her unhappiness. She's been through enough already. And in some ways, I blame myself. I'm trying to right a wrong.'

He chuckled softly. 'Yes, she has a way of working beneath your skin, doesn't she?'

'What do you think of my idea, then?'

Vittorio rose from his chair. 'In principle, it has its merits, but I'm not about to sell out. A small share, perhaps – just to put the police off the scent. But I will never relinquish my control, not completely. Give me some more time to think it over. I'll get some figures together and we'll talk further. Now it would give me great pleasure to take you downstairs and buy you dinner.'

Getting up from her seat, Rachel gave a wicked grin and

retorted, 'I would insist on it. I want to see what I might be investing in.'

As they reached the door, it opened and Lily entered. Her look of shocked surprise made Rachel laugh. 'Hello, darling!' Smoothing the expensive cloth of her coat, she asked, 'Like the *schmatte*?'

Chapter Twenty

Lily was flabbergasted to see Rachel all dressed up to the nines, closeted in with Vittorio. But she was even more surprised when the two of them told her of the possibility of Rachel becoming involved in the club.

'Nothing is definite yet,' said Rachel. 'If this villain tries to charge me too high a price, I'll tell him what to do with his business! And it depends on the quality of the meal and the wine that I am served with tonight.'

Vittorio was highly amused by her banter.

Looking at her dear friend Lily asked, 'Why are you doing this?'

'To make a lot of money, my dear. Why does anyone, especially a Jew, invest? I told you I was looking for a business – well, maybe I found one.'

Lily turned to her lover. 'Is this what you want?'

'It'll get the police off my back, darling.'

'But does it mean you'll move out?'

'I'm not moving anywhere.' He saw Rachel purse her lips. 'I may sell you a share of the business, but Lily is still an important part of my life. You understand that, don't you?'

'Of course.' She held his gaze. 'But once everything is settled, you don't step foot over the door, do you understand that?'

'Not over the front door, Rachel. But I will most certainly be using the *back* door. I'll be keeping a close watch on my investment. When it comes to money, I trust no one.'

Rachel flushed, knowing she'd been put in her place. 'Just as long as the punters don't see you.'

With a grin Vittorio said to Lily, 'She drives a harder

bargain than you do. But you too must understand, Lily, that although I'll only be watching from upstairs, you are still mine. Your independence is only on the club front. Nothing else changes. With me not around, some men might try it on. I wouldn't put up with that.'

Lily looked from one to the other. Rachel's expression gave nothing away but Vittorio was staring hard at her, looking for any trace of betrayal. He hadn't forgotten when Tom McCann had visited the club. He remembered his gut feeling about the two of them. It still filled him with unease.

Lily softly touched his face with her hand. 'Why would I want to be with another man when you've done so much for me?'

Kissing her palm he said, 'I can't imagine.'

Early the following evening, Lily put on her coat. She didn't sing in the club during the early part of the week and tonight she'd made plans.

'Where do you think you're going?' asked Vittorio.

'I'm going out. There's nothing to do here and I'm bored. I'm meeting Amy.'

'Where?'

'At The Sailor's Return. I haven't been back there since I came to work for you. It's the only place Amy can face going. You know, being among friends. You don't mind, do you?'

Shaking his head he said, 'No. You go ahead. I've lots of bookwork to see to. But take care, Lily.'

'What's that supposed to mean?'

'Keep out of trouble is what it means. Remember our conversation over dinner last night?'

'I don't know why you persist with this, Vittorio. After all, everybody knows I'm your mistress.' Her cheeks flushed with irritation. 'No man is going to come near me. He'd be too bloody scared.'

He laughed aloud. 'This is true.' The laughter faded and his tone became more serious. 'I don't like you wandering around at night without me, that's all.'

'I can take care of myself.'

He hesitated. 'Another thing, Lily. Please don't tell anyone about our plans with Rachel Cohen. Nothing is yet settled and I don't want the police to find out until it's official and too late for them to try and intervene.'

'What could they do?' she asked with a worried frown.

'Legally probably nothing, but I don't trust those bastards.'

'Well, they won't hear it from me, rest assured.'

'I know you'll be tempted to tell your friend Amy, but once one person knows . . .'

Nodding her understanding she said, 'Please don't worry. I'll see you later.'

'Don't be late!'

She turned at the doorway, her eyes flashing. 'Christ, Vittorio! You sound like a father.'

'I don't care who I sound like. You get home in good time.' He stared hard at her. 'I wouldn't like to have to send George out to find you.'

She knew better than to argue and left, bristling with indignation.

Earlier the same day, on hearing that Burt Haines, his ex-foreman, had retired through ill-health, Tom McCann had made his way to the office in the docks to try and get his old job back. After much discussion and many promises to curb his temper, he was once more employed as a caulker. It had been common knowledge to the powers that be that there were faults on both sides and, such was Tom's skill, the office was pleased to have him back with assurances that there would be no further trouble.

After leaving the office, Tom walked to the dock-gates and just stood watching the hustle and bustle of the life within the area. He loved the docks and was completely at home in the atmosphere . . . the smell of salt in the air, the sounds of the ships' funnels, the cry of the tugs' whistles and the clanking of chains as anchors were lowered. He watched as a huge crane, stark against the skyline, lifted a large cargo and swung it effortlessly into a ship's hold. He observed the dockers and stevedores rushing about. He'd missed the camaraderie.

His pride in his profession had been sadly dented. Working for Knocker had been enjoyable in its way, but he was happiest working on ships; being part of a team. And soon he would be back among his mates.

He was jubilant as he eventually made his way home after spending time with Knocker, passing on his good news. At last he'd made a start towards solving his marital problems. Now Mary would have reason to be happy, and he hoped that would put paid to her constant carping about money – or the lack of it.

Mary, looking pale and tired, was sitting down when he burst in the door with his news.

'I'm back working in the docks, Mary. I start next week.'

'About time too. These past four months have been a nightmare.' There was no joy at the good news. 'With the baby coming, we'll need the extra money.'

Mary was secretly relieved at Tom's news. Apart from worrying about the lack of money, she was due to give birth in a week's time and she was terrified. Her mother had tried to explain that every woman feels this way and that when she held the baby in her arms, she'd forget the pain. But Mary wasn't convinced.

Tom felt thoroughly deflated. He'd thought she'd be pleased. His smile faded. 'I thought at least you'd be happy. You know how much the job means to me.'

'Yes, well,' she said truculently, 'had it not been for your temper, you wouldn't have lost it in the first place. Look at the money we've had to do without.'

His anger boiled over. 'There really is no pleasing you, is there? You'll have your money – enough for you and the baby, but as far as I'm concerned, that's it.'

With a startled look she said, 'What do you mean?'

'It means I've had it. To be sure, how can any man live with a woman such as you for the rest of his life? It would take a saint, and I'm just an ordinary man, so I am.'

She was shattered. 'You mean you're leaving me?'

His tone softened. 'It means I'll stick by you until you've had the baby, but after you've got over the birth, then we'll have to make other arrangements.' Seeing the stricken look on her face, he knelt beside her. 'I didn't mean for this to happen now, but you don't love me, Mary. You only want me as a provider. It's not enough to build a marriage on. I'll provide for you and the baby, don't you fear. I'll honour those commitments, but I want my freedom. I want a divorce.'

Her face flushed with anger. 'You want to go to this other woman. This Lily you call for in your sleep.'

He looked at her in surprise. 'I do?'

Her mouth narrowed spitefully. 'You make me pregnant and you call another woman's name while you are in bed beside me. How do you think that makes me feel?'

'I'll not lie to you,' he said with a grim expression. 'I've always loved her and I always will. I thought you and I could make a life together, but you put an end to that with your grasping ways.'

'All I wanted was a decent home and a decent husband. What's wrong with that?'

He glared at her. 'And all I asked for was a woman who knew how to be a wife.'

'You'll never see your child – I'll make sure of that,' she threatened.

'Look,' he said, 'I don't want to fight with you, not in your condition. I've been honest and truthful. After the baby is born, we'll work out an arrangement between us. You'll not go short, I promise you. But remember, the child is mine too.'

'A lot you care about your child.' She put her hands on her swollen stomach. 'What interest do you have in this baby? *None!* But I'll be better off without you.' She spat the words out. 'I don't like married life. *She* can sleep with you, with my blessing. At least I won't have to put up with that any more.'

His hazel eyes flashed angrily. 'You made that quite clear on our wedding night.'

'It's dirty and disgusting.'

He nodded. 'To you it is, but thank God, not everyone is as inhibited as you in the bedroom.' He turned towards the door. 'I'm off to see those who appreciate me.'

'Go to your fancy woman!' she yelled. 'See if I care!'

All the locals greeted Lily and Amy with enthusiasm when they walked into the bar of The Sailor's Return. Sandy struck a chord of welcome on the piano and Declan leaned over the bar greeting them both warmly with a smacking kiss.

'My but the sight of you makes this Irishman a happy fellow. What'll you both have? And Amy, love, how are you?'

Sandy came over and hugged Lily. 'Hello, you old tart. We must stop meeting like this. Perhaps a bit later you'll give us a song. How about it?'

'Why not?' Lily laughed. She was relaxed and happy. Some of the best days of her singing career had been spent here, among her friends. And it was good to be back.

'How's Vittorio?' asked Sandy. 'I hear the club's being watched. I forgot to ask when we met.'

She nodded. 'Well, you know about the other trouble. The police have been watching the place ever since and it scared away some of the business for a time, but it's picking up again.'

'I do hope so,' said Sandy. 'I don't want to play to an empty house!'

At that moment the bar door opened and Tom walked in. He was surprised when he saw Lily. 'What are you doing here?' he asked. 'Slumming, are you?'

She ignored the sarcasm. 'I came with Amy. I'm trying to get her back into circulation. It's not easy for her, so be nice.'

He smiled and waved at Amy and asked, 'How is she coping?'

'She doesn't say a lot. Time is the thing that will help, just being among friends. How are you?'

'So so. Today I got my old job back in the docks. The foreman has retired, thank God.'

Lily was pleased for him. 'That's wonderful, Tom. Now perhaps things will work out at home for you.'

He shook his head. 'I wouldn't think so. Tonight I told Mary I want a divorce.'

She was deeply concerned. 'Should you have done that when she's due to have a baby? Wasn't that a bit heartless?'

'It just happened that way, Lily. I didn't plan it. But a man can only stand so much.'

She looked at him with horror as she heard his easy words of dismissal. She knew that Tom wasn't happy, and in all probability neither was Mary. Yet the woman was heavily pregnant, about to give birth. Tom's words sounded both brutal and callous. And, above all, selfish.

Lily was angry. 'You say you can't stand it, but you were the one to make her pregnant. How does she feel, do you think? The woman needs sympathy and understanding at this time, and a fat lot she's getting from you! How long before the baby's due?'

'About a week.'

Her eyes blazed. 'Your wife has only a matter of days to go and you tell her you're leaving! How could you have been so cruel? She's heavy with child, probably scared out of her wits, and all you can think of is yourself. It seems to me that's all you ever think about. You are not the man I thought you were, Tom McCann.' She glared at him, shaking her head in disbelief. 'To think I could ever have loved someone like you.'

She went over to Amy and sat beside her.

'What's up, love?' asked her friend.

Lily looked at Sandy. 'I'd like to leave now, but I don't want to spoil Amy's evening. Would you take her home?'

'Yes, of course.'

Looking at Amy she asked, 'Do you mind?'

'No, of course not. You go on.'

Lily made her way quickly towards the door and with a final glare at Tom, she left.

He was shattered by her reaction.

'Blimey! What did you say to Lily to send her away like that?' asked Declan.

Tom, filled with guilt, snapped, 'Just give me a pint and mind your own business.' He drank his beer quickly and left, any wish to celebrate his good fortune far from his mind.

He let himself into the house, only to find Mary doubled up with pain.

'Get the midwife, Tom,' she gasped. 'My contractions have started!'

Three hours later, Tom was still pacing up and down the living room, flinching every time he heard Mary cry out with pain. It seemed an eternity since he'd gone for the midwife and sent for Mary's parents. After examining her patient, the midwife insisted on having the doctor in attendance. They were both with Mary now.

Jessy was making yet another pot of tea, her face pale and drawn. Bill, her husband, sat before the range puffing on his pipe. The atmosphere was tense.

There was another cry of pain from the bedroom and Tom gripped hold of a chair. His knuckles were white. 'God! When's this going to end?'

Jessy put a mug of tea on the table. 'Drink this, son. The first baby sometimes takes a while. They won't come into the world until they're ready. The next one will be easier.'

'The next one!' Tom looked at her with horror. 'I couldn't put any woman through that again.'

She placed a comforting arm on his hand. 'You'll both forget all this when you hold your child in your arms.'

He grinned wryly. 'I might, but will Mary?'

'She will,' she insisted. 'You'll see.'

The midwife came downstairs. 'It's a difficult birth,' she explained. 'The baby is a breech, you see. Your wife is so tense, it's making things difficult.' She looked appealingly at Tom. 'Perhaps if you could come upstairs, comfort her, try to make her relax.'

'Of course I will, if you think it will help.'

When Tom walked softly into the bedroom and crossed over to the bed, he was shocked to see how pale Mary was. Beads of perspiration shone on her forehead. He was filled with guilt, remembering his cruel words to her earlier that evening. Kneeling beside her, he took her hand in his. 'Hello, darlin'.'

She turned on him. 'Get out of here! It's because of you I'm in so much pain. How could you do this to me and then ask for a divorce?'

'I'm sorry, darlin'. I was angry. Now, don't you fret none.'

He spoke calmly. 'Listen, Mary, try and relax. The doctor said it will make things easier for you.'

She became even more petulant. 'When did he last have a baby?'

The doctor hid a smile. 'Take deep breaths, Mrs McCann,' he urged. 'Please try and do as I ask.'

Another contraction gripped her and she screamed out, 'I hate this bloody baby!'

Tom squeezed her hand as the pain subsided. He smoothed her forehead. 'Come on now, breathe deeply.' His soft lilting voice calmed her, at last.

The doctor listened for the baby's heartbeat through his stethoscope and frowned. 'So far the baby isn't in any trouble,' he said quietly to Tom. 'But it could be if this goes on much longer. Try and get her to breathe in and out slowly and evenly.'

Tom coaxed Mary to do the doctor's bidding and she started to make an effort.

'That's better,' encouraged the doctor. 'Carry on like this and it will all be over soon.'

But Tom observed the worried look that passed between doctor and midwife, and he was filled with apprehension. He stayed beside the bed, calming his wife between contractions, bathing her forehead, talking to her. Deep inside he was filled with shame that he could have been so insensitive to her needs at this time.

The doctor and midwife worked hard trying to deliver the child. The sweat poured off the doctor's brow and the midwife looked even more worried with every contraction.

Mary's cries of pain went through Tom like a knife. He became more worried with every passing minute; seeing his wife's exhaustion, he wondered if she would survive the trauma.

Eventually, ten hours after she went into labour, Mary gave birth to a son. They showed her the baby but she was too weary to hold the child. She looked at Tom and whispered, 'You promised to take care of us both.'

He kissed her on the cheek. 'I'll keep my word, darlin'. Have no fear. You just rest and get better. Don't you worry about anything now. We'll talk about it much later, when you've recovered.'

The nurse wrapped the baby in a towel and handed him to Tom. He looked at the puckered little face and his eyes filled with tears. Taking the child back from him, the nurse said, 'Go down and tell the grandparents the good news. We have to take care of the mother now.'

Looking at the doctor Tom asked, 'She's going to be all right, isn't she?'

The doctor took him aside. 'She's had a bad time, Mr McCann. She's suffered greatly. Now leave us to do our job, and try not to worry.'

Tom made his way unsteadily down the stairs. 'Mary's had a son,' he said in a flat voice.

'And?' asked Jessy.

'The doctor said she's had a bad time and sent me down here.'

Jessy covered her mouth with her hands. 'Oh my God! I hope she's going to be all right.'

Putting an arm around her shoulders, Tom said, 'Of course she will be. We just have to wait.'

As he sat at the table, his head resting on his arms, Tom thought the silence was worse than the cries of pain. What was going on? He'd seen for himself that it had been a difficult birth. The look of fear and pain on Mary's face would live with him for the rest of his life, as would the greyness of her complexion.

He felt so guilty about telling her he wanted a divorce. Even Lily had thought that was cruel, and now so did he. If only he'd not lost his temper, rushed into things. But it was too late for recriminations. The damage had been done. Had it added to the stress of the birth? If anything happened to Mary, how could he live with himself?

It was an hour later before the doctor summoned them all upstairs. Outside the bedroom he told them, 'Mary is very tired and weak but, thank God, I think she'll be all right. Stay for just a moment.'

Mary lay back against the pillows, her eyes closed. Her skin was almost translucent. Tom walked over to the bed and took her hand. Jessy and Bill stood on the other side. Bill struggled to hold back the tears.

His face white, Tom said, 'Oh, my dear Mary, you didn't deserve this. I'm so sorry.' The baby stirred in its crib. 'I promise you I'll give our son everything you ever wanted him to have.'

She opened her eyes and looked at Tom as if she'd heard his words. Then she gave a weak smile, looked at her mother and father and closed her eyes.

The midwife ushered them all from the room.

Downstairs, the doctor had a word with Tom. 'A breech is always a dangerous birth, Mr McCann. And your wife was so tense it made it worse. She's badly torn. We had to stitch her.'

'Nothing else?' There was a tentative note in Tom's voice.

'What is it, my boy? You've something on your mind.'

With a sigh, Tom explained. 'We were not happy, doctor, and earlier today we had a row and I told her I wanted a divorce. I feel dreadful now.'

The doctor took his arm. 'Best not to dwell on it, my son. Just help her get over it all. Kindness goes a long way, you know. It's none of my business, but you have a new life to care for. A child needs both its parents. Try to work things out.'

Tom nodded. 'I will. Thank you, doctor.'

'I'll look in on her tomorrow, and I'll leave the nurse here for tonight just to be sure. The mother is far too weak to breastfeed the baby, so it'll have to go on the bottle.'

Jessy looked up as Tom entered the kitchen. Her heart went out to him and she felt pity for him. She'd been aware of the tension in the marriage, and she also knew that Mary was not the easiest person to live with, but it was the future of her grandchild that was her prime concern now.

'Sit down, Tom. Let me get you a hot drink and a sandwich.'

He shook his head. 'I'm not hungry.' He looked at Jessy. 'How am I going to be able to look after him until Mary's better?'

'Bill and I have been discussing that very thing. I'll take

care of the baby for the time being, until Mary's back on her feet and able to cope.'

'I can't expect you to do that.'

'Why not? Look, you have to work to provide for your son. How else can you manage? I'll take care of them both. After all, Mary's my daughter, and women are better at these things. You go about your work.'

Tom slipped upstairs and looked for the second time at his child. His little fist was closed tightly. His face was red and on top of his head grew a wisp of hair. Tom smiled as he studied him. 'Look,' he said to the nurse, pointing at the small fist. 'He looks as if he's ready for a fight.'

She tucked the blanket tighter around the small figure. 'Well, if you think about it, he had a fight to come into the world, didn't he?'

Tom nodded and, remembering the difficult birth, said, 'That he did.' He smoothed the little hand gently. 'If I can make life easier for him, I will,' he promised. He gazed at his wife, now asleep. She looked so frail, so unlike the strident harridan he'd known. He knew now he couldn't leave her. They would have to work out their future together. Somehow.

For once the club was really busy. Vittorio had put on a special gourmet meal at a reduced price which had tempted several clients to return. And as one of the liners was in dock, it was full of catering officers and other of the ship's higher echelons. They were not concerned with the scandal and the bad name of the club. Why should they be? They were constantly in and out of the port, so it didn't affect them at all. They just wanted an evening's entertainment within easy reach of their ship. Tonight was ideal.

Vittorio was making his round of the tables, joshing with his clients, making sure they were happy, when he saw Ned Saunders, Chief Steward of the *Olympic*, arrive.

Slapping Vittorio on the back, Ned said, 'Got a table for me?'

Vittorio said, 'I'm sure we can fit you in somewhere. I heard you were away on a cruise.'

'Yes. We docked this afternoon.' Once he was settled, Ned ordered his meal and waited for Lily to perform.

The girl was even lovelier than he remembered. Her black sequined gown clung to her curvaceous figure, and her magnetic personality dominated the room. He looked over to the bar and saw Vittorio watching her too. Ned's eyes became thoughtful as he saw the expression on the other man's face. Over the years he'd seen him with many women, some who for a time had become his mistress, and he'd admired the casual, even contemptuous way in which The Maltese treated them. But this was different.

Up on the stage Lily was singing, thrilled to see the club so busy. It would be wonderful if they could work up this amount of trade when they refurbished the rooms. When she noticed Ned among the patrons, watching her, she felt her skin crawl. After their first encounter, she'd always managed to make an excuse if she saw him in the club, and avoid any further contact. She knew that Vittorio and Ned had a business arrangement, and was aware that much of the meat and spirits for the club came from the *Olympic*. She was determined that if she had the opportunity, that arrangement would cease.

When she finished her act, she pretended not to see Ned's wave and walked towards the bar. Soon he was standing beside her. He placed a hand around her waist and she angrily pushed it away. 'I told you once before I don't like being mauled!'

Ignoring her comment he said, 'How would you like to work for me?'

Lily wasn't expecting this. 'What?'

The Chief Steward looked around the club. 'I wouldn't mind a little place like this. Set me up nicely for my retirement. Perhaps Vittorio would sell it to me.'

She burst out laughing. 'This place isn't for sale, Mr Saunders, and I would rather starve on the street than work for you.'

He watched her walk away, his body rigid with anger. 'Little jumped-up bitch!' he muttered under his breath.

Upstairs, Lily walked into the bedroom, tired out and

longing just to creep into bed and sleep. She prayed that Vittorio would be as tired. Laid out on the bed was an exquisite ivory-coloured nightdress and matching negligée. She stood, staring with disbelief and delight, and inspected the gowns, which were obviously expensive.

She ran a bath and soaked in the hot water, scented with crystals. What a very strange man Vittorio was, she mused. But lately he seemed to have changed towards her. After that night when he'd taken her so roughly, he'd become more gentle. She knew she wasn't in love with him, but there was something indefinable between them. She respected him and they shared a deep affection. In business he might be a hard man, but not with her. In their own way, they were happy together.

She dried herself, then slipped into the nightdress and looked at her reflection in the mirror. The satin clung to her body, emphasizing her curves. The thin straps topped a lace bodice which showed the soft contours of her breasts. She slipped on the negligée as the bedroom door opened.

Turning, she looked shyly at Vittorio as he walked towards her. He undid his tie, took off his jacket and, to her surprise, threw it casually over the back of the chair. He removed his shirt, then putting out his hand, slowly drew her into his arms.

'You look adorable, my dear,' he said in a deep husky voice.

'I don't know what to say, Vittorio. I know you usually like me to wear black when I'm in bed.'

He drew her closer. 'You look tantalising in black, but tonight I wanted you to look more virginal. Don't say anything. Just kiss me.'

Coiling her arms around his neck, she put her lips softly on his. He responded gently, moving his mouth over hers, exploring the contours of her lips. His hands caressed her back, pressing her body into his.

She ran her fingers through his hair, over his bare chest, feeling the taut muscles there, returning his kisses until she felt her skin quiver at his touch.

He released her, and slipped the negligée from her shoulders. As it fell to the floor, he took her hand and led her over to the bed. Lily lay waiting, wondering what was to happen next, but Vittorio just looked at her as he stroked her soft breasts.

She was unnerved. What was going on here tonight? Vittorio had never been quite like this before. There was a different look in his eyes.

He held her closer. 'You know, Lily darling, I'm going to really miss being around you. I didn't realise how much until tonight.'

'You won't be far away. I've only to walk upstairs to the office.'

'It's not the same, but I don't have a choice. Rachel is right – with me about, the club doesn't have a chance.'

He bent his head to kiss her again. This time Lily could feel the passion in him as he teased her with his tongue. His hand slipped beneath her gown.

'Shall I take it off?' she asked breathlessly.

He shook his head. 'Not yet. I love the feel of the material, it's very erotic.'

As they kissed, Lily thought she would go crazy with the need for him. His fingers touched all the places that set her on fire, making her yearn for him to be inside her.

'Now! Now!' she begged him, but he made her wait. Then he was astride her, entering her, slowly. She arched her back to meet him, and clung to him with all her strength and longing.

At the moment of climax, Vittorio did not withdraw. With a deep moan, he shuddered and came inside her. He lay on top of her, smothering her face with kisses. 'Lily, oh Lily,' he murmured. Their bodies still entwined, he rolled over, pulling her on top of him.

She smoothed his forehead, feeling the beads of sweat on her palms. Looking at him she asked, 'What is it? Tonight was different. You were different. You didn't withdraw as you usually do.'

'You're mine and I wanted to be a part of you. For us to be one. Truly. I'll kill any man who tries to come between us. You know that, don't you?'

'Don't be foolish, darling. I don't want anyone else.'

Lying in his arms, Lily relished her feeling of contentment. She had spoken the truth, she realised; she *didn't* want anyone else, not any more. Tom was no longer the man of her dreams. He would always have a place in her heart, but that place belonged in the past.

She'd given herself willingly to Vittorio. Wantonly. Enjoying every moment. Now she snuggled against him and fingered the square emerald and diamond ring hanging on the chain around his neck. 'Tell me about your mother, Vittorio.'

He looked at her with a tender expression in his eyes. 'She was the one person I've ever loved. She was warm and tender. You would have liked her, Lily.' He paused, lost in thought. 'She died when I was five. It's a terrible thing for a child to lose his mother.'

Lily held him close. This was the first time he'd ever let down his defences and told her anything about himself. And sad though it must have been for him, her own mother had never loved her, so in a way, he'd been lucky. At least he had the memory to cherish, which was more than she did.

Chapter Twenty-One

It took almost six weeks to complete the redecoration of the upstairs rooms of the club, but Lily and Vittorio were both pleased with the result. The décor was exclusive and tasteful, which was ideal for their purpose. In the publicity released about the change of ownership, it was clearly stated that Vittorio Teglia had sold the business, and would have nothing more to do with running the Club Valletta. It had also taken several weeks for Rachel and Vittorio to reach an agreement about the price she should pay for a share of the club.

'Christ, Rachel,' he complained, running a hand through his thick dark hair. 'You are a hard woman to do business with.'

She looked at him calmly. 'So what's so difficult? If you had listened to me from the beginning, this could all have been sorted out days ago.'

'Yes . . . to your advantage, if you'd had your way. Now it's settled, to all intents and purposes, you and Lily have gone into a partnership with a hotel company backing you. No one will be able to trace it to me – I've made sure of that. You and Lily will get forty per cent of the profits between you, and the rest will be paid into the company account. The public, however, don't know the details. As far as they are concerned, you are the main shareholders.'

He poured them both a drink and handing Rachel a glass, he said, 'Here's to our success. We'd better call Lily in and give her the good news.'

Lily was delighted and excited. 'I can't believe it. But thank goodness I don't have the books to worry about. That would be too much.'

Before Vittorio had the chance to say anything, Rachel put in: 'I don't mind doing them.'

The Maltese looked across at her. 'No!' he said. 'I'll be keeping them as I've always done. You have only purchased a small share, Rachel – you seem to forget that. I'll keep a copy for you to see at any time, and each month you'll be given a statement of the figures, OK?'

She shook her head in admiration. 'My life, you've got it all worked out, haven't you?'

'Of course I have.' Turning to Lily he said, 'In time, I'll teach you how to do them. But for now, you've got enough on your plate. The rest you'll learn later.'

'It's all a bit much to take in.'

'The important thing in business,' Vittorio told her, 'is the costing of it all. We have to work within a budget or we'll be in trouble. Isn't that right, Rachel?'

'It's the secret of success.' She smiled benignly at them. 'We are all starting out on a new road – for you, my friend, even more so.' She grinned wickedly at Vittorio. 'A legitimate business, already! Who'd have thought it?'

'I just hope that the police will. I don't want any trouble from them.' He lifted his glass. 'To a new way of life.'

Rachel and Lily planned advertising posters to be distributed around the town and advertisements to be run in the local paper, declaring that the Club Valletta was under new management. Vittorio had approved their idea and encouraged them. He was no longer in the building during the day, but occupied with setting up and staffing his new finance business in the centre of Southampton.

Lily was thankful that, in the restaurant, the ordering of supplies remained in the chef's capable hands, while the dining room also remained the responsibility of the friendly head waiter. She spoke to both of them, laying out her hopes for their future. She had a happy knack for motivating people, filling them with the same enthusiasm as herself. There was a new air of excitement about the place.

Sandy, who by now was established as the day-time pianist, remarked on it when he saw Lily. 'You know, darling,

I think this place is really going to take off.'

'Do you think so?' Lily said eagerly. 'I do hope you're right.'

He patted her hand. 'You haven't failed yet, my dear. Not since I've known you.'

'And what about you, Sandy? Are *you* happy here?'

He raised his eyebrows. 'Sweetie, I'm in seventh heaven. The barman and I are having a *torrid* affair.'

'Sandy!' she exclaimed, and burst out laughing.

He put his fingers to his lips. 'Shh. It's all very cloak and dagger. We both want to be discreet. We don't want The Maltese to find out.'

'He'd better not,' she warned.

'There's no need to worry. Neither of us can do without the money. He's a nice boy though, don't you think?' Sandy was obviously smitten.

'I don't want to hear. I don't know anything about it, understand?' she said as she walked away, shaking her head.

There was to be a special gala evening to celebrate the grand opening of the revamped Club and Hotel Valletta. Lily hired various vaudeville acts to appear, and planned to end the show with her own performance. The preparation was hard work, but Lily enjoyed it, apart from the fact that she'd not been feeling at her best lately. She'd had one or two occasions when she thought she'd faint away and now she was feeling nauseous in the mornings.

The day before the opening, Lily received two visitors. The first was Detective Inspector Chadwick. He looked around the dining room then gazed at Lily suspiciously. 'Looks very nice, Miss Pickford. And where does our friend Vittorio Teglia fit into all this?'

'Mr Teglia has sold out to Rachel Cohen,' she lied. 'She and I are partners.'

'So I've been told, but you don't expect me to believe that The Maltese doesn't have a finger in this pie somewhere.'

With a haughty look she said, 'I don't care what you think, Inspector. Mrs Cohen has a legally signed bill of sale.'

He walked towards the door. 'I would like to believe you,

Lily. But we'll be keeping an eye on things to make sure.'

'Any time you want to call in, please do so. I can give you my word this place is being run on the right lines.'

'Does this mean that you and Mr Teglia have terminated your relationship then?'

'Not that it's any of your business, but no. We are still close. But his business and mine are no longer connected.'

'Mmm,' he said. 'That makes me very nervous. I'd like to see you succeed because I think, despite your relationship with Teglia, that you're a decent woman. Just make sure you keep your nose clean, all right?'

No sooner had he left, than Ned Saunders put in an appearance, demanding to see her. Not wanting to be in the confines of the office with the lecherous Chief Steward, she went to see him in the bar.

The predatory look in his eye made her skin crawl.

'So . . . no wonder you told me the club wasn't for sale. You already knew that Vittorio had sold out. Why didn't you tell me?'

'It was none of your business!' she retorted.

'Sparky little thing, aren't you? Well, me and your old man had a business arrangement. When I'm in port I supply him with meat and spirits and any other things that might be on offer. I assume that arrangement will stand?'

She looked at him coldly. 'Then you assume wrong, Mr Saunders. I have made my own arrangements and I'm afraid you don't fit in with them at all.'

He stood there, blustering with anger. 'What do you mean? It's first-class goods!'

'I run this business on a strictly legitimate basis. Your goods have no place here any more.'

His mouth narrowed. 'You little whore. To think I was going to offer to take you on too!'

Lily started to laugh, which made him even more angry. 'You think I'd look twice at *you*? My, what an inflated idea you have of your own importance. You have nothing to offer me that I would be the least bit interested in, thank you. Now, I'm a busy woman and I must ask you to leave.' She told the barman to show him to the door.

Then she bolted to the ladies' room, where she was violently sick.

That evening, she told Vittorio that Ned would no longer be doing business with them.

'What? Has something happened to him?'

'No. I told him his goods were no longer required.'

'You did what?' He was furious.

Lily stood her ground. 'How can we be legitimate and take his dodgy gear?'

'You never make these kind of decisions unless you consult with me first. Do I make myself clear?'

Lily said quietly, 'He was angry that he didn't know the club was for sale. He wanted to take it on . . . and me with it.'

'He what?' Vittorio's face was pinched with anger.

'He's always fancied me from the first day I was here. You know that. Remember when we all had lunch together?'

'Yes. I remember.'

'When he touched me under the table?' she added, pushing her point home. Making sure that Vittorio would never again accommodate Ned. 'Now do you understand why I sent him packing? He would always be pestering me when you weren't around. You wouldn't like that, Vittorio, would you?'

He glared across the desk at her. 'No, I wouldn't. But that doesn't mean you can take over like this. Don't ever do anything like this again without you ask me first, all right?'

'Of course.' Smiling inwardly with triumph, she left him alone to fume.

At last it was opening night. Outside, the name of the club was emblazoned in lights. A smartly uniformed doorman stood ready. As Lily had predicted, he gave an air of respectability and look of class to the place.

People soon started to arrive. She noticed that there were not many ladies in the gathering but hoped that eventually, as the clients realised that this truly was to be a legal establishment, they would feel free to bring their womenfolk.

Rachel, beautifully gowned, stood at the bar, her face flushed with excitement. As the dining room began to fill up and Harry's band played quietly in the background, waiters scurried about taking orders. Rachel turned to Lily, who had paused beside her, and said, 'This is only the beginning, my dear. In a month or two, there will be a waiting list to book a table here, you see if there isn't.' She stared at Lily with a worried frown. 'Are you all right, darling?'

Lily dabbed at her top lip with a lace-trimmed handkerchief. 'I'm fine, why do you ask?'

Shaking her head, Rachel said, 'You look a bit pale.'

'It's the excitement, that's all.' She walked away and began to work the tables, seeing that the clients were comfortable and satisfied.

Rachel watched her carefully, a knowing look in her eyes.

As she spoke to the clients Lily was aware of a few whispers from the females. She heard the words 'mistress' and 'Maltese' murmured in conversation, but she didn't let this faze her at all. She just smiled at the women and took note of the way they admired her gown and her jewels. There were looks of envy from some and hostility from others. None of this gave her a moment's worry. She was not a fool and knew her notoriety would work more in her favour than against. There would be a few who disapproved, but enough of them would be fascinated to swell the business, until the time came when it wasn't important any longer. People would come because the food was excellent and the entertainment first class. And expensive – which would make it select.

As Lily took the stage to thunderous applause, she looked across at Harry, the band leader, and winked. Within the first few bars of her song, she knew she had the punters in the palm of her hand. Many newcomers were surprised at the sweetness and purity of her voice. She thought that perhaps a few might have expected lewdness, knowing her position in life. But if so, instead of being disappointed, they were won over by her professionalism and her talent.

She made a short speech as her act came to an end, thanking them for coming to the opening night and hoping they would be returning as regular clients.

After closing, Lily and Rachel, exhausted after the long night, sat with Vittorio in the office, counting the takings.

Rachel's eyes were shining. 'We've done really well, Lily.' Turning to Vittorio she said, 'You should be very happy.'

He gave his enigmatic smile. 'I am. You did well, Lily. I watched you, swanning around the customers. I must say they all looked very satisfied. Good. It's an excellent start. Do you want me to call a taxi, Rachel? You must be tired.'

'I am,' she said. 'But I'm so excited I'm sure I won't sleep.'

Lily waited downstairs with her for the car to arrive.

Patting Lily's hand Rachel said, 'You make sure you have a good sleep. You need to look after yourself, especially now.'

With a startled look Lily asked, 'What do you mean, especially now?'

'Now you're pregnant.'

'Now I'm what?'

Rachel sat back in the chair. '*Oy vey!* I don't believe it. You don't even know, do you?' She paused, taking in the shocked expression on Lily's face. 'I hear you being sick sometimes when I come in early in the morning. I know about these things. I can spot a pregnant woman a mile away.'

Lily put her hands to her face. 'Oh my God!'

Rachel sat watching her. She could hardly believe that this young girl, able to fend for herself, capable of taking The Maltese as her lover and now a partner in what she hoped would be a thriving business, had not realised that she was with child. She knew so much, yet she knew so little.

Lily was stunned. Her periods had always been somewhat unpredictable, and she'd thought her symptoms were caused by her nervousness and excitement. Although inwardly she was convinced that her endeavours would eventually be successful, she'd been overwrought with the burden of the responsibility upon her young shoulders.

'What am I going to do, Rachel?'

Coming straight to the point as usual, the Jewess said, 'You have two choices. You have the child or an abortion.'

Lily's eyes widened. 'I'm not having any bloody abortion!'

'Then it's settled. You have the child.'

'But what about the business? We're trying to start on the straight and narrow. Me being Vittorio's mistress is bad enough, but having his child . . .' She suddenly sat up straight. 'Vittorio! What will he say about it?'

Rachel raised her eyebrows. 'What can he say? He made you pregnant.'

'Oh Rachel. What a mess. The gossips will have even *more* to talk about now.'

Getting up from her chair, Rachel put an arm around Lily and held her close. 'So what's another mess? We've both had plenty. Maybe Vittorio will make an honest woman of you.'

'What do you mean – marry me?'

'There's a different meaning?'

Lily slumped back in the chair. 'I won't tell him.'

'So where are you going to carry this child – under your arm?'

Shaking her head, Lily said, 'I can't believe it.'

'What's to believe? You lie with a man, what do you expect? You won't be able to hide it for long.'

'Long enough to get the business off the ground, do you think?'

Shrugging, Rachel said, 'Maybe. You'll have to get bigger gowns to cover your belly as it swells. Maybe you'll get away with it for three months. But in bed . . . you think he won't notice?'

The taxi arrived and Lily kissed Rachel good night. 'I'm going to bed. I'm knackered. I can't think about anything.'

Rachel said, 'Best thing. No need to get up too early. The staff will be in. You won't be needed until later in the day. Bye, see you tomorrow!'

Rachel sat in the back of the taxi, with a feeling of satisfaction, but a fracas outside The Grapes public house made her sit up. A bottle came flying through the air and hit the side of the car and the driver cursed. Several drunken men were fighting and Rachel heard the sound of glass breaking, followed by a scream of pain. But such savage scenes could not mar her happiness.

Tonight had lived up to all her expectations. If only it would continue, for Lily's sake. For Rachel, financial considerations were not important, but she wanted Lily to be independent – especially now a baby was on the way. How would The Maltese feel about being a father, she wondered.

She reached her destination and paid off the driver, then put the key into the door of her sizeable Edwardian house and walked into the entrance hall. As she locked the door behind her, she smiled softly. The Maltese had good taste; he would feel quite at home here, in these comfortable, well-furnished surroundings.

Once inside the large drawing room, she put on the light and pulled the heavy rich-green velvet drapes together and, sitting down on the comfortable easy chair, covered in damask the colour of port wine, she kicked off her shoes. She reached out for the cut-glass decanter on the table beside her and poured a large brandy. It was a nightly ritual which she enjoyed to the full.

A pity, she thought, there was no man to share these comforts with her, but she was used to living alone. On the whole, men brought nothing but trouble, and she enjoyed having the big double bed to herself.

Tipping the last of the nightcap down her throat, she made her way slowly up to bed, aware that the excitement of today would rob her of the sleep she so badly needed.

As Lily lay, equally restless, in the big bed on the other side of town, waiting for Vittorio, she stretched her arm across the empty space beside her. Tonight, she needed the comfort of his arms. She couldn't accept that she was pregnant . . . now of all times. She pulled back the bedclothes and looked at her stomach. It didn't appear any different. Foolishly, she'd never thought about getting pregnant. And Vittorio had once said he didn't want a family. What would his reaction be when eventually she told him her news? Too tired to think straight, she fell into an exhausted sleep.

While Lily was engrossed in her plans for the Club Valletta, Tom McCann was trying to come to terms with being a father and attempting to mend his broken marriage. He loved his son, Thomas William, with all his heart. He played with the child constantly, enamoured with his every move and expression. He even sat with him, feeding him from the bottle. But he drew the line at changing nappies, saying it was woman's work.

Mary, after being confined to bed for fourteen days following her labour, had been very weak and was only now getting back to normal. Because of her physical condition, and following the doctor's advice, Tom had not attempted to make love to her.

He sat with her one evening, trying to sort out their future. 'I'm sorry I upset you so much before the birth of the baby,' he apologised.

Mary gave him one of her baleful looks. 'What's that supposed to mean?'

Patiently he said, 'It means I'm not leaving you and the lad. We must start again. Put all this behind us.'

He noticed her look of relief, quickly followed by one of fear.

'What is it, darlin'?' he said tenderly. 'What's bothering you?'

'I don't want any more babies!' she declared.

'That's understandable, after what you went through. Do you think I would want to see you suffer like that again?'

'I thought I was going to die. I *wanted* to die.'

'Mary love, don't take on so.'

There was sheer terror in her eyes as she looked at him. 'It's all right for you men. You don't know the pain. It was like something tearing my insides to pieces. I couldn't face it again.' She closed her eyes as she mentally relived the traumatic birth. No man was worth it, she concluded.

'I promise you I'll be careful. I won't make you pregnant.'

Glaring at him she said, 'Well, you won't get the chance, Tom McCann.'

'What do you mean?'

'It means I'll be a mother to our child and I'll cook and clean for you and share your bed, but I won't have sex with you. Not ever again!'

He was astonished. 'How can you be a wife to me, without it?'

'I'll be an understanding wife. I know that it's important to you.' She grimaced. 'Men can't seem to do without it, but that's fine. You just get it somewhere else.'

He couldn't believe his ears. 'Are you telling me that I can sleep with another woman?'

She looked at him quite calmly. 'Yes.'

'Are you out of your mind?'

'I've never been more sane. You can have your women, I'll take care of the rest. You'll provide a home and food for me and your son. I think it's an excellent arrangement.'

Tom sat in his chair puffing on a cigarette, pondering her words. Many men he knew would welcome such an arrangement! He thought it had its funny side and grinned to himself. After all, his sex-life with his wife had never been satisfying. Now his house would be clean, his food cooked, clothes washed and ironed, his child cared for and he was free as a bird. Wasn't life strange? Looking across at Mary, he said, 'Is that really what you want?'

'Yes, I do. Mind you, I expect you to be discreet. Don't make me appear a fool.'

He was bemused. 'I've never heard anything like it in me whole life.'

'Look, Tom,' she reasoned. 'I know I haven't been the best wife in the world. You wanting to leave was partly my fault. But this way we can both have what we want. You're earning again. I can have back my standard of living. You were always a generous man when you were earning. That's all I want from you.'

'Thanks. That makes me feel a right eejit!'

Ignoring his remark she added, 'There is one more thing.'

'And what on earth might that be?'

'I don't want you to tell me anything about it.'

His face flushed. 'What sort of a man do you take me for? Do you think I'd come home and flaunt it in your face? That's supposing I take a woman.'

Giving him a knowing look she said, 'Oh, you will, Tom. You will.'

And she was right. Free of any guilt, Tom found a pretty young maid whose passionate nature matched his own and who was more than pleased to be seen with such a handsome man. Tom was shrewd enough not to take her to his usual haunts, thus keeping his amours discreet. He was straight with the girl, telling her he was married and wouldn't dream of leaving his wife and child, that this was just a fling. The girl was still willing.

He had of course immediately thought of Lily, of hopefully renewing their love. But her disgust at his behaviour when last they'd met kept him at bay. And when he heard that she and Rachel Cohen had taken over the club, he felt she was no longer within his reach. Therefore he was a little nonplussed one day when he saw her walking towards him in Kingsland Square.

Lifting his cap in greeting he said, 'Hello, Lily.'

She was studying a shopping list and was startled to hear her name. 'Tom,' she said with surprise.

He noticed the coldness in her voice. So she hadn't forgiven him. He thought she looked well, though she had put on a little weight. Her complexion was as smooth as ever and her eyes as blue, but there was something different about her that he couldn't put his finger on.

'Lily. You're looking well.'

'Thank you.'

She seemed to have even more poise than usual, thought Tom. Well of course, nowadays she'd moved up in the world. 'Congratulations. I heard about you and Rachel owning the club. I wish you both luck. What's happened to Vittorio?'

Cocking her head on one side she asked, 'Happened? What do you mean?'

He looked deep into her eyes, searching for some faint sign of what had been between them. There was nothing. 'Is he still around?'

She ignored his question. 'I hear your wife gave birth to a son. Congratulations. Try and be a good father, even if you're no good as a husband. It's important to a child.'

She walked away before he could answer.

Threading her way through the shoppers Lily headed for

home. As she did so she thought to herself, You bloody hypocrite. How could you say such a thing when you haven't even informed the father of the child *you're* carrying?

She was surprised, too, that seeing Tom again had failed to interest her. She'd been so disillusioned with him at their last meeting that it had doused the flames of love that had burned within her for so long. And now, with her own pregnancy to consider, she scarcely ever thought of him.

At Rachel's insistence, Lily had paid a visit to the doctor. After an examination, he informed her she was ten weeks pregnant, by his calculations.

When she told Rachel, the older woman asked, 'How long are you going to wait before you tell Vittorio?'

Lily prevaricated. 'I don't know. When the time is right.'

Two weeks after the club reopened, four well-dressed strangers came into the bar. They ordered drinks and spoke with the barman, who then came over to Lily.

'Excuse me, Miss Lily.' He looked perplexed.

'What is it?'

'Those men at the bar, they're asking for Mr Vittorio. Something about gambling.'

'I'll come and see them. Perhaps they're old clients.'

'No, miss. I've never seen them before.'

Walking over to the men, Lily said, 'Good evening, gentlemen. Can I help you?'

The tallest one spoke. 'We're looking for Vittorio Teglia. He told us where we could find a card-game, but we've lost the address.'

Lily was puzzled. 'There is no gambling here.'

'We know that. It was some other place he has. Do you know where it is?'

She went cold. 'No, I'm sorry. I've no idea.'

They drank up and left.

Lily stayed at the bar, trying to fathom this puzzle. Soon after the opening, when Vittorio could see that everything was running smoothly, he'd occasionally disappear for a couple of hours, returning just before closing time, telling her he'd had business to attend to. Now she began to wonder, what kind of business? She'd imagined it had to do with his finance company. Now she was worried. She had a sick feeling in the pit of her stomach.

After the club closed that night, she tackled him. 'Some men came here tonight looking for you.'

'Oh. What did they want?'

'They wanted to gamble. Apparently you told them of a place where they could play cards. A place that was yours.'

'Oh, those chaps. Yes, I know.'

'How do you know?'

'Because they found me later.'

She sat down and asked, 'What's going on, Vittorio?'

'I've rented a small house. It's a very select place – only a few invited clients use it. Nothing that need concern you.'

Lily was speechless. She couldn't believe what she was hearing. She had really thought Vittorio was going straight. 'How could you?'

He glared at her. 'It's none of your business, Lily.'

'Are you mad or what? You know the police are keeping an eye on you.'

He was unconcerned. 'They can't do anything about it. It's a private house. I only have a small gathering and if the police should ask, it's a get-together with friends, not a business.'

'For which your so-called friends pay.'

'Of course.' He smiled. 'And pay handsomely.' Seeing the expression on her face he said, 'You must realise, Lily, that this is my business. My way of life. I'm not able to do it here, so I have to do it elsewhere. How do you think I make my money?' he went on irritably. 'There are no prostitutes now, no gambling. How do you expect me to buy your clothes, that jewellery you wear – on the modest profits of my legitimate loan-brokering business? You can't be that naive! Besides, it's what I do best, and I get a kick out of it.'

'So much for your new way of life!' Lily stormed out of the room, tears in her eyes.

As she undressed, she raged inwardly. How could he take such a chance, just as things were working out? Huh – that was a laugh! She was pregnant and Vittorio was breaking the law. Maybe nothing was working out. Yes, business was good in the club . . . at the moment. But it could all blow up in their faces. Poor Rachel, how disappointed she would be if it did fail. It was all right for Vittorio, he was well off. But if he was caught, everything would be ruined. All her hard work would be for nothing. And Rachel's expectations would be shattered. She couldn't tell her.

When Vittorio climbed into bed beside her later, Lily turned away from him.

'You're still angry,' he said.

'Well, what do you expect?'

'I expect you to have faith in me, Lily. You know that I never do anything without calculating the risks. And in this case there are none.'

She was not convinced. Impulsively, she blurted out: 'Well, there's one thing you didn't calculate. I'm pregnant!'

She hadn't meant it to come out like this.

He sat up. 'You're pregnant?'

She nodded. What would his reaction be? She held her breath.

He stared hard at her and asked, 'Is this child mine?'

Still angered from the earlier revelation, Lily blazed at him. 'How dare you ask me such a thing?' She threw back the covers, got out of bed and stormed across the room. Picking up one of his silver-backed hairbrushes, she repeated her words, 'How dare you!' and threw the brush at him.

Vittorio ducked under the sheets, then leapt out of bed and swiftly crossed the room, grabbing her by the wrists. 'How do I know it isn't that man's? That Tom McCann who came here and upset you.' His dark penetrating gaze burned into her. 'You said he wasn't your lover but I didn't believe you.'

Lily was so enraged she spoke before thinking. 'We were lovers,' she spat. 'For just one night! Long before I met you. Now are you satisfied?'

'When was this? Tell me.'

'It's none of your bloody business!' she yelled at him.

His grip tightened, making her wince. 'Indeed it is my

business. You are mine. You belong to me.' His voice was full of menace. '*When?*'

For the first time, Lily saw in Vittorio what caused so much fear in others, but she was too incensed to be cautious.

'I don't ask you about your women!'

'If I thought you were carrying another man's child, I'd kill you. When did you have this night of passion?'

'It was a year before I came to live with you. Now are you satisfied?'

'How many others have there been?' he demanded.

Lily glared at him. 'Millions!' she cried. 'They could all be the father.'

Vittorio released her. 'Don't be so stupid.'

'Stupid! Me? It's you who are stupid, Vittorio.' But she could find no more words. She was incredibly hurt that he could doubt her loyalty. How could he even think of her taking a lover whilst she lived with him?

He sat on the chair, took a cigarette out of his case and lit it. Looking back at her he saw that she was trembling. 'For goodness sake get under the covers before you catch your death of cold.'

'I'm not at all sure I want to share a bed with you,' she said tearfully.

His jaw tightened and he said evenly, 'Do as I say.'

Lily was feeling so chilled and unwell, she did as she was told. She'd been deeply shaken by their angry exchange.

Vittorio put his cigarette out and climbed into bed.

Lily turned her back on him.

He put his arm around her. She stiffened at his touch, but he ignored this. 'You're frozen,' he said and held her closer until she stopped trembling. He put his hand over her stomach, gently stroking the soft mound. 'Inside here is our child?' he asked quietly.

Lily said, 'Yes. You can believe it or not. I don't care any more.' Her shoulders shook as she tried in vain to stem the tears that started to flow.

He gathered her even closer. 'Please, Lily, stop this,' he coaxed her. 'It isn't good for your condition.'

Her condition. The words seemed strange, but she did

have a condition. She was carrying a child in her womb.

'You aren't angry any more?' she whispered.

'No.'

'But you told me once, you didn't want a family.'

He suddenly chuckled. 'That's right, and at the time I didn't, but now, I must say the idea appeals to me.' He turned her round so that she was facing him. 'And you, Lily, how do you feel about it?'

She was relieved that his anger had faded. That he knew. 'I really don't know.' She looked at him anxiously. 'It's been such a surprise. But when I think about it I wonder how the club patrons will react. Will it make a difference to the business? Oh Vittorio, I want this child very much and I so want the club to be a success, but if I was the reason it all failed, it would be terrible.'

'Darling,' he said, his voice filled with concern, 'so much worry on so young a pair of shoulders.'

'And now to learn about your gambling. It's too much.'

'I have to earn a living. I've explained that,' he said patiently. 'Especially now, with the baby coming.'

'I suppose so,' she reluctantly agreed. She suddenly found her spirit. 'Why should I care what the customers think, anyway? As long as the food and the entertainment's good, they won't give a toss.'

He became thoughtful. 'I'm not so sure about that. You are already notorious as my mistress. This, of course, will only add fuel to the fire. Are you prepared for it? You could be in for a rough ride, you know. People can be very cruel. I don't want you getting hurt any more.'

She snuggled against him. 'I really don't know. I was hoping that before my pregnancy showed, the club would have taken off. I'll just have to wait and see.'

He kissed the tip of her nose. 'You are a wonderful girl. Bright, and very brave. Some women might have rushed to have an abortion.'

'Not me! I'll not let some back-street woman shove things up me.'

Cringing at the thought, Vittorio pulled her to him and kissed her softly. 'Promise me you won't ever consider putting yourself in such danger.'

'No, of course I won't. I know there are girls who have died after such a thing.'

There was a moment's silence, then Vittorio said, 'We could always get married.'

This was as big a shock to Lily as when she realised that she was pregnant. She looked at him anxiously.

'Would that be so terrible?' he asked.

'I'm just so confused,' she said. 'All this is a bit much to handle at once. First the club, then the baby and now this. My mind's in such a whirl I can't think straight.'

'It would make the child legitimate, darling. And you respectable. And it would make me very happy. Think about it. But right now I want you so much, I can't wait.'

Later, as she lay in his arms, Lily looked at the sleeping figure beside her. Did she want to marry Vittorio? It would give the child his name. After all, he was the father – but again he was living beyond the law. What if he went to prison? What would happen to her and the baby then?

Chapter Twenty-Two

The first month of the new enterprise was coming to an end and everyone was pleased with the obvious success of the venture. Word had spread quickly that things at the club had changed. It was now the place to be seen and the bookings were much sought-after.

'Didn't I tell you, Lily!' exclaimed Rachel with obvious glee as the head waiter showed them his book of reservations.

'You did. And we are getting a decent kind of crowd too. More women are coming and that's good.'

'Well, how else would the young flappers be able to say they'd spent an evening in a former brothel without having their reputation in tatters?' was Rachel's cynical retort.

With a grin, Lily had to agree. 'At the moment that certainly adds to the attraction, but that'll soon pass.'

'Yes, I know.' Rachel rubbed the palms of her hands together. 'But by then, we've got them.'

Rachel was standing with her back to the main entrance, unaware of the new customer who had just entered, but Lily, looking over her shoulder, recognised him immediately.

'Oh well, better get on,' she said calmly. 'Rachel, why don't you go up to the office? Vittorio is working on the first month's figures and I know you're interested to see how well we've done.'

'Bloody slave-driver,' her friend grumbled with a smile, and made her way upstairs.

With bright eyes and a brittle edge to her voice, Lily greeted the newcomer. 'Good evening, Manny. This is a bit posh for you, isn't it, even if you have improved your appearance.' She looked at the well-tailored dark suit he was wearing. She'd never seen him look so presentable. But hate burned in her heart as she stared into the hooded eyes of Rachel's son.

He leered at her. 'You are the one who's moved up, or so I hear. Is it true that you and Mama are in business together?' He looked around the dining area, and she saw the calculating look in his eyes.

'Yes, that's right. News travels fast. What do you want? There are no prostitutes here any more.'

'I've come to see my mother. She sold the business in The Ditches.' He glared at Lily. 'That was supposed to be my inheritance, but . . .' Looking around he added, 'This doesn't look so bad.'

Lily felt anger rise within her like a volcano and she fought to keep control. It was because of this man she'd lost Tom, had spent time on the streets, selling her body for a crust of bread. The humiliation still lived hidden deep within her, and Manny had brought it all racing to the surface. She was choking on the memories of that wretched period in her life.

'I'll tell her you're here. Give this man a drink,' she sharply instructed the barman.

Lily marched into the office upstairs and shut the door behind her. She looked across the room at Rachel, poring over the books. Her glasses were perched on the end of her nose, making her look like a wise old owl. 'Where's Vittorio?'

'Popped out for a moment. He won't be long. Something wrong, darling?'

'You have a visitor,' Lily announced.

With surprise Rachel said, 'I do?'

'Your son is downstairs. I thought I'd better warn you, before I brought him up to see you.'

Taking off her glasses Rachel asked, 'And what does he want?'

'He says he wants his inheritance!'

Rachel's eyes narrowed. 'They soon come crawling out of the woodwork at the smell of money. You'd better ask him up here. I wouldn't like the clients to be put off by the sight of blood.' At the look of dismay on the face of her young friend, she cackled with laughter. 'Don't worry. I'll smother his screams of pain.'

Manny was shown into the office. As the door closed behind him, he looked around the well-appointed room, then at his mother seated in the large leather chair. He took in every detail of her elegant apparel and sneered, 'Well, well. You're doing all right for yourself, aren't you?'

She eyed him up and down. 'I'm surprised you clean up so well. You'd better sit down.'

He walked across the room and she was filled with bitterness as she watched her son. Things could have been so different between them. 'What do you want? I know you're not interested in my health.' She leaned back in the chair and waited.

Beneath his mother's steely gaze, Manny became a little nervous. But he had come with a purpose. 'You sold the shop without consulting me.'

'What the bloody hell did it have to do with you, might I ask?'

'It was my inheritance.'

She laughed loudly. 'You *shlemiel*! It's what kept you in pocket-money to spend on women. My indulgence, as your mother. Well, I threw you out – disowned you. Remember?'

His pudgy face seemed to swell even more as his anger rose to the surface. 'Only because of that bitch downstairs. I want what is mine. I want a piece of this club.'

Raising her eyebrows she said, 'You think you are capable of running such a business, I suppose?'

'Of course I could. There's nothing to it. Any fool could do it.'

'And that just about sums you up, Manny. What brains you got you carry in your trouser pockets. Beyond that you have nothing. You *are* nothing.'

'Look at you,' he said scornfully, 'sitting there filled with your own importance, like the bloody Queen of Sheba.'

Rachel remained calm. 'Such a brain you have. You have just proved my point, Manny. You come here wanting money and you sit and insult me. Hardly a good business move, would you say?'

He flushed with anger. 'Don't lecture me, Mama. You've nagged me all my life. Now I'm too old to be spoken to like that.'

Her raucous laughter filled the room. 'My God! The boy is standing up for himself. *Nag* you? It was the only way to get you off your fat, lazy arse, try and make a man of you. But it was wasted effort.' Her expression hardened. She leaned forward and in a low voice said, 'You listen to me, you little runt. Nothing I have belongs to you. You have no right to anything of mine. In my will I have stated as much, with a certificate from an eminent doctor that I was in my right mind when I signed it. So when I'm dead and buried don't think of trying to contest it in a court of law.'

'How can you treat me like this? Your own flesh and blood.' His expression darkened.

'I meant what I said when I sent you away. I'm ashamed to be your mother.'

'My father if he was alive wouldn't have this.'

'Such a threat you make. Your father is six feet under, his body rotten with the syphilis that killed him.'

Manny's eyes widened with shock. 'You foul-mouthed old woman! My father died of a bad heart.'

'That's what I told you, to save you shame. He got it from the whores he visited – like you. How do you know you ain't tainted too?'

'There's nothing wrong with me,' Manny blustered, his face white. 'I only went to clean houses. I don't go any more.'

She let out a cruel cackle, although inside her heart was heavy with grief. 'No, I don't suppose you can afford it now I'm not keeping you. You're working – earning a living. It should be enough.'

'Yes, with your brother, the slave-driver. He pays me peanuts. He made me buy this suit and I have to pay so much off a week out of my wages for it.'

She grinned. 'Well, at least you look halfway decent. Maybe if you get lucky, some woman will take pity on you, though I doubt it.'

He was incensed. 'That's where you're wrong. I'm

engaged to be married.' Rachel's expression of astonishment pleased him. 'There – what do you think about *that*?'

'So, who is this woman?'

'Miriam Goldburg.'

'The widow Goldburg? The one whose husband had a hump?'

'Yes.'

She grinned broadly. 'Manny, my son, *mazel tov!* She may have a face like an old bus, but she's got money, she's tight-lipped and tight-arsed, and she's just the woman for you. So you don't need anything from me. You got it all. She's got enough for both of you.'

He slumped in his chair. 'Yes, and she hangs on to it.'

'So she's tight-fisted too. Wise woman. You'd spend it all, given the chance.'

He thumped the desk with his fist. 'I want my own money. You owe me, Mama. I want what is rightfully mine.'

'I have nothing for you, Manny. Not any more. You forfeited the right when you let yourself into the shop that night. But for Lily, you might have been arrested and imprisoned for rape. Such shame you could have brought on me and your family. Did you care? Of course not.' She paused to take a shuddering breath. 'I don't want to see you in here again. You're not welcome. I've invested my money with someone who's willing to work for it – something you never did. You had your chance and you threw it away.' She glared across the desk at him. 'You walk into the club again, I'll have you barred!'

Manny got to his feet in such a hurry that he sent his chair crashing to the floor. He stood over the desk threatening his mother. 'You give me what's mine, woman, or you'll rue the day you were born.'

Behind him the door opened and Vittorio stood there surveying the scene. With a few quick strides he was across the room, hauling Manny away from his mother.

Turning, Manny looked into the eyes of The Maltese and froze.

'What's going on here?' Vittorio asked, still gripping hold of Manny.

'My son, who I disowned, came to claim what he thinks is his – my money. He should be so lucky!'

Manny by now was a shivering wreck, all his bravado gone.

Vittorio looked at him in disgust. 'God, how I hate parasites like you. You haven't done an honest day's work in your life. You lived off your mother for years.' He led him towards the door. 'I'm taking you myself down the back stairs. When you leave here, you don't ever return. Understand?'

Manny didn't reply.

'Understand?' Vittorio repeated. 'You come back here and I'll break your legs. Do I make myself clear?'

'Yes. Yes. I won't come back.'

Opening the back door of the club, Vittorio sent him flying. As Manny picked himself up out of the gutter, Vittorio said, 'Remember: you return at your peril.'

Back in the office, he asked Rachel, 'Are you all right?'

She nodded. 'Sure. I suppose I should have expected to hear from him, but to be honest I'd put him out of my mind a long time ago.'

'Do you think he'll cause trouble?'

Shrugging she said, 'I honestly don't think so. He don't have the balls for it.' But knowing Manny's avaricious nature, Rachel was not at all sure.

'Well, if he gives you any trouble, you let me know. I'll deal with him.'

There was a look of anxiety in Rachel's eyes. She despised her son but at the same time she knew that if the need arose, Vittorio would be ruthless. Despite everything, she was still a mother.

'No, Vittorio!' Her voice was harsh. 'You don't kill my boy.'

With a contemptuous look, he said, 'Boy! He's in his thirties. Old enough to take what's coming to him if he crosses me.'

'All right, to you he's a man and not much of one at that. But me, I remember the child.' She put her hands on her stomach. 'I carried him in here for nine months, felt him move. Gave birth to him.' Tears welled in her eyes. 'Held him to my breast. I can't stand by knowing what might happen to him. No mother could.' Her voice trembled with emotion. 'I have learned you can be a good man, a kind man. For Christ's sake, Vittorio, you're to be a father yourself! Can't you understand?'

The cold expression of The Maltese slowly changed as he saw Rachel's anguish. He thought of his own unborn child and was touched. 'Very well. But if he bothers me, he'll get the beating of his life.'

She walked around the desk and caught hold of his arm. 'But you won't kill him? Promise me that. You won't let him die?'

He stared into the older woman's eyes and patted her hand. 'I give you my word. But better for him that he keeps away. If you have any control over him at all, warn him of the consequences.' He turned and walked out of the room.

Rachel flopped into the nearest chair and angrily wiped the tears from her eyes. Bloody Manny, she thought. That a boy of hers could be the cause of so much trouble. With a deep sigh, she lit a cigarette, and put on her coat. She felt sick and needed to be in her own home, alone.

There was a further incident in the club that night.

Four young men were dining. They were flushed with wine and being raucous in their behaviour, disturbing other guests.

Walking over to them Lily quietly said, 'I'm happy to see you enjoying yourselves, gentlemen, but I must ask you to keep the noise down.'

The ringleader looked at her through glazéd eyes. 'Who do you think you are?' he asked rudely.

'I'm part-owner of this establishment.'

He looked her up and down. 'Were you one of the whores when this place was a brothel? I'd pay for you, my dear.'

Lily picked up a glass of wine from the table and threw it in his face. She looked at the barman and nodded towards the entrance. He quickly returned with the doorman.

'This young man is leaving,' she said. 'And his friends will go too, after they settle the bill.'

The troublemaker's companions were deeply embarrassed.

She turned to the other patrons. 'I'm sorry for the disturbance, ladies and gentlemen. Please continue with your meal.' She walked over to the bar and, with trembling fingers, lit a cigarette.

The doorman was surprised to see Vittorio waiting for him as he led the diner outside.

The Maltese grabbed the front of the young man's suit and pushed him up against the wall.

'What the hell are you doing? Let go of me.'

Vittorio looked at him. 'You were very rude to Miss Lily in the restaurant and I won't have it.'

'It was only a joke,' the man blustered.

'I'm not laughing. And I didn't see her look amused, did you?'

'I don't know why you're getting so excited, old chap. She's only a whore. She's the mistress of Vittorio Teglia.'

Vittorio released his hold. 'Have you ever met him?'

The young man looked at him. 'No, I haven't.'

'I am Vittorio Teglia . . . *old chap*.' And he punched the man viciously in the stomach.

The three friends emerged from the club, and saw their friend doubled up. They looked at the menacing figure beside him.

'I've just given your friend a lesson in manners. You'd better take him home. Don't bring him here again.'

In bed that night, Vittorio told Lily of the scene between Rachel and her son. 'He'll be back,' he declared. 'He won't be able to help himself. Manny always wanted to be in the money and now he thinks he's got a chance.'

'But he knows how Rachel feels about him,' Lily objected. 'Surely he must realise he's wasting his time.'

Her lover looked thoughtful. 'If he does, it makes the situation worse. He's a twisted little bastard. I'll instruct the staff to keep a watchful eye open for him. I won't put up with someone like him messing with my business.'

'What will you do if he does return?'

He pursed his lips. 'Whatever I have to, Lily. Whatever I have to.'

She knew the subject of Manny was closed.

Then: 'You had a bit of trouble tonight in the restaurant. I saw from the office,' he remarked.

Lily, who hadn't intended mentioning the incident, said, 'It was nothing. It was over in a moment.'

'He won't be back, I can assure you. We don't want his kind here.'

'What do you mean, he won't be back?' She saw the anger in Vittorio's eyes.

'I taught him a lesson outside he won't forget in a hurry.'

'Whatever did you do?'

'Never mind, Lily. I've told you – any trouble, I'll take care of it.' He smoothed her hair. 'Nobody treats you like that and gets away with it.' He drew her closer. 'Come here.'

As he held her, Lily wondered what had happened outside the club. She hoped Vittorio hadn't gone too far. She'd handled the situation the right way, as far as she was concerned, and it was over and done with. Would there be any repercussions? She hoped not.

Vittorio's voice interrupted her worried thoughts. 'I see you've dispensed with the black sheets.'

'To be honest, I hated them,' she admitted. 'And now I'm an expectant mother, they didn't seem appropriate.'

'You should have said, my darling.'

She gave a sardonic smile. 'Would it have made any difference?'

His eyes sparkled. 'No.' Nuzzling her ear he asked, 'Have you thought any more about our getting married?'

She shook her head.

'You don't think I'd make a good husband?'

Looking into his dark-brown eyes, she said, 'I'm sure you would, but I don't know if that's what I want.'

The expression in his eyes became watchful. 'And what's that supposed to mean?'

Easing herself away from his embrace, she sat up. 'I'm not sure I want to be married to anyone.'

Vittorio lit a cigarette and drew on it slowly. 'Even as my

mistress you kept your independent streak. I see it hasn't gone away.' There was no smile on his face as he asked, 'Are you trying to tell me you don't need me any more? Is that it?'

She sensed the menace in his voice. 'No, that's not it at all.' How could she explain her innermost feelings to Vittorio without upsetting him? 'I'm not interested in anyone else,' she tried. 'I'm happy with you.' She looked at him. 'Do I make you happy?'

His expression relaxed. 'Darling Lily, of course you do.'

'Then why do we have to change things?'

'I would have thought that was obvious. You are with child.'

She sighed and automatically placed a hand on her abdomen. 'Yes, I am, but would it matter to you if we stayed as we are? After all, your name will be on the birth certificate. I'm not trying to deny you your child.'

He gathered her to him. 'Oh Lily, don't you see? I'm only trying to protect you by giving the baby a name.'

'My parents were married. That didn't protect me when I was a child, or after. My father treated me like dirt and my mother didn't give a toss.'

Hearing the bitterness in her voice, he held her tighter. 'Oh my darling, I'm sorry.'

'Isn't it more important for a child to be loved?'

'Of course.'

'I don't want my baby mixed up in any illegal activities when it gets older,' Lily declared.

Vittorio's jaw tightened. 'You forget again, my dear, that such activities have kept me in luxury and you in clothes. They have also been the means of starting this business that you are so anxious to succeed in.'

'Yes, I know that. But the child will already have enough to cope with.'

'Another reason that we should be married. Besides, that scene in the restaurant tonight wouldn't have happened if you were my wife.'

Lily was silent.

Vittorio wasn't happy. He knew how difficult her life would be with an illegitimate child. At least with his name, he could safeguard her. But he didn't want to push her at the moment.

'If you can be brave enough to put up with the scandal and taunts you will undoubtedly receive, then we'll stay as we are – if that's what you want.'

She looked at him with trusting eyes. 'You will love the baby, won't you, Vittorio?'

His slow smile touched the corners of his lips. 'Of course I will. How could I not do so?'

Lily was relieved. She hadn't lied to him. By marrying him, it would make the child legitimate, but as the wife of The Maltese, she would be even more notorious. So what was the difference? She didn't care what people said about her. She would care for the child as a real mother should. She was confident that by the time she gave birth, the club would be up and running anyway. Besides, she'd made up her mind, and thankfully Vittorio had not been difficult.

When she told Rachel of their conversation, the older woman frowned. 'Well, I suppose you know what you're doing. You're not hankering after the wild Irishman still, are you? Is he the reason for not marrying?'

Shaking her head, Lily denied it. 'Of course not. Tom will always be my first love and I'll never forget him, but he's changed. He's not the man I thought he was.'

With a look of affection Rachel said, 'He loved you.'

'I know, but in the end the first thought in his head was that I was Vittorio's. His pride got in the way of love and that's not good.'

With a shrug Rachel said, 'He's a man. What do you expect?'

Lily said, 'Women should run the world and keep men only for breeding and moving heavy stuff around.'

'*Oy vey!* I like the sound of that.' Rachel's eyes twinkled mischievously at the thought. 'I'd have a couple of young ones in my house at my beck and call . . . day *and* night!'

'Go on,' Lily teased. 'You're past it.'

'You don't know that. Neither do I, but I'd like to find out!'

'You are a disgusting old woman.' The smile on Lily's face

faded as she said, 'Why is life always so complicated? It would be nice if just for once there were no problems, no worries.'

Rachel grimaced. 'Once upon a time is for fairy stories, girl. We're dealing with life and that's different. You of all people should know that.'

Life in the McCann household had settled to its strange existence. Tom came home on a Friday night and handed Mary her housekeeping money which she took, without thanks, and put carefully in the biscuit barrel on the sideboard.

She kept their home spotless, ironed his shirts to perfection and baked every Friday afternoon, filling the house with the delicious aroma of homemade bread and cakes. She cared for little Thomas William in an efficient manner, but it was from Tom that the baby received unstinting affection.

With the child, a comfortable home and complete sexual freedom, Tom should have been a contented man, but apart from the times he spent with young Thomas, he was deeply unhappy.

His former girlfriend the maid had been replaced by a young lady who worked in a shoe shop in the High Street. His sexual appetite catered for, Tom spent the rest of his free time in the pub with his friends. He thought constantly of Lily. He questioned Sandy about her, asking, 'Have you seen her lately?'

Sandy shook his head. 'No, me old love. Lily's a busy lady, the club's a huge success. Amy goes round there sometimes during the afternoon and has a cup of tea and a chat, and occasionally they go shopping. But I've not seen her for ages.'

'Still with The Maltese, is she?' Tom's jaw tightened as he waited for the answer.

'Yes, she is.'

'But I thought he didn't have anything to do with the club any more.'

'Maybe not, but they're still very much together. Best you forget about her, Tom.' Not wanting to get any deeper into this conversation, Sandy drank up and left Tom to stew on his own.

But Tom couldn't forget. Lily had become an obsession with him. Thoughts of her seared into his brain, building on the jealousy that fermented inside him every time he thought of her in Vittorio's arms. He'd taken to watching the club, hoping for a glimpse of her, but in this he'd been unlucky. The sight of the many patrons entering the club only fired his anger instead of making him pleased for her success.

One day, Tom saw Lily standing outside the door with two members of staff, taking delivery of two enormous tubs containing tall bay trees. She instructed them carefully in the placing of the tubs, one on each side of the entrance. As she stood sideways he was shocked to realise that she was pregnant. Without thought for the consequences, he strode across the road.

'Lily!' he called.

She looked around at the sound of her name.

When he reached her, he angrily caught hold of her arm. One of the staff stepped forward to protect her, but she said quietly, 'It's all right. I know this man. Just wait by the door.'

Tom looked at her accusingly. 'You're pregnant.'

Coolly she said, 'How observant of you. What on earth are you doing here?'

'Why didn't you tell me when you first found out? I could have taken you somewhere to get rid of it.'

Her face turned pale. 'What are you suggesting?'

'You can't want this child! Not that gangster's brat!'

Anger blazed in her eyes and she shook off his hold. 'How dare you talk to me like that! It's none of your bloody business whose child I have. And for your information, both Vittorio and I are happy about it.'

He looked at her as if she was a stranger. 'What happened to the lovely, innocent young girl I used to know?'

She gave him a hard stare. 'She went with the young Irish boy who used to be caring, who would never treat any woman the way *you* did! Especially when your wife was about to give birth.'

'I was wrong to do that,' he admitted.

'And look at you now.' Lily prodded him in his chest. 'You still don't care about me. All you can see is that it's Vittorio's child I'm carrying. You can't bear the idea. You would rather have put my life at risk by having an abortion, than see me pregnant.'

'I would do anything to stop you having his child.'

Lily looked at him with disdain. 'It's my child too, Tom. It hasn't even occurred to you that I may want this baby, has it? You just can't stand the idea that I might be happy with any man other than you. If you thought anything about me, my happiness would be your main concern.'

'How can you ever doubt my feelings for you?' he protested.

'It's not love you're feeling, Tom McCann. It's jealousy. Obsession with something that you want and can't have. That's not healthy. Now leave me alone.' She turned away, then paused and turned back to him. 'Don't ever think of visiting the club. You won't be welcome.'

Lily walked back to her room on trembling legs, shaken by the altercation. How could Tom, the man she'd once loved so much, have even thought of putting her life at risk, rather than have her give birth to Vittorio's child? The callousness of his words hurt her deeply. What had happened to the man she'd once known? He'd changed so much. There was nothing – *nothing* left of the wild Irishman she'd so admired. With tears of sorrow for the lost past, she caught hold of the gold cross and chain Tom had given her, and which she'd cherished and worn ever since as a token of their true love, and tore it angrily from her neck, throwing it aside.

Sitting in a chair, she tried to calm herself. It was hard enough to cope with the whispers as her condition became apparent, but the scathing accusations from Tom angered her, because he made it all sound so sordid.

Leaning back in the chair, she entwined her fingers and cradled her swollen stomach. She would lie in bed at night and press the soft mound gently, trying to feel the baby's head. These were precious moments. It thrilled her to think that in four months' time she would be able to hold her child in her arms. She silently prayed to God, Who had looked after her through troubled times, to deliver the baby safely. She desperately wanted this child, and Tom's wicked suggestion that she should do away with the life growing inside her had cut through her like a knife. Now Lily vowed that she would protect this child from anyone and anything until the day she died.

Vittorio had been so solicitous towards her since he'd known about the baby, so tender and thoughtful to her needs that she'd felt loved and cosseted. She couldn't help but compare the reactions of the two men.

Not that Vittorio had ever put his feelings into words, but she didn't need to be told. She could tell he cared by the soft expression in his eyes when he looked at her and her swollen belly. She just wished his business wasn't so precarious and longed for him to make his living a different way. She wanted an upright, solid citizen as the father of her child, but she knew he would never change.

Deep down, Lily still hankered to be respectable. She had said it didn't matter – that she didn't care what people said. But it did and she knew it.

The women who came to the club whispered among themselves. At the moment she didn't care about that. But she worried about what it would be like when the baby was born, when she could hold it in her arms, take it out in a pram. When people could see the child, that's when it would really hurt.

She knew she would have to be strong to shelter the child. She knew too that as her offspring grew older she would have to teach it to stand up for itself. She feared for the future, but if the club continued to succeed, she would have money, and she'd learned the power of that since living with The Maltese. She would just have to cope with the situations that arose. But no one would be allowed to do the child harm if she could prevent it. She would be a force to be reckoned with.

Chapter Twenty-Three

Lily was in labour. Vittorio, ever calm, had called a taxi and was sitting with her in the dining room, holding her hand, letting her grip it tightly with every contraction.

Rachel was fretting away in the background, muttering to herself about the time it was taking for the taxi to arrive. She was the first at the door when the driver parked the car. 'Where the hell have you been? Building the bloody thing?'

Vittorio helped Lily into the vehicle, carrying her case and getting her settled. Then he climbed in beside her and waved goodbye to Rachel.

Lily eased herself into a more comfortable position. 'I could have had the baby at home, you know.'

Shaking his head Vittorio said, 'No, my darling. It's better this way. With you in a private nursing home I will feel more content, knowing you and our baby are in safe hands.'

He stayed in the waiting room until Lily had been prepared, then shocked the nurse in charge by insisting he would stay with Lily throughout the birth.

'You can't do that, sir!' she exclaimed.

He stared at her with an expression that forbade argument. 'Indeed I can.' And he did.

Lily was grateful. He was a calming influence on her with his mellifluous voice coaxing her, telling her how lovely she was, soothing her throughout the pain. He encouraged her to push when it was time, and bathed her forehead. And when eventually their daughter was born, his eyes shone with happiness.

He looked at the bundle held in Lily's arms. 'She's so beautiful,' he whispered and Lily, noting the smooth olive skin of her child, thought so too. The baby looked so like her father that Lily smiled, amused.

'What is it, darling?'

'Well, take a peek at her. No one could possibly say she was fathered by the milkman.'

He looked at her in mock horror. 'I should hope not! What are we going to call her?'

'Victoria,' said Lily immediately. 'What else could she be called?'

Catching hold of his daughter's small fist he said softly, 'Victoria. Yes, I like that.'

During the following days, Sandy, Amy and Declan visited the new mother and baby, their arms overflowing with gifts. Soon Lily's room was festooned with flowers and baby clothes, fruit and toiletries.

One wet afternoon, a few days after the birth, Lily was sitting up in bed as Rachel held Victoria in her arms, crooning softly in Yiddish. Looking up she said, 'This child is so beautiful, you'll have men beating their way to her door.'

'I hope not!' retorted Lily. 'I want a peaceful life for her.'

'No chance,' Rachel scoffed. 'She's got your looks and Vittorio's colouring. *Aiy yi!* Such a combination. You'll have your work cut out as she grows, mark my words.'

Gazing at her child, Lily hoped Rachel was wrong. She wanted Victoria to have a good life, free of the deprivations Lily herself had experienced, shielded from the sexual appetites of unsuitable men. She would protect her daughter from such things. When she was old enough, the little girl would go to a good school and be well-educated, prepared for a life away from the docklands far removed from the seedy world that she, Lily, had grown up in. With Vittorio's help she could plan a start in life for Victoria such as she'd never experienced as a child.

Later that evening, Vittorio sat beside the bed watching Lily feeding his daughter. He looked on in delight at the child suckling. 'That is the most beautiful sight in the world, a child at its mother's breast.'

Lily was overcome with maternal love as she held the small

bundle in her arms. But in the back of her mind she wondered how it was that her own mother had shown none of these feelings for her, had never held her in a warm, motherly embrace. How could a mother not love her own flesh and blood? Lily knew she would be willing to make any sacrifice for Victoria, yet her own mother had been completely indifferent and heartless.

Seeing the shadow cross her face, The Maltese asked, 'What is it my darling? What's wrong?'

Shaking her head she said, 'I was only wondering what sort of mother couldn't love her own child.'

Holding her hand, he said, 'Only someone who is very sad and unhappy. You are thinking of your own mother, aren't you? You should feel pity for her. Think of what she's missed all these years, how empty the life of such a person must be.'

Watching Victoria's little mouth working away, Lily agreed. Whatever lay ahead for this beautiful child of hers, she wouldn't want to miss it for the world.

It was now the month of June. Lily was fully recovered from the birth of her child and back at the club working full-time. She'd hired a nanny to look after Victoria when she was busy, but spent every free moment with her baby.

Vittorio was besotted with his child and he too would slip into the back entrance of the club whenever he was free.

The club was thriving. The rooms were always fully booked and, as Rachel had prophesied, the tables in the dining room were reserved weeks in advance. Examining the monthly accounts, Rachel had suggested to the couple that they should look around for a second establishment, to be run on similar lines, but in a smarter area of Southampton.

'Can we afford it?' Lily asked. 'Isn't it a bit too soon?'

'My life!' exclaimed Rachel. 'Don't you have no faith? You got to speculate to accumulate – isn't that right, Vittorio?'

He was in agreement with her. 'As long as it's a small enterprise. This is not the time to go too big, but yes, I think it's a good idea. I'll start looking around for a suitable property.'

Later, when she and Lily were alone, Rachel confided, 'I

have a dream, Lily. A small chain of hotels, offering the best service . . . at the highest prices naturally,' she added with a gleam in her eye.

Lily raised an eyebrow. 'If Manny gets to hear about this he'll come running.' Seeing the look of concern on Rachel's face she asked, 'Have you heard from him again?'

'Sure I hear from him – about once a month. He's now married to the widow Goldburg. She's got plenty but wisely she keeps a tight hold of it.'

'What does he want?' asked Lily.

'What do you think he wants? Money! I get begging letters, then when I don't answer, he sends letters threatening me. He's a *meshuggener*. I don't have a son – I have a leech.'

Lily was worried. 'What will he do? Do you think he'll be any trouble? Will he come here again?'

With a derisive laugh, Rachel said, 'What, and face Vittorio again? Never! He's a gutless little sod. But I don't give him nothing, not after the way he treated you.'

'Oh dear,' said Lily. 'I feel awful. I didn't mean to come between you.'

'Look, Lily, don't you understand? I don't do him any favour if I shell out my money. He's got to learn to fend for himself. Be a man. Stand on his own two feet. I give him some – he comes back for more.'

We all have our problems, thought Lily the next day as she walked the baby in her pram around the market. Her presence had caused quite a stir. She was aware of the glances at the sleeping child, the whispers, the speculative looks in her direction. There were a few who knew her of old who genuinely wanted to look at the baby and congratulate her. But she was very aware of the others. Holding her head high, she continued with her shopping, but in her heart she worried for the future of her daughter.

Mary McCann, Thomas' pram at her side, was buying vegetables at one of the stalls when she suddenly became aware of the buzz around her. She turned and looked at the pretty girl pushing her own pram who seemed to be the centre of so much attention and gossip. Her curiosity got the better of her and, turning to the stallholder, she asked, 'Who is that woman?'

'That's Lily Pickford, owner of the Club Valletta. Great girl. Sings like an angel.'

'What does her husband do?'

The man winked at her. 'She ain't married, love. She's the mistress of The Maltese. Baby looks just like him.' He turned away to serve another customer.

Mary froze. She had learned from a spiteful friend that her Tom used to go out with the notorious Lily Pickford.

Lily came to the same stall but before she could ask for her wares, the man said, 'Here's another new mum – Mary McCann. You know Tom, her husband, don't you?'

Lily saw the hostile look in Mary's eyes. 'Yes, I knew Tom.' Glancing into the pram she said, 'Congratulations. I heard you had a baby. What's his name?'

'Thomas,' snapped Mary. She looked at the olive skin of Lily's child and said, 'I'm told yours is like her father.'

Lily felt her hackles rise at the spiteful tone in Mary's voice.

Mary was awash with jealousy. This was the woman her husband had called to in his sleep; the one he loved far more than her. 'You used to be close to my husband, I believe.'

A crowd started to gather. They all knew of Lily's friendship with Tom, as they used to shop together in the market during their courting days, and, sensing the strained atmosphere between the two women, they moved closer to witness the encounter.

Lily gave a friendly smile. 'That was a long time ago.'

'Well, now he's a happily married man, so you keep away from him!'

Mary's attitude was getting to Lily. She could well understand Tom's unhappiness as she saw the woman's tight mouth. 'As long as he's happy with you, my dear, and you keep him satisfied, you won't have anything to worry about, will you?'

Knowing the situation in her marriage was more than precarious put Mary even more on her mettle. 'At least my child isn't a bastard, like yours.'

There was a gasp from the listening crowd. Lily looked at Mary and burst out laughing. 'You really are a bitch – just as Tom said you were, but I'll give you this . . . you had the courage to put into words what everyone around us is thinking. Yes, my child is a bastard, but I'm not ashamed of her. And I'll do for anyone who tries to harm her. As for your Tom, I wouldn't touch him with a barge-pole.' She leaned closer to Mary and said softly, 'I believe there we are both in agreement. You may have a marriage certificate, Mary McCann, but I'm more of a wife to Vittorio than you ever were to your husband. You could crack walnuts between your knees, you keep them so tight together!'

She walked away, leaving Mary open-mouthed.

That evening as she was serving Tom his dinner, Mary, still seething from her earlier encounter, said, 'I met Lily Pickford today in the market.'

Tom's knife clattered onto his plate. Picking it up again he said, 'Lily Pickford?'

'You know her, Tom, so don't lie to me. She's the mistress of Vittorio Teglia. Her baby, Victoria, looks just like him – so I'm told.'

He glared at her. 'Really? So what?'

'So she's the one you used to talk about in your sleep.'

He looked up. 'Used to. Don't I do it any more then?'

She shook her head. 'Get fed up with you, did she?' She couldn't help the snide remark. Although she didn't want any physical contact with her husband and she didn't care about his girlfriends, she knew that this woman had been something special to Tom and she was jealous. 'Mind you, you couldn't keep her as well as The Maltese. The clothes she was wearing were very expensive. Far beyond your pocket.'

His mouth tightened. 'Don't go on, Mary. You've got what you want, a home and money coming in. Don't push your luck.'

'At least your child isn't a bastard, like hers. I told her as much.'

'You *what?*'

'I told her what I thought of her and I told her to keep

away from you. She said she wouldn't touch you with a barge-pole.'

He looked at her with hatred. 'And what else did she say?' Mary's cheeks flushed scarlet. Seeing her embarrassment he persisted, 'Knowing Lily, she would have given as good as she got. Did she?'

'She said she didn't care, and at least I had the courage to put into words what everyone was thinking.'

'You couldn't help yourself, could you, Mary? Courage . . . my arse! You were filled with spite – you just had to have a go.' He picked up his plate and threw it against the wall. Mary stepped back in horror. He stood up slowly. 'You rotten bitch! Never talk to me about her again – you understand? She's more of a woman than you'll ever be!' He stormed out of the house.

Mary cleared up the mess with trembling fingers, at the same time knowing that although Lily and Tom were no longer seeing one another, Lily was a woman he would never forget.

'What do you mean, he hasn't paid up?' Vittorio's eyes flashed angrily as he looked across his desk at George.

'He keeps making excuses, guv. Says he'll ask his old man for the money, but all he's interested in is gambling and dancing. Last week he won a Charleston competition. He was full of it.'

Vittorio sat back in his chair. With a thoughtful expression he said, 'He wouldn't be able to dance with a broken ankle, would he?'

'Not very well, guv,' said George with a smile. 'That would really throw a spanner in the works.'

'Then see to it – and tell him if he doesn't settle up with me by the end of the week, you'll break the other one. Then pay his old man a visit – and tell him what's going on.'

'Right, guv.'

Shaking his head, Vittorio said, 'This all makes me sick. You help these people out and they mess you about. I'm pissed off with it.' He gazed across at George, who'd worked faithfully for him for years. 'No doubt you are too.'

'Trouble is, guv, we're getting older. A few years ago it wouldn't have bothered us at all. It would have been sorted and forgotten.'

When he was alone, Vittorio considered George's words. It was true. And it wasn't just his age. Since he'd become a father, his whole outlook on life had changed. He was already thinking of buying a house, a proper home for him and Lily to live in and bring up their child. He really didn't want all this bother any more – trouble with the police, having to cover his tracks over every deal. There was no longer any excitement in cheating the law.

He would enjoy a quieter life, running the hotels and making an honest living, watching his child grow. He gave a wry smile. Good heavens, he was contemplating becoming respectable! Who would believe it? Certainly not Lily, although he knew she'd be pleased if he told her how he felt. If they opened another establishment, he could give up the finance company altogether, and the house he used for gambling. He'd more than enough money as long as the hotels were successful. The whole thing needed some serious thought. He'd go to the estate agents today and ask about properties for a new hotel, and at the same time, he'd pick up the prospectuses of a few houses.

He smiled to himself. If he did all this, maybe Lily would seriously consider marriage. It was time they settled down and became a proper family.

Manny Cohen was walking up and down the well-furnished living room, raging at his wife. 'You tight-fisted old bitch! Why did you marry me? Why? You don't give me money to enjoy myself. You make me work for that uncle of mine when you know I hate it there. We could afford for me to stay at home.'

Miriam looked at him and quietly said, '*I* could afford it . . . not so much of the *we*. Besides,' she added, 'I don't ask you to give me money for housekeeping. I pay all the bills, I dress you well. You've got your pocket money from your weekly wage. What's to complain about?'

He held out his hands and pleaded, 'What can I do with

that pittance? I can't afford to go nowhere.'

Speaking as if to a child, she said, 'Where would you want to go, Manny? We go to the pictures. To the theatre. Visit friends. We eat out once a week. We're going to Bournemouth for a holiday later this year.'

'Bournemouth! Who wants to go there? We could travel to the South of France and live like millionaires for a couple of weeks, staying at the best hotels.'

'You'd like that, wouldn't you?' Her eyes narrowed. 'You'd like to visit the casino, no doubt, and the brothels. I know you so well. You are a pitiless excuse for a man.'

'Then why did you marry me?'

'For convenience. A widow woman doesn't get asked out so much and I like my social life.'

Manny gave her a sly look through his hooded eyes. 'You and your wealthy friends. How can I impress them if I'm not as well-heeled as they are?'

She laughed at him. 'You've never been so comfortable in your life. When I first saw you, you were a mess. Your clothes were shabby and dirty; you never bathed. Now you're well dressed with a wardrobe of expensive suits. You live in a nice house, and I have someone to sleep with without losing my reputation.'

He looked at her in disgust. 'The truth is, Miriam, that you're so bloody ugly no man worth his salt would look at you!'

Instead of being angry, she smirked. 'I know I'm no oil painting, my dear, but any woman with money can get a man, even if she has only one leg and one eye. But I decided you would do.'

'You talk as if I'm a piece of merchandise.'

'That's precisely what I think. And you ain't worth a great deal either, but you'll do. You fit my needs. You do as you're told, only because without me you'd have very little. You should feel privileged instead of whining all the time. Others would give their right arm to be in your shoes. Now go and put the kettle on and make me a cup of tea.'

Manny knew he was beaten. Without Miriam, he had nothing. But he was her slave, fetching and carrying, having to make love to her. It was the only hope he had of satisfying his sexual urges and he hated himself for it.

He meekly made his way to the kitchen, cursing his mother and Lily beneath his breath. It was all Lily's fault. Until she came on the scene, he'd had enough money. His mother was generous. He'd had the women he wanted whenever he wanted and he didn't have to work hard. He'd pay her back one day. By God he would.

Lily and Rachel were planning a huge fancy-dress evening at the club. 'We could use the old gambling room for extra tables, then move the other tables around to give a bit more space for dancing. If we pack them tightly together, we should get in extra punters. You know how the toffs like to dress up. We could make it a masked ball.' Lily's eyes shone with excitement. 'We'll do a special menu. Advertise well in advance. Make it a ticket-only do.'

Rachel grinned. 'They'll sell like hot cakes. It's a great idea.'

Lily gave her a sly look. 'As it's going to be a masked affair, Vittorio will be able to come down into the club. No one will know it's him.'

'Such a crafty girl you are, Lily Pickford. As you say, who's to know? We'll discuss the idea with Vittorio, but I can't imagine he'll object.'

Vittorio didn't. He thought the idea was inspired, and was tickled when Lily told him she'd hire a costume for him too.

'I'll enjoy that, wandering around in disguise. It should be a great night, my darling.'

'And we'll make a lot of money,' said Rachel happily.

Lily went over her plans, sorted out the menu with the chef, hired extra staff and put her advertisements in various papers. The bookings poured in.

Manny Cohen was one of the first to purchase a ticket.

Chapter Twenty-Four

It was the day of the fancy-dress ball and the club was in chaos. Florists arrived to decorate the interior with ropes of flowers. The bandstand was suitably bedecked. Waiters busily carried cutlery, tablecloths and napkins, squeezing through the narrow spaces caused by the extra tables. Lily was running around like a scalded cat, making sure that all was in order.

Walking into the kitchen she checked with the chef that he had all he required. 'Everything's fine, Miss Lily, don't you fret.' He grinned broadly at her. 'This is going to be a big night.'

And it was. All their tickets had sold and many people had been disappointed. To appease them, Lily promised to put on another gala evening in the near future.

Vittorio closed his office early and was going over the bar stock, ringing up the suppliers for more champagne. 'I have a feeling we'll need it,' he said.

With an hour to go, he dragged Lily away. 'Come along upstairs, the staff can manage. Why not take a bath and play with Victoria before she goes to bed, and then you can get into your costume. After all, you must be there to greet the clients. I'll slip down a bit later, when there are plenty of people about.' He drew her to him and kissed her on the forehead. 'There's nothing more for you to do here for the moment.'

Having relaxed in her bath and seen Victoria fall asleep in her cot, Lily changed into her costume. She smiled to herself as she stepped into the gown made of sky-blue taffeta, trimmed with exquisite cream-coloured lace around the low neckline and around the cuffs of the big puff sleeves. The boned bodice nipped in her waist. The dress was covered in delicate embroidery and fine ribbons were threaded through the skirt. It was a beautiful piece of craftsmanship.

She was dressed as an eighteenth-century courtesan, which she thought wholly appropriate and highly amusing. She put on her make-up and stuck the black beauty spot to her cheek before carefully placing the white powdered wig upon her head. She was amazed at the difference to her appearance when she looked into the mirror; ringlets fell over the silkiness of her shoulders, and the décolletage of the dress revealed the smooth rise of her breasts to perfection.

She swirled around in delight just as Vittorio emerged from the bathroom. There was an expression of surprise and admiration on his face as he watched the beautiful creature before him.

'What is it? Don't you like it?' she asked, placing her hand coquettishly on her bosom.

Holding her at arm's length, he drank in the sight of her. 'You look absolutely ravishing. I think it's just as well I'm going to be around tonight, keeping an eye on you.'

'You don't think this is too much, do you?' she asked, pulling the front of the dress higher.

He stayed her hand. 'Leave it, Lily. All the men will look at you and envy me. I'll enjoy that.' To her surprise, he then took the gold chain from his neck and removed the large emerald ring. 'Tonight I think you should wear this.'

'But it's your mother's ring!'

'I know, and tonight I want you to wear it. It was a family heirloom. Many times my father wanted to sell it, but my mother refused. Just before she died, she gave it to me. Tonight I give it to you.' He placed it on the slim finger of her left hand, brushed her hand with his lips. 'Now that makes it official,' he said softly.

Lily looked at the ring on her finger. The large square-cut emerald nestled between two diamonds; the light caught the gems, making them sparkle. She was overcome by the beauty of the ring and the sentiment of the gesture. Tears glistened in her eyes. 'Thank you, Vittorio.' She reached up and kissed him.

He glanced at his watch, his voice suddenly husky. 'You'd better get down those stairs, darling. The clients will be arriving at any moment. I'll see you later.'

Her scarlet mask, decorated in matching sequins and fine feathers, was mounted on a slim stick. She picked it up, and with a provocative look, held it to her eyes and gave a deep curtsey before leaving the room.

As she descended the stairs, the staff looked up and gasped, then broke into applause and cheers. Lily bowed gracefully. Looking around, she checked that all was ready.

Rachel was sitting in front of her dressing table. She took a sip of her gin and tonic and, peering into the mirror, carefully drew black lines above the roots of her eyelashes and the lower rim of her eye. Smudging the last one, she cursed and tried to rub it out. 'I bet bloody Cleopatra didn't have this trouble.' She then slipped into the gold lamé gown, tied the jewelled belt, put on the Egyptian headdress and looked at her reflection with a sardonic smile.

Deciding there was time for one more drink before the taxi arrived, she sat quietly in her living room and thought back over the past exciting months. She'd had no doubts whatsoever that the club would be a success without Vittorio's presence, and was more than a little satisfied at her own part in it. But more importantly, she'd secured a future for Lily . . . and her child. In her own way, she had helped pay back a debt. No matter what happened, financially Lily was safe.

Vittorio had been quite a revelation to her. She knew that in his business world, he was a force to be reckoned with – a hard man. But his affection for Lily was true and tender, and the way he cared for his child was a joy to behold.

Manny, she had ceased to worry about; she no longer even opened the letters that came to her from him. He was set up for life, if only he would accept the fact. The widow Goldburg had what she wanted and he should be content.

Hearing the taxi arrive, she put her fur coat around her shoulders and left the house.

Rachel sat in the back of the vehicle as it left Wilton Avenue and turned into Bedford Place, past W.J. French and Son's shoe shop that she often frequented. She gave a sigh as they eventually drove through the Bargate and threaded their way among the traffic, lined up to go through the narrow archway. She preferred the days when everything was horse-drawn. Things were moving too quickly now as more cars were in use.

The lights were on in the shop window of Shepherd and Hedger's, and she leaned forward to see what was on display. Only last month she'd purchased a very nice secondhand velvet-covered chesterfield there – a bargain at sixteen pounds, she thought. As the taxi drew up outside the club, Rachel felt a thrill of excitement at the forthcoming event, and prayed it would be a success.

In a small hotel near the docks, Manny Cohen sat on the edge of the bed, his costume laid out beside him. On the table by the bed was a half-bottle of Scotch and a glass. Lighting a cigarette, he blew three perfect smoke rings into the air. There was a look of satisfaction in his hooded eyes as he watched the circles float away. He wished he had a woman with him – he'd been a fool not to think of it before. But never mind, later . . . *after*. Then he could bring one of the local prostitutes back. Early that morning, before Miriam was awake, he'd taken some money from her hand-bag. By the time she realised this, it wouldn't matter. He'd have had his fun.

Tonight was the night that bitch Lily Pickford would get her comeuppance, and his mother Rachel would be taught a lesson she would never forget.

Manny stubbed out his cigarette and started to dress. First the trousers and shirt. Then the white bow tie, the waistcoat and the red frockcoat. Finally he placed the top hat on his head, picked up the whip and cracked it viciously. At the sound, he smiled to himself. He'd chosen his outfit carefully. The ringmaster was always in control. Tonight *he* would be the master. He'd have them all jumping through hoops.

Full of his own importance, he strutted about the small room. With the plain black mask on his face, not even his own mother would recognise him. Looking at his watch, he decided there was no rush. He didn't want to arrive until dinner was about to be served. He would slip in among the crowd. It was common knowledge that it was a sell-out, which would be all the better for him. Checking that all his things were ready, he poured himself another drink and waited.

The club was packed. Lily was doing what she did best, stopping at all the tables, talking to her punters. She eyed the bottles of champagne that were already open, recognising Vittorio's wisdom in ordering even more.

The array of costumes took her breath away. Among the men were pirates, French kings, vicars, devils and several sheiks. The latter made her smile, Vittorio, too, was to be a sheik. She'd thought it perfect with his olive skin and now he'd blend in even better than she'd hoped with the others.

Rachel was standing with a drink in her hand, being teased by the staff about her costume. They were warning her to look out for an asp. She took it all in good part.

The meal was a great success and once the tables had been cleared the dancing immediately began. Lily jumped as an arm came around her waist. 'Shall we dance, my little courtesan?' She recognised the deep voice of her lover and turned with him to the dance-floor. There was little room to move, but Lily was content to be held.

Several of her regular customers had spotted the exquisite ring on her finger, but none had the nerve to ask her about it directly. She sensed curiosity in the eyes that were watching her and her partner, but no one knew his identity.

During the evening, Lily slipped upstairs to see Victoria. The nanny was asleep in the chair but Lily didn't disturb her, just crept over to the cot to her baby. The child's hand was closed with her thumb covered by her small fingers. Lily stroked them gently, leaned over and kissed the soft cheek, then slowly crept out of the room.

'She's fast asleep,' she whispered to Vittorio. 'I wondered if the noise would disturb her.'

He shook his head. 'No. After all, she's two floors up.' He looked around at the crowd. 'This has been a wonderful evening, Lily. I've been listening to the various comments.'

'Oh, really? I hope they were complimentary?'

'Oh yes, they all seem of the opinion that it was money well spent.'

'Is that all? No gossip?' There was a speculative look in her eye.

He shrugged. 'A few caustic comments about your choice of costume. Some thought it a brazen choice, others like you could see the humour of it. But you must have expected that when you picked it.'

'Of course.'

He took her hand in his and looked at the emerald. 'This has caused a lot of curiosity.'

'I bet it has. Is that all?'

He nodded. He didn't want to tell Lily of the sarcastic remarks he'd heard from some. It angered him that she should be the subject of such ribaldry, but it made him all the more determined to insist that they marry . . . and soon. It was the only legal way he knew to deal with it. To give her some form of respectability.

Lily had returned to working the room, talking to her punters, joshing them along as she did so very well, when suddenly her attention was caught by a blonde woman dressed like a flapper, in an expensive-looking red gown. Around her head was a black velvet band with a single osprey feather tucked in to the back, and a black feather boa was flung carelessly over one shoulder. Long black gloves completed the outfit. She seemed to be the life and soul of the party among the crowd around her – but what puzzled Lily was the fact that as the woman turned away and made her way to the bar, she was carrying a tray of empty glasses.

She watched her carefully and suddenly recognised the sway of the hips. Walking over to the bar, she said, 'You seem to be very busy.'

Sandy turned in surprise. 'Hello, darling,' he said, and kissed her lightly. He did a small pirouette. 'What do you think?'

He wore a blonde wig and full make-up. Lily couldn't help but admire the results – the slightly rouged cheeks and the blackened eyelashes – though she thought the red bow-shaped lips were a little too much. 'Never mind what I think, you old tart. What the devil do you think you're doing?'

He smiled sweetly. 'I'm just helping out my boyfriend and the other barmen. It's so busy, they're running out of glasses.' He looked her up and down. 'Simply lovely, darling. You quite take the shine out of my effort.'

Lily started to laugh. 'Sandy, you're outrageous.'

He shrugged. 'Well, you always knew that, Lily, my dear.'

She suddenly had a brainwave. 'Look, Sandy,' she said, 'the band is in need of a break. How about you and I performing whilst they have a drink and a sandwich?'

His eyes shone. He placed one hand on his hip and smiled provocatively. 'What, me perform, dressed in a frock?'

'Why not?' she said. 'It's fancy dress, isn't it?'

'It may be fancy dress to you, duckie, but this is a normal part of my wardrobe!'

'Come on,' urged Lily, 'what do you say?'

'You know me, dear. I love to be the centre of attention. Let's go.'

As the band came to the end of their number, Lily told them to take a break. Then, after a drum roll, she announced there would be a short cabaret, performed by herself and her ladyfriend, Sandy.

The two of them were so used to working together from earlier days that the absence of a set programme was no problem at all. They put on the performance of their lives.

They started with 'Alexander's Ragtime Band' and followed it with 'I ain't got nobody', and 'Some of these days, you're gonna miss me, honey'. The customers, filled with champagne and bonhomie, joined in lustily.

The band returned and, after a quiet word from Sandy, started to play The Charleston. Lily and the crowd stood in admiration as he gave his rendition of the dance, which ended to rapturous applause.

As they stepped off the stage, Lily said, 'I didn't know you could dance.'

He looked a little coy. 'Well, you see, I started my career as a chorus boy.'

She shook her head. 'You,' she said, at a loss for words. 'Come on, you deserve a drink.'

A little later, Vittorio came over to Lily and kissed her on the cheek. 'I've never seen you quite so animated on the stage as you were tonight. You really enjoyed it, didn't you?'

She hugged him. 'It was such fun and Sandy's such a riot.'

He looked bemused. 'Do you know, I didn't recognise him. What a character he is!'

She laughingly agreed. 'Have you been up to see Victoria?' she asked.

'Not for some time. Let's go up together. You need a moment of peace after all that,' he said.

They walked upstairs to the second floor, holding hands. Opening the bedroom door quietly, they crept into the room and walked over to the cot.

'Just look at her,' said Lily as she smoothed the baby's face. 'Isn't she just perfect?'

'She's beautiful,' he whispered. 'Almost as beautiful as her mother.' He pulled Lily gently towards him and kissed her softly on the lips. 'Don't you think it's time we became a proper family?'

'What do you mean?'

He gathered her closer. 'I want us to get married – have a real home away from the business, so that our daughter can have everything a normal child has. Somewhere to bring her friends as she gets older. A garden to play in.'

Lily looked at the gentle expression in Vittorio's eyes and saw the unspoken love shining there. Suddenly she knew that what he was describing was what she wanted too. Flinging her arms around his neck, she said, 'Yes! That sounds wonderful. Let's get married as soon as we can.'

He didn't answer, but just smothered her with passionate kisses.

Catching her breath at last, Lily reluctantly drew away. 'We'd best go back to the party before this gets out of hand.'

He caressed her cheek. 'Tonight, I'll make love to you like never before.'

They went back downstairs, to rejoin the festivities.

Towards the end of the night, Vittorio suggested to Lily that it would be prudent to empty the takings from the bar tills, leaving just the float; the money could be locked away in the office safe. She agreed and, collecting the cash into a bag, handed it over to him.

'I'll put it away and look in on Victoria again whilst I'm upstairs,' he said.

He was about to open the office door when he noticed a strange smell in the air. Frowning, he sniffed again as he walked towards the stairs leading to the upper floor. Then suddenly he leapt up them two at a time. Smoke was seeping beneath Lily's bedroom door. 'Christ! A fire!' He flung open the door, only to be repelled by the sudden burst of flames caused by the draught. Running along the corridor to the nursery, he burst into the room calling to the nanny to get up. 'Grab a coat and put on some shoes,' he ordered. 'The building's on fire.'

He picked up Victoria, wrapped her in a blanket, covered her face and, pushing the nanny ahead of him, rushed down the stairs.

By now the smell of smoke had travelled to the dining room and the revellers were panicking.

'Get everybody out!' yelled Vittorio. Pointing to the telephone he told the barman to call the fire brigade. Grabbing Lily by the arm, he handed over the baby and the bag of money. 'You two get out of the building.' He caught hold of Rachel, who had just hurried over in her tight gold lamé dress. 'Take care of them for me,' he ordered.

'Where are you going?' she demanded.

'Back upstairs to see what I can do.'

'Don't be a fool,' she cried. But he was gone.

Vittorio took off his flowing robes and dashed upstairs in his trousers and shirt. By now, the main bedroom was ablaze. He tried to close the door to contain the fire, but the wood burned his hands. He cursed to himself. He searched the other rooms in the vicinity to make sure they were empty then made his way to the floor below to do the same.

The office door was open. In the half-light he saw a figure fiddling with a pile of papers on his desk. Flames caught in a sudden flash; there was a smell of petrol. 'What the bloody hell do you think you're doing?' he called.

The figure turned and he looked into the wild eyes of Manny Cohen.

'I'm teaching my mother and that bitch Lily a lesson,' he said, pulling down a curtain to add to the blaze.

Vittorio was across the room in a second, hauling Manny away. 'Are you mad? Get out of here.'

Strengthened by the adrenalin of revenge coursing through his veins, Manny picked up a heavy vase and smashed it over Vittorio's head. The Maltese dropped to the floor, unconscious.

Outside, the patrons gathered, appalled and bewitched by the sight before them. The upper storey of the hotel was burning brightly. The fire was out of control, huge flames licking the window frames after the heat had blown out the glass. All the rooms on the first floor were aglow.

Lily and Rachel watched, horrified. 'Where is Vittorio?' cried Lily, clutching her child. 'Why doesn't he come out?'

'He'll be all right, darling, you'll see. He's just doing all he can to save it.' But Rachel was silently praying as she tried to comfort her young friend.

Inside, Vittorio was slowly regaining consciousness. His throat was burning; the smoke was choking him. Where was he? Then he remembered. The office was ablaze. He staggered to his feet and made for the door, but a burning beam crashed down, brushing his shoulder and he cried out with pain. Fighting his way to the door, he flung himself into the hall. All around him were flames. He thought of Lily, of Victoria and knew he had to escape. He must survive – for them.

He made it to the bar downstairs, where he soaked glass cloths in water and covered his head. In the distance he could hear a fire engine, but looking around at the devastation, he knew they were too late. The bandstand was ablaze, the tablecloths burning, the drapes a curtain of fire.

He made a desperate dash for the entrance, and staggered out into the air, where he collapsed. His lungs felt as if they were about to burst.

'Vittorio!' cried Lily, and rushed over to him. 'Someone get some water – call an ambulance!' she wept. Feverishly she undid the neck of his shirt. Looking at the crowd, now gathered closer, she shouted, 'For God's sake move back! Give him some air!' She cradled him in her arms.

A woman dashed out of her house with a jug of water and a glass. Lily poured some of the water into the glass and held it to Vittorio's lips. He drank from it slowly and then, taking the jug from her hands, he poured the remaining water over his burnt shoulder. He winced with pain.

'I thought I'd lost you,' Lily murmured, her voice full of emotion. The tears welled in her eyes.

Vittorio got painfully to his feet and, putting his good arm around her, held her close. 'Don't get upset, darling. I'm fine.'

'Oh, Vittorio,' she cried, tears streaming down her face, and they clung together oblivious of the others around them. He kissed the top of her head and stroked her face as you would a child.

'Is the baby all right?' he asked tenderly.

'Nanny's got her, she's fine,' Lily assured him as she wiped her tear-stained face with the back of her hand.

He looked at the club and said, 'Which is more than I can say for the Valletta.'

At that moment, Sandy came over. He was holding his blonde wig in his hand, and his heavily made-up face looked incongruous. He shook his head and looked at Lily, 'I can't believe this is happening.'

For a brief second, the old friends clung together, united in their distress. The sense of devastation was total, but the warmth of that embrace gave them both new strength.

A pace or two away, Rachel was standing in a state of shock, the flames reflecting off her glorious costume, staring up at the building, mesmerised. Suddenly, she saw a figure at the window of the office on the first floor, screaming 'Mama! Mama!'

Rachel covered her mouth. 'Oh my God! It's Manny.'

'I thought he'd left the building,' Vittorio said, puzzled. 'He was busy setting the office alight. That's right – he's the one who started the fire. My God! He knocked me out and left me there to die.'

Manny screamed again. 'Mama! Mama! Help me, Mama!'

Rachel reached out her hand towards the figure as if she expected to touch him. 'My son! My son!' she wept. She made to run to the building but Sandy held her back. She looked at Vittorio, anguish and desperation etched on her face. 'My son,' she whispered.

Vittorio looked up at the figure of the man who'd caused this mayhem, and then at the face of his mother, remembering her pleading for Manny's life once before and his promise to her. 'It's all right, Rachel,' he said quietly. 'I'll get him.'

Lily clung to him, screaming, 'No! No! Vittorio, please don't go. Please, I beg of you!'

He released her hold. Several people tried to stop him, but he threw them off and ran towards the entrance. Behind him, he could hear Lily's frantic cries, but he carried on.

Inside, the building was an inferno. The smoke filled The Maltese's lungs. Pulling his shirt-front out of his trousers, he covered his mouth. The heat from the fire scorched his bare skin.

He managed to get to the stairs. 'Manny! *Manny!*' he bellowed. The bannisters were alight but the stairs themselves seemed solid enough against the wall and so, clutching the shirt to his mouth, Vittorio dashed up them to the office.

Burning beams lay across the room where the ceiling had fallen in and there at the far end, standing by the window, stood Manny. He called his name again, urgently. 'Try and get over here,' he shouted, but he knew it was hopeless. There were great gaps in the floor and what was left was alight.

'I can't!' screamed Manny. 'I'm going to die.'

'We're both bloody well going to die unless you try.'

But terror had paralysed Manny's limbs. Thinking of the look in Rachel's eyes, Vittorio stepped into the room, carefully picking his way forward. Just as he reached the middle of the room and Manny had taken a few tentative steps in his direction, the floor collapsed beneath them. They both fell to the room below, burning timbers falling with them.

Only minutes later, the firemen who had been fighting their way into the club, located the bodies and trained their hoses upon them, but knew it was of little use.

Outside, Lily was going frantic. 'Vittorio! Vittorio!' she screamed. The firemen had to restrain her from rushing into the building.

It was some time before the charred bodies were carried outside.

The nanny was holding Victoria in her arms, tears streaming down her face. Rachel and Lily clung to each other, sobbing.

The large crowd was silent as they watched the despair of the two women. The fire chief came over and, placing a hand on each of them, said, 'I'm sorry, ladies. We did everything we could to save them.'

They both nodded, too grief-stricken to speak.

The ambulance driver approached. 'I think you two should bring the baby and come with me to the hospital to be checked over. You are both suffering with shock and should be treated.'

As if in a daze they followed him and climbed into the ambulance. They sat side by side, clutching each other by the hand, unable to speak.

That night they shared a private room, with a cot for the child. Victoria hadn't suffered by her experience as her father had removed her from the fire so quickly. And as he'd covered her face, she'd not suffered from smoke inhalation at all.

The two women washed and put on hospital gowns. Both

of them were silent, lost in their own thoughts. Imprinted on Lily's mind was the figure of Vittorio, rushing into the flames. Oh, why hadn't someone stopped him? Now he was gone for ever. She couldn't believe it. Didn't want to believe it. She wanted to wake in the morning and find it had all been a dreadful nightmare.

Picking up Victoria, she held her close. But for Vittorio, she might have lost them both. She would never have survived such a loss.

Rachel could still hear the voice of Manny calling to her. She put her hands over her ears to block out the sound. How could one person cause such devastation? She looked across at Lily, the innocent young baby clasped to her breast, and her eyes filled with tears.

Once Manny had been an innocent babe like Victoria. She remembered how proud she had been when the nurse had first placed him into her arms, then how he'd cried when he'd been circumcised. There was a deep and empty pit of sorrow within her. Her child was dead and in such terrible circumstances. It was not meant to be like this. Children were supposed to outlive their parents, weren't they? She felt despair welling up inside her and wondered how she was going to cope with the loss. Yet as she looked across at Lily and remembered the sacrifice that Vittorio had made, a profound guilt icily filled her mind.

It was her son who had brought about this great sorrow. Perhaps if she'd given him money . . . but she knew that wouldn't have stopped him. Manny was born to be trouble and as his mother, his guilt was hers. It was as if she herself had started the fire.

Lily and Rachel were both given a strong sedative before they were settled for the night. They were too full of grief to utter a word to each other, but they clasped each other for a moment before getting into bed.

The following morning, Lily held Victoria in her arms and smoothed the child's face. She wept as she saw the likeness to Vittorio. She couldn't believe she'd never see him again.

She looked up in surprise as the door opened and Tom

McCann stepped into the room. He went over to her. 'Lily. I'm so sorry. I just heard.'

Lily wanted to scream. Why wasn't it Vittorio walking through the door? It was him she wanted to see, not Tom. In her despair, she held up Victoria. 'Look,' she said. 'This is what you wanted me to abort. My beautiful baby. She's all I have now.'

He held out his hand towards the child.

'Don't you touch her! Don't you ever come near her again – or me. Her father was a better man than you'll ever be. And now he's dead.' Her voice faded away as the sobs increased.

Rachel got off her bed and, taking Tom by the arm, she said, 'It's better you go.'

Cap held tightly in his hand, he nodded. 'I'm sorry too for your loss, Rachel.'

'I know.'

As he walked away from Lily for the last time, Tom cursed silently. Lily could have been his life. They could have had a family, a big one, but it wasn't to be. He couldn't.get the picture of her deep distress from his mind. How could she have such feelings for The Maltese, the man he hated. The man who was now dead, but for all the good it did Tom, he might just as well be alive. He pulled his cap onto his head in a savage gesture and strode out of the hospital.

Seeing Lily's despair, Nanny took the child away to feed and change her, leaving Rachel and Lily to have a cup of tea as they sat up in bed, their faces gaunt and pale. On a couple of hangers behind the door were their costumes from the night before, covered in soot and dirt.

Lily drew her legs up and cuddled them. Shaking her head she kept murmuring, 'Vittorio. Vittorio.' Tears streamed down her face.

Rachel sat on the side of her bed, her expression hard, like a block of granite, her eyes cold.

Looking across at her friend, Lily said, 'It doesn't seem real. Vittorio and Manny – gone. What are we going to do? Oh Rachel, what are we going to do?'

Rachel looked at her with eyes that blazed with anger. 'My son – he deserved to die! Twice he ruined your life. He could have killed the baby. What did he care? He could have killed us all. Maybe that was his intention.'

Lily quickly got out of her bed and rushed over to Rachel. 'You mustn't talk like that. He was your own flesh and blood.'

'I rue the day I gave birth to him and I'll not waste any more tears on him. I'll call the widow Goldburg. She can have what's left of him. If I hadn't been such a weak fool, Vittorio would never have gone back into the building. He would still be alive. That guilt I will have to carry for what's left of my life.'

Lily looked devastated. She fingered the ring on her left hand. 'He gave me this last night.' Tears choked her. 'It was his mother's ring. He said she gave it to him just before she died. And he did the same – gave it to me before he died.'

She sat holding her head, her shoulders shaking. 'We were going to be married. He asked me last night, just after the cabaret, when we went up to see Victoria together. And now it's too late.'

Rachel took a deep breath. 'Now then, girl,' she said raggedly. 'At least you and the baby are all right. We've got plenty to do. I suggest we order a taxi, take the baby and Nanny back to my place, pick up some clothes and make a start. We have got to try and get our lives back together.' She picked up the bag with the previous night's takings. 'For a start, we mustn't lose this.'

The next few days were hard for both Rachel and Lily, but they were so busy, their own private grief was held at bay. It was at night when she was alone in bed that reality loomed, and memories returned to haunt Lily. She would hold Victoria close, praying her silent thanks for her child's safe delivery. She cursed Manny Cohen and wished that he'd been left alone to die. Vittorio had been a good man really. It was such a waste of a life – all because of that waster.

The local and national papers had been full of the disaster. The headlines made Lily very angry.

'*Local villain dies a hero.*' The various articles had given the story a more scandalous slant, making Lily even more notorious as Vittorio's mistress. At the end of the week, the club was declared beyond repair by a builder Lily had called in. Everything inside was either burned or ruined by fire.

Lily stood with Rachel, looking at the debris. 'So much for our success. We're back to square one.'

'Hardly,' said Rachel. 'Vittorio had the place well insured. He gave me the papers to keep for safety.'

Lily looked at her with surprise. 'He did?'

'Yes. So we'll have the money to start afresh. That's something.'

Lily said, 'I don't know if I can go through all that again.'

'Rubbish! Of course you will. In time, when we are able to think straight, you'll be champing at the bit, wanting to sing again. Besides, we have Victoria's future to consider.'

'We?' said Lily. 'Victoria isn't your worry, Rachel. Why should my problems be yours?'

'Trying to get rid of me, are you?'

Lily looked at her with affection. 'Never. You are an important part of my life, you know that.'

'Then stop talking a load of old cobblers. We must find another place and start again.' Her voice faltered. 'You see, darling, if we don't then that little sod Manny has won. Now we can't have that, can we?'

Looking at the remains of the Club Valletta, Lily pulled back her shoulders and a look of determination crossed her face. 'No. I would rather die than have him destroy us.'

Rachel squeezed her hand. 'Thank God! I thought I was going to have to do battle on my own.'

Looking at her Lily said, 'Never! We are in this together . . . always.'

It was not until Vittorio's funeral that the full impact of the tragedy hit Lily.

Two magnificent black horses bedecked with black plumes pulled the hearse, bearing a rich mahogany casket with brass handles, slowly along the road. Behind them followed a car in which Lily and Rachel sat silently. Lily was wearing black mourning clothes – smart widow's weeds, while Rachel wore a stunningly chic black hat with veil.

The church was packed. Vittorio might have been a villain, but he'd been admired by many. He'd also been a hard man, but a fair one. It was only those who had tried to cheat him who had felt his wrath. George Coleman stood at the back of the church, his eyes filled with tears. He'd been with The Maltese for years and felt his loss deeply.

Lily saw no one but Rachel, to whose hand she clung throughout the funeral service. She stood tall as the coffin was lowered into the ground, staring down at the deep pit, knowing that inside the wooden box was Vittorio's charred body. She remembered his smooth olive skin, his deep-brown eyes, his mellifluous voice. Suddenly she felt the deep void in her life. She would never see him again, be held in his strong arms. Be loved. It was only at this moment that she realised how much she'd loved him in return. Silently she wept.

The mourners left her alone to pay her last respects, a small figure dressed in black yet surrounded by a myriad of colourful blooms from the funeral wreaths. Her own was a sheaf of roses, next to a childlike posy from Victoria.

After a while, Rachel walked over to Lily and squeezed her arm. 'Come along, darling. Leave him with God.'

Chapter Twenty-Five

Rachel and Lily, both still dressed in mourning, sat in the office of Vittorio's solicitor. George Coleman, too, had been summoned.

The solicitor opened Vittorio's will and started to read.

' "This is the final will and testament of Vittorio Teglia, made on the fourteenth day of May 1923.

' "If in the event of my death, my finance business is still in operation, I wish all outstanding monies to be collected and added to my estate.

' "George Coleman is nominated to this task. For this and the faithful service he has given to me over the years, I bequeath the sum of three thousand pounds in the hopes that he will use it to enjoy what's left of his life." '

George looked stricken. He turned to Lily. 'I didn't expect this.'

Laying a hand on his arm, Lily said softly, 'He thought a lot of you, and you've earned it.'

The solicitor continued: ' "I have set up a trust fund for my daughter, Victoria, which will be administered by my solicitor. It will pay for a private education and ensure that if she uses it wisely, she will never be financially embarrassed. I have insisted on certain clauses in the said fund, to protect her from spending it foolishly. But I wish her to carry my name." '

Lily saw Rachel smile.

' "To Lily Pickford, I bequeath the rest of my estate in recognition of the happiness she has brought to my life. I hope before she ever has to listen to this I will have told her how much I have grown to love her. I ask her to bring our daughter up to be as honest as she is and to teach her the true values of life.

' "To Rachel Cohen, my partner, who I know is financially secure, I leave five hundred pounds with which to do something completely frivolous. But at the same time, I entrust her to use her astute financial acumen to help Lily in her business endeavours. Knowing she has Lily's future at heart, I ask her to be Lily's adviser.

' "I do not want Lily to wear mourning for me. As she well knows, I don't associate black with anything so sad. I don't want her to grieve, but to be the bright and happy woman I've always known. I ask her to get on with her life. With her indomitable spirit and the financial security she now has, I don't want her to mourn my passing, but to remember the happy times we spent together." '

There were tears in Lily's eyes as the solicitor came to the end of the document.

'I've not been able to arrive at a final figure of Mr Teglia's estate, Miss Pickford. That won't be clear until the finance company is wound up. But I can tell you that you are a very wealthy woman.'

Lily sat shaking her head. 'I would willingly give it all up if Vittorio could still be alive.'

That night, in Rachel's home, Lily was still stunned by the day's events. 'It all seems so unreal,' she said.

'Well, he took good care of you. That's all you ever wanted. But he loved you too and I suspect you loved him in return.'

There was sadness in Lily's eyes as she said, 'Yes, I did, but I didn't realise it until the day of the funeral. When it was too late. Isn't that awful?'

Rachel shook her head. 'I'm sure he knew. Now, my dear, as your adviser, I suggest that tomorrow you and I go forth and find some premises to open another Club Valletta.'

Lily brightened. 'I'm so glad you think we should keep the name.'

'We have to,' retorted Rachel. 'It will be a definite part of our success. A continuation. And, awful though it may seem, the dramatic events that led to the fire will only add to the attraction. After all, the spread in the papers will have, in its own funny way, been good publicity.'

Lily remembered the headlines and shuddered. 'I would like to move away from the docks.'

'You can't do that!' Rachel was adamant.

'Why not?'

'Because the area only serves to make it more exciting. We must have our first place in the docks. The second one can be in a smarter area, but never the Club Valletta. It has to be there.'

As Lily sat gazing into the firelight, she gave a wry smile. It seemed that, even as a wealthy woman, she was never to be rid of the docklands. But perhaps that was fair. If she had a lot of money maybe, in her own way, she could help the people who, brought up in similar circumstances to her own, were unable to rise above them. She had been lucky, thanks to Rachel, Fred and Vittorio. Without them, what would have become of her? There must be youngsters on the street in similar circumstances with nowhere to go. Maybe that was to be her way forward in life.

She would be successful, Lily knew. She would have several hotels. And she would bring up her daughter the way Vittorio wanted, but maybe she could do much more. After all, Vittorio had helped her; it seemed only fair to use his money to help others.

Gazing at the emerald on her finger, she wondered just what Vittorio would have thought of her idea. What was it he had once said about lame dogs? No more . . . but then she always did get her own way in the end.

Looking at her sleeping child, she whispered, 'Well, Victoria Teglia, it seems your father left us quite a legacy. Now we have to use it wisely.' She gazed across at her dearest friend.

'Right, Rachel! Tomorrow we start again.'

Rachel raised her glass. '*L'chayim*. To life!'

When Tomorrow Dawns

Lyn Andrews

1945. The people of Liverpool, after six years of terror and grief and getting by, are making the best of the hard-won peace, none more so than the ebullient O'Sheas. They welcome widowed Mary O'Malley from Dublin, her young son Kevin, and Breda, her bold strap of a sister, with open arms and hearts.

Mary is determined to make a fresh start for her family, despite Breda, who is soon up to her old tricks. At first all goes well, and Mary begins to build up an understanding with their new neighbour Chris Kennedy – until events take a dramatic turn that puts Chris beyond her reach. Forced to leave the shelter of the O'Sheas' home, humiliated and bereft, Mary faces a future that is suddenly uncertain once more. But she knows that life has to go on . . .

'Lyn Andrews presents her readers with more than just another saga of romance and family strife. She has a realism that is almost tangible' *Liverpool Echo*

0 7472 5806 6

HEADLINE

Maggie's Market

Dee Williams

It's 1935 and Maggie Ross loves her life in Kelvin Market, where her husband Tony has a bric-a-brac stall and where she lives, with her young family, above Mr Goldman's bespoke tailors. But one fine spring day, her husband vanishes into thin air and her world collapses.

The last anyone saw of Tony is at Rotherhithe station, where Mr Goldman glimpsed him boarding a train, though Maggie can only guess at her husband's destination. And she has no way of telling what prompted him to leave so suddenly – especially when she's got a new baby on the way. What she can tell is who her real friends are as she struggles to bring up her children alone. There's outspoken, gold-hearted Winnie, whose cheerful chatter hides a sad past, and cheeky Eve, whom she's known since they were girls. And there's also Inspector Matthews, the policeman sent to investigate her husband's disappearance. A man who, to the Kelvin Market stallholders, is on the wrong side of the law, but a man to whom Maggie is increasingly drawn . . .

'A brilliant story, full of surprises' *Woman's Realm*

'A moving story, full of intrigue and suspense . . . a wam and appealing cast of characters . . . an excellent treat' *Bolton Evening News*

0 7472 5536 9

HEADLINE

*If you enjoyed this book here is a selection of
other bestselling titles from Headline*

WHEN TOMORROW DAWNS	Lyn Andrews	£5.99 ☐
MERSEY MAIDS	Anne Baker	£5.99 ☐
THE PRECIOUS GIFT	Tessa Barclay	£5.99 ☐
THE CHINESE LANTERN	Harry Bowling	£5.99 ☐
RICHES OF THE HEART	June Tate	£5.99 ☐
LOVE ME OR LEAVE ME	Josephine Cox	£5.99 ☐
YESTERDAY'S FRIENDS	Pamela Evans	£5.99 ☐
FAIRFIELD ROSE	Sue Dyson	£5.99 ☐
SWEET ROSIE O'GRADY	Joan Jonker	£5.99 ☐
NELLIE'S WAR	Victor Pemberton	£5.99 ☐
CHILDREN OF THE STORM	Wendy Robertson	£5.99 ☐
MAGGIE'S MARKET	Dee Williams	£5.99 ☐

Headline books are available at your local bookshop or newsagent.
Alternatively, books can be ordered direct from the publisher. Just
tick the titles you want and fill in the form below. Prices and
availability subject to change without notice.

Buy four books from the selection above and get free postage and
packaging and delivery within 48 hours. Just send a cheque or postal
order made payable to Bookpoint Ltd to the value of the total cover
price of the four books. Alternatively, if you wish to buy fewer than
four books the following postage and packaging applies:

UK and BFPO £4.30 for one book; £6.30 for two books; £8.30 for

... rface

... point

... Park,

... ld be

... 1235

... hour

... ax on

If you would prefer to pay by credit card, please complete:
Please debit my Visa/Access/Diner's Card/American Express (delete as
applicable) card number:

Signature .... Expiry Date...............